For Monica

With my thanks

help at the altar.

Janice B Scott

Heaven Spent

By
Janice B. Scott

Eloquent Books

Eloquent Books
An imprint of Strategic Book Group
P.O. Box 333
Durham, Ct. 06422
www.StrategicBookGroup.com

ISBN: 978-1-60860-947-5

Printed in the United States of America

Book Design: Prepress-Solutions.com

Disclaimer

This book is a work of fiction. All characters are fictitious, but some places are factual.

Diss is a delightful market town in South Norfolk, with a mere and the parish church of St Mary. The current rector of Diss is the rural dean, but bears no resemblance at all to the Reverend Charles Burgess.

The Bishop of Norwich does live in a lovely house with beautiful gardens within the shadow of Norwich Cathedral. He and his wife generously open their gardens several times a year for charity events, and the bishop does sit in the House of Lords but, again, does not in the least resemble Bishop Gerald.

Likewise, the Bishop of Lynn does live at Castle Acre and the Bishop of Thetford at Stoke Holy Cross, but neither of them bear any resemblance whatsoever to Bishops John and Percy.

Thorpemunden and the surrounding villages are fictitious.

Acknowledgements

I wish to express my thanks to all those many people at AEG Publishing for all of their efforts in putting this book together. And a special thanks to my editor, Reba Hilbert, for her keen eye and expertise in helping me polish my story.

Dedication

This book is dedicated to Ian, with my love and thanks for forty wonderful years.

Also to Fiona, Alexander, and Rebecca, for the way in which each of them has made (and continues to make) my life so memorable and worthwhile. Thank you for being you. You will probably never know how much you mean to me.

Table of Contents

Chapter One

"Welcome, Polly. Come in." The tall, thin woman, with faded brown hair beginning to turn gun-metal grey, sounded anything but welcoming. There was no smile, just a measured glance over Polly from top to toe. The door was opened a further crack as the woman turned away into the house.

"Well, come on, if you're coming."

Perhaps it was the Norfolk way, thought Polly. "Um, thank you, er—Mrs. Winstone—um, Mavis."

Polly giggled nervously, trying to shrink her cleavage back into its rather low-cut shirt. Well, it was the hottest day of the year so far. She felt very conscious of her tattered jeans, covered in dust now from all those boxes. Astonishing how moving house can generate so much filth from the cleanest of homes. Not that Polly's previous student residence had been exactly clean, she reflected ruefully. Polly ran her fingers ineffectually through her blond curls, wild at the best of times, positively ferocious now.

"Henry," called her hostess. "Here's Polly."

"My dear!" As Henry Winstone emerged from his study and took Polly's hand, she tried to remember how fortunate she was to have landed a job at all, as the principal of her theological college had never tired of reminding her. In these days of rising prices and falling numbers in church, not every curate could find a post and there was no guarantee whatsoever that your first position would suit you. You had to make yourself fit it, the Reverend Doctor Theodore Grimes had said.

"Would you like to wash before luncheon?" asked Mavis.

"Oh! Yes. Thank you."

Clearly she looked even more of a complete mess than she had realised. Although how anyone could expect her to dress decently when she didn't even know where her clothes were, beat Polly. But she wished she'd thought to bring a comb and maybe turfed out some makeup.

She washed her hands quickly in the downstairs cloakroom and splashed water on her face, scrubbing at the dirt which had somehow managed to install itself just above her left eyebrow. The cloakroom was so spartan and devoid of any comforting touches that Polly felt forlorn. She sighed and reminded herself how kind it was of Mavis and Henry to invite her to the rectory for lunch on her moving day. An evening meal would have been preferable, but Henry had explained in his letter that they always ate at lunchtime, so who was Polly to object? At least it was food, the only meal she was likely to get that day.

The savour of roast lamb guided Polly to the dining room. In a quaintly courteous way Henry pulled out a chair for her, before seating himself at the head of the table. Mavis was already seated at the other end.

At over six feet tall, Canon Henry Winstone was an imposing presence, with his thick and floppy silver hair and his heavy, dark-rimmed glasses making him look like a kindly professor. The wide dog collar, which completely encircled his neck and was fastened with studs at the back, was as embarrassingly old-fashioned as both his outdated sports jacket and Mavis' narrow-belted, polyester dress in dull shades of lilac and grey. Polly feared the Winstones' dress sense might indicate an expression of their outlook on life and church.

At her ordination service in Norwich Cathedral, Polly had worn a shocking pink clergy shirt to protest against the ban on women becoming bishops in the Church of England. This modern style had just a small piece of plastic slipped into the front of the collar. Henry hadn't commented on her choice at the cathedral, but Polly wondered what he would think about her colourful shirts. Still, for starting work in Thorpemunden she had a reasonably sombre, dark green shirt which showed off the new dog collar to advantage and which she planned to team with a pair of well-cut tan trousers and high-heeled tan sandals. The shirt, with side vents, was designed to be worn outside trousers, and Polly was pleased with the overall effect. The loose style suited her outsize boobs and she felt she would look sufficiently serious to be a curate without having entirely abandoned the fashion industry.

"Help yourself to vegetables." Mavis proffered a large tureen with new potatoes at one end and runner beans and carrots at the other.

Even though it was too hot to eat, Polly filled her plate in case it was days before she ate again. About to tuck in, she picked up her knife and fork, but replaced them in a hurry and bowed her head as Henry intoned,

"For what we are about to receive, may the Lord make us truly grateful."

"Amen," chorused Polly and Mavis.

They ate in silence for a few moments until Mavis asked, "What brings you to Thorpemunden, Polly?"

Polly laughed. "I was, like, so late applying, it was the only place left!"

"Oh, really? So we are your last choice?"

"Oh no! Oh, I'm sorry—I didn't mean—it's just that—I—um—haven't lived in a village before. I'm really looking forward to it. I grew up in Streatham, South London, then it was university and college, both of them in cities. I don't really know Norfolk at all. But I think this'll be so cool. I love trees and things."

Mavis smiled without humour, her blue eyes remaining cool behind their brown-rimmed spectacles. "Tell us about your family, dear."

"My family?" Polly thought for a moment. How much was it safe to reveal? "Well, Mum lives in Streatham with Toby, my younger brother. He's still at school. Took his exams this year. Doesn't yet know what he wants to do with his life, but that's boys, isn't it?" She thought to herself, *I didn't lie. I didn't say what exams. None of her business that it was SATS. If she finds out Toby's only ten, she's bound to probe*. Aloud she added with a sorrowful face which she hoped would forestall further questioning, "Sadly, Dad went years ago. Mum never really got over that." Then she brightened. "That's one reason why I wanted to come here. Mum's delighted that I'm so well settled in such a lovely spot."

Henry said, "Perhaps she'll visit from time to time? We'd love to meet her, wouldn't we, dear?"

Over my dead body, thought Polly. Aloud she said, "The countryside is so peaceful, isn't it? Like a retreat for the elderly."

Polly had just had her first retreat. All the ordinands had been taken by coach to the Diocesan Retreat House at Ditchingham, South Norfolk, where they had stayed together for a three-day silent retreat. Polly had dreaded spending three days in silence, seriously doubting her ability to do so, but the days had been punctuated by ten-minute homilies from time to time given by the retreat director. And Polly had found that the surrounding countryside and the grounds of the Retreat House were perfect for solitary walks. Meals were silent, which could have proved difficult, but they had been accompanied by quiet music. So although trying to mime "Pass the salt" had resulted in helpless giggles from time to time, Polly's experience had been extremely positive. As the ordinands had nervously donned their new clergy shirts and dog collars for the coach ride back to the cathedral for the ordination service, Polly had been filled with a deep peace and a genuine sense of gratitude that she was on the right path.

So she had meant her remark as a compliment, but intercepting the glance that passed between her hosts, she had a sinking feeling that it had not been received in quite that way.

Henry frowned. "Rather more than that, I should say. I shouldn't make too many assumptions just yet, if I was you. You might be surprised. You might find the country rather different from your expectations, although I admit there isn't much to do round here, not for young people. There's a film club in Diss and the theatre in Norwich, of course, but nothing in Thorpemunden itself. Still, that won't bother you, I'm sure. After all, most of your evenings will be taken up with meetings and you'll be busy enough during the day.

"Do you like walking? There are some lovely walks around here. I myself am interested in trains, so Mavis and I often migrate to Diss to the railway. Do you have any interest in trains?"

"Er, well, not a lot. Not at the moment, that is, because—because I've not had the opportunity..." As soon as the words had left her mouth, Polly wished them unspoken.

"Well!" said Henry, glancing at Mavis. "We must see about that, mustn't we, dear? Now then, Polly. Obviously you need a day or two to settle in—and anything you want, just ask. Mavis and I are only too willing to help, aren't we, dear? But when you're settled, I say Morning Prayers at seven-thirty a.m. daily in Thorpemunden Church. Breakfast after that and we begin work at nine o'clock. Will that suit, do you think?"

Polly gulped. He was joking, wasn't he? But a glance at Henry's face soon disabused her of that forlorn hope.

Polly thought quickly. "Um, well, that might be a little difficult for me, living in the next village. I was, er, hoping to cycle as much as possible—to, like, reduce my carbon footprint—so I wouldn't have time to get back for breakfast. Would it be possible to have breakfast first and meet a little later?"

Henry and Mavis exchanged glances. "What do you think, dear? Could we manage that, do you think?"

"I suppose we'll have to, if Polly is unable to fit in with your plans." Mavis tossed her head.

"We'll say eight-thirty for prayers on Monday, then," Henry conceded, "and come straight back here to organise the day. How does that sound?"

"That's cool," said Polly, "thank you. I won't be late, I promise."

***

She was glad when the meal finished and she was able to get back to Mundenford, to her new home. Polly had never had a whole house to herself before, although she had shared with others. It felt strange to have so much space all to herself and she spent a couple of minutes wandering through the rooms, savouring the feel of her own place. Although it was considerably smaller than the rectory, Polly's new house was still a good size, since many curates these days came into the church late with fully established families. What's more, the house had been fully redecorated by the diocese prior to Polly's move. With ivory walls and paintwork it wasn't entirely to Polly's taste, but she reckoned she could brighten it up plenty with curtains and posters and a few ornaments. She especially loved the study. Like Henry's study in the rectory, the whole of one wall was covered in bookshelves, so several of Polly's boxes could be opened immediately and she could spend hours lovingly arranging her books on the pristine shelves. She had had book grants from the diocese throughout her training, so had amassed an interesting theological library during her three years at college. And if she visited the local auction for a desk and couple of old armchairs, this would quickly become a snug room.

Although she had few possessions, it was hard work getting the new house straight. By nine o'clock, Polly was exhausted but figured it was too soon to go to bed. She picked up her mobile.

"Sue? Hi! How are you doing? Me? Oh, fine thanks. Got most of it unpacked now, although it's a bit like a tip in here at the moment. Had lunch with my new boss and his wife. That was an experience and a half! I already know who wears the trousers. Yeah, well, you'll never believe, but he actually wanted to start at 7:30 a.m. Me! Can you imagine? Anyway, I managed to knock him back to eight-thirty. That wife, though. She's something else. I got the impression she really didn't take to me."

"Oh, Polly! Do be careful. Don't make any unnecessary enemies, especially at the rectory—"

"—what? Oh, stop worrying! I'll be careful, 'course I will. Anyway, it's all cool, and the house is brill. Just thought I'd give you a ring, keep you in the picture. See you later. Bye."

***

The Reverend Susan Gallagher replaced the phone thoughtfully. She loved being a mentor to Polly, but from the beginning had been worried about Polly's new post. Polly just didn't seem the type to settle into village life. Sue could see her dashing about in a big city centre parish or relishing ministry in the poverty of an inner city council estate, but the remote Norfolk countryside? Sue shook her head. She thought of Polly as an exciting livewire, terrific fun and with a huge personality but with the sort of impulsiveness that often led her into trouble.

Indeed, trouble had ensued from Sue's very first meeting with Polly, who had wandered into her church in Bayswater after an unexpected encounter with God. Polly, a non-churchgoer at the time, had suddenly perceived a thought in her head which had come from nowhere. It had said, *I want to be a woman priest.* Polly had laughed uneasily and tried to dismiss the thought, but when it had refused to disappear, instead growing so large that it took over her whole life, she had sought help. Sue's church happened to be the first one Polly had seen, and Sue had happened to be there at the time. She had taken Polly back to the vicarage and listened carefully to her story. Then she had poured them each a large gin and tonic and they had talked for hours. She'd finally sent Polly away with instructions to come back if she wished to do so. Sue had reckoned that actually voicing the words would clear the unwelcome thought from Polly's head, unless, of course, the thought really had come from God. In that case, Sue knew it would never disappear, however much Polly might wish it to do so.

The thought had not disappeared. Consequently Sue found herself thrust into the position of mentor, and her friendship with Polly had blossomed and deepened. Sue set about encouraging Polly in her change of direction, initiating her into the mysteries of Anglicanism, talking to her about God and life and possibilities, enrolling her as a chalice assistant and a member of the pastoral team at St. Bartholomew's, and arranging for her confirmation as a member of the Church of England. When it became clear that Polly's vocation had no intention of vanishing, Sue shepherded her young charge through a maze of interviews and assessments until Polly was finally accepted to begin training. Then, despite the Bishop of London's reservations over Polly (he thought it was far too soon for this new Christian to be thinking about ordination to the priesthood and besides, he was none too keen on female priests), Sue persuaded Polly to apply to St. Symeon's, a theological college known for its liberal agenda. But even there Polly discovered trouble.

Sue grinned to herself as she recalled the time when Polly had been charged with producing and printing an order of service for the senior students' final Eucharist. The first hymn had been "Now thank we all our God," but Polly had inadvertently typed "Now spank we all our God," which the spellchecker had failed to pick up. The students had loved it. Later, Polly had sworn to the principal that it was a genuine error, but Sue had never been entirely sure. Neither had she been sure about the liturgical dance which Polly had initiated at a "Fresh Expressions" service. There was a very fine line, Sue reflected, between passion in worship and sex. There had been, she thought, distinctly sensual elements in the dance, which had had the college staff writhing uncomfortably in their seats but which had kept the students enrapt.

How would Polly get on in Thorpemunden? Although Sue had never met the Winstones, she had looked up Canon Winstone in Crockford's, the Church of England's repository of all clergy details. When she learned that Henry Winstone had not only been born and raised in Norfolk but had also spent his entire career in Norwich Diocese, Sue was worried. Henry sounded very traditional in his beliefs and had never made archdeacon. Could he be one of those aging clergy full of resentment at being "passed over" by the diocese? Did he even approve of women priests? How would he cope with a young female curate fresh from theological college, full of exciting new ideas and with a decidedly wicked sense of humour? Somehow, Sue doubted that Polly's favourite mealtime graces of "Rub-a-dub dub, thank God for the grub" or "Bless this bunch as they munch their lunch" would go down well in Thorpemunden.

***

As they prepared for bed, Mavis Winstone was expressing her own reservations over Henry's new curate.

"You'll have to say something about her appearance, Henry. I hope she doesn't imagine she can go visiting in the parish in jeans. And wouldn't you have expected her to wear a dog collar for lunch with her rector? You are a canon, after all."

Henry sighed. "She has only just arrived, Mavis. Perhaps she hadn't unpacked her clothes. I'm sure she'll settle in. And don't worry, I'll make sure she looks the part. You know what I think of trendy, young vicars who think they can wander round in shirt sleeves and take a service wearing a suit."

"What about that hair? Have you ever seen such a mess? Is it permed, do you think? I'm sure she must dye it. Nobody can be that blond at twenty-eight. She'll have to tame it somehow. Whatever will she look like in the pulpit? The congregation will be so intent on staring at her that they'll never hear anything she has to say. Which I don't suppose is much anyway, since she's only just out of the cradle."

"I shall keep a close eye on her, my dear. I intend to peruse her diary every week—as my first incumbent did at St. Saviour's where

I served my title—so that I know exactly what she's up to. But you know what they said at that meeting of incumbents I went to at the college. They told us that curates should only work for two sessions out of each day. Apparently now they divide the day into three sessions—morning, afternoon, and evening—and curates should only work two out of three, so it might need some careful handling."

"What, political correctness has even breached the Church? Oh, Henry, you've devoted your whole life to the Church of England, but what have they ever given you in return? When I think of all the time you've given this job, working all the hours God sends and never complaining. Only two sessions out of three! It'll never work. Don't they know anything about the demands of parish ministry?

"No wonder pastoral care has gone by the board with these youngsters. No priests except you visit their parishioners these days, Henry. You're one in a million, you know.

"Why should the young be pampered like this? I'm quite sure it does them no good at all. No wonder the churches are empty. And to be honest, I'm not at all sure you started on the right foot with young Polly. I don't know that you were right to give in to her over the time of Morning Prayer. That girl needs a firm hand; that much was obvious. I do hope she's not going to prove to be lazy or expect her own way all the time. I can't abide a lazy priest."

"I don't think I had much choice there, my dear. If she wants to cycle—and I do wish to encourage that—it was quite reasonable to propose having breakfast first. Otherwise it would have meant having her back here to the rectory for breakfast every day, and I'm not sure you would have wanted that."

"Indeed I would not. Not after seeing how she piled her plate at luncheon. No wonder she's overweight. Let's hope a bit of cycling helps to shift a few pounds."

"Mm," murmured Henry. He had heard his wife's views on the current state of the Church of England many times before and had no wish to waste another thought on his new curate. He turned over very deliberately. "Good night, my dear. Sleep well."

Chapter Two

"I think," began Henry as they settled into the two worn armchairs in his study on the Monday morning, "that we'll need to spend the morning together in here, sorting out what you are going to do this week. I've asked Mavis to kindly bring us coffee at ten-thirty. Milk? Sugar?"

"Just milk, please."

While Henry disappeared to relay his orders to the kitchen, Polly took the opportunity to inspect the study. Like the rest of the house, it was sparsely furnished and there were no photos or, indeed, pictures of any kind apart from a rather severe icon on one wall. A large desk, sporting a small wooden cross and placed against the far wall, was equipped with a blotter, much to Polly's amusement. Did Henry use a fountain pen, then? Had he never heard of rollerballs or biros? Polly looked in vain for a computer and sighed. If Henry was a Luddite it would be so much more difficult to communicate with him. And this was the neatest desk that Polly had ever seen. She recalled her principal's desk at college. Dr. Grimes was not known for tidiness and his desk had been overflowing with piles of books and papers, migrating in due course to the floor, which soon resembled an obstacle race.

By contrast, Henry's study was obsessively neat. It was a drab room, with a thin, biscuit-coloured carpet and similarly coloured curtains brightened only by a flowery pattern picked out in white. The two brown armchairs were beginning to show signs of age. Polly, with short legs, could have done with a cushion in her chair, but clearly that was a comfort too far.

She was scrutinising Henry's bookshelves when he returned.

"Ah, Polly! I see you are a reader. Good, good. Study must continue throughout your ministry. A priest who ceases to study ceases to learn. You may borrow any book you wish. No doubt you'll need plenty of books for your Potty Training?"

"My what?"

Henry chuckled. "Post Ordination Training? Always known jocularly as potty training in my day."

"Oh! You mean CME—Continuing Ministerial Education."

"I must remember that. Talking of which, do you know when your training weekends are? I need to include them on the rota. And presumably you have one afternoon a month for training? In Norwich?"

"I think it's a whole day, actually," Polly said hastily, thinking longingly of pub lunches with her tutorial group.

"Dear, dear, dear! They certainly do look after you young people these days. Now, about working just two sessions out of every three. That may not always be possible, Polly. Unexpected events tend to crop up in parish ministry, requiring us to respond immediately."

"Not a problem, Henry," Polly replied. "I'm flexible. I can always make up the time off later."

"Hmm, well, we won't discuss that now. We need to decide which will be your day off. I take Fridays, so I suggest you have Wednesdays since there's a mid-week Eucharist every Thursday and we need to meet on Mondays. Will that suit you, Polly?"

Polly shrugged. Since she had nothing at all planned, a Wednesday off was as good as any other day. "Mm. That'll be fine, thanks."

Henry gathered a sheaf of papers from the desk and passed them to Polly. "I've worked out a rota for services for the next three months. We have five services to cover each Sunday. The two smallest parishes only have two services a month each, so they alternate. All the other parishes have one service per week. We start at eight a.m., then nine-thirty, eleven, and six-thirty. Any baptisms are extra, during the afternoon."

"That's only four services. I thought you said five?"

"Father Brian helps us out. He's retired but he lives in Middlestead so covers one service a week somewhere in the benefice. You'll meet him later on. He's opposed to women priests, but it's nothing personal. He's a lovely man. I'm sure you'll get on well together."

Polly was less sure. "It may not be personal for Father Brian, but it certainly is for me. I'm female! How can it not be personal?"

Henry sighed. "I do hope you're not going to be difficult about this. You must understand how hurt Father Brian has been over this issue, especially now that women are likely to become bishops. It's very painful for someone of his persuasion who has given his whole life to his beloved church, and I think you should remember that."

"What about women's pain? Doesn't that count? Women have suffered for two thousand years and have been prevented from giving their whole lives to their beloved church! What about that?"

"Polly, there's no need to get upset. I hope this isn't going to be your reaction every time this particular issue arises. This is neither the time nor place to discuss the rights or wrongs of women's ministry. Anyway, since you're merely a deacon for this first year, you won't be presiding at Holy Communion, so no problem will arise for at least a year. When you're priested in a year's time, the circumstances may be different. Meanwhile, I merely ask that you show some consideration for Father Brian. He's an old man and he is extremely generous with his time. I couldn't manage six parishes without him. I don't want you upsetting him over this or any other issue. So please keep your opinions to yourself."

Polly compressed her lips, wondering whether there would ever be a time to discuss women's ministry or whether she would be expected to be subservient and silent for three whole years.

She said coolly, "I know how to behave, Henry. I hope Father Brian does, too."

"Yes, well, just so long as you remember to respect other people. In the New Testament deacons were servants and that's what we all have to learn first. How to serve others. Although I'm a priest and now also a canon, I'm still a deacon. Once a deacon, always a deacon, as my old training incumbent used to impress upon me. It's a good lesson for all of us in ministry to learn."

"I am aware of that, Henry. I'm looking forward to learning from you."

Henry nodded. "Good. As long as we understand each other. Now, let's look at these rotas. You'll share services with me for this first year, as I'm your supervisor. You'll preach once in every six weeks and you'll lead both Matins and Eucharistic services, although of course, I shall preside at the altar. When you preach, I shall expect you to lead the congregation in intercessory prayers."

"But if that's only every six weeks or so, what will I be doing for the rest of the time?"

"Leading worship is an art, Polly. It requires careful preparation. Just because the service is written out in full in the Prayer Book doesn't mean it's easy to lead, as you will discover. I don't want you to run before you can walk."

"But I—"

Polly's protest was cut short as Mavis tapped on the door and came in bearing a tray of coffee. They busied themselves with their drinks before settling down again to Henry's rotas.

"I have a list of people for you to visit, Polly. You need to visit every member of each Parochial Church Council—"

"—but that's more than fifty people!"

"I don't expect you to visit them all in one day! The names and addresses are on your list. You may organise the list as you wish. You should manage three visits in half a day, so it will only take you three weeks or so. And parochial visiting is a very good habit to develop."

"Can you tell me why I'm going? What's the purpose of these visits? Do you want me to find out something?"

"The purpose is for you to get to know these people, and the best way you can do that is in their own homes, believe me. Members of the PCC are the ruling body of the church, and you need to know them well. Young priests visit far too seldom these days and it's proving to be the death of the Church of England."

Polly bit back the retort which sprang to her lips. She had three years in which to fight her battles. She nodded. "I'll start this afternoon."

"Good. That's the spirit. But don't forget that we meet for Evening Prayers at five p.m. sharp. We'll meet at each of the churches in rotation, so let's meet at Mundenford Church this week. That way, you'll be close to home when we finish."

"That's nice of you, Henry. Thank you."

"We have a PCC meeting on Thursday evening at 7:30 p.m. at Middlestead, but you won't meet Father Brian there, as retired priests are not permitted to serve on PCCs. I'll let you have an agenda and a copy of the minutes before then."

"I don't see a computer," said Polly. "Only, if you had one, you could have emailed me. It makes life a lot easier."

"I can do that. At least, Mavis can. She's the computer expert in the family. She has her own little office upstairs and kindly copes with all my secretarial needs. Mavis will email the minutes if you write down your email address for me."

Polly nodded, reflecting that Mavis doing all the paperwork explained the abnormal tidiness of the study. Probably Henry never used the room, except for meeting people. She was also aware of a slight uneasiness at the thought of Mavis being party to all her communication with Henry, but there was nothing to be done about that.

Henry continued, "When we meet on Monday mornings we will discuss all that you have done during the previous week and study the theology behind your actions."

"What?"

"Part of your formation as a priest is the ability to consider every situation theologically. I shall be asking you how your conversations and your actions relate to God."

Polly thought, *Oh my God!*

Aloud she said, "All right, Henry, I'll do my best, but I may need your help."

Henry smiled. "That's what I'm here for, Polly."

***

Since they were meeting at Mundenford Church later that afternoon, Polly decided it made sense to start her PCC visiting in Mundenford. She picked a name at random, located the tiny cottage tucked away down a loke behind the village green and, as there was no doorbell, hammered on the front door with her fist.

After a disconcerting length of time, she heard bolts being drawn and keys turned. The door opened a crack.

"Yes?"

Polly smiled brightly. "Hello, Mrs. Cranthorn? I'm Polly Hewitt, the new curate. Just thought I'd call and see how you are."

The door was flung open. "Come in, come in! And call me Ivy. How lovely to see you. I'm so glad you've called. Come on in and sit down. I'll put the kettle on."

The birdlike, white-haired old lady beamed. She had a face full of wrinkles but twinkly blue eyes filled with merriment, and Polly warmed to her immediately. She ushered Polly into a comfortable armchair. "You sit down there, my love, and tell me all about yourself. And let me advise you now, next time you visit, come to the back door. Nobody round here uses the front door. You need to go round the back."

"Oh!" said Polly, surprised. She couldn't recall ever going to a back door before. "Is that all right? Won't people mind?"

"Lord bless you, my love! They'll be that pleased to see you, you'll be like a member of the family before you've set foot in the house. And they'll be expecting you. By now the whole village will know you're here, so I'm right glad you decided to call on me first. They'll all be waiting for you."

"Really? How on earth do they know I'm here? I've only just come."

"There's an instant communications system in all villages, far quicker than the Internet. Better get used to the idea that everyone will know your business almost before you know yourself. But it's not always a bad thing. You'll find folk are very responsive, and if they take to you, they'll support you through thick and thin."

"What if they don't take to me?"

"Lord love you, girl! You don't need to worry about that. They've already taken you to their hearts."

"They have?"

The old woman chortled. "Anyone who can work with Mavis Winstone hovering in the background has their admiration and their sympathy, I can tell you! And I'm not speaking out of turn, just in case you were wondering. We all know Mavis from of old and we all know your life won't be easy, girl. But if life gets tough, just you call on a member of the Cauliflower Club."

"The what?"

Ivy Cranthorn laughed delightedly. "See my hair? All these white curls just like a cauliflower? All of us old ladies in Mundenford Church, we all look the same. So we call ourselves the Cauliflower Club. And we're so thrilled to have a female curate that we've already pledged our support for you. Never thought old Henry would have a woman. Never thought Mavis would allow it!"

Polly laughed. "To tell you the truth, I don't think she's overjoyed by my presence. But I suppose she'll have to put up with me for three years."

"She won't find that easy, you being young enough to be her daughter. You'll be a constant reminder to her of all she's missed over the years. They never managed to have any children, you know. I think that may be the cause of her bitterness. It's as though she's become increasingly dried up inside with unresolved grief for what never was."

"Did she have miscarriages, then?"

The old lady shook her head. "Nobody really knows. They've only been here fifteen years, so Mavis was well past childbearing age by then. But they have always been in Norfolk, and the web of family relationships which stretches all across Norfolk has to be experienced to be believed. Of course, it's stronger locally. You'll find that everyone you speak to is related to someone somewhere, cousin or aunt or something. So remember to be careful what you say. Anything you say will soon get around."

"Even this?"

Ivy laughed. "Not this! You're safe here, my love. If ever you want to speak confidentially, come here. Although you'll soon pick up who you can trust to keep their mouth shut."

Clearly Mrs. Cranthorn was a fount of information. "Tell me, Ivy," began Polly. "What about Father Brian? What's he like? Henry's already told me he doesn't approve of women priests, so I'm feeling a wee bit nervous about him."

The old woman gave a snort of laughter. "Lord love you! You don't need to worry about him, daft old fool! He's got Old Timer's disease, you know."

Polly laughed. "How d'you mean?"

"Never remembers to turn up for services. We always have to ring him about five minutes before he's due to leave home. He's usually late even when he does turn up. Fumbles and bumbles his way through the service, forgets half his lines even when they're written down for him, and has never yet completed a sermon without losing his way in the middle. Still, having said all that, he's a dear old boy. Vague, confused, and muddled, but his heart's in the right place."

***

Polly continued to enjoy her visiting. She was welcomed into every home and discovered that Henry was right; this was a good way of getting to know folk. Polly was a people person, with a natural warmth and an ingenuous openness which invited confidences and brought out the protective instinct in older people. Blessed with an outgoing personality, Polly was never shy and rarely at a loss for words. She soon had the most retiring of indigenous Norfolk villagers revealing their whole life-story to her and she listened intently, with care and gentleness.

She learned that the churchwarden of Thorpemunden, James Mansfield, who was a retired local farmer, together with his wife, Daisy, had the beautiful, sixteenth-century manor house in Thorpemunden and were revered as the village squires. But they lived with the sorrow of a grown-up son with severe learning difficulties. Frank had been in trouble with the police on a number of occasions caused, according to his parents, by village youths who goaded him beyond endurance. Frank, with a mental age of around ten, was unable to understand their teasing, so reacted with anger to their jeers and ridicule, lashing out when it became too much to bear. Since he was a big man, this could result in injury to the lads, who were never slow to report him. James and Daisy, growing old now and fearful for the future of their only son, lived on a constant tightrope, trying to balance Frank's needs with the needs of the village and resisting an undercurrent of village feeling which wanted Frank "put away."

From that beautiful home standing in five acres of manicured grounds and crammed with priceless antiques, Polly visited Arthur Roamer, a widower living in an ex-council house. Arthur was quite the grumpiest person Polly had met so far. He resented folk like James and Daisy, whom he referred to as "toffs" and seemed to be full of a simmering anger which emerged as a giant chip on his shoulder. He was a Yorkshire man who had retired to Middlestead twenty years ago but whose wife had died just two days after their move. Arthur had never come to terms with her sudden death and tended her grave in the churchyard every week, always leaving fresh flowers supplied by his garden. But he used his Yorkshire heritage as an excuse for his rudeness.

"Yorkshire born and bred, that's me," he declared proudly. "You'll find I says what I thinks. You'll know where you stand with me, right enough."

"I'd like to stand in your garden," replied Polly. "It's fantastic. Do you do it all yourself?"

"What, you think I'm too old to look after my own garden?"

Polly sighed. "That's not what I meant! Are you always so cranky or have I caught you at a bad time?" Then she added, "I'm Surrey born and bred. We speak first, think afterwards."

To her relief, Arthur laughed. "You'll do, right enough. There's not many as would answer back like that. Reckon you'll be all right. Come on, I'll show you the garden."

His garden was a riot of colour but cleverly designed, with hidden corners producing unexpected pleasures. One area was filled with perfumed plants, which were a delight to the senses.

"In memory of my wife," Arthur said gruffly. "She was blind. I promised her a sensory garden when we moved to the country. This is it."

Polly resisted the temptation to express conventional sympathy, instead saying simply, "It's lovely." She sat down on a cast-iron bench and closed her eyes to savour the full fragrance of the garden.

"You can come here, if you like. If you want to, I mean."

"Thanks, Arthur. It's a brilliantly peaceful spot. Might take you up on that."

He was lonely, she realised, but too proud to ask for help or to seek out company. Perhaps she would drop in from time to time, not ostensibly to see him but just to enjoy his amazing garden.

It was going to be all right, she reflected happily as she cycled home. The people she had met were struggling with their own problems, but Ivy Cranthorn was right. They had accepted her and were warmly welcoming. All that nonsense she had been fed when she had first mooted the idea of moving here, of Norfolk people being unfriendly. It was complete rubbish, fabricated through ignorance. People were people and if you were pleasant to them, they were pleasant back. It wasn't rocket science. There was nothing here to cause her to lose any sleep. She was going to enjoy her three years in the Thorpemunden benefice, and nobody was going to prevent her.

Chapter Three

Ella Wim wondered whether she should attempt to tidy the flat before she left. After all, the others had let her crash on their floor and had even found her an old sleeping bag and a cushion. Perhaps tidying the flat was one way in which she could repay them, since she had barely a penny to her name. But when she looked around at the overflowing ashtrays, the empty lager cans, the magazines strewn on the floor, the dirty clothes left where their owners had dropped them, and the scuffed table piled haphazardly with textbooks and old newspapers and computer printouts, her heart failed her. She wandered through to the kitchen, but the sink was stacked so high with dirty dishes that she was unable to fit the kettle under the tap in order to fill it with water for a mug of coffee. And she knew exactly what she would find if she opened the dishwasher. Half of the contents would be clean, but rather than empty the clean dishes and replace them in the cupboards, one cup would be removed, replaced by a dirty one, and the cycle started again. Some of those dishes, Ella reckoned, probably had been washed five or six times without ever leaving the dishwasher.

It would take her hours to begin to straighten any of this mess, and for what? The others probably wouldn't notice. They didn't, usually. And even if they did, within ten minutes it would be just as bad again. Was it worth the huge effort it would take?

Ella knew she was going to move on. But where? Where could she go and what could she do? Without an address she would never land a job. "No fixed abode" they called it, and good-bye to employment. And without any papers whatsoever, there was zilch chance of getting anything out of social security. If only her mother had kept something—anything—a birth certificate, for instance. Ella's dark, almond eyes filled with tears, which she impatiently brushed away. Don't go there. Not yet.

Almost without thinking, Ella began to straighten the lounge. She picked up Siobhan's rumpled cardigan and folded it neatly together with the discarded bra that she was almost certain Siobhan had been wearing last night, ready to take them into Siobhan's bedroom. Siobhan was a brilliant friend, generous, supportive, and huge fun to be with, but the untidiest person Ella had ever known. She was the mainstay of the flat, but so full of life that she never knew when to stop. All-night parties were common, and so many friends crashed on the floor from time to time that it was difficult to know who actually belonged in the flat and who didn't. And nobody, apart from Ella, ever seemed to clean the flat.

Ella emptied all the ashtrays, along with the lager and beer cans, the old newspapers, and torn magazines, into a plastic Sainsbury's bag she found in the kitchen. She ran down the steps to dump the lot in the outside dustbin, then collected a duster from the kitchen drawer and set to work. It took her two hours to straighten the furniture, tidy, and dust the room. Then she unearthed the ancient Hoover from under the stairs and cleaned the carpet. By the time she'd finished, she was quite pleased with the result. The lounge looked presentable and, for once, quite welcoming. It just needed one addition.

Ella pocketed a pair of scissors, ran down the steps again and over the road into the park. Glancing round to make sure no park keepers were in sight, she began to snip at the roses in the centre bed, just taking one from here and one from there so as not to spoil the display. When she had around a dozen beautiful and highly scented, deep red roses, she ran back to the flat and placed them on the table in the lounge, in a cracked vase she found under the sink. The addition of the flowers transformed the lounge, so Ella wandered through to start work on the kitchen. She emptied the dishwasher, put away the clean crockery, and reloaded the dishwasher with all the pots from the sink. Then she made herself a coffee and took five minutes' break. But she only allowed herself five minutes before she began to scrub the cooker, followed by the sink. As she finished washing the kitchen floor, her eyes filled again, for she would be sorry to leave this place.

Not for the first time, Ella wondered whether she had been wise to drop out of university. At the time, it had seemed the obvious solution, but now in retrospect, it didn't seem obvious at all. With her mother being so ill, university had seemed utterly irrelevant. But Ella knew now that she hadn't thought it through. She had simply upped sticks and left, to nurse her mother. That was a year ago. Ella had vaguely thought her mother's illness would be brief. She hadn't expected to be her mother's sole companion and nursemaid for so long. Neither had she expected her mother to die. Now without finance, there was no way Ella could resume her studies.

The only good thing to come out of all this was her friendship with Siobhan. Although she hadn't made contact for the entire year, as soon as Ella had turned up at the flat, Siobhan had flung her arms around her and made her welcome. It was as though Ella had never left. The other people in the flat were strangers to Ella. They had been pleasant enough, but there were no deeper ties of friendship. No one had objected to Ella sleeping on the floor for a few days, and even when those few days stretched into weeks and months, no one had said a word. Ella was grateful for that. For her part, she had tried to keep out of their way, to clean up now and again, and to make herself as inconspicuous as possible. That, she felt, was only fair.

Now the time had come to move on. The flat was too small to house an extra person, especially with all the rubbish that was constantly strewn around. And although Ella had contributed to the food, her meagre supply of money had now run so low that she was relying on charity from the others. But they were all students, so none of them had any money. Clearly, they could not support Ella as well as themselves.

Ella quickly collected her few belongings and shoved them into the backpack, making sure that the gold locket was safely hidden under her clothes. She pulled the knitted cloche hat of many colours firmly down over her ears, not because it was a cold summer but because she felt her identity as a person was somehow bound up in the hat. When she wore it, she felt complete. She had one remaining twenty-pound note and a handful of change that she pushed deep into the pocket of her jeans. Then she hoisted the backpack over her shoulders, took a last look round, and quietly slipped out of the flat. She left no note, no forwarding address, and no telephone number. Once again, Ella Wim was about to disappear.

With no clear idea of what she was going to do, Ella is sauntered across the park, enjoying the scent of the roses and the sight of the trees in full leaf. Somehow, nothing seemed as bad during the summer, but Ella was well aware that within a month or so, the summer would be ending and she would have to find somewhere to spend the winter. There were no relatives, no uncles or aunts or cousins or grandparents, and Ella had no brothers or sisters. Apart from her friend Siobhan, Ella was alone in the world.

Obviously, her first priority must be to find work. She could probably survive for a month by sleeping rough if the weather remained relatively fine, but after that, she would need to find accommodation as well as work.

As she stood in the park gazing up at the statue of the young Queen Victoria, her mind a blank, Ella suddenly knew what she was going to do. It wasn't a conscious decision, it was just there. It was as if the solution had been deep inside her all the time, but she had needed a nudge to discover it. Dear old Queen Vic had been that nudge. Ella ran across the park to the subway and clambered down the stairs to the underground tunnel. She found a good position leaning against the wall, placed her backpack on the ground, and then removed her hat. Her long, dark hair cascaded over her shoulders as a shining mantle and Ella's face assumed a vulnerable expression. Blessed with the oriental features and the slightness of build of her mother combined with the height, she presumed, of her father, Ella was a striking figure.

As people began to scurry past in the evening rush hour, Ella held out her hat. Many of the older women continued to rush past her without a second look, but the young women of about her own age quite often stopped with a sympathetic smile, dropping a coin into her hat. And nearly all the men stopped, as she had known they would. Most of them could not prevent their eyes from raking her body, from the top of her glossy black hair over her slender figure in its tightly hugging white tee-shirt, down to her long legs in their narrow jeans with the right knee torn out and the appliqué on the left lower leg, and ending in high, cork-heeled sandals.

One man dropped in a five-pound note and made a lewd suggestion. Ella removed the note and handed it back to him with a smile. He began to pester her, but Ella continued to smile, gently ignoring him. And as other men came up, dropping coins and occasionally notes into her hat, the man shrugged, replaced the five-pound note in her hat, and left. By the time the rush hour had more or less finished, Ella had doubled her money.

She emptied the contents of her hat into her pocket and jammed the hat back on her head. Then she walked to the ticket office and purchased a tube ticket for Victoria. Since the flat was nearly at the end of the underground system, it was an hour's journey, and Ella had to change to the Victoria line when she reached Central London.

She walked briskly from the underground station to Victoria coach station. She bought her ticket but discovered to her disappointment that the last bus had left at six-thirty and the first one next day wasn't until twelve noon. So that meant a night under the stars unless she could find some other accommodation.

The middle-aged man in the ticket booth had noticed her forlorn expression. "Nowhere to go for the night, love?"

Ella grimaced. "Didn't think the buses would finish so early."

"Know your way around here?"

"Not really. Lived in Essex for a while, but don't know this part at all."

"There's a Backpackers Hostel, quite cheap. Only about twelve quid a night. Can you manage that?"

Ella nodded. She might have to do a bit more scrounging, but she was sure she could run to twelve pounds. "Whereabouts? Is it far?"

"About a mile and a half. It's in Soho, so keep your wits about you. Look, here on this A to Z. Go down here, then left there, round here, and into Pall Mall. Then take a right here into Waterloo Place and keep on until you get to Piccadilly Circus. Then you're nearly there. It's called the Piccadilly Backpackers Hostel and it's got around seven hundred beds, so they should be able to squeeze you in. Look, I know the guy on the door there. Would you like me to ring and tell them to expect you?"

Ella's smile widened at such unexpected kindness. "That would be brilliant. And I wonder—do you think you could possibly jot down those directions? I'm hopeless at remembering."

The man surprised himself by saying, "I'll do better than that, love. I'm off in ten minutes. If you can wait that long, I'll take you there myself. It's only about a half-hour walk, not far. Look, get yourself a coffee out of the machine. By the time you've finished drinking it, I'll be with you."

Ella smiled her thanks and did as he suggested. She was an ingenuous person, one of life's innocents who always presumed the best in others. It didn't occur to her to question the ticket man's motives since she automatically took him at face value.

The ticket man was as good as his word, reaching Ella as she drained the last dregs of her coffee. A thickset man with a large beer belly and a few strands of greasy hair which he combed over his head, he introduced himself as Ray and offered to take Ella's backpack. She thanked him but refused.

He led the way at a brisk pace, grabbing Ella's hand to dodge the traffic when they had to cross the road. His touch was hot and damp and his breath soon came in quick gasps with the exertion.

"Do you walk much, Ray?" asked Ella.

He laughed. "I get free transport with the job, so no, why would I?"

"Is this taking you out of your way?"

He shook his head. "I can get a bus from anywhere. Just as easy from Soho as from Victoria, and they'll be a bit emptier come half-past eight. I live in Notting Hill."

"You married?"

"Was. Not anymore. She upped and left. Took the kids with her, the cow. Got a partner, though. Louise. Been together three years now."

"That's nice," said Ella.

Ray shot a sidelong glance at her. "You got anyone?"

"No."

"I could wait around a bit, if you like. Get you some food, take in a movie?"

"What about Louise?"

Ray laughed, shortly. "She won't care. Probably out herself, anyway."

"You're lonely," said Ella, gazing directly into his eyes.

Ray looked a little uncertain. She was strange, this girl. A bit forthright for his liking. Was that what they called "oriental fatalism" or something?

He blustered, "Me? 'Course not! Got plenty of friends, me." Then he added nastily, "Needn't think I want you, love. I can do better 'n you. I was just being friendly, seeing as you're a young girl all on your own."

Ella kept her liquid eyes focussed on him and simply smiled. She didn't seem to be aware of the malice behind his words. When they reached the hostel she shook hands with him and said, "Thank you, Ray. You've been a good friend. Good-bye." She went straight in, without looking back.

Ray waited for a moment, not sure whether he was angry or flummoxed. Then he shrugged his shoulders and wended his way to the nearest bus stop, puzzling over Ella and the odd effect she had had on him.

***

Ella paid her twelve pounds at the desk and was given a room for the night. It was small and basic, but there was clean linen on the bed, a clean towel on the rail, and the use of a hot shower. She luxuriated in the shower, washed her hair, then climbed into bed and fell into the first dreamless sleep she had enjoyed for months.

***

Next morning Ella wandered round the coach station until she found the bay where bus number NX 497 was standing. As the first bus of the day, it was already half full. Ella climbed on board, smiled at the driver, and found an empty seat. She kept her hat on, but stashed her backpack in the overhead rack. Then she settled down in the seat, hoping no one would sit next to her.

She stared out of the window as the bus rumbled through the London traffic, but was glad when they left Stratford and reached the open road, where the traffic was lighter and the bus picked up speed. As they travelled through increasingly long stretches of rolling English countryside, Ella felt her heart quicken. The bus stopped at Newmarket, disgorging a few passengers and taking on more, and Ella was thrilled to see the racehorses in their paddocks as the bus drove on towards Bury St. Edmunds. With each succeeding stop the scene became increasingly rural and, to Ella's city eyes, increasingly quaint. She loved it. But her greatest thrill was when the bus drove along the coast road from Lowestoft to

Gorleston and finally, finally to Great Yarmouth. With mounting excitement, Ella could hardly wait for the bus to stop.

She leapt from the bus, swinging her backpack up onto her shoulders, and set off at a run from the coach park down Euston Road, following the scent of the sea until she stood on the sea-shore, gazing out across the breaking surf and the vast expanse of the ocean.

This was it. Remembered joy from her childhood surged through Ella's veins and she slipped off her sandals to stand barefoot on the sand, drinking in the smell of mingled ozone and seaweed. She was home in Great Yarmouth, the seaside holiday town in which she had felt truly happy for three whole months.

Chapter Four

Frank Mansfield flipped on a Friday, at some ungodly hour in the morning. Polly was in bed asleep when the call came.

She struggled to consciousness. "Um, yes? Who? Sorry, I'm not quite with it—what?"

Then she shot up in bed, sleep forgotten as the full impact of Daisy Mansfield's anguish communicated itself to her. "Hang on, Daisy; can you slow down a bit? Start again, could you. What exactly has happened?"

"Oh, Polly, it's Frank. He's gone and we don't know where. His father is frantic with worry. He was gone when we got up just now. His bed hasn't been slept in. James made a cup of tea like he always does first thing, but Frank wasn't there." Her voice quavered and raised several tones. "What are we going to do? How shall we find him? You must help us, please!"

Polly responded in her most calming voice. "Of course I'll help you, Daisy. Give me half an hour to reach you. Meanwhile, have you called the police?"

"No! No police! We don't want the police involved. Don't call the police!" And Daisy rang off.

Polly shrugged into her clothes in record time, dashed to her car, and roared over to The Manor in Thorpemunden. She ran into the house and impulsively flung her arms around Daisy, who immediately collapsed into sobs. Polly led her to a sofa and sat down next to her, waiting until the paroxysm began to ease.

"Where is James now? Is he out looking for Frank?"

Daisy nodded. "He dressed and rushed out straight away. I'm so worried about him, too. He's diabetic, you know, and he hasn't had anything to eat since last night. And he needs his insulin injection."

As the weeping began again Polly hurriedly said, "Have you any idea where Frank might have gone? Has he done this kind of thing before?"

"Never like this. He has wandered off once or twice before, but he knows he shouldn't go out of the grounds. He's such a good boy, usually. He has walked down to the village by himself—well, I wanted to encourage some independence—but you know what happened each time. I told you, he got into awful trouble with those dreadful village boys. It's them that should be locked up, not our Frank."

"Did that put him off going to the village?"

"We haven't allowed him to go there again. He's never been out since then without one of us going with him. We take him for walks around the grounds. He likes that."

Privately Polly thought that any man of forty-three, with or without severe learning difficulties, would soon become somewhat frustrated if kept virtually under lock and key and allowed out only for sedate walks with his elderly parents.

Aloud, she said, "Did anything set him off? I mean, do you have any idea what might have precipitated this? Was Frank upset for some reason?"

Daisy convulsed with renewed sobs. "I'm so afraid he's run away! He's never done that before. How will he manage? We didn't mean it! But he can be difficult sometimes. It was just to calm him. We're getting old now and he's so strong. Not that he'd ever hurt us," she added hastily.

"But— ?" Polly prompted, gently.

"He was naughty last night. He didn't mean anything by it, but we can't allow that sort of behaviour. I mean, it was a perfectly good meal. I know he doesn't much care for spinach, but it's good for him. I told him it would give him muscles like Popeye—he likes Popeye—but he threw the whole plate at me. Such a waste. James was so angry. He marched Frank off to his room and locked him in. Frank was very noisy for a while, banging and crashing as he always does when he's upset, but then it all went quiet and we thought he'd calmed down and put himself to bed. He does that sometimes, when he's tired. It wasn't until this morning when James went in and saw the open window…"

She tailed off and gazed beseechingly at Polly. "It's all my fault, isn't it? I knew he didn't like spinach. I shouldn't have tried to make him eat it."

Polly squeezed her hand. "Too late to worry about that now, Daisy. We must find him. Now think, Daisy. Does Frank have a favourite place on the estate where James might have gone to look for him?"

"There's the pond—we used to take a jam jar and fishing net, Frank used to love that. But we haven't been for ages."

Then James Mansfield came in. He seemed suddenly old and shrivelled; with drooping shoulders and a deeply despondent expression he looked every one of his seventy-something years.

Polly sat him down next to his wife and bustled about in the kitchen, making tea and toast for all of them.

"Here, both of you, eat some of this. You'll feel better with some food inside you. And you need to keep up your strength for Frank. James, better get your insulin injection. Look, I've had an idea. I wonder if he's gone to Diss? You've taken him there on a number of occasions and you said he liked it. I guess it's like the big city and the bright lights for Frank. Why don't you two stay here and get some rest while I nip into Diss and see if I can spot him?"

Daisy looked unsure. "How would he get to Diss? It's nine miles away."

"If he's been gone since last night… He's young and strong. He could walk there."

James nodded. “She’s right, Daisy. It’s worth a try. He’s not on the estate, I looked everywhere. And I don’t think he’d go into the village; he was frightened last time.” He stood up. “I’ll come with you, Polly.”

“Er—no! Frank will need you both here when he returns,” Polly said, thinking that the sight of his father bearing down on him might tip Frank all over again. She’d have a much better chance of bringing him home if she was alone. She added, “But if I can’t find him there, we really will have to notify the police.”

The elderly couple looked at each other and nodded. Daisy clasped Polly’s hand. “Thank you so much, Polly. God go with you.”

Polly floored the accelerator on the road to Diss, a small market town with just one street of shops and a small arcade round the corner at the top of the town near the bank. If Frank was anywhere, either he would be by the mere, the large pond at the start of the town, watching the swans and the ducks, or he would find his way to the town’s toyshop. He was quite distinctive, with his dark hair flopping over his forehead, his beetling brows that nearly met above his dark eyes, and his shuffling gait, all of which gave him a somewhat forbidding appearance. Unfortunately, he might well have approached children as he loved to play, but most children reacted to him with fear, so there could be trouble ahead.

Polly sped towards Diss as fast as she dared along the narrow, winding road. Some of the bends were treacherous and it was single track in places, but at least there was little traffic. She parked in the Tesco car park at the entrance to the town and set off on foot.

She walked all round the mere and across the recreation ground on the far side, but there was no sign of Frank nor of any recent disturbances, so it was unlikely that he had dallied by the mere. Polly wandered up the High Street, glancing into the shops on either side without much hope of spotting Frank in any of them. He would hardly be interested in the organic food store, the charity shop, or the photographers. At the top of the town she made her way towards the toy shop.

"Can I help you, love?"

Polly turned. "I'm looking for a man with learning difficulties. I thought he might have come here—he loves toys. I don't know whether you've seen him?"

"About six foot, dark hair, couple of sandwiches short of a picnic?"

"That's him! When did you see him? Do you know where he is?"

"He was sitting on the doorstep when we opened. We let him in, but he was something of a nuisance. We had to turn him out in the end."

"How long ago? Do you know where he went?"

The shopkeeper nodded. "I've a pretty good idea. I think you'll find him in the Amusement Arcade. He had a stack of money with him and no idea how to use it. He's only been gone from here half an hour or so. Shouldn't be too difficult to find. Better keep your eyes on him in future, love," he called after Polly as she ran out of the shop.

Frank was the only customer in the Amusement Arcade. He was intently feeding ten-pence pieces into a slot machine and pulling the handle. Polly edged up to him.

"Hello, Frank. Good to see you. How are you doing?"

Frank ignored her.

Polly tried again, injecting a little more authority into her voice. "Frank, it's time to go home now. Come on, I'll give you a lift. Frank. Frank."

At this he turned. His black brows drew together as he glared at Polly. "Not yet. Not ready. Not finished. Playing."

Polly took his arm, but he threw her off so violently that she stumbled and fell against the machine, banging her head. She put up her hand and felt blood. She fished a clean tissue out of her pocket and held it to her head to staunch the flow.

"Frank! That was so naughty. You've hurt me—look, I'm bleeding."

But Frank was paying no attention to her. Having used up all his ten-pence pieces, he had drawn a wad of notes from his trouser pocket. Polly's eyes widened as she realised that he held several hundred pounds.

"Frank! Where did you get all that money? What have you done?"

"Nothing," mumbled Frank, defensively.

"Wanna change them, mate?" The arcade attendant, a youth of around seventeen with spiked, dirty, blond hair, a stud through his lip, two rings through his left earlobe, and heavy jewellery all over his hands, had sidled out of his kiosk at the appearance of the notes.

"Yeah!" Frank turned to Polly for the first time. "My friend," he confided. "We're mates. He gives me pennies for the machines."

"That's right, mate," agreed the attendant. "You give me one of them notes and I'll give you a pocketful of pennies."

Polly turned on him angrily. "Now just hang on a minute! How much has he given you already? This cash isn't his to give, you know. That makes you an accessory to a crime. Receiving stolen money."

The boy jeered, "Sez who? What's it got to do wiv you, darlin'? You his minder, or what?"

"He must have stolen this money," argued Polly. She turned to Frank. "Where did you get the money, Frank?"

Frank said sullenly, "Not stolen. My dad's. Keeps it in a tin box in his study, I seen him. And I seen where he keeps the key," he added proudly.

"I thought you were in your room last night? How did you get it?"

Frank beamed. "Climbed out the window and down the tree. S'easy. And I done the burglar alarm, one, two, three, four," he added proudly.

"You went back in through the front door with your front door key and into your dad's study?"

Frank nodded. "Remembered where the key was, second drawer in the desk, under the whisky. Remembered where the box was, too, top drawer of the filing cabinet."

It was the longest speech Polly had ever heard him make. Clearly, he was pleased with himself. She said more gently, "But, Frank, that's your father's money. It wasn't yours to take, was it now? Come on. Your mum and dad are worried about you. Let's go home. You can come back here another day."

But the attendant intervened, grasping Frank's arm. "C'mon, mate. Don't you take no notice of her. Bitch. Nothing to do with her. Tell her to mind her own business."

Frank laughed delightedly. "Go away, Polly. Bitch. None of your business. He my friend. We mates." He shoved Polly roughly out of the way. She staggered at the unexpected onslaught, caught her heel, and fell again, crashing her head against the side of the fruit machine.

***

Polly felt groggy, as though there were a huge weight pinning her down. She struggled to move, but the attempt resulted in a searing headache thundering through her temples and spreading across her forehead. She felt violently sick. When she found that she was unable to open her eyes, a whimper of fear escaped her lips.

At once, there was a rustle of movement and a hand caught her wrist. "You just lie there," ordered a firm, female voice, and Polly fell back, giving up any idea of movement.

"I feel s-sick," she croaked.

A cool glass was thrust between her lips. "Sip some water," instructed the voice, and a hand behind her neck held her forward a little to enable her to swallow.

Polly felt marginally better and this time was able to prise open her eyelids sufficiently to allow in some light. Gradually her eyes opened. She became aware that she was lying on a firm bed with metal cot sides, her left wrist attached to a drip. All of this informed her that she must be in hospital.

Polly opened her eyes wider and looked around her. She was in a single room and a nurse was checking her pulse.

"That's better," declared the nurse approvingly. "You've had a nasty bang on the head, but you'll be right as rain in no time. How are you feeling?"

"Bursting head and still a little sick," admitted Polly.

The nurse fetched a metal, kidney-shaped dish and rested it on Polly's chest, under her chin. "Hang onto this. If you need to use it, ring this bell." She placed the end of a long cord in Polly's hand. "See? Just press this buzzer and someone will be with you in no time."

"Where am I?"

"In the Norfolk and Norwich, the Assessment Ward. But I don't think you'll be here too long. The doctor will be along presently to fill you in on what's going to happen. Meanwhile, why don't you get some rest?"

"It's this vicious headache," said Polly. "Can't rest. It's thumping away like a sledgehammer and feels like someone is boring into my brain with a screwdriver."

"The doctor will give you something for that. He'll be along soon." The nurse patted Polly encouragingly on the shoulder, offered a warm smile, and bustled out of the room.

Polly lay back against the pillows and tried to recall just what had happened. She remembered begging Frank to return home with her and she remembered being shocked by the amount of cash he was carrying, but she couldn't recall much after that. She had no idea how she had ended up in hospital, and although she was aware that she had hit her head and had used a tissue to stem the blood, she had not thought that such an injury was severe enough to warrant hospital treatment.

The doctor who shortly entered her room was dark-skinned, slight in stature, and looked as if he had been qualified about three weeks. He wore a new white coat and sported a stethoscope in a deceptively casual manner around his neck. His name tag identified him as Dr. Azar Mir.

He spoke with a gentle Indian lilt, and despite the crashing and insistent throbbing in her head, Polly was instantly attracted to him.

He stood at the foot of the bed and gazed at her with a serious expression. "How are you feeling?"

Polly managed a weak smile. "Not too bad, thanks. It's just my head. Really hurts."

"I will prescribe some painkillers. You have been unconscious for some hours. We have X-rayed your skull; you have no fractures, but perhaps a little remaining concussion. We have stitched your head. You had two nasty wounds, one on your right temple—that only needed butterfly stitches—but a deep gash on the back of your head. I'm afraid we had to cut away some of your hair." He glanced apologetically at Polly's blond frizz.

"Ouch!" Polly grimaced. "Will it show?"

"I don't think so." He smiled, revealing a set of white, even teeth. "You have much hair. It will cover the area we had to cut."

Polly thought she had never seen such beautiful teeth. She smiled back. "Yeah, point made. Look, Dr. Mir, can you tell me what's happened? How did I get here? And how long will I have to stay?"

"You must stay overnight. We are always careful with head injuries. It's just to make sure."

***

The painkillers worked quickly and Polly began to feel better. She was left alone for a couple of hours and just as she was beginning to feel hungry, the door opened. Two police officers entered the room.

"Ms. Hewitt?" asked the older one.

Polly felt suddenly cautious. "Reverend Hewitt, actually."

"My apologies, Reverend. I'm Sergeant Hooper, and this is my colleague, PC Dachery."

They both flipped open warrant cards, holding them briefly in front of Polly, and the young female officer partly hidden behind the sergeant nodded to Polly and half smiled.

"How are you feeling?" continued the sergeant.

"Okay, thanks. But I'd like to know what's going on. How did I get here?"

"You don't remember?"

Polly said, "Well, I remember hitting my head, but I didn't think it was all that bad. Oh, and the money! I do remember the money."

The two police officers exchanged glances. PC Dachery took over. "What can you tell us about the money, Polly? Do you mind if I call you Polly?"

Polly shrugged. "Can't tell you much. It looked like there was a lot, but that's only a guess. It always looks a lot if it's in a bundle like that, doesn't it?"

"A bundle?"

"I watched Frank peel off a twenty-pound note from this bundle he was carrying, so I assumed all the rest of the bundle was twenties. But it may not have been. It might have been tens or fives."

"Did you handle the notes yourself?" asked Sergeant Hooper.

Polly shook her head. "But I was concerned. Frank hasn't a clue about money. Oh, where is he, by the way? Is he all right? I promised his parents I'd find him and take him home. Made a pig's ear of that one," she added ruefully.

"Frank's fine. He helped us with our enquiries."

"You arrested him? Oh no! His parents were afraid of that very thing. They didn't want the police involved. I promised! Look, I know he pushed me, but I don't want to press any charges."

"That's out of your hands, Reverend. Circumstances beyond your control," said the sergeant. "Anyway, we didn't arrest him, we briefly questioned him. You see, we have a witness who claims that you tried to take the money off Frank and it was in the ensuing struggle that you fell and hit your head. What do you have to say to that?"

Polly glared at him. "That's not true! What witness? There was no one else there except—oh! You don't mean that sleaze ball who runs the place, do you? That skinny bit of a kid with studs and rings and bling?" She laughed. "You're taking his word for it?" she asked incredulously.

"I thought you couldn't recall what happened."

Polly responded angrily. "I do know I wouldn't have tried to snatch anything off Frank, especially not money. I'm not completely stupid."

The sergeant closed his notebook. "We're having the notes fingerprinted," he said in a matter-of-fact way. "That'll be all for now, but we will need to see you down at the station when you're well enough. We'll need to take your prints for elimination purposes. We need to establish the truth."

"I'm telling you the truth," shouted Polly. "Why don't you believe me? I'm a curate, for God's sake! I don't lie."

Chapter Five

Henry was feeling distinctly grumpy, which was rather unlike him. Normally of a benign and placid disposition, Henry was seldom unduly fazed by events in his parishes, which after fifteen years ran almost entirely to his liking.

Today being a Friday, he had enjoyed the morning on Diss Station checking on the trains to London and expressing suitable ire at hold-ups on the line causing delays in the Eastern region. Since this was something of a familiar occupation with Henry, the ticket office clerk had suddenly become extremely busy at Henry's approach and advised him brusquely to contact National Express direct. This, Henry had every intention of doing. Meanwhile, it had satisfied his inner need for straight lines and an ordered life to spend a couple of hours sitting on the platform seat watching the trains come and go, discharging and recharging with passengers. Mavis had opted out of this exciting pursuit, pleading the need to tidy the garden and prepare lunch.

Although they always had a cooked lunch, on Friday it was a more elaborate affair than usual. Feeling satisfyingly full and distinctly sleepy, Henry was now sitting in his favourite armchair in the lounge in his slippers with his feet resting on a small footstool, the top of which had been lovingly embroidered by Mavis for their tenth wedding anniversary many years ago. Henry had a mug of tea on the elegant occasional table by his right-hand side, *The Times* on the floor to his left, and golf on the television. He was happy.

Until the phone rang.

Henry lifted the receiver. He put on his courteous-but-keep-at-a-distance clergy voice. "Thorpemunden rectory. Canon Winstone speaking."

"Henry? Percy Thetford here. Hope I haven't caught you at a bad time?"

Henry groaned inwardly, wondering why it was impossible for bishops to open the Diocesan Directory to ascertain their clergy's day off. Thorpemunden Benefice had long since learned that Henry's day off was sacrosanct and left him well alone on Fridays. Not so his suffragan bishop.

Percy, Bishop of Thetford, lived not in the London overspill town of Thetford, with its reputation as one of the few areas in Norfolk that could legitimately be described as "urban priority," but in the far more salubrious area of Stoke Holy Cross, a small and picturesque village close to Norwich. He had responsibility under the diocesan bishop, the Lord Bishop of Norwich, for the area of the diocese south and east of Norwich. His counterpart John, the Bishop of Lynn, lived not in King's Lynn (parts of which also approached "urban priority" status) but in the far more salubrious area of Castle Acre, another picturesque village, with the ruined abbey of Castle Rising within spitting distance. He had responsibility for the area north and west of Norwich. The Lord Bishop of Norwich lived in a palatial house in the centre of Norwich, with a large and extremely impressive garden that he regularly opened for fund-raising events throughout the community. Naturally, he did not tend the garden himself, instead employing a full-time gardener. The bishop's house had the added advantage of being in the shadow of the cathedral, which the bishop could easily reach via his garden. Since he was a very busy man with his seat in the House of Lords and his packed timetable of important meetings and important people (the press numbering among them), he had direct responsibility only for Norwich itself, although his ultimate responsibility was for the whole diocese. And as Bishop Percy well knew, Gerald, Lord Bishop of Norwich, was very definitely in charge.

Bishop Percy, who had never served as a parish priest but had attended all the right schools, had risen through the ranks via the cathedral route. He had started singing treble at an early age, so had been schooled via the St. Paul's Cathedral Choir, which had opened many doors for him. After his voice had broken he had gone on to sing tenor in what he considered to be a fine, rich tenor voice, but which musicians in the diocese considered to be merely a competent choir voice. Nonetheless, after theological training and a spell as a bishop's chaplain, his voice had assisted his move to become Precentor of Gloucester Cathedral, responsible for liturgy in the cathedral and, by extension, in Gloucester Diocese. From there it had been but a short step to his appointment as Bishop of Thetford, especially as he had followed a well-known hymn writer into the post, which had thus become associated with church music.

Nevertheless, Bishop Percy was reckoned by many of his clergy to be a disappointed man who would have given his expensive dental implants to be a diocesan bishop and even more to have sat in the House of Lords.

Wealthy or not, it was clear he was going no further in his career. When trying to soften a refusal to his clergy he was renowned for saying, "I'm only a curate, really. Like you, I have to obey those of a higher station," thus reinforcing the Church's rigorous hierarchy system while at the same time evading direct blame for his own actions.

He was a small, rotund man with a head so devoid of hair that he resembled a pink, polished egg. That, together with his strutting manner like a chicken, gave rise among his clergy to the nickname, "Humpty Dumpty." Bishop Percy was aware of this nickname and rather liked it, assuming it to be a term of affection. He was not aware of "Pompous Prick," the nickname privately afforded to him by some of his ruder and more recalcitrant clergy.

Henry did not number among the recalcitrant clergy and, indeed, would have been shocked had he ever heard their nickname for his suffragan bishop.

Irritated by the call interrupting his day off, Henry nevertheless responded, "Bishop Percy! How nice to hear you. No, of course you haven't interrupted. Lovely to speak with you at any time."

"Good, good. How are you, Henry? Things going well?"

"Yes, thank you," responded Henry, curious as to the bishop's motive for calling him. It certainly wasn't to ask after his health or well-being, since he had spoken with Henry at length at Polly's ordination in the cathedral only a fortnight ago. Henry waited for the bishop's next move.

"Good, good. And that curate of yours? Shaping up, is she?"

Henry was mystified. "Well, it's early days, of course," he began cautiously. "But yes, she seems keen enough, and as I told you in the cathedral, I'll make sure she's competent. We're meeting regularly."

There was a pause on the other end of the phone. Then the bishop said, "Supervising her, are you, Henry? You remember how we talked about the importance of supervision?"

"I do indeed remember, Bishop, and I can assure you that I have taken your words to heart. I supervise Polly very closely and shall continue to do so for at least the first six months."

"I'm extremely glad to hear that, Henry. So you can tell me exactly what she is engaged upon today?"

Henry thought rapidly. Clearly, he was not privy to some hidden agenda here. "As Friday is my day off, Bishop, I can only tell you what Polly is doing today in quite general terms. I can tell you the schedule I have set for her. As to whether she is following that programme today, well, obviously that's a matter of trust. Might I enquire as to why you are asking?"

"Indeed you might, Henry, and I have to say that I'm deeply disappointed in you. Whatever your intentions—and I'm sure they're good—" the bishop made it sound as if Henry's intentions were anything but good, "—your curate has managed to create mayhem which clearly you know nothing about. You should be on top of all this, Henry. It should not need me to ring you up in order to bring you up to speed with events in your own parish. Do I really have to remind you, Henry, that Polly Hewitt is your responsibility? You are to oversee her and make sure she is up to standard. Do I make myself clear?"

"Perfectly clear, Bishop, thank you," replied Henry coolly, "but you still haven't told me what Polly is alleged to have done or how the news of it has reached your ears so very quickly."

"I've had an extremely serious complaint from the Mansfields. They tell me that Polly Hewitt is not only in hospital, but is likely to be arrested as soon as she is well enough to leave."

"What?"

"I'm afraid so. The Mansfields are very influential people, as you know, so you had better get yourself to the Norfolk and Norwich straight away and sort this thing out before it goes any further. Oh and, Henry," the bishop paused for effect, then added, "your day off be bothered!" before cutting off the call.

Henry felt dazed. He ran through the house shouting for his wife and eventually found her outside weeding the flowerbeds.

"Mavis! Mavis, quick. Something terrible has happened."

"What? What do you mean, terrible? Tell me. No, on second thoughts come on inside. You never know who might be listening." Mavis quickly peeled off her gardening gloves, flinging them down onto the small paved patio built for them by the diocese, and followed her husband into the house.

Henry was shaking and his heart was beating at an alarming rate. He wondered if he was about to suffer a heart attack. "Mavis, it's Polly. I don't know what to do."

"What has she done?"

"That's the trouble, I don't actually know. I've just had Percy on the phone. I've never heard him like it before. He's usually so pleasant and polite to me, but this time! Mavis, he sounded furious and he was angry with me! I don't know what I'm supposed to have done, but he practically swore at me and cut me off."

"He did what? Percy? Are you sure you're not mistaken? I've told you before you could do with a hearing aid. You do mean the bishop?"

"Of course I mean the bishop! What other Percy do we know? It's something about Polly. I have no idea what's happened, but according to Percy she's in hospital and may be arrested."

The colour drained from Mavis' face and she sat down heavily. "And the bishop's blaming you?"

Henry nodded miserably. "Apparently he's had some dreadful complaint from James Mansfield, which he's taking very seriously—and somehow, it's entirely my fault."

"Even though you have no idea what's happened? That figures," Mavis said, grimly. "They move in the same circles. The bishop shoots over there at least twice a year and I'm pretty sure they're both Masons."

Henry didn't shoot, since an early encounter with his best friend's air rifle at the age of ten had accidentally killed a robin. The friend had been delighted and congratulated Henry on his accuracy, but the young Henry had actually been aiming at a nearby tree trunk and felt physically sick as he watched the robin fall to the ground. He had never been able to pick up a gun since, even though he would have dearly loved to move in the same circles as the bishop. Neither had he been invited to the local Masonic Lodge despite the hints he had dropped.

Henry groaned. "What am I going to do, Mavis? He told me to get over to the hospital, so I suppose I'd better go."

"Just wait a minute. Let me think." Mavis was more adept than Henry at weighing up the options. "Look, I think you should go over to the Mansfields. Why don't you ring the hospital, find out how long our wretched curate will be in, and then go over to James and Daisy? After all, they may only have rung Percy because they know him. Damage limitation there first, then you can go and see Polly. Not that she deserves it, but I suppose we should be Christian about this."

A look of relief flooded Henry's face. "You're right. Polly is safe. She can wait. My first priority is to the parish and that means James and Daisy."

***

The receptionist at the hospital was reluctant to reveal any information until Henry pulled rank, introducing himself as Canon Winstone. The receptionist, who thought a canon was something you fired, immediately transferred Henry's call to the ward sister. Although guarded and less susceptible to manipulation, the ward sister was sufficiently open to inform Henry that Polly had suffered nothing worse than a bang on the head and would be out next day.

To his shame, Henry realised for the first time that he hadn't considered Polly's well-being at all. He had somehow assumed that nothing major had happened, but nobody had actually said so. Perhaps it was because the bishop had seemed much more put out by Polly's misdemeanour than by her incapacity, which had not appeared to worry the bishop at all. Yes, that must be it. Through all the haranguing, the bishop had put Henry's mind at rest over Polly's condition. Otherwise, his first thought would certainly have been Polly's welfare. Thus, Henry comforted himself and he reinforced his self-justification by reminding himself that the Mansfields held a central position within the church and contributed heavily to its finances. If he upset the Mansfields, the whole parish and ultimately the diocese would suffer, since without the contributions from the manor, Thorpemunden Church would be unable to meet its parish share.

That led Henry on to reflecting gloomily upon the evil of the parish share, that vast sum of money all parishes were expected to pay to the diocese annually towards the cost of its clergy. Since as incumbent Henry was expected to make sure the parish paid in full by dragging money out of parishioners, it made

Henry feel uncomfortably like a kept man and forced him to temper his sermons to give his people something they wanted to hear rather than what he thought they should be told.

***

As he rang the doorbell at the manor, Henry assumed an expression of concern. “Daisy, my dear!” Henry held out his arms towards her, making sure to keep far enough away to prevent her falling into them. Henry was well aware of the dangers of physical contact with his vulnerable female parishioners. “Whatever has happened? How can I help?”

“Henry! On your day off as well. We didn’t want to disturb you, but James said we must tell someone in authority as soon as possible, that’s why he rang Percy.”

“And Percy very kindly rang me. But he didn’t really tell me what has happened, so other than knowing that Polly is in hospital and that somehow or other the police are involved, I’m all at sea.”

“You’d better come in, Henry. James will be so pleased to see you.” Daisy led the way into the lounge, where James was sitting with a subdued Frank. “I’ll make tea.”

“James!” Henry shook his hand vigorously and nodded towards Frank with a smile. “Hello, young man. How are you today?” This usually raised a giggle from Frank, but today there was no response. Frank merely stared stonily in front of him.

Henry turned back to James. “What has happened? How can I help?”

James indicated an armchair for Henry and sat down himself. “It’s that new curate of yours, Polly Hewitt. If you remember, Henry, I did warn you against employing a woman. And she’s no more than a young girl. Where did you find her, Henry? She’s a liability. She should be kept under lock and key.”

Henry forbore to point out that having Polly was hardly his decision. He had merely requested a curate and had expected a nice, young family man with two point four children. Instead, he had been landed with Polly Hewitt by the diocese.

"Oh?"

"Our Frank here went missing, so we called Polly, it being a Friday. As you know, we don't like to disturb you on your day off. She did come over straightaway, but then she just took over in a very bombastic manner. Insisted on going out looking for Frank herself. I tried to go with her, but she brushed me off and told me to keep out of it."

Henry's eyes widened.

James continued, "It was even worse when she found poor Frank, here. He was enjoying himself in the Amusement Arcade in Diss, a harmless enough pleasure you might think, but Polly ordered him to come home with her. Well, as you know, one does not order Frank. That is not the way to deal with him at all—I would have thought Polly would have known that. What do they teach them at theological college? Anyway, she tried to snatch Frank's money out of his hand and naturally, Frank resisted. Well, he thought she was stealing it, so he was merely guarding what was his. With that she caught her foot, fell, and hit her head. Luckily, the young man working at the Amusement Arcade had the sense to ring 999, and the paramedics apparently arrived quite quickly. They took one look and called the police. Sid Ellis, the young manager there, was most caring and thoughtful towards Frank."

Frank, who had been struggling to follow the conversation, heard Sid's name and suddenly interjected, "He my friend. We mates."

His father patted his hand. "Yes, yes, Frank. We know. That will do, now. Why don't you go up to your room? You can watch television, if you like."

Frank grinned delightedly and shuffled off.

"And it was this Sid Ellis who testified to the police what had happened?" asked Henry.

James nodded. "Seems a sensible young fellow. Not much of a job managing that little Amusement Arcade, but he seems to have his wits about him.

"Henry, I had to collect Frank from the police station, and you know how I feel about that. Daisy had particularly impressed upon Polly that the police were not to be involved, and look what happened."

"But it wasn't Polly who called the police."

"No, she knocked herself out cold. But that's hardly the point. Poor Frank was terrified. You know how badly he's been treated by the police on previous occasions. It takes us months to get him settled again."

Privately, Henry hadn't observed much wrong with Frank, who had seemed a little quieter than usual, surely a good thing. But Henry wasn't about to point that out to James. He thought it might be diplomatic to ask James' guidance.

"How do you think we should handle this, James? I can't help worrying over what it would do to Frank if Polly is charged. He'd certainly be interviewed again by the police and might even be required to give evidence."

James frowned, unwilling to surrender the high moral ground. But he was also horrified at the thought of exposing his vulnerable son to any kind of rigorous interrogation, being well aware that that he and Daisy only just managed to contain Frank at the best of times. He was also of the opinion that Frank was unfit to answer any questions, but that had never bothered the police in the past.

He was saved from responding by Daisy coming in with a tray of tea, sporting the best bone china cups and plates with dainty floral napkins and offering homemade flapjack.

As Henry took a cup of tea and a piece of flapjack, Daisy said carefully, avoiding her husband's eyes, "I don't know that it was all Polly's fault, you know. She was only trying to help."

James immediately turned on her. "Not the kind of assistance we wish to see again, thank you. I do not like interference at the best of times, and this was far from being the best of times. There is a fine line between legitimate support and intrusion, and Polly Hewitt was well beyond it. Look how she took herself into our kitchen without so much as a by-your-leave and helped herself to toast and marmalade."

As Henry's eyes widened further at this evidence of malpractice by his curate, Daisy raised a half-hearted objection. "But she did make it for us, James."

"Nobody asked her to! That is my point. You do not come into this house and take over. And it's just an indication of exactly the way she behaved towards Frank. Clearly, this is her pattern. So tell me, Henry, how will you deal with Polly?"

Henry said, "Don't worry about Polly, James. I'll handle her. She's still only a deacon, which is paramount to a probationary year, so we shall have a long and meaningful conversation as soon as she's out of hospital and well enough to return to work. If she wants to remain in ministry, Polly will do what I tell her. You need have no worries on that score."

James escorted Henry to the door and shook hands with him. "We'll say no more about it, for now, then," he said, with the air of a man doing his friend a great favour. Then he added, "As long as there are no more incidents. It is down to you, Henry. Your responsibility."

Yes, thought Henry darkly as he drove away. *I have a curate for two weeks and suddenly everything that happens is my responsibility. If this is what happens in two weeks, what on earth can happen in three whole years?*

Chapter Six

Ella ran down to the sea, to paddle in the warm surf at the edge of the shore. Memories came surging back into her mind, like her mother spending hours in the sea with her, teaching her to swim, and the terrific sense of achievement when she managed a few strokes on her back by herself. She remembered meeting other children on the beach, joining other families, playing in their games, accepted just as though she belonged. She remembered the sun, which seemed to shine daily, for she had no memories of overcast days or of rain.

It was as though a photograph album had opened in Ella's mind and odd snapshots from her childhood kept popping up. She couldn't remember any men around at the time and always put her happiness down to that fact. When her mother had men (and there were many of them), Ella's life was precarious. Some of the men were kind to her, but some regarded her as a nuisance, and the worst ones treated her badly, although her mother always got rid of them at the earliest opportunity.

But here in Great Yarmouth, for what had felt like forever, there had been just her lovely, slight, Korean mother and her, so Ella had had attention showered on her and had blossomed during that time. She wondered whether folk were still as friendly in Great Yarmouth as they had been during her childhood, and that immediately brought memories of Mrs. Bunn, the proprietor of the guest house where they had stayed.

Ella turned back towards Marine Parade, struggling to recall where they had stayed before. Perhaps Mrs. Bunn was still there, in which case Ella was sure she'd not only be welcomed, but be offered a bed for the night. Mrs. Bunn had become like an honorary grandmother during the stay, allowing Ella to help her bake cakes and cook and serve in the Guest House and even giving her a little pocket money for her assistance.

Ella wandered back up the beach and sat down to brush sand from her feet and replace her sandals. She was unable to decide which road she should try since she had no idea of the name of the road where Mrs. Bunn lived. But she knew it was quite near the beach, so she reckoned that by wandering up each road in turn she might recognise the little house on the corner with its gable ends and the intriguing gate which shut by itself.

It was, though, a hopeless task and Ella soon tired of it. When she found herself outside the Lord Nelson, she went in and asked for a telephone directory, thinking it might be easier to locate Mrs. Bunn that way.

The owner, a beefy man with a beer gut and long grey hair pulled back in a ponytail, suggested that she might like a drink. "While you're searching, like. Searching can be thirsty work."

Ella smiled and ordered a Coke.

"Who are you looking for, anyway?"

"A Mrs. Bunn. She used to run a guest house here somewhere."

"How long ago? I know some of the guest house owners, but I don't know no Mrs. Bunn. And you won't find her in there," nodding towards the telephone directory, "Bunn's a common Norfolk name. There's thousands of 'em."

"What'll I do then? Is there any other way I could locate her? A list of guest houses or something like that? How about the Tourist Information place? Where's that?"

"Look, love. If you want a bed for the night, why don't you stay here? You can look for your Mrs. Bunn tomorrow."

Ella considered. It looked and felt like a cheap pub, but her money was running low. "I don't know—"

"If it's the money you're worried about, you could do a couple of hours in the bar for me tonight in return for a room," the proprietor said, shrewdly. He had noticed the heads of the early customers turning as Ella walked in and the interest which the presence of this young woman of somewhat exotic appearance had caused. He added, "Why don't you come up and see the room? Then you can make up your mind. Up to you, love."

Ella nodded. It sounded like a reasonable plan, which at least would give her somewhere to sleep tonight. After that, she could reconsider her position and perhaps come up with some brilliant new way of relocating her childhood home. She exchanged a smile with the careworn woman behind the bar and followed her host through the back and up a narrow, winding staircase. The proprietor offered to take her bag, but Ella kept it slung on her back. Since it was all she possessed and contained her gold locket, she didn't like to let it go.

The room was snug, under the eaves right at the top of the three-storey building. Both Ella and the proprietor had to duck beneath the sloping roof, but the room was clean and the single bed looked inviting. There was one small wardrobe and a dressing table, both old and mismatched, but functional. The view from the dormer window was over the street, and if she craned her neck, Ella could glimpse the sea in the distance.

She turned to her host. "Thanks, it's nice. Do you want me to start in the bar straightaway?"

He looked at his watch. "Give it half an hour. Settle in first. The bathroom's that door over there, and there's no one else up here so it's all yours. I'm Melvyn, by the way, and my partner downstairs in the bar, she's Tracey."

"Nice to meet you, Melvyn. I'm Ella Wim. See you in half an hour. Is what I'm wearing okay?"

He ran his eyes over her and nodded. "You'll do very nicely, Ella. Ever done bar work before?"

"Yeah, several times. I know my way around a bar as long as you don't serve a lot of fancy cocktails."

Melvyn laughed. "No worries there! The locals wouldn't know a cocktail if they saw one. No, it's mostly beer and spirits, usual stuff. Tracey'll take you through it when you come down."

Ella had a quick wash in the tiny bathroom and tidied her hair. She applied some sparkly green eye shadow with black eyeliner and mascara and was pleased with the result. With her smooth, olive skin and delicate mouth enhanced with just a touch of lipstick, she felt she didn't look too bad at all.

Down in the bar, Tracey quickly initiated Ella into the mysteries of the bar and the rates charged at the Lord Nelson. Trade picked up at around seven-thirty and the start of the England match. Holidaymakers joined regulars, clustered around the giant screen showing Sky Sports, and Ella was kept busy pulling pints while Tracey disappeared into the kitchen at the back of the pub to produce bar meals. Ella wondered how Melvyn and Tracey had managed without any extra help, for the pace did not let up all evening.

Melvyn was pleased with his new acquisition. Male eyes were drawn towards Ella, who somehow combined stunning looks with a childlike acceptance and trust. She wasn't fazed by male attention, although she didn't respond to it except with that enigmatic smile, and she was so clearly unworldly that the women, too, accepted her. Since she didn't respond to flirting, there was no way Ella Wim was after any of their men.

Ella was tired by the end of the evening and glad when Tracey slipped her a bar meal of chicken and chips. She helped Melvyn and Tracey clear up, then headed off to bed, sure she would instantly sleep despite the continuing noise from rowdy holidaymakers in the street outside.

***

Even though Ella was up early next morning, Tracey and Melvyn were already hard at work cleaning up from the previous night. Tracey insisted on stopping to cook Ella a breakfast of egg and bacon, followed by toast and marmalade and washed down with coffee.

"I'll have to work tonight, too, for this!" Ella joked.

Melvyn said, "Funny you should say that. Tracey and me have been talking. If you want a job for the rest of the summer, it's yours. Can't pay you quite as much as minimum wage, but you get the room and meals thrown in. That's if you ain't got no plans."

Ella shook her head. "I don't have any plans and I am looking for work. Are you sure?"

"That's if you're not an illegal," Melvyn added and chuckled. "'Course, if you are, I wouldn't expect you to tell me anyway! But you don't have no accent so I s'pose you're on the level. Have to be a bit careful round here, what with the docks an' all. Our last bloke got caught by the cops and I can't afford to let that happen again."

"I've been in England all my life," Ella said, "although I don't have any papers with me to prove it. But I am English. My mother was Korean but my father was English."

"That's all right, then. The job's yours if you want it."

Ella didn't have to think for long. She had to find work, she liked Melvyn and Tracey, and she had enjoyed the previous evening. She would only be working for pocket money, but with everything found, couldn't see how she would need much money.

She nodded. "When would you pay me? Weekly?"

"That's what we usually do. On a Friday night. Works out at about three pounds an hour. So if you work a forty-eight-hour week you should net around a hundred and fifty quid. 'Course, if it goes slack we wouldn't be able to pay you quite that much, but you've got the room and your keep, so you won't starve. Then there's tips. If the customers like you, they'll tip well, so it's up to you. All tips go into the jar under the bar, and then we share them out equally at the end of the week. We each get a third, you, me, and Tracey. Okay?"

"Mm, that sounds fair. So apart from the bar work, what else do you want me to do?"

"Just a bit of clearing up, cleaning and the like. It's not that bad and at least there are no ashtrays to empty these days. Anyone who wants to smoke has to go out in the street. We don't have a smoking area here."

Melvyn stuck out his hand and Ella shook it. She felt she had been offered a good deal and it was serendipitous to have found the Lord Nelson.

***

Over the next couple of weeks, Ella got to know all the locals who regularly used the bar. They were a different crowd from the holidaymakers, tending to come in earlier, drink a pint or two, mardle with their mates, and then go home. The holidaymakers were younger, later, and noisier and tended to come in family groups, most of them with over-tired and whining children who could be a nuisance. Ella was soon able to distinguish between locals and holidaymakers the moment the door opened.

Ella enjoyed the work, for she liked being with people and especially liked being with people on a professional rather than an intimate basis. From her pay packet at the end of the first week, which was smaller than she expected and as far as she could ascertain contained no tips, Ella bought a new outfit of smart grey jeans, which she teamed with a scarlet, low-cut top gathered into a knot under the bust and falling softly over her hips. She wore her mother's gold locket for the first time for months and noticed Melvyn eyeing her with admiration.

"Wow! You look terrific," Tracey said, fingering the locket. "Who's inside here? Is it your boyfriend?"

Ella shook her head. "Don't have a boyfriend. Actually, it's my mother. It's the only thing I have which has any value."

"It's lovely. It really suits that outfit. Make sure you keep it safe."

"I will," Ella said.

***

Although the pub was open all day, they were generally quiet during the mornings and afternoons. There was often a rush at lunchtime, and Ella was kept busy helping Tracey produce basket meals for families who liked to use the beer garden at the back in fine weather, but in between times, Ella was free to amuse herself. Occasionally she cut the lawn in the beer garden, but mostly she would either wander the streets of Great Yarmouth, still searching for Mrs. Bunn, or go to the beach where she liked to walk for hours along the sand or along Marine Parade. Ella never minded being alone. Although she found other people pleasant enough, she was happy in her own company. Despite previous distressing experiences especially during her childhood, Ella continued to take people at face value, and since this could lead to disappointment, she tended to keep people at arm's length, a strategy she had perfected over the years without quite realising it.

***

Ella bought herself a street map of Yarmouth, hoping the sight of the street names might jog her memory. She concentrated on streets leading down to Marine Parade, although Marine Parade had been extensively redeveloped over the last fifteen or so years. Perhaps Mrs. Bunn lived further away than Ella remembered. On the other hand, perhaps the redevelopment had somehow obscured the route to the beach.

One day Ella wandered up Laundry Loke, a tiny alley which obviously had once contained a laundry but which now had just a few remaining dilapidated houses that had seen better days. One end of the loke had disappeared completely, swallowed up into a new supermarket and roundabout. Ella called into the supermarket to buy some much-needed toiletries, then turning the wrong way as she emerged from the store, found herself amongst the houses and noticed a further tiny alley leading between two of them. She walked up the newly discovered passage and, to her joy, suddenly found herself outside the house she had been seeking. She recognised Mrs. Bunn's guest house from the gable ends and the unusual gate which had so intrigued her as a child; a gate that was now hanging drunkenly from one hinge. Without a further thought, Ella pushed open the gate and walked up the path to the front door, now peeling and ancient. She rapped on the door.

"Yes?"

The young man who opened the door was wearing jeans and a ragged vest, which showed off to advantage the tattoos covering both arms.

Ella smiled. "Sorry to bother you, but I wonder if you know where Mrs. Bunn lives now? She used to run this place as a guest house."

"What, about a hundred years ago?"

"Well, yeah, I reckon it must have been at least fifteen years since I was here."

"Hasn't been a guest house here for years. I've only been here five years, but you wanna go next door. The old girl in there might remember, she's been here forever."

"Okay. Thanks, I will."

Ella failed to recognise the old person next door, but when she mentioned her quest was invited in. Ella judged her host to be in her eighties and thought that perhaps Mrs. Bunn might be around the same age. As a child, Mrs. Bunn had simply seemed old to Ella, so Ella had no real idea of her age.

The old woman proved to be garrulous and only too ready to chat. "Well, she's gone of course, poor old Sadie Bunn. Very sad, that affair. Knocked the stuffing out of her, she never had the will to go on after that. Sold up pretty quick and moved away. We did keep up for a while, Christmas cards and that, but then I heard she had died. Broken heart, I shouldn't wonder.

"Mind you, she sold at the right time. Can't sell these houses now, not since that supermarket came. Nobody wants to live in the shadow of a great place like that. And noisy? I should say so! Cars at all hours. They sell petrol as well, so everyone comes here to fill up. It's open all day and all night, you know, so we never get any peace.

"They was good days, back then when Sadie Bunn had the guest house. I used to help her out sometimes, when she was busy. I'd do the sheets and towels for her, save her taking them down to the Launderette.

"How did you say you knew her?"

Ella said, "I stayed here, with my mother. What happened, then? What made Mrs. Bunn sell? I really liked her. It was a great place to stay."

"It certainly was in its heyday, until that business. She had so many guests; they used to come back year after year. Well, what happened was this." She leant conspiratorially towards Ella. "There was this foreign woman, Japanese or something. You know what they was like, no offence. Lots of soldiers—boys from round here—got stuck in POW camps in the Far East during the war. Had a terrible time, they did. Came out half-starved after the war. So I wasn't a bit surprised when that Jap woman did the dirty on poor old Sadie. But she had a heart of gold did Sadie and she wouldn't think ill of no one.

"She took in this Jap woman and her child—about seven years old, she was, just a waif—and she looked after them like they was her own family. They stayed for months, but the woman never paid a penny. She was always going to pay and I said to Sadie, I said, 'You want to get the money out of her, you do, or you'll never see it,' but Sadie kept letting it go, longer and longer. She felt sorry for 'em, see, 'cos they was all alone and it was obvious they didn't have much money. In the end, she told the woman she needed the money and that was the last she saw of 'em. Packed up in the middle of the night, they did. A moonlight flit and Sadie never heard a thing. She'd grown that fond of them in the time they was here. Treated that child like her own granddaughter and that was all the thanks she got. Cleared off without so much as a by your leave or a word of thanks.

"What, you going already, love? Are you all right? You look a bit peaky."

Ella mumbled an excuse and stumbled to the door, the forgotten memory now brought to the surface and clearly etched in her mind. The whispered instructions from her mother to be silent because they were going on a big adventure, the coldness of the night air, her own sleepiness and the effort to stifle her yawns, and the frisson of excitement she had felt when the stair had creaked.

On numerous occasions, she had asked her mother when they were going back to Yarmouth and when they would see Mrs. Bunn again, but her mother had always evaded the questions. Ella had missed Mrs. Bunn, missed the seaside, and missed the happiness of those carefree months. And her happy memories were now sullied with the shame she felt over her mother's actions and the guilt she felt over Mrs. Bunn's death.

She left the cottage as quickly as she could and walked back to the Lord Nelson, her mind full of the unwelcome revelations she had just heard.

"You all right?" Tracey asked.

Ella shook her head and her eyes filled. At Tracey's concerned expression, she began to tell her about the events of the afternoon, and once she started, the words poured out in a torrent.

"So you didn't remember any of this?"

"Not until Mrs. Bunn's next-door neighbour this afternoon. As soon as she told me, I remembered it all vividly. I suppose I was blocking it out somehow."

"Did you tell her who you were?"

"No way! I was so ashamed, I couldn't get out fast enough."

"And you never knew why you left in the middle of the night? Didn't you think it odd?"

"I never thought about it. I was only a kid. Took it for granted as what always happened. You do, don't you, as a child?"

Tracey nodded. "Guess so. Anyway, it's over now, love. You can't do nothing about it now and let's face it, it wasn't your fault. What'll you tell your mother, though?"

Ella frowned. "My mother died earlier this year."

Tracey caught her breath. "Oh Ella, I'm so sorry! I had no idea. What happened? Was she ill?"

Ella nodded. "I nursed her for the last nine months of her life." Her shoulders began to heave. "It was so awful watching her deteriorate day by day and nothing I could do about it."

"What was it, cancer?"

"No," Ella said through her tears. "Not cancer. My mother died of AIDS."

Chapter Seven

Polly saw no more of gorgeous Dr. Mir and was discharged first thing on the Saturday morning. She was without transport and nervous of ringing Henry for a lift, so was forced to call for a taxi. She had no money with her and told the taxi to wait while she ran into her house at Mundenford to find some cash.

Although events at the Amusement Arcade that had caused her overnight stay in hospital were still mainly blank, she felt completely well and decided to spend the day continuing with her visiting, reckoning that she might find people at home on a Saturday morning. Besides, since she was only reading the lesson and serving at the altar for Communion at church next day, she had nothing to prepare for the services. She would be trailing Henry, first at Thorpemunden Church at eight a.m., then driving with him back to Mundenford, and finally rushing over to Middlestead for the eleven o'clock service. The afternoon, thank goodness, was free before Evensong at Beesthorpe at six-thirty.

Polly was looking forward to the next day's services, for she felt that her new calling was really about church on a Sunday. Of course, mid-week activities and pastoral care were important, but in Polly's eyes, the Sunday services defined priesthood. She wondered what Henry was like as a preacher, suspecting that he was impressive with his rich, melodious voice and the measured pace of his speech. And according to the figures in the Diocesan Directory, the congregations at Henry's parishes, although very small, were holding up reasonably well for rural Norfolk, which must say something about Henry's input.

Unaware that Henry knew about her hospital stay, Polly decided to say nothing to anyone about what had happened. She felt it was only fair to Frank to keep some confidentiality about his disappearance, and given James and Daisy's paranoia about the way their son was regarded by other people, she was certain that they would approve her decision.

***

Polly cycled to Thorpemunden on the Sunday morning, arriving twenty minutes before the service was due to start.

Henry, already robed for the service, looked at his watch. "Good morning, Polly. How are you? All right? Good. I like to give myself half an hour to prepare for services. I think it's a good policy and would be obliged if you could follow suit."

"Oh! Sorry, I thought twenty minutes was long enough."

"Not to prepare properly. One needs at least five minutes silent prayer, and some of the congregation begin to arrive fifteen minutes before the service starts. Besides, one needs to check that the altar is ready."

Polly reflected that with James Mansfield as churchwarden, the altar at Thorpemunden was certain always to be pristine. She couldn't imagine him being anything other than exact. "I'll robe now, then, shall I?"

Henry nodded and watched as Polly pulled out of her bag her black cassock and black preaching scarf with its colourful appliqué of gold on the lower ends, depicting the cross surrounded by a crown of thorns. Henry, who had plain stoles and a plain preaching scarf, eyed it askance, but said, "What robes have you brought with you? No, Polly. This is a Eucharist, a service of Holy Communion. You should have brought a cassock-alb—your white robe—and a green stole, as we are in the Trinity season. Surely you know that?"

Polly's cheeks burned. She felt like a foolish child. "I—I'm sorry. I never thought. What shall I do?"

Henry looked displeased. "You'll have to wear what you've brought, obviously. Please remember in future that we wear an alb and stole for Communions, and for non-Eucharistic services we wear choir robes. You do know what they are, I presume. Black cassock and black preaching scarf, although yours hardly qualifies as black, does it?"

Polly bit her lip. She was immensely proud of her scarf and of her stoles, all of which were equally stunning with different modern, embroidered designs. "It was given to me by my presenting parish in the Bayswater Road in London as an ordination gift. And all my stoles were gifts, too."

"As long as you realise that we're not here to make a fashion statement or to commend ourselves. The purpose of robes is not to show off ourselves but to hide ourselves beneath standard dress so that we can point away from ourselves and towards God. Therefore, I myself prefer a much plainer style. Do you not feel that so much finery can be a distraction for those who are trying to worship?"

Polly was rescued from the need to reply by the arrival of the earliest worshippers. There was no further opportunity to speak until after the service when they were driving to Mundenford Church in Henry's car.

Henry was strangely silent on the short journey to Mundenford and seemed so deep in thought that Polly didn't dare intrude. Thinking that perhaps he was engaged in silent prayer, she sat uncomfortably beside him, holding herself stiffly and saying nothing.

As she had at Thorpemunden, Polly processed down the aisle in front of Henry at the start of the service. After reading the set lesson from the gospel, she served at the altar, handing Henry the wafers, wine, and water, receiving the offertory plate from a member of the congregation, and handing it to Henry. Then she held a small bowl of water and a linen towel for Henry to ritually wash his hands before beginning the long, Eucharistic prayer through which the elements of bread and wine were blessed. She was also responsible for offering the chalice to each member of the congregation, but there her duties ended. For the rest of the service she sat and listened.

Henry had given only a short homily at Thorpemunden, but as the service here at Mundenford was an hour rather than half an hour, he expanded the homily to a ten-minute sermon. Polly listened carefully and was impressed by the content, but by the time she had heard the exact same sermon twice more, at Middlestead at the eleven o'clock service and at Beesthorpe in the evening, she was heartily sick of it and her mind was wandering.

***

Father Brian was in the congregation for Evensong at Beesthorpe, which attracted only nine people in all. Polly marvelled at his commitment, for he had already taken the service at Kirkby Thorpe that day. Henry introduced her to him after the service.

Father Brian was small and round, with a ring of white hair at the back of his head giving the impression of a monk's tonsure and adding to the feeling of holiness that Polly experienced as she took his hand. His blue eyes twinkled as they met Polly's and he shook hands firmly.

"So you're Polly? I'm very pleased to meet you. Henry needs some help here. No one can adequately run six parishes alone and I'm not much help. I do my best, but I can't manage more than one service a day. How are you finding it?"

"Great, thanks. I've really enjoyed today, going round with Henry."

"But you'd rather be on your own?"

Polly blushed, wondering what telltale sign had revealed her deeper feelings to the astute old priest. She laughed to cover her confusion. "I 'spect that'll happen in due course. Guess I have to learn some patience."

"And what would you do if you were on your own? Evensong or something different?"

Polly hesitated. "People seem to like Evensong," she said, without much conviction.

"Nine of us do, you mean," retorted the old man. "And look at us, all in our seventh or eighth decade! No younger people. How would you bring in the youngsters?"

Polly's eyes sparkled. This was her forte, where she was full of ideas. "Maybe have an occasional Taizé service or a Celtic service. Offer a picnic tea and games for the children and perhaps get a band for some modern music." She added eagerly, "We could even start a parish band. There must be young people round here who can play guitars or keyboards or a flute or something."

By now almost all the congregation had gathered round and were listening, most of them with despondent faces. Henry, too, shaking hands at the door with the one or two who were leaving, had overheard Polly's words. He came over.

He said, "Thank you, Polly. I'm not sure you will be able to recruit anyone here for any nonsense like that! Personally, the thought of guitars seems to me to be the very antipathy of worship. But I suppose that's modern ideas."

This drew relieved smiles from the people, but Polly felt betrayed and alone. She shot a hurt glance at Father Brian, suspecting that he had led her to reveal her inmost thoughts for the express purpose of seeing her put down, but to her surprise caught an expression of concern on his face.

Father Brian said, "We all have to move with the times, Henry, if the Church of England is going to survive at all in country areas. Much as I love Evensong—as we all do—in another twenty years, this little church here at Beesthorpe will be closed if we don't do something to attract the young. Polly here might be just the person to do that. I do hope everyone here will support her."

Polly could have hugged him, especially when Henry grudgingly conceded, "Well, well, you may be right at that, Brian. We shall have to see."

***

As soon as they were in the study on the Monday morning for their weekly session together, Henry demanded, "Well, what have you got to say for yourself?"

Polly wrinkled her brow. "What? What about?"

"Isn't there something you want to tell me?"

"What sort of thing?"

"Polly, do you really think that I'm in ignorance of your shenanigans this last weekend?"

"My what?" Polly was furious. Her brows drew together, her lips pursed, and her nostrils pinched. She had had just about the worst weekend of her life after doing a good turn to save this insufferable man's day off, ending up in hospital as a result, and he was somehow twisting it.

"Exactly what have you heard?"

"Polly, you've been here five minutes, you've upset the most influential parishioner we have, you have the police after you, and then you have the temerity to tell the evening congregation how their services should be run—"

"It wasn't like that! None of it was like that. What do you mean I upset the Mansfields? I was doing them a favour. Last night Father Brian asked me what I thought. I was merely replying. Anyway, you haven't asked me what happened. Why don't you listen to my side of the story?"

"I gave you every opportunity yesterday to share what had happened with me, but you chose to keep silent. That in itself tells me a great deal. Silence is generally reckoned a tacit admission of guilt, and you have given me no reason to think otherwise. If you can't trust me, Polly, maybe you should consider another post."

Polly blanched, trying to prevent her lower lip from trembling. She retorted, "Maybe I should. To be honest, Henry, at yesterday's services I felt like I was stepping back two hundred years into a kind of worship time warp. I really don't know how much I'm going to learn about the living church here in this benefice, and that does bother me. Why, there's nobody at all in any of the congregations under the age of sixty."

Henry bridled. "Older people aren't on the scrap heap, you know. They have plenty to offer. There is a real ministry for the retired and I like to encourage it. And the Church is about far more than worship. The sooner you realise that, the better. You know nothing about country life and even less about running six churches, yet you come here thinking you know everything. You've a lot to learn, young lady."

"I realise that, but exactly how am I supposed to learn anything other than how to look after old people? Why don't you let me start a Parents and Toddlers group or an informal evening service or a Communion for young people? It would be brilliant and bring in a few younger people, but you don't seem to want to let me breathe on my own. What's the matter, Henry, do you find me threatening or something?"

They glared at each other until Henry said, "You'd better sit down. We can't go on like this. Let me spell out what I expect from you as my curate.

"I expect you to be on time for services, and that means arriving at least half an hour before the service starts. I expect you to have the correct robes for each service. I expect you to learn to take services here so well that you can recite them in your sleep. I expect you to preach once in every six weeks, the maximum permitted by the diocese in this first year. I expect you to be guided by me in what you should be doing in the parishes. You have to learn your craft first, Polly, before branching out. Next year we'll look at some of your ideas and maybe take them forward."

"Next year?" Polly was dismayed. She was already bored by what she considered dreary services, enjoyed only by the very elderly. And she was already desperate for some company of her own age. “What about my expectations? Don’t they count?”

Henry said, “When I was a curate I was expected to do anything my training incumbent told me to do. And I might tell you, he was a lot less lenient than I am. He would never have permitted a conversation like this with his curate.”

“Oh please! That was a long time ago, Henry. Life really has moved on. If the Church doesn’t soon move on with it, there’ll be no Church—as Father Brian said.”

“I’ve heard doom-mongering like that for donkey’s years, but the Church is still chugging on. I do not think the situation is nearly as bad as you suppose. Why, in a few weeks, we will be having Harvest Festivals in all our churches, and you’ll find that the churches are full, as they are for Remembrance Sunday, Christmas, and all the other festivals.

“But listen, Polly. I’m not here to argue with you over every little thing. I hope we can sort out any difficulties between us like mature adults. So why don’t you preach at Thorpemunden’s Harvest Festival? It will be a big service, mind. Seventy or eighty people usually—and you may find some families are present. What do you think? Could you handle it?”

Surprised by the proffered olive branch, Polly nodded, although still aware of a vague, underlying feeling of discontent. But it would be brilliant to preach at Harvest Festival. She determined to prepare thoroughly, and her mind immediately began to revolve around ideas of global warming and green issues.

***

As August stretched into September, bringing an occasional nip in the air, Polly settled down to life in the Thorpemunden Benefice. She heard no more from the police about the incident in the Amusement Arcade, and Henry never referred to it again. James Mansfield was coolly courteous to her, but Daisy much warmer whenever she was out of James’ company. Polly saw

Frank only occasionally and reflected that it was as though nothing had ever happened. Everything was neatly swept away, out of sight under the stone church floor.

But Polly's feelings of discontent grew. Although she enjoyed her work and even began to get a genuine feeling for the old traditional Book of Common Prayer services, she still craved company of her own age. On Wednesday each week, her day off, she was lonely. She had no friends of her own age with whom to share her thoughts and feelings and even found herself going to the cinema alone. *How sad is that?* she thought.

The village people were warm and friendly towards her and she would often pop into Ivy Cranthorn's or Arthur Roamer's for a coffee and a chat. She got to know them both well and loved being with them, but it was like spending her whole life with her grandparents. Sometimes she met some of the village young people (Henry referred to them as "yobs"), who tended to gather in the church porch in the evenings for beer and a smoke, but they were all teenagers and regarded Polly as a kind of tolerated aunt. Besides, she was torn between concern for the peace of the villages, regularly shattered when the youngsters were fuelled with illicit alcohol, and making friends with the village youth. She didn't want to collude with their underage drinking, but neither did she want to be regarded by the kids as a typical church killjoy who was responsible for taking away their only pleasure.

Polly grew accustomed to spending part of her day off shopping in Tesco's in Diss. She had to shop once a week and it was at least a way of passing the time. One Wednesday morning in mid-September, she was greeted by a cheery voice behind her in the checkout queue.

"Hiya, Polly, how ya doin'?"

Polly turned to find the rural dean, the Reverend Charles Burgess, beaming at her. Her spirits immediately lifted. She liked Charles, who was twenty years younger than Henry and an evangelical priest, running Diss Parish Church, where he was incumbent, just as Polly considered a church should be run.

"Charles! Hi! Great to see you."

"Everythin' goin' okay?"

Polly pulled a face. "Yeah, guess so. If you like working in an old people's home."

Charles said, "Sounds like you need a coffee with your rural dean. Come on, we'll hive off to that little place tucked away behind the mere and you can tell your Uncle Charles all about it."

"It's just so frustrating," Polly began when they were seated in the little café, large cappuccinos in front of them on the blue gingham cloth. "I don't mind BCP services, I even quite enjoy them. But with nothing else at all to lighten the diet, it's so crushingly boring. Now the schools are back, I'm sure I could get a young mums group going. Maybe an Alpha—it would be great. I'd love to have them to a meal in my house, then follow with the Alpha course afterwards. I'm sure it would work and we might get a few spin-offs from that, like a toddler group or an informal service or something. But Henry won't even consider it. I mean, he's lovely but he's so old-fashioned. He says I have to spend this year—a whole year—'learning my craft,' whatever that might mean."

Charles grinned sympathetically. "Yeah, poor old Henry. Good man, but a bit stuck in the mud. I was amazed he agreed to have a female curate at all. I wonder if I could get you a three-month placement at Diss? I think we'd be more your cup of tea. We have a band to lead worship and loads of youngsters. Plus Tiny Tots and Sunday Club. We're running Alpha and our congregation numbers around three hundred altogether, a hundred or so at each service."

Polly gasped, thinking of the half-dozen regulars at Kirkby Thorpe and the dozen or so old dears at Hamblestead. "Sounds a bit livelier. Do you think Henry would go for it? Probably have to ask my tutor first. Then he could approach Henry. It would be so cool to spend some time with you. I mean, perhaps if I survive this first year, it won't be so bad. He can't always stop me doing what I've been trained to do, can he?"

"Think of it as a boot camp," Charles advised. "Something you have to get through. After three years, you'll be on your own and you can do whatever you like. The hierarchy don't like it if you rock the boat. They prefer good, quiet curates who just get on with it and don't cause waves."

"Oh, for heaven's sake! Not me, then."

"I'm only telling you this for the future. You don't want to mess too much with the bishops and archdeacons or you'll never get a permanent job in this diocese, should you want to stay here. Even if you move on, you need their support for references and things. You don't want to find yourself in limbo at the end of three years."

"I had no idea the Church was so political."

Charles laughed. "You'll learn! Once you're in its inner clutches, you'll find that politics rules."

"What about God? Doesn't God have anything to do with it?"

"Who?" asked Charles and they both laughed. Charles added, "I'll do that, then. I'll have a word with your tutor and see if we can't get you out of Henry's clutches for a while. Would at least give you breathing space."

And Polly was so happy she could have kissed him.

Chapter Eight

Henry flagged the letter in front of Mavis. "Just look at this! What on God's earth do they think I'm doing? If they think I'm not good enough to train a curate, why can't they come out and say so? I—"

Mavis snatched the letter out of his hand and was reading it. "She's behind this, that little minx. I can see her written all over it. How long has she been here now? A couple of months? Got her feet under the table and now she thinks she can do anything. I did warn you about her, Henry, right at the beginning."

"You and the rest of the world," muttered Henry. "I suppose I should be glad that they want to take her away for a while. Might give us time to breathe and recover. But it's the way it's been done, behind my back with no discussion whatsoever. She's been talking to someone, that's clear, and I'm going to find out who. I'll ring Percy."

"Do you think that's wise, dear? You shouldn't get across him. Why don't you ring that dreadful Charles or have it out with Polly herself, first? Find out just what's been going on. Then you'll be armed with the tools to confront Percy. But remember, he may not know anything about it yet. This letter is from Polly's tutor, and look, if you read it carefully, it's only a suggestion, not yet set in concrete."

Henry took the letter back and scanned it again. "You're right. I shall have something to say about this. It's such an insult to suggest that she needs 'a wider field of experience' when she's only just started. Do they think I can't handle things? Do they think I'm too old or something? Am I such a terrible person, Mavis, that they need to remove my curate so early in her career? How I wish I'd never mentioned the word 'curate' to anyone in authority. It's been nothing but trouble since she arrived."

Mavis took his hand. "Calm down, Henry darling. This is just typical of the diocese, so we shouldn't be surprised. It's exactly the way you've been treated all these years. Come on. Let's sit down together and think this thing through."

***

"Come in and sit down, Polly." Henry's voice was tight and angry.

Polly was aware that Henry might be upset, but she hadn't expected quite such a degree of chill. She sat back in the brown armchair in Henry's study, refusing to perch on the edge of her seat. Let him come out with it. She wasn't about to be intimidated.

"I presume you know why I've called you in?"

Polly shook her head and raised her eyebrows, refusing to help him out.

"Your tutor has asked my permission for you to have a three-month placement in Diss with the rural dean. He seems to think that your experience here is not sufficiently broad, whatever that might mean. I'd like to know your opinion."

Polly shrugged in what she hoped was a casual manner. "Perhaps he thinks an evangelical parish might stretch me a bit?"

"And why exactly might he think that?"

"Maybe you could ask him, Henry? I can't presume to know what's in my tutor's mind. He has a mind of his own!"

Her feeble attempt at humour fell flat. Henry glared. Then he rose and began to pace. Polly had never seen him so agitated.

"Are you pretending now that you had nothing to do with this? That you didn't set this in motion? Don't you even have the decency to own your opinions? How dare you do this to me! How dare you go behind my back and make arrangements over my head? How dare you talk about me to the rural dean? I'm disgusted with you, Polly. I do think you might have had the strength of character to approach me first. This is not a Christian way to go about things, so don't run away with the idea that your 'mates' on the evangelical wing have all the answers. If this sort of behaviour is what you learn from them, you're welcome to them."

"It wasn't like that—"

"No, it never is with you, Polly, is it? You're nothing but a traitor. I'm sorry to have to put it so bluntly, but for me, loyalty is a basic Christian principle, one that you don't seem to have grasped."

Polly felt hot tears sting her eyes and battled to keep them in check. "I only wanted to—"

"Yes, it's always about what you want, isn't it? You never consider anyone else. Did it even cross your mind to wonder how I might feel about this? Or the parishes? What do you think they will feel? Betrayed, like me. As though you don't care tuppence about them."

The tears began to roll down Polly's cheeks. "I didn't mean—"

"Polly, you never mean to do anything. That's half your trouble. You just don't think. It's time you grew up and discovered what life's really about. Therefore, because I think it will be in your best interests, no, I will not grant my permission for you to disappear for three months. Neither to the rural dean nor to anyone else."

"You can't do that!"

"Oh, Polly! Have you not yet learned about the freehold? I have the freehold to the rectory. That means I can do whatever I like, and there is not a thing anyone—including the bishop—can do about it. You are not going. Do I make myself clear? That's final and I do not wish to hear another word about it."

Polly smothered a sob and stumbled from the room. She felt hurt and humiliated, confused and angry. She wasn't sure just what holy laws she had violated. All she had done was ask for a few weeks of temporary respite and it hadn't even been her suggestion. How could Henry accuse her of disloyalty? Why, not only had she never said a word against him, she had also refused to listen to any gripes about him in the parishes. In Polly's view, Henry was the one who had been disloyal.

As soon as she reached home, she got on the phone to Sue Gallagher, her mentor back at her presenting parish in London. Polly's hand was trembling and she felt wobbly.

"Sue, something awful has happened. He's a bastard, he really is. He's accusing me of all sorts of things and I haven't done anything, honestly, Sue. And there's no one here to talk to and I don't know what to do and—oh Sue!" Her voice cracked and she began to sob in earnest.

Sue said, "Hush, Polly dear, it's okay now. We'll talk about it. The situation may not be quite as bad as you think. Have you prayed about it?"

"I can't! Why did God put me here? I hate it and I hate Henry and just at the moment I hate God too."

"It's difficult to pray when you're all wound up inside. That's why prayer partners help. Listen. I'm going to say a short prayer now over the phone, then we'll see what comes out of it. Okay?"

Without waiting for a reply, Sue closed her eyes and said what came into her head, ending with "Through Jesus Christ, our Lord. Amen."

Polly's sobbing on the other end of the phone quietened, so Sue remained silent, giving her friend time to recover and say whatever she wanted to say.

Polly said, "Sue, can I come down? I really need to see you. I've such a headache and my throat is sore. I think I may be heading for a cold. Could I come now?"

"Is it your day off?"

"It is on Wednesday. I feel so rough at the moment I can't see myself going in tomorrow. I can't visit anyone feeling like this and there's nothing else to do."

Sue felt a shock of surprise at Polly's words. Her experience of parish life was that there was so much to do you could work all hours and still never get done. It wasn't all visiting, either. Although she suspected that Polly's symptoms were merely the result of tears, she thought that perhaps she ought to find out what was going on. "Yes, of course you can, if you can square it with Henry. I'll see you in two or three hours then?"

***

Sue asked, "Do you really dislike him so much, Polly?"

They were sitting in Sue's comfortable lounge, with their feet on the small coffee table, a gin and tonic in their hands. Goldie the retriever was stretched out on the carpet, snoring. An Abba CD was playing quietly in the background, a bit dated for Polly's taste, but she knew it marked Sue's era and she found it surprisingly soothing. Having grabbed only a sponge bag, a pair of pyjamas, and one change of clothing before she rushed out to her car, Polly was still clad in her clergy gear of dark trousers and a yellow clergy shirt, but she had slipped the plastic dog collar out of the shirt and loosened the neck. Sue, having just escaped from a PCC meeting, was still formally attired in a navy pinstriped trouser suit teamed with a blue striped clergy shirt from Wippells, one of the earliest purveyors of clergy dress, according to its website. So early, Sue reflected, that when women had first been priested in 1994, it had measured female clergy shirts by collar size rather than bust, much to Sue's discomfort. The shirts were good quality, though, always looked clean and pressed and lasted well.

Polly hesitated, torn between her anger and resentment at Henry's treatment of her and the truth. Reluctantly, she opted for the truth. "No, I don't really dislike him. To be honest, I find him quite nice, when he's being reasonable. But you can't get close to him. He keeps everyone at arm's length. Anyway, he really dislikes me. He's quite cold towards me even on good days, and he won't let me do anything. There are so many things I'm longing to try and I'm absolutely certain they'd bring new people into church, but he won't hear of it. When I first went, he told me that old Father Brian was opposed to women priests, but he's not at all. I think it's Henry himself. Projection or whatever you call it."

"So what exactly do you do?"

"All the usual deacon stuff. You know, reading the gospel at Communions, serving at the altar, helping with the chalice. Visiting till it comes out of my ears, since Henry's view is that it's a lack of visiting that is causing the demise of the Church of England."

Sue grinned. "What do you think?"

"He could be right to some extent. You certainly get to know people when you're in their home, and most people are really pleased to receive a visit. But there's so much more to it than that. I mean, even I'm bored with a constant diet of BCP and I'm religious! I don't wonder that no one wants to come to church, at least not in the Thorpemunden benefice."

"But when you first went, I thought you told me the congregations were holding up quite well?"

"They are, but only with old people. There's no one under sixty and most are over eighty, so there'll be no church in twenty years unless Henry can be persuaded to pull his finger out."

"And you'd introduce bands and popular music and picnics and dancing?"

"Of course! Stuff people might be faintly interested in. More than that, though. There's no prayer group anywhere in the benefice, and without constant prayer, how can anything exciting happen?"

"Don't you and Henry say morning and evening prayer?"

"Oh yeah, but that's straight out of the book. There's no soul to it. It's just, like, routine. No emotion in it. We ought to have a prayer group which meets regularly, where people can say what's in their hearts. I'd love to run one."

"Perhaps prayer groups aren't quite to Henry's taste?"

"They damn well ought to be then," declared Polly, finishing her gin. "Susie, can I stay for a bit? Just a week or so to replenish my spiritual reserves. I feel so dry up there in Thorpemunden. Now Henry won't let me go to Charles on a placement, I feel like there's nowhere I can go to refresh my spirit. Please, Susie."

Sue yawned. "I'm bushed. This is too late for me! Let's talk some more tomorrow. See what things look like after a good night's sleep. I'll take some time off tomorrow and we'll take the dog for a long walk and see what we can sort out. Good night now, Polly. Sleep tight."

***

Henry pushed his plate away. "I'm sorry, dear, I just can't manage it."

"But Henry, it's only toast. You haven't eaten properly for two days now. You must have something to keep up your strength."

Henry sighed. "I'm so worried, Mavis. I just don't know what to do for the best. I keep wondering whether all this really is my fault. That is what Polly thinks. Should I have let her have her head and learn by her own mistakes?"

"You were only trying to protect her and start her off with sound principles which will stand her in good stead throughout her career. Why do you have to reproach yourself? You've done nothing wrong. And it's her that's gone haring off, not you."

"Yes, but where is she? Suppose she hasn't gone haring off, but something has happened to her? This is the third day without a word. I have no idea where she might be. Do you think I should call the police or tell the bishop or something?"

Mavis poured a second cup of tea and wrapped her fingers around the cup, savouring the warmth. "Have you asked around?

She's quite friendly with Ivy, always popping in there for coffee. Ivy and old Arthur Roamer. I'm told she sometimes sits in his garden for hours, doing nothing."

"The trouble is, as soon as I begin to make enquiries or knock at her door, the whole benefice will know that she's skipped and I don't know where she is. It's bound to get back to Percy via the Masonic Lodge, and he already thinks I'm a hopeless training incumbent. But on the other hand—what if she's lying unconscious in some ditch somewhere?"

"Nonsense, Henry!" Mavis declared robustly. "You've been reading too many of those detective novels you're so fond of. This is real life and nothing like that has ever happened in Thorpemunden. Yesterday was her day off, after all. Perhaps she was a little upset after your row on Monday and just decided to take an extra couple of days. Why don't you shut yourself in your study for half an hour and ask for God's help? Then maybe you'll know what to do."

"Huh!" said Henry. But he went off to follow his wife's advice.

***

"As long as you're sure it's all right with Henry." Sue was striding through the park, Goldie at her heels and Polly puffing a little to keep up. "It is rather early for you to be taking a week's leave, since you're not sick. What did Henry say when you told him you were coming here?"

"Um, well, um, I—er—"

Sue stopped abruptly, causing the dog to whine and look up enquiringly. "Polly! Don't tell me you haven't contacted Henry? Please don't tell me that!"

"He won't know whether I'm there or not," Polly said defensively, "and he certainly won't care. He'll be much happier without me. I told you. He doesn't like me."

"That's hardly the point. He's responsible for you. What possessed you, Polly, to leave without telling him?"

Polly mumbled, “I knew he’d stop me if I said anything, so I just came. Susie, I really need this break. Please don’t make me go back just yet.”

Sue Gallagher’s face was grim. “Come on. We’re going straight back to the vicarage and you are going to pick up that phone and ring Henry. And if you get a thorough bollocking it’ll be no more than you deserve.”

***

Polly’s face was ashen when she came off the phone. It wasn’t so much Henry’s biting words or even the coldness of his tone. It was more that faint note of both panic and relief she had detected. It genuinely hadn’t occurred to Polly that Henry might be concerned about her. Since early childhood, she had always been used to taking off whenever she felt the need. Nobody had ever bothered, neither her mother, who was usually so drunk she never noticed whether her daughter was there or not, nor her fellow students when she shared a flat. When she had returned, it had always felt like that verse in the psalm, “When the wind goes over it, it is gone and its place will know it no more.” She was shaken to hear the underlying concern in Henry’s voice and for the first time wondered what he had thought when she failed to show up for morning or evening prayer.

“What shall I do?” she asked Sue.

Sue busied herself making coffee and fetching the biscuit tin. She had noticed that whereas Polly had always had some discipline, taking only one biscuit or one piece of chocolate, she now seemed unable to stop. Her weight had ballooned since she went to Thorpemunden and her shirts, once loose because that was how Polly liked them, were now straining over her bust. Sue was more concerned about her young friend than she cared to admit.

She pushed back a few tendrils of brown hair, which as usual had escaped the knot at the back of her head and were trailing around her face, giving her the appearance of a bohemian artist. "What do you want to do?"

"That's just it. I don't know. What I'd really like is to stay here—get a transfer or something—and work with you. Could I do that?"

Sue looked dubious. "It's not completely unknown for a curate to change parishes, but it is frowned upon. It will be on your record and may affect a future living. You will be considered unsafe—someone who may not stay the course, who can't cope when life gets difficult. Is that true of you, do you think?"

Polly glared. "Of course not! It's not like that at all. It's not that I can't cope with Thorpemunden, I just don't feel I'm getting the right sort of training, and I do have questions about Henry's Christian commitment."

"Even though he's been there for hundreds of years?"

"That's just it. Everything is routine to Henry. There's no spark, no excitement. He doesn't seem to want anything which might disturb the status quo. There is so much I want to do for God, but I'm not being allowed to do it. I just have to sit there and watch a church devoid of any young people slowly crumble to death."

"So is it more than Henry's Christianity or gaining experience? Is there also something about your loneliness with no one of your own age anywhere near?"

Polly's face suddenly crumpled. She collapsed into a chair and began to weep, letting the tears fall in earnest.

Ah! thought Sue, *so that's the real problem. She's so lonely that she doesn't know how to cope with it. Never lived alone before and never lived in a village before. No wonder young curates usually opt for big city-centre parishes. There's time enough to migrate to the country when you have a family and want a better life for your children.*

Sue continued to muse over what she could do to help Polly. Should she ring Henry, whom she had never met? Alternatively, would it be better to ring Percy direct, since she had been with him at college years before? After all, Bishop Percy was Polly's father-in-God, so needed to be very concerned about her welfare. He ought to know the situation, for Polly couldn't be the only young curate in rural Norfolk suffering in such a way. If they weren't already aware, Norwich Diocese ought to be made aware of the pressures facing young curates serving their titles under elderly clergymen who were threatened by change.

Yes, the diocese should know. The decision made, Sue picked up the phone.

Chapter Nine

Ella spent the whole summer living and working in the Lord Nelson. For that time, she felt at home, coming more and more to regard Melvyn and Tracey as her family. The three of them grew quite close, although following her revelation about her mother, Ella was initially aware of a slight withdrawal on Tracey's part. However, since Tracey failed to find the nerve to ask Ella outright whether she was HIV positive herself and since Ella was exactly the same as she had always been, the reluctance gradually diminished and they returned more or less to normal. They seldom had time off together, but as Ella was happy in her own company, this was never a problem. She continued to enjoy the beach and even swam occasionally in the North Sea, when the sun shone.

The regulars soon treated her as though she had been there forever, often buying her drinks, which she seldom accepted, but put the money into the tips jar instead. She was also tipped for waiting at tables and noticed that the jar quickly filled and was emptied just as quickly. She presumed Melvyn emptied the jar and was waiting until the tips were substantial before sharing them three ways as he had promised. Although her weekly pay bought her a few luxury items like extravagant high-heeled shoes and a new bikini and one or two new outfits, it was not huge and never increased by any of the tip money. But Ella was happy enough. She never had much interest in money as long as she could get by, and it felt good to have regular work within a comfortable enough setting with people who liked her.

She occasionally experienced problems with men touching her inappropriately and making lewd jokes in her hearing. This minority seemed to regard her as fair game because she was working behind a bar, and Ella mostly brushed them off with a smile, ignoring their infantile humour, but one man became something of a nuisance.

He was a good-looking young man, clean-shaven with a square jaw and with black hair cut in a college boy style. He was smartly dressed in light chinos teamed with a pink short-sleeved shirt, open at the neck. Standing about five feet ten and aged around thirty-five, he appeared alone one evening, spending the whole time sitting on a stool at the bar counter.

Initially, Ella felt a little sorry for him, for he was unlike the usual run of customers attracted to the Lord Nelson. He gave the impression of being well educated and not short of money, and Ella feared that this, coupled with his pink shirt, might give rise to ribald comments from some of the more rowdy elements in the pub. She smiled at him and asked him what she could get for him.

He spoke in a cultured voice. "Do you stock Adnams?"

Ella nodded. "All the local beers. A half?"

"For starters. And have one yourself."

Ella smiled her thanks but explained that she had had enough this evening.

"Put the money in your cookie jar, then."

Ella was surprised he knew about the jar as he'd only just come in, but she smiled her thanks and accepted.

Then he said, "I'm Mark Winters. May I call you by your name?"

"Ella Wim."

"Pleased to meet you, Ella Wim. Has anyone ever told you how gorgeous you are?"

It was such an old line that Tracey, passing by with a tray of beers, rolled her eyes, and Ella laughed. But after that, Mark

Winters spent the entire evening following Ella's every move with his eyes. He bought her several drinks and she continued to add the money to the tips jar, but avoided further conversation with him. There was something odd about him, making her uneasy. Whether it was his intense, unrelenting focus on her, or the slight twist to his mouth when he smiled, she couldn't be sure. She just knew she felt uneasy anywhere near him.

At the end of the evening, he waited for Ella, asking whether he might walk her home, and seemed mildly offended when Ella informed him shortly that she never required an escort since she lived at the pub.

After that he was in every night, always watching Ella, constantly trying to start conversations with her, calling for her attention until she felt very uncomfortable in his presence.

Then the flowers started to arrive, delivered by courier. First, a relatively modest bunch that Ella quite enjoyed. She thanked him for them in the evening and he said,

"I'm in love with you, Ella Wim."

Ella moved away abruptly, saying over her shoulder, "Please don't say that. You know it's rubbish. And please don't send me any more flowers."

But the next day a dozen beautiful, long-stemmed red roses were delivered, with a card promising undying love. Ella threw them in the waste bin, where Tracey discovered them, fished them out, and arranged them in a vase in her and Melvyn's bedroom.

Ella said to Mark, "I've already asked you not to send me any more flowers. I threw the roses away and if you send any more, I will not accept them."

His face darkened, but a small, crooked smile played about his lips and he inclined his head.

There were no more flowers after that, but each day a gift arrived. Chocolates, perfume, even lacy underwear. Ella refused to accept any of them and did her best to avoid Mark Winters, but he was preying on her mind and she knew she was growing anxious.

The following week when Ella set out for the beach on the Monday afternoon, Mark was waiting for her and although she tried to avoid him, he walked to the seashore with her, refusing to leave her alone. She tried to move away, but he was like a limpet.

He said, "As you know, I'm in love with you, Ella Wim, and I can see by your eyes that you're in love with me."

Ella turned startled eyes on him. "Go away! I'm not in love with you at all. I don't even like you very much. You're stalking me and I don't want you or your gifts anywhere near."

He laughed. "I love it when you play hard to get, Ella Wim! That's why we're perfect for each other. I like the chase and you love being chased. You're panting for me. I can tell. You say these unkind things to tease."

Ella ignored him and began to run, but he caught up with her, grabbing her arm. "Not so fast, my darling. You can't get away. I shall never let you go now that I've found you. I've been waiting for you all my life."

Ella, really frightened now, began to scream.

As soon as Mark grabbed her, Ella had a flashback to her childhood. She was only small, around four or five years old and living with her mother in a one-bedroom flat. Ella never knew her father and, indeed, had no idea who he was. She was conscious of many "uncles" in her life; most of them would pat her on the head or chuck her under the chin. Some of them tickled her, which she half loved and half hated because it made her lose all control, and even at such a young age, she was uncomfortable not being in control of her own life. Other "uncles" brought her sweets or gave her coins or small toys, all of which she loved.

Mostly she went to sleep on the couch in the lounge, where she always slept when any of the "uncles" arrived, but on this particular occasion she was woken by screams coming from the bedroom. In a sleep-ridden daze, hardly knowing whether what she had heard was real or a horrible nightmare, Ella had climbed out of bed and padded over to the bedroom, needing her mother. When she pushed open the door she had seen the current "uncle" lying on top of her mother with his hand over her mouth, thrusting at her with his pelvis. All the small Ella could see was a huge male bottom, pushing and thrusting and driving into her mother, whose screams were stifled by the hand over her mouth. Ella, too, had begun to scream, and that was when the man had sworn furiously, leapt from the bed, enraged at being disturbed, grabbed the child roughly by the arm, and hit her across the side of the head again and again until she had fallen. Her mother had come to the rescue then, striking the man over the head with a heavy torch, and he had fallen asleep, so the young Ella had thought, on the carpet. After her mother had comforted her, making her hot chocolate to drink and putting her to bed, stroking Ella's head with her hand and singing to her in the soft, lilting voice which Ella so loved, she had fallen asleep. When she awoke the following morning, the man was gone and he didn't return. Ella never forgot that experience. She learned to be cautious around men and became deft at distancing herself from them with a smile that somehow discouraged any further communication from all but the most persistent.

When Mark Winters grabbed her arm, returning her instantly to that long-ago incident, the primeval scream that issued from Ella's lips was involuntary and came from somewhere deep inside her.

It caused passersby to stop, stare, and turn towards the commotion. That caused Mark Winters to drop her arm and move swiftly away, saying, "You'll regret that, Ella Wim, believe me. You'll regret it."

Ella didn't regret it in the least. She immediately took the opportunity to run back to the pub, where she poured out her story to Melvyn.

"Yeah, seen him eyein' you up," Melvyn said, "and no one could help seein' them flowers and presents he kept sendin' you. But don't you worry, love. I'll sort 'im out if 'e's in again tonight. 'E won't do nothing to you. I'll soon boot 'im out."

Ella's heart sank when she saw Mark Winters sitting on the bar stool as usual that evening, but Melvyn was as good as his word. Ella moved quickly in the opposite direction, spending more time than she normally did exchanging banter with a group of customers on the far side of the room, and when she looked again, Mark Winters had disappeared.

"What did you do?" she asked Melvyn at the end of the evening.

"You don't want to know, love," he replied. "But I'll tell you this, 'e won't be bothering you no more, that's for sure."

Ella said, "I'm so grateful to you, Melvyn. You and Tracey are such good friends to me. I find Mark Winters utterly creepy. I haven't been so scared for years."

Melvyn grinned with satisfaction. "You don't 'ave to worry no more, love. You won't see 'im again. I guarantee it."

And although for a week or two Ella was filled with trepidation every time she stepped out of the Lord Nelson, she did not see Mark Winters again.

***

By the second week in September and the return of all the children to school, the families had departed from Yarmouth. The weather was good, with a typical September Indian summer resulting in an influx of pensioners and the disabled, a few of whom found their way into the Lord Nelson.

Ella found a patience and acceptance in all the new visitors that had been less apparent in the younger holidaymakers. Although they still enjoyed their pints and their bar meals, few of this second wave of tourists became drunk or rowdy. It was a restful time in the Lord Nelson. Apart from local youths with nothing to do, the streets were generally quieter as the town began to wind down after the season.

Although nothing was said, Ella thought it unlikely that Melvyn would be able to keep her on for much longer, and she wondered what she would do when this seasonal work finally ended. But all those anxieties disappeared from her head the evening she went to put on her locket and was unable to find it.

Ella had taken to wearing her necklace most nights and distinctly remembered taking it off and laying it on top of the chest of drawers in her little room. When she went to put it on the following evening, it was nowhere to be found. Ella knelt down on the floor and shone a torch underneath the chest of drawers, in case the necklace had inadvertently fallen, but there was no sign of it. Then she wondered whether her memory was playing tricks on her and whether perhaps she had left the locket in the bathroom. It wasn't there either.

With dread in her heart, Ella systematically began to search every inch of her room and bathroom, pulling out the bed, taking her clothes out of every drawer, looking behind the radiator, and even throwing everything out of the wardrobe, but to no avail. The locket had disappeared.

Ella felt as if part of herself had been violated. Somehow, her identity was in the necklace and without it, she felt she was nothing. It seemed inescapable that some unknown person had been in her room, fingering through her belongings, someone who was well aware of the value of her locket. This thought filled her with horror.

As she started down the stairs to ask Melvyn and Tracey whether by any slim chance they had seen the locket, she found herself pausing by their bedroom door and pushing it gently.

The door swung ajar silently and without knowing quite what she was doing or why, Ella slipped inside. She had never been in this room before, usually running downstairs without even glancing at Melvyn and Tracey's room, but now she stood just inside the door, glancing around the room.

What she saw shocked her, for the room was even more untidy than the flat in Essex she had so recently vacated. Clothes were heaped everywhere, on the two chairs, on the bed, in a pile on the floor, and strewn haphazardly across the room. The bed was unmade and the sheets rumpled. Although Ella had been aware that the Lord Nelson was not in the top echelons of English pubs, she had nonetheless found it to be clean and tidy. The kitchen was always spotless, and Tracey worked hard at clearing up daily after the previous night. Melvyn helped, too, coping with the heavy lifting, and Ella lent a hand where necessary. The disordered state of Melvyn and Tracey's private room was unexpected and Ella found it disturbing.

Ella made her way through the clothes scattered on the floor to the dressing table, which was full of clutter; cosmetics, deodorants, cotton buds, combs, a hand mirror, and jewellery festooned the surface. Without any conscious thought, Ella began to rifle through the jumbled mass of jewellery; rings and necklaces, bracelets and brooches. Until that moment, she was barely aware that she was searching for her locket, but as she lifted the necklaces, letting each one drip through her hands, she began to sort more carefully.

Disturbed by a noise somewhere between a growl and a loud gasp behind her, Ella turned.

Melvyn, his face thunderous, his shoulders hunched like a rhino ready to charge, and his bulky frame filling the doorway, barked, "What the 'ell d'you think you're doin'?"

Ella, who was incapable of dissembling under any circumstances, said, "I'm looking for my locket. It's gone, disappeared."

"And what," he said, moving into the room, shutting the door behind him and leaning against it, "makes you think it might be in 'ere?"

Ella shrugged. "I'm just looking, Melvyn. I've searched everywhere upstairs and I just kind of stepped in as I came past."

"And 'ow exactly do you think it might have ended up in 'ere?"

"I don't know. Hadn't thought about that. It was just instinct, really. Not sure I knew what I was doing. I suppose if the clasp came undone and the locket fell from my neck without me noticing and one of you found it—"

"You little liar," snorted Melvyn. "You think we nicked it, don't you? That's what you think of us, me and Tracey, after all we done for you."

"No!" said Ella, who had not consciously considered any such thing until that moment. "You're my friends. I don't believe you'd do that to me." Even as she spoke, she felt suddenly uncertain. Nobody else lived in the Lord Nelson. Nobody else ever went up to Ella's floor. If the necklace was stolen, what other options were there? Now that the thought was in her mind, Ella was unable to think of any other explanation.

Melvyn noticed her uncertainty. His face turned a shade of beetroot and his eyes narrowed. He suddenly bunched his hand into a fist and rammed it into Ella's stomach. With a cry of pain, Ella doubled over and clutched at her stomach, retching.

Melvyn stood over her, his fist raised again, his face red and seething in anger. "Still think we're thieves, do you?"

Ella was coughing, spluttering, and fighting for breath. She turned as Melvyn brought his fist down again and he caught her face. Her nose began to bleed over Melvyn's hand.

The noise of the fracas had brought Tracey bounding up the stairs, her face already tired and careworn, now wrinkled in anxiety.

As Melvyn made to wipe his bloodied hand on his trousers, she shouted, "What on earth do you think you're doing, Melve? For God's sake, leave her alone. Don't you be using your fists on Ella."

Melvyn rumbled like a huge bear. "She thinks we're thieves, Trace. She thinks we stole her precious necklace. I caught her in here going through all your jewellery."

"You what?" Tracey stared at Ella in consternation, but Ella was still doubled up on the carpet. Tracey added, "And you think that gives you the right to beat her up? You fool, Melvyn! Don't you remember what I told you? About her mother? How she died of AIDS? You haven't made her bleed, have you? She's probably HIV positive."

Melvyn jumped back as though he had been stung and stared at his hand. Then he ran to the bathroom and could be heard running water into the basin. Tracey helped Ella to her feet. “Are you okay? He didn’t hurt you, did he? Sometimes acts before he thinks, I’m afraid. A bit too handy with his fists, sometimes, as I know to my cost.”

Ella said, “Oh Tracey, he doesn’t beat you, does he? I never knew. ’Course, I know he can act a bit rough sometimes, but he usually seems so calm.”

“He is, usually. It’s when he’s not calm that the trouble starts. He told me once that it’s like a red mist coming down in front of his eyes. He can’t think straight when that happens. He just starts lashing out. In a minute, he’ll be so sorry for what he’s done to you. He won’t be able to do enough to make it up to you. You won’t call the cops or anything, will you? Honestly, I know him. He won’t have meant any harm.”

“No, it’s okay. It’s not really his fault,” Ella admitted. “I don’t know what made me come in here. I shouldn’t have done it. I’ve never done anything like that before. I’m so upset about my locket. I can’t find it anywhere and it’s all I have of my mother. I don’t even have another photo of her. I don’t really believe you stole it, of course I don’t, but Melvyn thinks I do. Can’t blame him for reacting to that.”

“Come on downstairs and I’ll make you a cuppa. Then we’ll have a good look downstairs. Perhaps it did slip off last night and we didn’t notice.”

Ella followed her, grateful for her intervention and her solace. In her heart she knew that the locket wasn’t downstairs, and for some reason which she was unable to analyse, she was now more than ever certain that the necklace had been taken from her room during the day. She feared that she would never see it again.

Chapter Ten

"That was a lovely talk, Rector. I do so enjoy it when you come to Mothers' Union. Do you know we have some speakers who don't sound as though they're Christian at all? We have some interesting talks about beekeeping and the history of the Norfolk coast and global warming and so on, but nothing about God or Jesus. Oh dear," the speaker, little Alice Thompson, put a hand to her mouth and shot an apologetic glance at Mavis, "that's not a criticism, Mavis dear. You organize a wonderful programme. I know all the work you put in as Enrolling Member, but it is so good to have real meat, something to take home and think about. Don't you agree?" she appealed to the other members of the Mothers' Union as they sipped their tea.

Ivy Cranthorn said, "I thought Henry looked a bit peaky. Is everything all right, Henry?"

Mavis inhaled sharply. "Why do you say that?"

"He looks so pale. Those dark rings under his eyes. What's the matter, Henry? Haven't you been sleeping?"

Henry busied himself, selecting from the plate a pink wafer biscuit hidden under the plain rich teas. He was tired and the twice-yearly slot at the MU meeting was a chore at the best of times. He felt obliged to take a short service and preach to them on these two occasions, especially as Mavis was the sole organizer, but he had always hated it. He felt uncomfortable in a room containing only females and he was weary of the sycophantic nonsense bleated by sad people like Alice Thompson.

The plastic stacking chairs in the village hall were uncomfortable, and Henry was aware that he had spent the afternoon fidgeting, crossing and uncrossing his legs. Even in September, the village hall felt and smelt dank. It was uncarpeted and the floorboards creaked. The walls had been repainted a garish yellow only last year to try to brighten the place up, but after twelve months of the Brownies and Cubs with rambunctious games, they were already showing obvious signs of wear. One end of what had once been burgundy velvet curtains adorning the stage had come adrift, so that the curtain on one side, now old and faded, hung drunkenly from its rail, adding, Henry thought, to the general air of seediness. There was no doubt about it. This was an uncomfortable and depressing venue for the monthly MU meetings. For the first time ever, Henry wondered why the MU didn't meet in the rectory. *They could use our lounge*, he thought. *Why has Mavis never mentioned that?* As he glanced across at his wife he noticed her regarding him quizzically, which brought his attention back to Ivy's question.

Whatever Alice Thompson might say (and she always said the same, Henry had noticed) he knew that his talk on the topic of "Christian Forgiveness in Modern Life" had fallen well short of his usual high standards. His heart had not been in it today, and although he hardly dared admit it to himself, in view of his recent experiences he was beginning to have doubts about the efficacy of Christian forgiveness. Probably that had come through in his talk, making it weary, like him.

Ivy Cranthorn, who never missed a thing (Henry stopped himself thinking, "nosy old bat" even as the thought threatened to surface) had instantly noticed his discomfiture.

Now, twelve elderly, wrinkled faces framed by varying hues of grey, white, and impossibly black or blond hair, were regarding him with more interest than any of them had shown all afternoon. He pulled himself up and made the effort to smile. "I am rather tired, Ivy. You're right. I haven't been sleeping too well."

"Why not? Is something on your mind?"

Henry shrugged. "Who knows? You must all experience sleepless nights from time to time, eh ladies?"

That started the circle of women chattering, exchanging their own anecdotes of sleeplessness. Henry relaxed, avoiding Ivy Cranthorn's shrewd eyes.

Ivy hadn't finished. "I haven't seen that curate of yours for a day or two, Henry. Is Polly all right?"

Before either Henry or Mavis could reply, Daisy Mansfield interjected, "Haven't you heard? She's gone. No one knows when she's coming back. She may even move somewhere else."

There was a shocked silence. All eyes were riveted on Daisy, who reverted to her usual flustered self at being the centre of attention. She appealed to Mavis for support. "That's right, isn't it, Mavis?" Then, as she spotted Mavis' grim expression and realised that she may have spoken out of turn, added hastily, "Of course, I may have got that wrong. It was just something James, my husband, said. I may have got it wrong. Yes, yes, now I come to think about it, I'm sure I did. Oh dear, I'm so silly."

There was no way such a delicious morsel of gossip was going to be permitted to escape.

Jane Mattock pursued her with, "What exactly did James say, Daisy dear?" while Maud Tinton asked eagerly, "Is that right, Henry? Has she gone? 'Course, I always said she'd never last. Women in ministry! They just don't have the stature of you men. No endurance." She smiled winningly at Henry as she said it.

Ivy said coolly, "I don't recall you saying anything like that, Maud. Why, didn't you very kindly bake Polly an apple pie to welcome her here? I seem to remember that. Yes," nodding her head with her bird-bright eyes darting this way and that over the assembled group, daring them to support Maud, "we all made a little something to welcome Polly, and my recollection is that we were all very excited at the thought of having a female priest at last."

There was a general nodding of heads and murmur of agreement. Now the topic was raised, they wanted answers.

"So where is she, Henry? Mavis?" Bette Jarrold looked from one to the other. She was churchwarden of Hamblestead, a stout woman, well bolstered with old-fashioned corsetry concealed beneath a brown tweed suit. Having been a head teacher in her working life, she prided herself on always cutting straight to the chase.

Mavis said smoothly, "I don't know what Daisy has heard, ladies, but the truth of the matter is that Polly is staying with a friend for a few days. We're expecting her back shortly."

"So everything is all right, then?" Bette sounded a trifle disappointed.

Mavis put on her brightest smile. "Of course it is! Would you like me to invite Polly to one of our meetings when she gets back? She could tell us about her stay in London. She's staying with a friend in the Bayswater Road."

The extra detail effectively defused the gossip at the meeting, although both Henry and Mavis were aware that it would not only continue unabated in the car park outside, but was likely to be colourfully embellished before onward transmission by members of the Mothers' Union. Since those members were drawn from all six parishes in the benefice, before evening every village would have received a varying account of Polly's exodus, her present whereabouts, and the possibility of her permanent absence. But Mavis had done all she could in terms of damage limitation, so Henry had no further option other than to close the meeting by inviting the members to join him in saying the Grace.

***

With Daisy's revelation, the decision about whether or not to ring the bishop was taken out of Henry's hands. Clearly, the bishop knew as much or quite possibly somewhat more than Henry did, although how this had come about, Henry had no idea.

Surprisingly, the conversation with Bishop Percy was quite civilized and Henry thought that perhaps he had phoned Percy almost as soon as Percy himself had become aware of the situation, or that at last Percy was making an effort to support him. Henry agreed to a meeting with Percy and felt touched when Percy suggested that Mavis should attend too. Mavis was more circumspect.

***

As they drove to Percy's house in Stoke Holy Cross, Mavis voiced her fears. "I do hope Percy didn't invite me because he has unpleasant news to impart."

"Unpleasant news? What sort of news? What do you mean?"

Mavis shrugged. "I just wonder whether he's about to tell you that he's relocating Polly whether you like it or not." She forbore to add, "And wants me there to pick up the pieces."

Henry frowned. "I'm not sure he can do that. At least, not quite so easily. You know what they think about curates moving on. They usually insist on the full three years, even if the perfect job comes up just a month or two before the three years ends."

"I know that, but this is different. What worries me is how they will view you if they deem it necessary to move Polly. I'm afraid it might be considered quite a serious failure if they have to move a curate on after such a short period, even though we know the real story."

"Failure?" Henry swerved to avoid a cyclist who had suddenly turned out onto the busy A140 road, and swore under his breath with a quick sideways glance at his wife to make sure she hadn't heard his muttered imprecation. Mavis did not approve of foul language under any circumstances. Neither did Henry normally, but he felt that Mavis' insight coupled with the sudden manoeuvre to avoid hitting the cyclist justified some strong expression of emotion. He added, "I don't think we should jump to any conclusions, Mavis. And I certainly don't regard Polly's absenteeism as any failure on my part."

"Of course not, dear. That's not what I meant. As I said, we know the real picture. The bishop only knows what he's been fed, whatever that might be. So we need to make sure that he knows exactly what's happened before we leave this afternoon."

Mavis' fears redoubled when Bishop Percy kept them waiting for twenty minutes. They were perched uncomfortably on upright chairs in the tiny secretarial office, where the secretary ignored them, instead staring at her computer with a bored expression but doing no work, as far as Mavis could ascertain.

They could just hear the soft drone of Bishop Percy's voice through the walls. Although she could identify no words, Mavis reminded herself to make sure both she and Henry spoke quietly in their interview with the Bishop. Henry was usually so placid, but he was under great stress and just lately had occasionally raised his voice.

When at last the door to Percy's office opened, a young clergyman hurried out. He kept his face averted and rushed past Henry and Mavis without acknowledging them. He seemed very upset. Mavis and Henry exchanged a glance, wondering what had been going on, and on Bishop Percy's mood.

The young clergyman was shortly followed by Percy himself, his bald head gleaming as he wiped perspiration from his face. He greeted the Winstones urbanely. "Henry! Mavis! How good to see you both. So sorry to keep you waiting. Keeping well? Do come in. Emma," this last to his secretary, "have Mavis and Henry been offered coffee? No? Perhaps you could bring in a tray. Thank you, Emma."

He ushered Mavis and Henry into his office, showing them into armchairs that were deep and comfortable, covered in attractive chintz. The dark blue carpet had a thick pile and, as in Henry's study, books lined one wall of the room. Percy busied himself setting between Mavis and Henry an elegant occasional table on which he placed leather coasters. Mavis studied one. It bore a Scottish clan crest with three fleur-de-lis of the French monarchy and the name "Broun."

Mavis said, "This is nice, Bishop. I didn't know you had Scottish ancestry. And I thought you spelt your name B-R-O-W-N-E."

"Ah! The clan crest. Yes. They are rather special, aren't they? We have full place settings to match. The surname 'Broun' is the original Scottish spelling, from the French, 'Le Brun'—the brown one—descended from the Royal House of France, don't you know. Of course, there are all sorts of different spellings now and we ourselves do have the 'e' added onto the end of our name."

"Very distinguished," Henry remarked dryly. His mild sarcasm was lost on the bishop but not on his wife, who shot him a sharp look.

They chatted about the church and life in general as they finished their coffee. Then Bishop Percy set down his cup in a determined way and said, "Well, it's nice to chat but we must get down to business. Perhaps we should start with a prayer. Let us pray."

They all bowed their heads as Percy issued a short plea to God to be part of their discussions. What Percy really meant, Henry thought cynically, was that he wanted God to support everything he had already decided. Then Henry felt ashamed of his scepticism and issued his own silent apology to God.

Prayer and God safely out of the way, Percy continued, "Henry, Mavis, I'm concerned about Polly Hewitt, especially after your phone call, Henry.

"But I feel it's only fair to tell you, I have had a long chat with Sue Gallagher. Now Sue and I go back many years. We trained together. Of course, women couldn't even be deacons in those days, so Sue became a deaconess. She's come a long way since those early days and, as you know, now runs a large parish in London in the Bayswater Road area. She's a fine woman and a fine priest. I respect her judgment and I have a lot of time for her."

So that's it, Henry thought. *She rang Humpty Dumpty as well as me. Clever old Humpty immediately let it slip to James Mansfield, so now it's all over the benefice. Thank you very much.*

Aloud he said, "Yes, she seems very sound and a good friend to Polly, so I believe."

The bishop nodded. "I've asked you both here because I believe we need to work together to support Polly. It is difficult for young curates in rural situations, and to be honest, I don't think the Church has grasped that. Like the rest of the world, we sometimes tend to assume that as soon as our people are ordained they just get on with the job, as we used to, Henry, in our day.

"But times have changed. Most of our curates are at least in their forties nowadays and some are considerably older. They have their families, and their lives are pretty well sorted out, although obviously problems can arise even then with the change of direction. It's rare to find a curate as young as Polly. And of course, none of the problems that Polly is experiencing came to light at college."

Henry contented himself with nodding solemnly. Mavis said, "What sort of problems, Bishop?"

Henry held his breath, expecting a tirade against himself. His face lengthened and his lips pursed.

Percy said, "That's particularly why I asked you to come, Mavis. Sue Gallagher has had a long talk with Polly and has reached the conclusion that loneliness is at the heart of Polly's problems. Apparently she told Sue," here the bishop laughed apologetically, "that it's like living with her grandparents. Now, I don't think she meant that rudely, Henry. I think it's a cry for help and I wonder how, between us, we might respond to that cry."

There was an awkward pause as Mavis and Henry digested this unexpected information. Then Mavis asked cautiously, "Did you have anything in mind, Bishop?"

Percy nodded. "As a matter of fact, I have. Now I know Charles Burgess, your rural dean, suggested a placement at Diss for Polly. But I'm not convinced that's the answer."

Hallelujah! thought Henry, still in cynical mood.

The bishop continued, "I really don't agree that simply transferring her to a big, evangelical parish will help Polly in the long term, and that's what we all want, obviously, her long-term good. She needs a different kind of churchmanship to broaden her experience, which is why we placed her with you, Henry. She also needs to see what church life is like out in rural areas. Too many young curates of Polly's age have no idea of church life outside big city centres in these huge evangelical churches. When they reach fifty, sixty, they decide they'll go to the country to wind down prior to retirement. But you and I both know, Henry, that life in the country is no rest cure."

"It certainly isn't!" Mavis interjected. "Henry works all hours. Why, he's hardly ever at home."

"Quite so. That's another reason why we placed Polly at Thorpemunden. We recognize Henry's sterling work and we wanted to give him some help, after all these years."

"And presumably you thought I might have some talent for training a young priest? Some wisdom to pass on? Some experience to share?"

"Exactly, Henry." Percy still seemed unaware of Henry's sarcasm, but Mavis looked at him anxiously.

Percy continued, "Historically, the Church of England has always been much stronger in country areas than in cities or towns, and we expect this to continue. We want to encourage younger curates to experience the countryside and bring their own talents to it rather than migrating to big churches in city centres. So we want to keep Polly with you, Henry."

Mavis said hurriedly, "How can we help, Bishop?"

"Ah, Mavis. This is where I think you may come in. It seems that Polly's greatest need is for some friends of her own age. Young people that she can get to know, visit on her day off, and go out with in the evenings from time to time. I think if we could help her there, she might settle down much better. Then we'd all be happier. I wonder whether you have any contacts? Does your Mothers' Union operate a baptism visiting policy?"

"Funny you should say that, Bishop," Mavis lied smoothly, "we've been seriously considering starting just such a policy. So good for lay people to visit on behalf of the church, don't you think?"

Percy beamed. "I knew I could rely on you, Mavis. Oh, and you, of course, Henry," he added hastily. "Not that I'm asking you to vet Polly's friends, but you would know suitable young people who might be encouraged to invite Polly out now and again."

"We're also thinking of starting a Pram Service, for mums and preschool children. Polly might be interested in that."

Henry looked startled at this revelation from his wife, but the bishop failed to notice.

Percy clapped his hands. "Capital, Mavis, Henry! I think everything will work out just fine. You clearly have many new ideas in the pipeline. I'm sure Polly will return refreshed next week—oh, did I tell you I've given her a week's leave?—and will be delighted to help out with some of these exciting innovations."

He shifted in his chair, a sure sign of dismissal. Mavis and Henry stood and shook hands with him.

Percy said, "Good-bye. Thank you so much for coming. Be assured I shall keep you in my thoughts and prayers."

***

Henry grumbled, "What did you say all that for? I can't begin to imagine your old dears in the MU visiting young married couples, and as for a Pram Service! We have no plans of the sort."

Mavis waited while he negotiated the exit from the bishop's narrow gate onto the road. Then she said, "We have now, my darling. Don't you see? What we've done is pre-empt Polly. She'll jump at the opportunity to start some sort of Toddler group, but the initiative will have come from you, not her. That kills two birds with one stone. It makes you instantly concerned about and responsive to Polly's needs and also makes you a forward-thinking priest who is eager to encourage youngsters into the church. The beauty of it is, you won't have to do a thing. You won't have to relate to babies or small children. You can hand it all over to

Polly, take the credit if it's a success, and look sorrowful if it's a failure, because it won't be your fault."

Henry felt a little shocked. He suspected that there was something unethical about Mavis' pronouncement, but couldn't immediately put his finger on what it was. He said,

"This isn't like you, Mavis. I've never seen you like this before. What's got into you?"

Mavis grinned and squeezed his arm. "My man has never been threatened before. We've been through a lot together, Henry, but all this strikes at the heart of who you are. I'm not about to stand by and watch you go under because of some tuppeny ha'penny girl who can't stand the heat. You know what they say. If you can't stand the heat—"

"—get out of the kitchen," chorused Henry.

Chapter Eleven

"What did they say?" Polly was lying on her back on the floor, her favourite resting place, her bare feet up on the sofa and crossed at the ankles. She was dressed casually in blue jeans and a loose, rugby-style shirt in blue, green, and white stripes, with a white collar and cuffs. She was still wearing the multicoloured bandana which she had tied around her hair prior to walking Goldie.

Sue came in from the kitchen bearing two mugs of steaming coffee. She set one down on the coffee table, and Polly moved to a sitting position, legs outstretched, leaning against the sofa.

Sue said, "Henry was a bit stiff and starchy, but then he doesn't know me. But dear old Percy—do they still call him Humpty Dumpty? He was as bald as a coot even back in college days—he was lovely. Sounded quite pleased to hear from me after all this time and he was very concerned about you."

"Does that mean he'll put pressure on Henry to let me go to Charles' for a couple of months?"

Sue sipped her coffee, made a face, and went back into the kitchen to find the sweeteners. She called out, "He didn't say. I put him in the picture as best I could without slagging off Henry. Didn't want to make him too defensive." She came back to the lounge with the sweetened coffee and sat in one of the armchairs. As she had a big study in which she could hold church meetings, Sue kept the lounge all to herself. It was a much smaller room than the study, but big enough to hold three armchairs and a sofa. Having spent a year or two as a naval chaplain, Sue referred to it as “The Snug,” which in Polly’s estimation described it exactly. It was a warm and cosy room.

Sue continued, “I think it would be counterproductive to heap blame on Henry. As soon as you get into the blame game, people retreat into defence mode. And some of them defend themselves by attacking, so no one gets anywhere.”

“Oh! I hadn’t thought of that. I kinda thought that if it was someone else’s fault, you should be honest about it. Surely people should face their own shortcomings?”

Sue hid a smile. “And Henry has plenty of shortcomings, you think?”

“Well, you yourself said he was stiff and starchy on the phone. That’s how he always is. Like he’s playing some part. The perfect village rector, with no faults or foibles, standing on some celestial pedestal.”

“And what about you, Polly? Any pedestals for you?”

“Me? I’m just me! I know I’m not perfect. I tend to leap into things and think afterwards, I know that. But at least I’m sincere. God means everything in the world to me and I really, really want to serve him.”

“And if God sends you somewhere you’d rather not be?”

“I’d go there,” Polly declared without hesitation. “Honestly, Sue, I really think I’d go to the ends of the earth for God, if only he’d ask me. Changed my life when I met God.”

Sue raised her eyebrows. “Hmm, yes. I seem to remember someone else who protested about as strongly as you that he was ready to die for Jesus. But if you remember, he denied Jesus three times less than three hours later.”

Polly’s lower lip stuck out. “That’s not fair, Sue. I thought you were my friend.”

“I’m merely pointing out that God seems to have sent you to Thorpemunden, but here you are, only two or three months into it and already crying out to go somewhere else.”

"That's so different! I'm not being fed spiritually in Henry's parishes. How can I give out if I can't take in what I need?"

Sue sighed. "You're sounding like so many of my parishioners. They all want to worship God in their own way, and if the worship in church doesn't suit them, they immediately hive off somewhere else where it's more to their taste."

"So what's the problem? I'd have thought you of all people would be pleased that folk were worshipping at all, not worrying about where they worshipped. As far as I'm concerned, they can worship at the bottom of the garden if they like."

"It brings us back to that age-old question of who worship is for. Is it for us or is it for God? If it's for us, then yes, I suppose you have a point. Although even then I think we need to take account of other people as well. What does it do to the remaining congregation if half the rest hive off to the bright, new church down the road? But it's more than that. If worship is for God, then our own feelings are not particularly important. We just need to offer our best—like a kind of sacrifice. Giving of our best to God."

Polly said, "It's all very well for you. You can do what you like, you're in charge. If things don't suit you, you can just change them. It's not so easy as a curate, where you're expected to do as you're told and not ask questions! It wasn't a bit like that at college. We had brilliant theological discussions and everything was alive. Now I'm suddenly dumped in the middle of nowhere with a rector who doesn't even like me."

Sue said carefully, "I'm not sure you're right about that, Polly. Henry may be feeling just as disorientated as you are. He hasn't worked with a curate before. Perhaps you need to help him."

"How can I do that when he won't let me breathe?"

"I think you need to go back to Thorpemunden and talk to Henry. Now," Sue raised her voice as Polly made to object, "I'm not suggesting you go back to another slanging match with him. But you might try asking him what he wants before you tell him what you want. And I think you need to apologise to him. You've treated him badly."

"That's all I ever hear," Polly grumbled, "what he wants and what I've done wrong."

"Would you like me to come back with you and act as referee for a meeting? Not that I would necessarily be on your side; I'd want to avoid taking sides at all. But I might be able to act as a facilitator, if you and Henry both agree. What do you think?"

***

Since Henry, with the bishop's words about the attributes of Sue Gallagher still ringing in his mind, had agreed to using her as mediator, Sue and Polly soon found themselves sitting in the lounge at Thorpemunden.

Henry was pale and even thinner than usual. But he had greeted them courteously, and Mavis had clearly gone to some trouble to provide them with a substantial tea of sandwiches and cake, which Polly particularly tucked into with a will. Mavis seemed quite perky and even Polly drew comfort from the fact that they were meeting in the lounge rather than the study. Not that it approximated in any way to "The Snug," but at least it had a couple of pictures on the walls and a reasonably modern television in the corner.

Henry asked Polly how she was feeling and appeared to be genuinely interested in the answer, especially when she apologised to him for her rudeness. Sue and Mavis chatted amicably together, comparing Mothers' Union stories and discovering one or two MU friends in common.

When the last cake had been finally refused and the teapot finally emptied, Sue said, "Henry and Polly, this is between the two of you. It's your shout. Mavis and I will do our best to act as mediators. We will only interrupt to move you on if you seem to be stuck or to act as referees if necessary. Of course, it goes without saying that everything stays in here. We must all be satisfied that our discussions will be fully confidential. Is that agreed?"

There were nods all round, although Henry looked strained and Polly anxious. Sue continued, "I suggest that you each have your say without interruption. There will be an opportunity to ask questions or to object later on. But first, we all need to hear what you both think. Then, perhaps, we can begin to build some bridges. Polly, why don't you begin?"

Polly swallowed. She wasn't very happy having Mavis privy to all she intended to say, but couldn't see how to avoid it, especially as she had Sue supporting herself. And now that the moment had come, she wasn't sure what to say. She risked a glance at Henry and thought that he looked grim. But she took a deep breath and began, "It's just that, like, I'm not used to the way things are here. College was so exciting and I learned so many new ways to present the gospel to people today. But Henry won't—"

She was interrupted by a cough from Sue and a warning glance. She amended her words. "I—um—I feel kinda frustrated not being able to try anything out. I do know I've got to learn the old ways, too, and I really appreciate the way you take services, Henry," she hoped it didn't sound too patronising, "but I guess I'd like to try something on my own. Maybe take assemblies at the school, or start a Youth Club or something. Perhaps I just need to feel responsible for something myself." She glanced round at the silent room and shrugged, ending lamely with, "Well, that's it, really. I think that's all."

Sue smiled at her encouragingly, then turned to Henry. "Henry?"

Henry cleared his throat and looked uncomfortable. "I'm not sure quite what you want me to say at this point. Is this where I reply to Polly?"

Sue shook her head. "This is your moment, Henry. Your opportunity to say what you think and feel. There'll be time to reply to Polly later."

"Oh, I see. If that's what you want. Well, in my view Polly is here to learn the nuts and bolts of the Church of England, and it's my job both to teach her and to protect her." Polly rolled her eyes at this point, but Sue ignored her, smiling at Henry to encourage him to continue. "I think Polly needs to become fully cognisant of the type of services we offer here before branching out into something new which may or may not succeed. It can be quite destructive to spend hours preparing new services only to find that no one turns up —"

"—Oh, but," began Polly, but was quelled by a glance from Sue.

Henry continued, "And I think Polly has a lot to learn about traditional Anglicanism and all that it offers. Once the basics are firmly in place, then we can turn our attention to new ideas. But if I allow Polly to spread herself too thinly at this stage, she may burn out. It happens to many new priests. I don't want that to happen to Polly, who has a great deal to offer."

"Mavis." Sue turned to her hostess. "Anything you want to add?"

Mavis looked at Polly and her eyes were cold. "I think it needs to be said that Polly has shown herself to be thoroughly irresponsible, running away at the first sign of difficulty and leaving poor Henry worried to death over her whereabouts. Whatever else has gone on, that sort of behaviour is inexcusable."

Polly clenched her jaw and looked at the floor.

Mavis continued, "But Henry is a wonderful Christian and therefore is a forgiving person. Not only is he willing to let bygones be bygones, but he has also indicated to me that he wishes Polly to take on a new responsibility within the benefice, thus showing true Christian forbearance."

Polly thought she had never heard anything quite so nauseating. She glanced at Sue, but Sue was looking to Henry for his response.

Henry fingered his collar and cleared his throat. "Hmm, yes, well. I have been thinking." He turned to Polly and addressed her directly. "Perhaps you're right, Polly," he conceded. "Perhaps you do need something to call your own. I've been thinking for some time of starting a Pram Service—you know, something for the preschool children and their mothers—but I've never had the time to get round to it. Would you like to start one, Polly? I won't interfere. It will be all your own project. I merely ask that you keep me informed because I do have overall responsibility for the benefice, so I do need to know what's happening. What do you think?"

Polly stared at him, open-mouthed at such breathtaking effrontery. Since she had suggested exactly this not more than a couple of weeks previously and he had turned her down flat, she was astonished. But she was also delighted, for she felt it really did mark a change.

With eyes shining, she grinned at Henry. "Thank you so much," she said. "You won't regret it, Henry, I promise. And I'll keep you informed every step of the way. This is so brilliant! It's just what I've been wanting. Thank you!"

***

As soon as Sue had returned to London, Polly set about her new task. She mapped out a short order of service, to last about thirty minutes. She decided to start with an action rhyme which toddlers could manage, then move on to a story, followed by an activity with paint and glue. Then some sort of physical activity, like a simple game or a dance, a short prayer time, and another song, finishing with a blessing and with orange juice and biscuits to follow.

Polly thought it sounded good and was sure she could encourage young mums to bring their children along. She took it to Henry for his comments.

Henry read the order of service through carefully, his face revealing nothing. Then he nodded and handed it back to Polly. "You don't have any space for confession and forgiveness, but the rest is probably all right."

Polly was disappointed with his lukewarm response, but determined to prove her openness and cooperation. "We could include that in the prayers. Would that do? Or would you like me to write in a special slot for confession?"

"Do it your way," Henry decided. "But you can't start too soon teaching children about sin and impressing upon them the need for continual forgiveness."

"No, Henry," Polly said meekly.

"Have you thought how you're going to gather your clientele?"

Polly nodded. "I've got some time tomorrow at the Nursery School. I thought I'd hand out some flyers. And I'll put some in the surgery, too, for the pre- and postnatal groups and perhaps in the Primary School. Lots of them have little brothers and sisters."

"Which church are you planning to hold it in? And when?"

"Um, well, actually I was thinking of Hamblestead Village Hall. I know it's a little way out, but they only have church once a fortnight at Hamblestead and I thought it might be a way to bridge the gap. It might just boost their sense of self-worth at Hamblestead if something is set up especially in their patch." She looked at him anxiously. "The church is so cold in winter and it will save on the heating bills. If I get them to contribute fifty pence, we'll collect enough to pay for the village hall rental and for the refreshments."

Henry thought for a long moment. He was opposed to church services of any sort, even what he considered to be a pretend service like this, taking place outside church buildings. But finances were always low, and the church took hours to heat adequately. He nodded. "All right. How often are you planning to hold it? I suggest once a month to see how it goes. You can always increase the frequency later on if it proves to be popular."

Polly bit her lip. She had reckoned on a minimum of once a fortnight. "Don't you think people will forget about it with such a long gap?"

"That will be up to you, Polly. I'm afraid you don't just set these services up and expect them to happen. I think you'll find that it's hard work keeping the momentum going. Part of your job will be to make sure that people remember it and turn up. How you do that is up to you."

***

Polly planned to launch her services after Harvest Festival. Henry had said that plenty of people attended the harvest services, so she could make sure leaflets were handed out at each service. And since she was due to preach at Thorpemunden, she thought that perhaps some of the younger villagers might attend on this one occasion and be impressed by her. She had already decided to include a children's talk, building her sermon around it, so hopefully young parents and their children would respond to that.

Polly booked the village hall at Hamblestead for the first Monday afternoon of each month, passing Henry the invoice for the benefice treasurer to pay. She handed out plenty of her leaflets and was gratified to see that they were being scrutinised with interest.

The next time she and Henry went to Hamblestead for a service Polly was full of excitement, anticipating the delight of the congregation at this new venture in their parish. But she was met by a disapproving and angry churchwarden, who squared up to Henry.

"Why was nothing said to me?" demanded Bette Jarrold, her back like a ramrod and her brows drawn.

Henry said, "Perhaps you should ask Polly that question. This is her venture."

The full force of Bette's gimlet eyes was turned on Polly. "Well?"

"Um, er, well, I'm sorry," Polly said lamely. "Since it's to be held in the village hall rather than the church I thought I only needed to book the hall."

"I imagine this is a church event wherever it's being held. As churchwarden I should be informed of all that is going on in my parish. Besides, as a retired teacher myself, I do think I might have been invited to take part. I have plenty of expertise with children and I should be delighted to share it."

Polly's heart sank. She couldn't think of anyone worse for small children than the formidable Miss Jarrold. She glanced at Henry and was surprised by the small smile playing around his lips. *He knew!* Polly thought. *He knew this was going to happen and he didn't warn me! I'm sure he wants me to fail.*

Aloud she said, "That's so generous of you, Miss Jarrold. But I couldn't ask you to waste your expertise on this. They're only very tiny tots, preschool age. Your skills would be put to so much better use with older children. May I keep your offer in hand, for when we start a Sunday School or Youth Club?"

Bette Jarrold snorted and said forcefully, "If you don't want me, at least remember in future to consult the churchwardens whenever something is arranged for our parish. We churchwardens are responsible in law for what goes on here in Hamblestead. We need to know. Isn't that so, Rector?"

Henry inclined his head. "Quite so, Bette, quite so. I'm sure Polly won't make the same mistake again. But your offer of support is most valuable." He turned to Polly. "Have you considered inviting the Mothers' Union to organise the refreshments, Polly? It would be good to involve church members in this new venture and I have no doubt that they will wish to support you. What do you think, Bette?"

Bette Jarrold concurred, her good humour nearly restored. "Of course we would, Rector. Only too delighted. I'll pass the message on. We'll sort out the refreshments, Polly. No need for you to trouble yourself about that. And it means we'll be there to help out if necessary."

Polly's heart sank still further. Was the Pram Service to be doomed then, before it could start? For how on earth would she manage a service for preschool children with a load of disapproving old grannies looking over her shoulder, clucking their tongues at the antics of unruly toddlers, and looking down their noses at the young mums? Was this Henry's subtle way of torpedoing her new venture?

Chapter Twelve

"I'm truly sorry about your necklace, Ella," Tracey said, "but I wish you hadn't destroyed our room like that. I don't blame you going in to look—I'd have done the same—but you've made such a mess of it. I guess that's why Melvyn lost it."

Ella turned startled eyes on her friend. "You think—you think I did that? I assumed it was how you live when you're on your own. I came from a student flat which always looked like that, so it didn't occur to me that it wasn't how you lived in private. I didn't touch anything except your necklaces. I was looking for my own and I suppose I thought it might have got jumbled up with yours."

"You actually thought that's how we live? Ella, don't you know me at all? You've been here almost the whole summer. Have you ever known me to be anything other than neat and tidy?"

Ella shook her head. "I'm sorry. I just didn't think. But it proves that someone has been in both our rooms."

"Do you want to call the police? I haven't checked properly yet, but from what I saw, I don't think anything is missing from us. All my jewellery seems to be there and there's nothing else to steal. If the thief was just after your locket, maybe he thought that it was your room. It's the first one you come to up the stairs." She looked anxiously at Ella. "You won't say anything to the police about Melvyn, will you?"

Ella shook her head. "There's no point in informing the police. I have no idea how much the locket is worth, probably not much. It is gold, but I don't suppose it's hugely valuable to anyone except me. No, I think it must have been taken out of spite, and I'm already resigned to the fact that I won't ever see it again."

"Mark Winters?"

Ella nodded. "Can't think of anyone else who has reason to hold a grudge against me. No, let it drop, Tracey. There's no proof of anything and I don't want to be involved with Mark Winters in any way ever again. If I go to the police it'll just stir things up."

Melvyn came in as they were finishing their drinks in the kitchen. He sat down heavily without looking at Ella. "Sorry, love," he said gruffly. "Thought you'd trashed our room. Still, shouldn't have done that. Don't know what got into me. Don't know me own strength sometimes. No excuse, though. Can't forgive meself. Won't never happen again."

Ella smiled. "It's okay. I've no desire to involve the Old Bill and I'm not surprised you reacted if you thought I'd caused the state of your room. But actually I'd only just gone in."

"So we 'ave a thief?"

Tracey and Ella both nodded. "But he only took Ella's necklace, nothing from us. And Ella doesn't want to involve the police because we think it might have been that Mark Winters, who so pestered Ella."

There was a look of relief on Melvyn's beefy face. "Your shout, love. We can call the police if you want. But if you think it's him, do you want me to go after him? Get your necklace back?"

Ella said hurriedly, "No, thanks very much, Melvyn. I'm just going to write it off. I mean, it's really sad to lose my mother's picture, but I hold her in my head. No one can take that away from me."

Tracey suddenly said, "What about the CCTV? Does that reach behind the bar? Could it show someone sneaking up the stairs?"

Melvyn shook his head. "We had it to stop trouble and to register people coming in. Didn't expect no one to be out back, so it don't cover that area."

"Would it show us who was in the bar, though?"

"Yeah, but we don't know 'e came in through the bar. Might have sneaked in round the back when we was getting in the new supplies. That's more likely, 'cos we leave that side door open."

Not knowing what else to suggest, the three of them looked at each other. Then Ella said, "I've been thinking, anyway. The season's more or less finished now and you're not going to be able to afford to employ me much longer."

Melvyn, anxious to erase his earlier behaviour, said, "Now you stop that talk right there. You can stay as long as you like, love. We're glad to 'ave you, me and Tracey. Ain't that right, Trace?"

"Yes, we'd be sorry to see you go, Ella. But realistically, you're right. Not just because the income will drop over the winter months, but because you need something better for yourself. You're a bright girl, Ella, and you need to be thinking about your own future. We all knew this was just temporary work to tide you over."

"But it's not just that." Ella drummed a rhythm on the table-top with her fingers as she thought about her words. "It's this whole Mark Winters thing. When you got rid of him, Melvyn, I thought he'd gone for good, and it was great to be able to go out again without being afraid he'd appear. But now I'm not so sure. If it was him—and I can't think of any other explanation—then I want to be as far away as possible. I can't go through all that awful business again."

Tracey looked at her sharply. "What are you saying? That you'll just up and go one day and we'll never see you again?"

Ella made a gesture of apology. "Not because I don't want to see you again, but because if you don't know where I am, no one can put pressure on you to reveal my location. It would be safer for us all that way."

Melvyn began belligerently, "Now see 'ere, we wouldn't tell no one—" but he subsided at a glance from Tracey.

She said, “Ella, love, we won’t ask any questions if that’s the way you want it. But we want you to remember, Melvyn and me, that’s there’s always a home for you here. You can come back any time you want. We’d always be pleased to see you, wouldn’t we, Melve?”

And Melvyn nodded until Ella thought he looked like one of those Chinese dolls which used to sit in the back of cars.

***

Although Ella had made her decision, she was unable to bring herself to depart. She had been more frightened by Mark Winter’s unwelcome attentions than she had cared to admit, and with the further suspicions that he was still around, she found herself unwilling to leave the shelter of the pub. She went out from time to time with Tracey and there was more opportunity for this now that life had quietened down in the Lord Nelson, but even then she was constantly gazing fearfully over her shoulder, expecting Winters to pounce at any moment.

But neither was she quite as easy in the pub as she had been. Melvyn’s attack had unsettled her, and try as she might, Ella was incapable of regarding him in quite the same light as she had previously. She avoided being alone with him and was more silent in her tasks. Although Ella had always given the impression of self-containment, Tracey noticed that she was becoming more withdrawn and less inclined to pass the time of day in a friendly manner, even with the customers.

Curiously, this withdrawal did her no harm with the patrons, for it added to her general air of inscrutability and made her seem even more exotic.

Ella herself was unaware that she was grieving, for it wouldn’t have occurred to her that anyone could grieve over the loss of a material object. But she was making the difficult transition between her childhood with her mother and her adulthood without her mother. The locket symbolised her past life, and without it she felt that she had no anchor, no roots, either here in Yarmouth or anywhere else. She had given up her university career to care for her mother, a task which had been much more demanding and distressing than she had expected. When her mother died, Ella had returned to the flat she had shared with student friends only to find that everything had changed and that with such a long and unexplained absenteeism, she had forfeited her university place. It was only now, after a short period of relative stability in her life and with the catalyst of the lost locket, that the effects of all these unresolved losses began to make themselves felt in Ella's life.

She herself was aware only of her growing fears and the desire to be alone. And she found that she was unable to quieten her fears however hard she tried. But both Tracey and Melvyn absorbed Ella's general air of gloom, and with the now half-empty pub, were themselves depressed by it.

Melvyn grumbled a week or so later, "She said she was goin', but she's still 'ere. Lord knows, I don't want to chuck 'er out, but it ain't doin' none of us any good with 'er mopin' around like this." He continued to feel guilty over his assault on Ella and assumed her gloominess was all his fault, which made him feel worse. And her constant presence was a sore reminder of his wrongdoing. He had reached the stage where he wanted her gone from his life.

But Tracey hankered after the way things were, when the three of them laughed and chatted comfortably together. She was determined to make one final effort. "Why don't we all go out?" she suggested. "There's not much work on at the moment. We could get someone in just for one evening to run the bar, and take in a film and a meal. Might brighten us all up. Just what we need to set us up for the winter. What do you think?"

Melvyn, who hadn't been to the cinema for five years, was enthusiastic about the proposal. Ella was less sure but unwilling to disappoint Tracey and Melvyn.

"Why don't you two go by yourselves? I'll look after things here; then you won't have to get anyone else in."

But Tracey refused. "We've had a really good summer. What with problems on the airlines and the credit crunch, lots more holidaymakers settled for home this year. Despite the weather, we've done better than usual, and since East Anglia is the driest part of the country, we've fared pretty well here in Yarmouth. You're part of that success, Ella. I think we should all go out and celebrate. Besides, it wouldn't be the same without you."

So Ella had capitulated.

They elected to go to *The Quest of the Silent Soldier*, which didn't particularly appeal to either Ella or Tracey, but which was very much Melvyn's choice. Having been in the Territorial Army for a short while, he was riveted by any film to do with soldiering, and since this one starred Keira Knightley as well as Halle Berry, he was sold.

***

They all chose Italian for the meal, as they wanted something as unlike bar meals as possible, and hit upon La Trattoria, a local Italian restaurant with a good reputation.

Not wanting to disappoint her friends, Ella dressed carefully for the occasion in an emerald green satin sheath with a cream pashmina. She wore matching emerald green high heels, which showed off her long, slender legs to full advantage, and, as a final touch, added a white daisy to her sleek black hair. With eye make-up and a smidgeon of lipstick, the effect was stunning, and both Tracey and Melvyn stared open mouthed at the transformation.

They, too, had made an effort. Tracey had washed and set her brown hair, which now shone and fell in gentle waves about her face. She had chosen a panelled skirt in maroon linen teamed with a white blouse, and looked much smarter and younger than usual. Even Melvyn had changed his jeans for grey slacks and a red checked, open-neck shirt.

They sauntered to the restaurant chatting in the old, friendly way, ducking inside the doorway, which was abnormally low since the restaurant was located in a seventeenth-century building, and were shown to their table in the window. Set with a white cloth covered by hand-embroidered Italian place settings, they settled down to a relaxing evening. As it was Italian, the two women decided on Campari and soda, but Melvyn stuck to his usual Norfolk Woodforde's ale, named after Parson Woodforde, an eighteenth-century Norfolk clergyman whose diaries revealed his passion for good food and good ale.

Their tastes differing in food, too, Melvyn opted for a Neapolitan pizza, which he considered to be fairly safe for a man who never stirred much beyond beef burgers and chicken and chips. The women were more adventurous, Ella choosing tomato and mozzarella salad, and Tracey going for Parma ham and two-cheese pasta. It was when Ella was trying to decide whether to have a tiramisu or panna cotta for dessert that she glanced out of the window for inspiration. And she froze.

Tracey noticed the sudden tensing of her posture and followed Ella's glance. "What? What is it? You look like you've seen a ghost."

Ella tore her eyes away from the street. "Him! It's him! I saw him out there, he was staring straight at me."

Tracey looked startled. "I didn't see anyone." She craned her neck to look both ways up and down the street. "Are you sure?"

"Of course I'm sure. It gave me such a shock."

Melvyn got up. "I'll go out. If 'e's there, I'll find 'im."

He went outside and stood for a few moments surveying the whole of the street. Then he crossed the road and looked back. Finally he shrugged and held up his palms as if to say that he could see no one.

Tracey said, "Are you really sure, Ella? Mark's been so much on your mind lately. Could it have been a trick of the light? Or someone else?"

By then Melvyn had returned. "Couldn't see no one. Nowhere for 'im to have gone, neither. Yer mind playing tricks, is it?"

Ella tried to smile. She felt confused. She was certain she had spotted Mark Winters, but there had been no one there when she had looked again just a moment later. Perhaps she had been mistaken.

She looked all around when they emerged from the restaurant, but the road was clear, devoid of any people. With Ella somewhat reassured and firmly encased between them, they wandered to the cinema, bought their tickets, and settled down into their seats.

Despite its all-star cast, in Ella's estimation the film was rubbish. It took place in the unlikely setting of South Africa, where Ella enjoyed the many shots of game parks with wildlife of every description, but the plot, which had nothing to do with war but was about poachers and gamekeepers, was thin and the dialogue laboured. Melvyn, with eyes fully appreciative of the two female stars, hardly noticed the plot, and since Tracey had been a long-time fan of Johnny Depp, the male lead, she was happy enough to watch him. The stars carried the action along, but Ella found her mind wandering.

Even wedged between Melvyn and Tracey, she felt uneasy in the dark of the cinema. It wasn't so noticeable when her attention was caught, but when the action slowed practically to stopping point and when the tediously inevitable love scenes were shown, she felt a tingle at the back of her neck. She turned sharply, but other than the somewhat offended stares of the couple immediately behind, was unable to penetrate the darkness sufficiently to see anyone.

Ella felt a tremor run through her body. Had he followed them to the cinema? Was he watching her even now? Her heart beat faster and she wiped sweat away from her face with a tissue.

Tracey leaned towards her. "All right, love?"

At a furious "Ssh!" from the row behind, Ella merely nodded and smiled at her friend. But when the film eventually ended and they wended their way in the semi-darkness towards the exit guided only by the tiny blue lights set into the edges of the stairs, she could feel tension in her neck and shoulders and was unable to prevent herself glancing over her shoulder to right and left every few moments.

Tracey was aware of Ella's discomfiture and took her arm as they hurried home. Despite her constant scrutiny, Ella saw no further glimpses of anyone remotely resembling Mark Winters, and when they reached home Tracey was at pains to reassure her.

"I know it must have been a terrible shock for you, thinking you saw him on the street outside the restaurant, but maybe you really were mistaken. I mean, why would he come there and then disappear? And you didn't see him at the cinema, did you?"

Ella took a sip of her hot chocolate and tried to smile. "But maybe that's just his sort of strategy. To somehow make sure I'm the only one that sees him, then to clear off again. He's really messing with my head, Trace."

"I know that, love. And I wish I could help. But if you're the only who sees him…" She shrugged and left the sentence hanging.

Ella's shoulders drooped. "You don't believe me. You think I'm mad and I imagined it."

Tracey took her hand and looked very deliberately into her eyes. "Now you listen to me, Ella Wim. There's no one here thinks you're mad or daft or barmy or anything else. But I do think you've got yourself into a state over this creep and you're right, he is messing with your head. But you're the only one who can stop that. If you see him in every shadow whether he's there or not, you'll never get him out of your head. And then he'll have won even if he's over the other side of the world by now."

Ella smiled wanly. "I know you're right. It just isn't that easy. But look. It's not your problem. Let's get a good night's sleep. Perhaps I'll feel differently tomorrow. And thank you so much for trying to help. I enjoyed this evening, I really did, despite all my twitches."

***

But Ella knew that her reassurances to Tracey were hollow and she knew that there was only one way she would be able to get the odious Mark Winters out of her system. With a heavy sigh because she felt that once again she was leaving relative safety for the unknown, she pulled out her backpack and began to gather her clothes together. She had acquired a considerably greater wardrobe since earning money in the Lord Nelson and there was no way she could stuff everything into the backpack. She slipped down to the kitchen and helped herself to a couple of plastic carriers.

While she was there she wandered through for a last look at the bar, for she was aware that she was unlikely ever to return to Great Yarmouth. The cookie jar with the week's tip money was under the counter. There wasn't much in it since tips had virtually dried up now the season had ended, but Ella emptied out the few pound coins and dropped them into the pocket of her jeans. She hadn't been paid this week and, as far as she knew, had never had any of the tips, so she didn't think Melvyn would be too bothered.

Some of her stuff she left behind. There was a purple blouse that Tracey had much admired, so Ella left it folded neatly on the bed. Her oldest pair of jeans was consigned to the waste bin, as were her ancient trainers. Clothes which had wear left but which she no longer particularly wanted, she left in a pile on the bed. The rest fitted into the backpack and two carriers.

Ella was ready. She glided noiselessly down the stairs, took a last look round at the Lord Nelson, and slipped out silently into the night.

Chapter Thirteen

It was after the Harvest Festival service in Thorpemunden Church that Henry woke in the middle of the night with severe, cramping pains in his chest.

The service had attracted many more Thorpemunden villagers than usual, and for the first time in around twenty years, a dozen or so children ranging in age from three to thirteen had solemnly processed up the aisle carrying fruit, vegetables, and packets of dry food to present at the altar. Henry, who had not known that this was going to happen, was enraged. But the professional in him took over and he managed to keep his anger in check, looking as though this sort of thing happened every week and was decreed by him. It wasn't that he had any objection to the children (who had swelled the congregation because they had been accompanied by their parents), but he did object very strongly to being unaware of this innovation and thus being made to look foolish. Laying the gifts on the altar with his back to the congregation, Henry took the opportunity to glare at Polly. But she was happily impervious to him, bouncing around imperturbably in the sanctuary as she, too, received the harvest produce. This made Henry even more furious. For him the sanctuary was sacrosanct, a part of the church where solemnity was of the utmost importance. He was ashamed of what he considered to be Polly's ungainly capering, feeling that it desecrated the holy space of the High Altar.

Matters were made worse for Henry when Polly preached. He had tried to persuade her to let him look over her sermon in advance, but she had consistently resisted, and in view of their meeting and his avowed intention to allow her more freedom, he had capitulated. Now, he deeply regretted his decision, for Polly had preached a sermon aimed at children instead of adults, which was bad enough, but it was also full of what Henry regarded as tasteless and inappropriate jokes, which in Henry's view were not particularly funny, taught nothing about Jesus, but which had the congregation rocking with laughter. Such frivolity, plus noisy, bumptious children who had no idea how to behave in church and were never corrected by their parents, was almost more than Henry could stand. Henry's sermons were always carefully scripted and delivered with dignity. He abhorred humour in Church devotions and he hated the feeling that Polly was revolutionising worship by removing all solemnity and allowing it to degenerate into entertainment. He was especially furious because by failing to consult him, she had forestalled any objections he might have had, thus effectively rendering him helpless. Henry felt emasculated.

At the Harvest Supper after the service he had sat well away from Polly, hardly able to look at her. And in a sort of compensation for his feelings he had eaten more than his usual abstemious portions of cold meats and salads and apple pies, all provided by the ladies of the parish.

Used to eating at midday rather than the evening and never normally eating anything at any time past eight o'clock, the meal had been too late for him. And the pastry particularly had lain heavily on his stomach. He had gone to bed in a bad mood.

Now here he was in the small hours, sitting up in bed, clutching his chest and gasping for breath.

Mavis was lying on her side with her back to Henry, snoring rather loudly. As best he could while still holding his chest, Henry nudged her on the shoulder.

"Wh—what?" Mavis turned over groggily, rubbing her eyes. It took her a moment or two to focus. Then she sat up in alarm. "Henry! Henry, whatever is the matter? Henry, talk to me."

Henry wheezed and coughed, his face distorted in pain.

"I'm going to call the doctor. Henry, just stay quiet while I go down to the study. Why didn't you have a phone put in here? I just knew something like this would happen. Try and breathe deeply, more slowly. That's better. I'll be back in a minute."

But she was more than a minute and Henry began to panic. The pain in his chest worsened and he found his breath coming in short gasps.

Mavis had dialled 999 but was now being forced to speak to some idiot at the other end who failed to grasp the urgency of the situation. He was saying, "Now slow down, please, madam. Can you give me your name?"

"It's not me, it's my husband. I think he may be having a heart attack. Oh, do be quick! I need an ambulance."

The voice took on a soothing tone. "Yes, of course, madam. Our response time is very speedy. The ambulance should be with you within ten minutes. But you need to tell me your name and address and describe your husband's symptoms to me."

"Mavis Winstone, if you must know. But it's my husband. I keep trying to tell you. He's Canon Henry Winstone, Rector of Thorpemunden and we live in Thorpemunden rectory."

"Can you give me your post code, madam?"

"For goodness sake, hurry up! Why do you need the post code? Everybody knows where the rectory is."

"But we are in Norwich, madam," the voice said patiently. "If you could just tell me your post code, the ambulance will be with you very soon. Please leave the front door open and put on an outside light if you have one."

"IP23 8DG," Mavis said angrily. "Now can I go back to my husband?"

"Of course. Do you have any aspirin in the house?"

"Aspirin? Yes, I think so. Why?"

"Go and find an aspirin, preferably a soluble one. Dissolve it in water and give it to your husband. Aspirin given in the first few minutes of a heart attack diminishes the symptoms and reduces any long-term damage. If it is a heart attack."

But Mavis had already gone, and he was speaking into an empty phone.

Mavis raided the medicine box in the kitchen. She kept all medicine in an old plastic biscuit box, a relic from Christmas long ago. She found an ancient packet of soluble aspirin, dissolved a couple of tablets in half a glass of water, and carried it up to Henry.

"Here." She supported him with her arm and held the glass to his lips. "Drink this. It's only aspirin. That's what they told me to do."

Henry took the glass with a trembling hand while Mavis anxiously took his pulse, piled up the pillows behind him to make him more comfortable, and continued to support him with her arm behind him.

Henry lay back against the pillows, exhausted by the effort. Mavis put on her full-length pink candlewick dressing gown and pulled the belt tightly around her waist. She ran a comb through her hair, thought of applying some lipstick, but decided against it. When the ambulance men came, she wanted to look presentable as befitted the wife of a canon, but not as though she were about to go out on a date.

Screaming sirens were soon heard, and a car with flashing blue lights raced into the drive.

A male voice called out, "Ma'am? Are you up there?"

Mavis flew to the top of the stairs. "Up here. Do be quick."

"Now then, let's have a look." The paramedic held Henry's wrist, checking his pulse against a watch. "Can you tell me the course of events? What happened, exactly?"

Henry's breathing was less laboured now that professional help had arrived. "I was fine when we went to bed. Well, a bit tired, perhaps. We'd had a long evening. I went off to sleep quite quickly, but awoke with this awful pain in my chest."

"What sort of a pain is it?"

Henry grimaced. "How do you describe pain? It's intense, like something has hit me in the chest. Almost like cramp."

"Like a squeezing pain?"

Henry thought. "No, I don't think I'd describe it quite that way. More a tightness in my chest and, as I say, as though I've been kicked by a mule."

"When did you last eat?"

"We were quite late. We'd had a Harvest Supper, you know. I did think the apple pie was lying a bit heavy, but it didn't stop me sleeping so I suppose it was all right."

"How's the pain now?"

"As a matter of fact," Henry said in surprise, "it's not as bad. No, it does seem to have eased a bit. But I can still feel it."

"I gave him aspirin," explained Mavis, "like they told me on the phone. I expect that's had an effect."

The paramedic listened to Henry's chest with a stethoscope and straightened up. He attached a rubber cuff to Henry's arm and took his blood pressure. Then he attached electrodes to Henry's chest and wired him up to an electrocardiogram. He watched for a while as the machine disgorged a paper tape covered in a continuous graph. He chatted amicably to Mavis and Henry, both of whom were watching anxiously. Then he perused the tape, tore it off, folded it carefully, and put it in his pocket, removed the electrodes, and switched off the machine.

"All fine," he declared. He sat on the bed and smiled at Henry. "You know, I think it might have been that apple pie. Your heart is fine, your blood pressure is normal, and your pulse is good. I think this might have been a spot of indigestion brought on by the late food. Have you been worrying about anything lately?"

"Parish ministry always has its worries. But yes, perhaps I have. Just a little." Henry was unwilling to admit to any negative feelings.

The paramedic nodded. "I think that might have exacerbated the situation. Caused the problem with your breathing. How are you now?"

"I feel all right now," Henry admitted.

Mavis said, "Sorry for bringing you out like this if it's a false alarm."

"Nothing to be sorry about, ma'am. I'd rather come out to a hundred false alarms than miss one heart attack. And your husband has a problem, but fortunately not one requiring hospital treatment. Reverend, I think you should see your own doctor in the morning and I'd be surprised if he didn't order you to rest for a day or two. I'm going now, but any further problems, don't hesitate to ring. We'll be out in a flash."

"Thank you so much," Mavis said as she showed him to the door.

"Make him rest, ma'am," advised the paramedic. "Might not be so simple next time."

***

Dr. Peter Lambert repeated all the tests performed by the paramedic the previous night and added a few more of his own. The urine test for diabetes was negative, but Peter explained that it would be a week before the results of the blood tests were known.

"We have to send the blood away for analysis. If you haven't heard from us within a week, give me a ring."

"So if it wasn't a heart attack, Peter, what was it?" Peter Lambert wasn't a member of any of Henry's congregations, but along with Henry was a trustee of a village charity which administered funds to needy parishioners, so the two men knew each other quite well.

"Henry, have you been overworking lately? Now don't give me all that squat about clergymen constantly overworking, I know all that. And it has never affected your health before. But if there's something else, I need to know about it. I need hardly remind you that this office is like the confessional. Complete confidentiality, or my life wouldn't be worth living."

Mavis said, "Tell him, Henry."

She had insisted on going in with Henry because, as she put it, "Two heads are better than one. You're bound to forget something, Henry."

Peter Lambert looked quizzically from one to the other, his head tilted slightly to one side. He was a pleasant-looking man of around forty-five, with sandy hair now thinning. He sported a small moustache and goatee, which teamed perfectly with the red and white spotted bow tie he always wore in surgery.

Henry frowned at his wife. "There's nothing to tell."

"I'll tell him then, if you won't." She ignored his protest of "Mavis, please!" and turned to the doctor.

"You may know that we have a new curate, a woman."

"Yes, Polly Hewitt. I've met her."

Of course he has, thought Henry. *She'll have had to see him after that hospital business.*

Mavis continued, "I'm sorry to say that she's been nothing but trouble since she came. It's very unfair on poor Henry, who's been worried to death. He hasn't been eating properly or sleeping properly for some weeks now."

"Is that right, Henry?"

Henry nodded disconsolately. He felt as though he was somehow an invalid who couldn't be trusted to speak for himself. But strangely, it wasn't a wholly unwelcome feeling. Part of him wanted nothing more than to lean back and let other people make all decisions for him.

Peter said, "Henry, I suspect that you're suffering from stress. I don't want to put you on medication at this stage, but neither do I want this to develop into a full-blown depression. So I'm going to suggest a course of treatment. No need to make notes, Mavis, I'll give you a fact sheet.

"Henry, you need to have at least a month off work and I'll write a certificate for you. No, this is not up for negotiation. You will have a minimum of a month's sick leave. I want you to use that time in learning to relax, and I'm going to suggest some classes for you. You need to take at least half an hour's exercise daily. Now, you don't have a dog, but you can still get out for a thirty-minute walk. I'd also like you to see a counsellor and I can arrange that for you."

"No!" The old Henry suddenly reasserted himself. "I'm not doing all that and if I do take this time off—and I haven't agreed to it yet—what would the parish do? I don't want it known that I'm off with stress."

Mavis looked at the doctor helplessly. He said, "Could you go away for a while? Take a holiday?"

"I suppose. And I don't mind taking the exercise or, indeed, learning to relax, but I'm not going to see some shrink."

Mavis rolled her eyes at the doctor. He said, "Henry, there's no stigma attached to illness these days. No one will think any the worse of you because you're sick. They all know what sterling work you've done over the past years and they all know you constantly go the extra mile. It's now time you begin to look after yourself and everybody knows that."

"Huh!" Henry snorted. "Tell that to my bishop. The Church is still in the dark ages as far as illness goes. There's no such thing as stress. We priests are definitely not expected to go under."

But Henry took the proffered certificate and, after further cajoling from Mavis once they reached home, agreed to take the time off.

In truth he was relieved. He wanted nothing more than to be in a place where he wasn't known and do nothing but sleep as long as he wanted. Let someone else take the strain of parish ministry for a time and see how they got on with it.

***

Polly was sorry to hear that Henry was off sick, but was unable to prevent a tremor of excitement at the news. She rang Charles, the rural dean, to ask what she should do.

"I'll call a benefice meeting of all the PCCs," Charles decided. "The churchwardens are legally responsible for running the parishes in the incumbent's absence, but I suspect they will be looking to you, Polly, for spiritual guidance. If you like, you and I could meet together first and have a chat about the situation."

"Thanks, Charles, that's cool. Would you like to come over to mine?"

"I could do that. I need to pay a pastoral visit to Henry anyway, so I'll go there first, then come over to you."

Recognising that the parishes needed to get rotas reorganised and meetings either cancelled or rearranged, Charles visited Henry next day. At first Henry insisted that he could organise the parishes from the rectory, taking phone calls, answering queries, and setting up meetings from his armchair, but both Charles and Mavis insisted that rest meant forgetting all parish business until he was fully recovered. Afraid that Henry would gradually revert to running the benefice after two or three days' rest, Mavis handed over to Charles all the paperwork and announced that her computer would be out of action until Henry was back at work. That way, no one would be tempted to email her with tasks for Henry.

Charles offered to bring weekly Home Communion to Henry, but filled with horror at the thought of having to meet with Charles every week, Henry adamantly refused, saying that he wouldn't dream of troubling Charles since the rural dean had enough work without him, but that he would ask Father Brian to call. Henry had never had much time for this young rural dean, whom he considered to be so evangelical in churchmanship that he was barely an Anglican at all. He knew that the pews of Diss Church were filled every Sunday, but he despised the sort of worship offered by Charles, regarding it as no more than a superficial diversion devoid of theological meat of any depth.

Mavis, who was equally dismissive of the rural dean behind his back, was not above using him when it suited her. Since Henry had refused point-blank to go away on holiday, she asked Charles to spread the message that Henry was to be kept quiet in order to rest, so he was to have no visitors. Charles promised to relay that information to the benefice meeting and to set up a bulletin point through the churchwardens where news of Henry's progress could be garnered and relayed. That way, there would be no need for anyone to ring the rectory.

When he visited Polly she offered to be the bulletin organiser, but Charles dissuaded her. "You'll have plenty to do without taking on that as well. Surely one of the churchwardens has a computer? It's an easy enough job. Just requires contacting Mavis once a week for an update on Henry."

"If we had a pew slip, we could write a little message about Henry every week. Then everyone would see it. And we could use it for other information, too, times of meetings and things like that. It would save all that reading of notices at the beginning of the service."

"You mean you don't have a weekly sheet for people to take home?"

Polly grinned and shook her head. "I told you Henry was about two centuries behind the times."

"We must see about that, then. I'll suggest at the benefice meeting that someone should start a pew slip, to make communications easier while Henry is laid up. Anything else you'd like me to put in motion?"

"Communions will be difficult. Can't expect Father Brian to take many more. He's so old he gets exhausted just taking one. Are there any spare priests who could come in just to do the magic bits?"

"Now then, Polly! What would Henry say to hear you talking like that?"

But they both laughed and Charles said, "Shouldn't be too difficult to find someone if all they have to do is say the Eucharistic prayer. Can you manage all the rest of the service?"

"Easily. In fact to tell you the truth, I'm really looking forward to taking on a bit more responsibility. It's a fantastic opportunity for me. Do you realise that if Henry hadn't been laid up like this, I wouldn't get to do any of these things for another year? I hardly dare say it, but I really do wonder whether God has had something to do with Henry's illness."

"You mean you think God has sent it? Because Henry needs to be moved on somehow?"

"Not exactly. But I do think God may be using it to help the benefice move forward. And it's brilliant for me."

"God uses every situation, Polly, as you must know. The question is, how are you going to use this opportunity?"

"How much can I do? Am I allowed to change things? Or do I have to keep everything exactly as it already is?"

"What do you think God is calling you to do?"

"That's easy," Polly said. "I think God has put me here because the Thorpemunden Benefice is ready for a shake-up. And I guess it looks as if God has decided I'm the one to do it. This is my big chance."

Chapter Fourteen

Polly took a back seat at the benefice meeting. Thorpemunden Village Hall was packed with PCC members from every church in the benefice, and since Polly had suggested starting the meeting with free cheese and wine (Charles passed the bill to the Thorpemunden treasurer), people were talking to each other and enjoying themselves. This, Polly thought, was probably a first for any kind of PCC meeting. They were often miserable affairs held in cold churches, where everyone wanted to get home as soon as possible and where tempers had been known to flare.

Following his conversation with Polly, Charles opened the meeting with prayer, then introduced a number of suggestions and asked for opinions. Since the people of the benefice were used not to being asked but being told and since Charles as rural dean was a figure of authority, they readily agreed to all his ideas. Bette Jarrold offered to undertake the editing and printing of a weekly pew slip. She came from a long family tradition of printers and prided herself that at the age of sixty-eight she had taught herself the rudiments of computer use. She was now proficient with email and word processing and fancied trying her hand at desktop publishing. And since she had the latest colour laser printer, she would be happy to run off the eighty or so copies required each week. There was some discussion as to how these pew slips could be delivered to all the churches, but as Sam Herbert was the postman covering the whole area, he volunteered to pick them up from Bette's porch early on a Saturday morning and drop them off in the course of his round. The meeting was pleased and readily agreed to pay all expenses.

The idea of pew slips had generated some excitement, and people waited expectantly for Charles to speak again.

"As you know, Polly is going to start a Pram Service once a month in Hamblestead Village Hall, and I understand that the Mothers' Union has very kindly offered to help her by providing refreshments for these little ones in God's family. It would be wonderful to encourage young families to become more closely associated with the Church, and I understand Thorpemunden had a very successful Harvest Festival service this year, with quite a number of new younger families attending."

At this there was some anger and murmurs of dissension amongst the Thorpemunden people, most of whom were of Henry's persuasion.

James Mansfield stood up. "Mr. Rural Dean, as churchwarden of Thorpemunden I think I need to point out that this was a very different kind of service, not altogether appreciated by our regular members. Of course, we are delighted to have parents and children worshipping with us," at this there were nods of support from the Thorpemunden PCC, "but we would not like to think that our usual service was going to be—" he hesitated, "—well, can I say 'hijacked' for something completely different? Our regular members are the backbone of our church, and until or unless we have a new backbone, I think we need to stick with something we all know and love. After all, we shouldn't be regarding poor Henry's illness as an opportunity to slide in all sorts of new ideas through the back door. And I need hardly remind you as rural dean that the PCC is responsible for worship in the church."

There were murmurs of assent and a few muted cries of "Hear, hear!" throughout the hall as he sat down. Polly felt her heart sink.

But Charles smiled easily and said, "Thank you, James. Your finger is exactly on the pulse, as usual. You're quite right, of course, hence the calling of this meeting of all PCCs, to consult you all. No, I understand the Harvest Festival was a one-off, to try to ascertain whether there would be any support in the village for a more informal service, but this was never intended to replace the services you already have." He glanced round at the signs of relief on the various faces. "No, the idea is to start something completely new. A new, informal service on a Sunday afternoon, perhaps at four o'clock, designed for young people and their families. You would be able to feed the Pram Service people into it and hopefully liaise with the school to attract older children as well."

A hand was raised. "Would this be at Hamblestead too?"

"Not necessarily. Is there another parish who would like to host it? It will mean some work, mind you. A commitment from the PCC and others to help run the service, and it would need to be followed by tea."

This produced both uncertainty and excitement. Although some members of the congregations acted as chalice assistants and read the lesson in church, no one had ever helped run a service before.

Another hand went up. "Would it be in the village hall? What would we have to do?"

Charles beamed. It was definitely going his way. "No, as it would be on a Sunday, it would be in church this time. You'd meet with Polly once a week to plan the service. She will have plenty of ideas. Then you'd need to personally invite youngsters to attend. And run off some suitable publicity and plaster the neighbourhood with it, so that everybody knows what is going on."

Jonathan Eckerby, churchwarden of Kirkby Thorpe, stood up. "We'll do it. We'll take that on, with Polly's help." As one of the smaller parishes and sharing services with Hamblestead, he felt that Kirkby Thorpe was often unnecessarily ignored by the rest of the benefice. A success like this, building up a strong youth group, would show the rest of them, prevent Hamblestead from gaining any advantage through their Pram Service, and bring some much needed new blood into Kirkby Thorpe. The other members of his PCC, although less sure, murmured their assent. Jonathan had been the local bank manager before he retired seven years ago and they were used to following his lead.

Polly was delighted with the outcome of the meeting. Charles had handled it brilliantly and just as she thought, people were eager for change. She arranged a meeting with Jonathan and the Kirkby Thorpe PCC for the following evening, determined to start her new service as soon as humanly possible.

***

After a night's sleep and in the much less forgiving light of day, many of the parishioners felt anxious about the proposed changes. Even Ivy Cranthorn felt that perhaps they had all been carried along on a sort of public wave of animation, rather like the unreal atmosphere generated at a football match. She got out the car and drove over to Arthur Roamer's at Middlestead to see what he thought.

Arthur was in the garden, an electric hedge cutter strapped to his chest. He wore earmuffs to minimise the noise and goggles to protect his eyes, so Ivy had to walk slowly into his line of vision in order not to startle him. She didn't want to cause an unfortunate accident.

Arthur spotted her quite quickly and switched off. He removed his earmuffs and unstrapped the hedge cutter, laying it on the grass. "Come on, I'm ready for a break. We'll have coffee in the kitchen."

Ivy followed him in and sat down at the kitchen table while he produced the coffee. She liked Arthur's kitchen, which was always toasty and although neat and well kept, not so pristine that she was afraid to sit down. "What did you think of the meeting last night?"

Arthur pulled a face. "Hope we're not about to become like Diss. If I wanted to worship like that I'd go there. Don't want his way-out ideas coming over here. If I wanted to dance in the aisles I'd go to *Strictly Come Dancing,* not church."

"Know what you mean. But Polly is right, we do have to attract the young somehow, don't we?"

"Do we have to do it so quickly? We've hardly had time to breathe, yet I understand it's all set to start next Sunday. But can you really see that Kirkby Thorpe lot tripping the light fantastic in church? The only thing they trip over are their own feet. Besides, there's only about nine regulars. They're all on the PCC. The PCC is the church, there's no one else."

Ivy laughed. "You're right there! Full of enthusiasm last night, but I wonder how many will stick it out. My bet is, they'll fade away within a month."

"They're too old for that sort of caper. No, Polly will find she'll have to do it all herself. But she's young, plenty of energy. She should do all right. Anyway, if you're right and it only lasts a month, it'll all be over by the time Henry comes back. I heard he was going to be off for a month. What's wrong with him, do you know?"

"They're not saying. Mavis was very tight-lipped at Mothers' Union. She tried to make it sound as if he was terminally ill, but we all reckon it's nothing more than stress."

"Huh! No such thing in my day." Arthur bit into a shortbread biscuit and handed the tin to Ivy. "Can't cope, more like. Do him good to be stirred up a bit by young Polly. He's had it his own way far too long. And I like that girl. Got a bit of spunk about her."

"I like her too," agreed Ivy. "That's why I'd be sorry if her new venture fails. But I am worried about the speed of it all. Still, she's that enthusiastic, I expect she'll carry it along. And I think she'll get new, younger people to start running this informal service. People who don't come at all at the moment."

Arthur frowned. "Huh! So we'll have a two-tier church before long?"

"I suppose we might. Can't see many of us oldies wanting newfangled worship, and the youngsters have already voted with their feet. They don't come anywhere near our services. So yes. I suppose that's the way it'll go. Two churches which never meet, using the same building but running alongside each other. Doesn't feel quite right, does it?"

***

Polly went ahead with the new Sunday afternoon service, managing to persuade Kirkby Thorpe PCC that they would much prefer to organise refreshments after the service rather than take part in the service itself. This led to relief all round, and one or two PCC members took the opportunity to bring their grandchildren to church for the first time.

Polly had been busy recruiting young mums for the monthly Pram Service and used that mid-week base to convince the younger generation that it was worth trying church on a Sunday afternoon. She used the enticement of an old-fashioned high tea, with scones and cake and sandwiches, jelly and ice cream and orange juice for the children, as the draw. Until she got her own band going in the Thorpemunden Benefice, Charles had agreed to loan the Diss band of two guitars, a drummer, a flautist, and a violinist to provide music. He also lent a data projector and a brand-new screen for Polly to show the service and all the words of the songs ("They can't be called hymns, can they?" Diana Courtney from the Kirkby Thorpe congregation asked Jonathan, the churchwarden) on a PowerPoint presentation to save printing out service sheets.

Polly was thrilled and the Kirkby Thorpe PCC amazed when thirty adults and twelve children arrived for the service. Polly gave a little talk on the man who built his house upon the sand, which she illustrated with cardboard boxes, inviting the children to knock the boxes over at the appropriate point in the story. With noisy action songs, a great deal of moving about and dipping into different "worship stations," plenty of heartfelt feeling in the songs, and some Bible-based games, everybody had a good time and tucked into tea afterwards with gusto.

***

Polly was unaware that the Kirkby Thorpe organist had stayed away in a huff. Rosemary Grant, a Mothers' Union member, had been playing the organ devotedly at Kirkby Thorpe for thirty years and was most put out that Polly evidently thought her playing was not good enough for the new service. She was incensed that a band from elsewhere had been invited in without ever consulting her. Rosemary, who was in her early seventies, with her yellow-white hair cut in a straight bob and her half-glasses perched precariously towards the end of her rather sharp nose, had been ready with plenty of advice about suitable music for the new service. But she had not been asked and felt rejected and deeply hurt. Although she had reached no further than grade six piano in her youth, she had done her best on the somewhat rickety Kirkby Thorpe harmonium and had always considered herself to be the musical expert at Kirkby Thorpe. True, she played the odd wrong note—and nobody was more aware of this than Rosemary—but she was always given the responsibility to decide on which hymns they would sing. That this was because Henry was aware of the limitations of her repertoire had never occurred to Rosemary; neither had she realised that the Kirkby Thorpe hymn singing was restricted to around fifty hymns repeated endlessly throughout the year. Never having heard a modern worship song and being unaware that any hymns had been written post 1935, Rosemary had already sorted out what she considered to be suitable hymns for the new service. Amongst others, she had chosen for the kiddies "All Things Bright and Beautiful" and "Jesus Wants Me For a Sunbeam," her two all-time favourites. But Polly had simply looked at the proposed hymn list, laughed, and handed it back to her without comment. Rosemary was simmering and unable to forgive or forget. While the service was going on, she was tucked up in her armchair at home, feeding her misery and debating whether or not to resign.

***

To her surprise since she was only twenty-eight years old, Polly felt exhausted by the time that first Sunday ended. Quite apart from the new service, which was exhausting in its own right keeping control of a dozen children while at the same time engaging with their parents, she had taken three services in the morning and an Evensong after the new service.

She had started at eight o'clock in the morning, when she had had to shepherd an unknown priest to preside at Communion. Then she had collected Father Brian for the same purpose for the nine-thirty and eleven o'clock services. He had not been ready when she called, having forgotten that he had agreed to help out in this way, so they had been late starting the nine-thirty service, which had irritated the waiting congregation and increased the rush for the whole day. By the time the day finished, Polly reckoned she had driven over forty miles, dashing about from place to place.

***

At the Kirkby Thorpe planning meeting for the following Sunday's service, Polly was disappointed that four people had sent apologies, and those who did turn up were already grumbling about the cost of producing a full-scale tea every week.

"This should be a benefice expense," Jonathan Eckerby told Polly. "If families and youngsters are coming from every parish, the other churches should help cover the cost. And I must say, Polly, I do think you should have taken a collection. These things don't pay for themselves."

"This was their first experience of church, Jonathan. What sort of a message do you think it would have given them to have started by asking them for money as soon as they set foot through the door?"

"A realistic one! Nothing runs on air and they know that. You'll have to find some way of raising money from them, so you might as well bite the bullet now."

"Surely we need to consolidate their commitment first. Maybe in six months' time we can broach the question of giving."

Jonathan's lips set in a thin line. "At least put a plate out on the refreshment table. If you don't do that, you're effectively taking away people's right to give if they wish to. You're always full of people's rights. Give them this right."

So in view of all the opposition, Polly had reluctantly agreed.

She found the meeting heavy going. She discovered that although it had been easy to plan one session of new worship, planning the second, bringing back some of the songs and prayers heard last week but adding a new flavour to the worship to keep it fresh, was rather more demanding. And since no one from Kirkby Thorpe had any ideas at all, the meeting soon deteriorated into Polly deciding what was to be done and informing the gathered people.

To add to her difficulties, Polly learned that although Father Brian and one or two visiting priests were happy enough to come in to preside at Holy Communion during Henry's absence, none of them wished to take the whole service. So Polly found herself responsible for preaching at every service, every week. Where once she would have been thrilled at this opportunity, with all the extra work generated by the new service and the monthly Pram Service, especially the hours it took to prepare the PowerPoint presentation, she found herself struggling. Not used to preaching, it took her ages to prepare a sermon. Ruefully, she recalled the words of the Reverend Doctor Theodore Grimes at college: "It takes an hour's preparation for every minute of a sermon." At the time, Polly had laughed, assuming with youthful arrogance that he was exaggerating. Now she wasn't so sure. Reading and mulling over the Scripture passages set for the Sunday, deciding on a theme and researching it, then finding suitable illustrations, and finally writing the ten-minute sermon took all of ten hours.

She was also finding Father Brian quite hard work. Well into his eighties he was extremely slow, fumbling at the altar and losing his place in the Prayer of Consecration, which he thought he knew by heart but kept forgetting. For Polly, who knew she could have presided much more efficiently, this proved frustrating, and the astute old man picked up on her frustration as they travelled between churches in the car, apologising for his slowness in such a humble way that Polly felt ashamed. She longed for next year when she would be priested and all this nonsense of having to import priests to bless the elements would be over.

Then, on the Saturday morning when she thought everything was in place for the following day, Polly received a letter.

"Dear Reverend Hewitt," she read. "It is with regret that I feel I must tender my resignation both as organist of Kirkby Thorpe Church and as a member of the PCC, to take effect immediately.

"As you may or may not know, I have been organist at Kirkby Thorpe for over thirty years and have, I hope, during that time played to the glory of God. My music has been my offering to God and while this may not be good enough for some people," (this last was heavily underscored) "I feel sure that God has appreciated my poor efforts, knowing that I have given of my best.

"I have lived at Kirkby Thorpe all my life and cannot remember a time when I did not attend church. When I was a girl, we children all went to church with our parents and sat quietly through the service until such time as we were old enough to understand and appreciate what was going on. It never did us any harm. I have to say that in my opinion it would do children a great deal more good to learn to sit quietly at church rather than all this running about up and down the aisles and singing rubbishy pop songs. That is not, and never will be, Anglican worship.

"I deeply regret leaving a post I have loved all these years, but in view of the terrible changes being wrought upon our beloved little church and the clear message that my services are no longer needed in this modern life, I am left with no alternative.

"Yours very sincerely in the name of Christ,

"Rosemary Grant (Miss)."

Polly put her head in her hands and burst into tears. She suspected that the letter had been carefully timed to produce maximum embarrassment, for how could anyone find a new organist in a rural area like Thorpemunden with less than twenty-four hours' notice? And although the congregation could possibly scrape by tomorrow morning by singing unaccompanied, she had no idea what to do about the long-term future. Should she go and see Rosemary Grant, begging her to return? On the other hand, why should she? It was obvious that this was exactly what the old bat wanted her to do, but Polly was not at all sure she wished to be manipulated by Rosemary Grant. Especially after dropping Polly in it in such a vicious way. So what should she do? Call the old girl's bluff by doing nothing but calmly carrying on as though nothing had happened, or effectively allow Miss Grant even more power by bending to her wishes? Polly didn't know.

Chapter Fifteen

It was the first time Ella had been to Great Yarmouth train station and she was disappointed to find that at such an early hour no waiting rooms were open, nor were there any refreshment facilities. She was in no particular hurry, so consulted the train timetable to find out times of trains for London and noted that she would have to change and probably wait for an hour or so at Norwich. So she wandered back into the town to find an all-night transport café where she could while away the hours and get some breakfast.

The Greedy Pig had an unfortunate name, which conjured up in Ella's mind mountains of greasy food, but although basic, it was clean and warm. She sat at a table in the far corner out of the sightline of the door and windows and ordered a full English.

"Tea or coffee, love?" asked the waitress. Middle-aged and thickening around the waist, she appeared weary.

Ella said, "Coffee, please. You look tired."

"Been up all night, love. Night shift. We're the only twenty-four-hour place for miles around. Get a lot of business from the docks." She eyed Ella's bags. "You going far?"

"London. But there's not much open on the station and you can't get a cup of tea, so I came here."

"We'll give you a good breakfast then, love, keep you going for the day."

She was as good as her word and Ella, one of those fortunate beings who never increase weight no matter how much they eat, put away bacon and egg, baked beans, tomatoes and toast, finished off with more toast, marmalade, and two mugs of tea. But as she was enjoying her food, the breakfast immediately reminded her of Tracey and she wondered disconsolately whether her absence had yet been discovered and, if so, what Tracey and Melvyn's reaction would be.

Ella felt a sadness at her departure. Although this had been the pattern for her life as long as she could remember, preventing her from becoming rooted anywhere, she still experienced a sense of loss whenever she felt the urge to move on. But now she was in her twenties, alone and responsible for herself, and she began to notice a new feeling of regret which hadn't been apparent before. In happier times her mother had been the solid rock of Ella's life and as long as that rock was always there, Ella had felt safe. It had never occurred to her before that it might be possible to have roots in a geographical area, but now she thought wistfully of how wonderful it would be to have a place she could call home, somewhere she belonged, where she could return whenever she needed stability. Somewhere which would always be there for her and which would never change.

That led Ella on to reflecting on her father, that shadowy man she had never met. All she knew was that he was a professional man, but her mother had never revealed what his profession might be, nor had Ella ever seen a picture of him. In her darker moments Ella had wondered whether her mother even knew his identity. But on the few occasions her mother had spoken of him, she had spoken with warmth and sincerity and described him to Ella as a "good and kind man."

Ella wondered exactly how good he was. Was he the one who had made her mother HIV positive all those years ago? The clinic had been unable to trace all Ella's mother's sexual partners because she could not remember them all, and Ella wondered whether her mother had contracted the disease prior to or after Ella's birth. Upon reflection, she assumed it must have been afterwards or she herself would perhaps have been HIV positive when she was born. And it wasn't until Ella was twelve or thirteen that the first symptoms had shown themselves. Ella knew that HIV commonly presented around five to ten years after infection, which probably meant that like she herself, her father was clear. She hoped so, even though the man, whoever he was, had shown no interest in her or her mother. Watching her mother die from AIDS had been horrendous, as the beloved person Ella had known had gradually slipped away both physically and mentally until Ella's mother was but a shell which hung grimly onto life for several months. Ella shuddered. The memories were still raw.

Thinking about her mother had made Ella nostalgic. She suddenly needed one last look at the sea before she departed forever from Great Yarmouth. She paid for her breakfast, gathered up her bags, and cautiously left The Greedy Pig, glancing all around her before she dared venture down the street. It was a fair walk to the front, but the streets were only just coming to life at that early hour and Ella was undisturbed.

The beach was completely deserted, which gave Ella confidence to remove her footwear for one last paddle in the sea. But the water in late September was already beginning to take on its winter chill, and her nostalgic mood abruptly ended. She said her own farewells and repeated a ritual she had developed as a child, finding a flat stone and spinning it over the surface of the water as she chanted her good-byes to the ocean. Then she was ready.

She replaced her shoes and socks, hoisted the pack onto her back, picked up the carrier bags, and this time walked briskly to the station, with only a few furtive glances around her.

***

Henry was not doing well. Mavis worried about him and wondered whether she was doing the right thing by keeping all news of the benefice away from him. Perhaps he would have liked to hear the gossip, if only to protest against it. She had even ventured as far as, "I don't think Rosemary Grant at Kirkby Thorpe is too happy. Apparently Polly had some sort of pop band in there last week." But other than briefly raising his eyebrows, Henry had shown no interest. Neither did he show interest in anything else. Mavis herself went out each day to buy the paper for him as she didn't think it would be a good idea for him to venture into local shops. But he often failed even to open the paper, spending long hours simply staring into space. Mavis tried the television and the radio, but although Henry made no move to turn either of them off, neither did he seem to be listening.

Bearing in mind Dr. Lambert's words, Mavis made an effort to bundle Henry into the car each afternoon, driving out of the benefice to find somewhere pleasant like Thetford Forest where they could walk. Henry dutifully walked without complaint, but he seemed turned in on himself and his conversation was almost exclusively limited to monosyllabic responses.

Mavis pleaded with Henry to visit the doctor again, but he adamantly refused, saying that he had no intention of taking tablets, so it was a waste of time. He had one visit from the bishop, who wished him well, said a prayer, heartily clapped him on the shoulder, and escaped as soon as possible. He had two visits from the rural dean, but Mavis managed, without saying a word, to make it plain to Charles that he was unwelcome. And Henry ignored him, so Charles settled instead for a short, weekly phone call.

Henry himself was not really aware of what he was doing. Once the parish work had been removed from him, he had lost his anchor. Without his work which had identified him for so many years, Henry no longer knew quite who he was. He had played the role of vicar for so long that without realising it, he had become the role. Now that he no longer had the role, he felt faceless, an unknown nonentity.

But to Henry's surprise, being a non-person was not altogether unpleasant. He left Mavis to make all the decisions. If he didn't feel like responding to her, he simply didn't respond, not worrying what she might think or what it might do to her. Without the need to wear as nearly a perfect façade as he could, Henry dropped all pretence and found it a great relief. He no longer cared if he appeared brusque or withdrawn. Henry became self-absorbed and discovered he rather liked it.

Having been utterly firm in his faith all his life, Henry was no longer sure what he believed about God. When he bothered to think about it at all, he supposed he would eventually have to resign from ministry since he could no longer say with his hand on his heart that he believed in the existence of God. But this unbelief did not alarm him. He merely put it to one side and forgot about it. As long as Mavis continued to look after him, placing meals on the table in front of him at regular intervals and washing and cleaning and shopping for him, he was content. He simply sat in his favourite armchair with his feet on the footstool, staring into space for long hours at a time, letting his mind wander at will, thinking about nothing in particular. Had he but known it, he was allowing his mind and soul to heal, rather like being put into a drug-induced coma to allow the body to heal.

Mavis was far less sanguine than Henry. She could see her husband visibly slipping away from her and felt both helpless and rejected. On her knees in Henry's study she implored God to return her husband to her, but nothing happened.

However, Mavis was a strong woman, accustomed to taking the lead, and she was determined to pull Henry out of his self-absorption by any means at her disposal. Early in October when the weather was starting to wear its winter apparel, she pulled Henry into his anorak, placed a woolly hat on his head, sheepskin gloves on his hands, and drove him to Diss Station.

Although the station master followed his usual habit of hiding at Henry's approach, Mavis took no notice, but led Henry onto the platform and sat him in his customary seat to watch the trains thundering by.

It was a good move. Henry's eyes immediately brightened and he began to display a certain amount of interest in his surroundings. They stayed there all morning, punctuated by coffee at frequent intervals purchased by Mavis from the station buffet when she could stand the cold and the boredom no longer. But it was worth it just to see Henry with a little colour in his cheeks and that almost forgotten spark of brightness in his dark brown eyes.

***

Ella caught the mid-morning train from Yarmouth to London not knowing how long she would have to wait at Norwich. But she didn't much care. She had nothing particular to go to London for. It was merely an anonymous city where she expected to be able to find work.

She entered a long, open carriage, where the seats faced each other with a table between them, and stowed her bags on the rack, taking out a novel before she sat down. But she passed the journey staring out of the window at the fields racing by, wondering what she was going to do with her life.

She dozed a little on the short journey to Norwich, jerking awake as the train slowed to enter the station. But as she opened her eyes to orientate herself by glancing out of the window, she thought she caught the reflection of a man in the glass. She turned in panic, but nobody was there. Even so, Ella was unable to prevent a shudder running through her body as her mind began to play with the possibility that Mark Winters had somehow spotted her in Yarmouth and silently followed her onto the train.

She stood up to collect her bags, trying to shake off what she suspected had been simply a trick of the light in her just-waking state and to convince herself that it was only her mind playing tricks again.

Ella climbed down onto the platform, looked up at the announcements on the monitors, and made her way over to the end platform, where the train for London would come in. But she couldn't help frequently looking over her shoulder and walking with her back as close to the wall as possible. Her neck was prickling and she wasn't sure whether it was all imagination, as she tried to tell herself, or whether she ought to be worried.

She sat on a remote seat well down the platform where she could see all the comings and goings, but didn't dare to pass the time reading her book. She was glad when the train drew in, even though she knew it wasn't due to depart for another half hour.

Ella was one of the first on the train and selected a carriage way down the track, hoping that few people would bother to walk that far. She sat in the first seat with her back to the engine so that she was near a door and could clearly see the whole carriage. This time she kept her bags hugged to her and didn't bother to take out her book. She sat with shoulders hunched, unable to relax.

As she kept glancing towards the other end of the carriage, she again thought she spotted a shadowy shape flitting past the door at the end. She contemplated jumping out of the train onto the platform, but by then it was moving and picking up speed. After keeping her eyes trained on the far door for ten minutes, Ella could stand it no longer.

She quickly slipped out of her seat and into the vacant toilet. She locked the door, took off her jacket, exchanged it for a scarlet sweater, and stuffed the jacket into her backpack. Then she fished out her striped, woollen cloche hat, bunched her hair under it so that no hair was showing, and pulled it down low over her face.

Noticing the slowing of the train, she cautiously unlatched the door and peered out. No one was near as the train pulled into a station. Ella waited for five minutes as passengers got on and off and until she heard the station master's whistle; then she opened the door and tumbled onto the platform just as the train was beginning to pull away.

But she had left it a little late and the speed of her momentum caused her to fall in a tangled heap of bags. The station master ran up, angrily berating her for her stupidity, but someone else reached her first.

Henry put his arm around Ella and helped her to her feet.

"It's all right," he said to the station master. "She's with us."

Ella stared up at him in dismay. But as Henry smiled, his dark brown eyes crinkled and his face lit up and Ella felt something like a bolt of electricity shoot through her. As they held each other's gaze for a long moment, the middle-aged man and the young girl, they were both aware of unexpected chemistry.

Then Ella smiled back and said, "I'm all right. Really. It was stupid of me, but I'm not hurt."

"No, but you must come with us and have a cup of tea," Mavis said firmly. She had noticed Henry's almost involuntary instinct to help the girl and thanked God for it. For the first time in weeks he seemed to be coming out of his trance-like state. It was just like the old Henry to help someone in distress without a thought, and Mavis wanted to capitalise on such a welcome change. Besides, she'd had enough of Diss Station for one day.

After glancing fearfully around to make sure she hadn't been followed onto the platform, a movement that wasn't lost on Henry, Ella allowed herself to be guided to the station buffet and accepted a coffee and a Danish from Mavis.

As Ella pecked at her Danish, Henry said, "Not hungry?"

"I had a big breakfast. Didn't expect to eat again until tonight."

Mavis asked, "Where are you headed?"

Ella looked a little sheepish. "London, as a matter of fact. But I—well, I've had a difficult time and—"

Henry said shrewdly, "You're hiding from someone?"

Ella turned astonished eyes on him. "How did you know? I am, actually. I've been stalked and now I keep thinking I see him everywhere I turn. Stupid, I know."

"Not stupid at all. Did you think he was on the train with you? Is that why you hurtled off at the last moment?"

"Yeah, that was stupid, too! I don't know now what I thought. I kinda thought I saw his reflection on the train from Yarmouth, and since then I've seen him in every shadow. I just wish I could get him out of my head. I'm not even sure it was him in the reflection. I dozed and it was just in that waking moment, you know?"

Henry looked around. "I don't think he's here now. We're the only ones in the station and there's no one hanging about outside. But how are you going to get to London? Wait for the next train?"

Ella sighed. "I suppose so. Not that it matters. I've nothing to go there for. It's just somewhere to go."

"Well, if you don't have a deadline or anyone waiting for you, why don't you come home with us for the night? We have plenty of spare rooms and I can make up a bed in no time." Mavis' eyes gleamed.

"Oh, I couldn't possibly trouble you! You've been so kind already. No, there'll be another train before too long. I'll just wait."

But Mavis had a plan to save her husband and wasn't about to be deflected from it. "Hmm. Let's hope he wasn't on the train, then. It would be too awful to get to Liverpool Street and find him waiting beside the track."

There was a sharp intake of breath from Ella. "You don't think—?"

"No, I very much doubt it! But if time's not important at the moment, perhaps one night here would make doubly sure that you're safe. He certainly won't wait for every train for twenty-four hours, will he?"

Ella was still uncertain. "I don't know—"

Henry said easily, "We haven't introduced ourselves, but we can remedy that without difficulty. I'm Henry. The Reverend Canon Henry Winstone, Rector of the Benefice of Thorpemunden, if you want my full title. And we live in the rectory at Thorpemunden, which is a small village about eight miles away. This is my wife, Mavis. There. Will that do for a formal introduction?"

Ella turned relieved liquid eyes upon him. "You're a vicar! That's all right, then. I'm Ella Wim, I'm twenty-two years old, I don't come from anywhere much, and I have nowhere in particular to go. Does that make it all right?" She looked anxiously at him. "I mean, if you're a vicar you look after homeless people and all that, don't you?"

Henry hid a smile. He said solemnly, "We do. That is part of our remit. And we would like you, Ella Wim, to be our special guest for today."

Chapter Sixteen

Ella had felt safe immediately when Henry had stopped to pick her up, but in company with both Mavis and Henry she felt ultra safe, safer than she had felt since her mother died. As they left the station, she didn't even glance around. She felt as if Mark Winters, real or imagined, was at least temporarily banished from her life. There was something indefinably stable about these two people she had so inadvertently met. Perhaps it was because they were of her mother's generation.

To Mavis' delight, Henry insisted on driving the short distance home, the first time he had driven since his illness began. Mavis was already planning how she might lengthen Ella's stay, perhaps until Henry was really well with no possibility of a relapse, however long that might be. Mavis was, however, a naturally cautious person and was hesitant about making any promises, even to herself, until she really knew this girl. Ella Wim seemed like a pleasant enough character, and it was clear Henry had taken to her in a big way. What was not clear was whether Henry's fascination with her would be sustained for more than an hour or so and whether the girl herself would prove to be of sound character.

Mavis invited Ella to sit in the front of the car next to Henry, while she herself sat in the back. Mavis was content to occupy the rear seat, listening to the continuing drone of conversation as Henry pointed out the various sights of Diss on the homeward journey. Well, nearly content. It was difficult from behind to make out what was being said and Mavis soon gave up the effort. She was delighted to hear the old Henry chatting away, but a tiny part of her felt hurt and rejected. Why couldn't he chat like that with her? Why did he sit there silent all the way to the station, hunched beside her like a mute, only to come suddenly and miraculously to life for someone he'd just happened upon? Although most of her was thrilled at this evidence of recovery, Mavis was unable to repress a tiny shaft of resentment.

Back at the rectory, Mavis took a chance by inviting Henry to make a pot of tea and some sandwiches while she prepared a room for Ella. Since Henry had never even boiled a kettle since his break-down, she was unsure how he would respond. But he immediately set to work after fussing over Ella and making sure she was seated in a comfortable armchair in the lounge.

Mavis was the first to finish her task, and Ella elected to transfer her bags to the bedroom before settling down to a spot of lunch. Although Thorpemunden rectory was not the warmest place she had inhabited, she was delighted with her room, which was spacious and light, overlooking the large rectory garden where she could already see a couple of pheasants strutting across the lawn and a squirrel scampering up the trunk of a large horse chestnut tree. Ella pulled off her hat, allowing her black hair to escape, cascading over her shoulders. And she changed the red sweater for a crisp white blouse with an upstanding frilly collar, covered by an attractive short-sleeved maroon vest which buttoned under the bust. She had a quick wash, applied a little makeup, brushed her hair until it shone, and went downstairs.

Henry's mouth fell open. He breathed, "You are so beautiful!"

Embarrassed by her husband's evident adulation and his failure to be circumspect (both of which she attributed to the illness) Mavis took over, gaining some return to normality by sitting them all down and handing round plates, sandwiches, and paper serviettes. She poured out tea for all of them and pulled up an occasional table on which to place Ella's cup. Mavis, too, had been taken aback by Ella's beauty, which had been disguised by the hat, and she was again aware of a slight feeling of discomfiture. But she was more concerned about her husband's health than her own feelings and determined that they should both get to know Ella.

Ella refused sandwiches, claiming that her big breakfast really would last her all day, but accepted the cup of tea which Mavis handed her. She found the atmosphere in the rectory a little forbidding but assumed that was because of her own nervousness and because the rectory was so unnaturally (to Ella's eyes) neat, with not even a cushion rumpled or out of place. She wasn't at all sure why she had been invited back on such a chance acquaintance; it seemed weird. Unless vicars did this sort of thing all the time? Ella had no experience whatsoever of the church and to her knowledge had never even met a churchgoer, but assumed the church was something to do with caring for people. Anyway, it was a bed for the night and she could always disappear if she found it all too oppressive. On the other hand, Ella felt strangely drawn to Henry, and to Mavis as an extension of Henry, so she was curious to see where all this would lead.

"You said you've come from Yarmouth?" Mavis began.

Ella nodded. "I've been there over the summer, working in a bar. The Lord Nelson. Do you know it?"

As both Mavis and Henry shook their heads, Ella's hand flew to her mouth. "Oh, I'm sorry. I don't suppose vicars go into pubs, do they? I mean, you're not allowed to drink, are you?"

Henry glanced at his wife and grinned. "It's not unknown for Church of England vicars, actually. We clergy are permitted to have a drink from time to time, and Mavis and I have occasionally partaken of a pub lunch. Very good they are too, usually."

"Oh, they are! Tracey—she's the landlady at the Lord Nelson—she's a brilliant cook. I lived there for the summer. Tracey and—and Melvyn were good to me."

Henry had noticed the slight hesitation. "Melvyn?"

"He's the landlord. When I had this trouble I was telling you about, you know—the stalker—Melvyn went after him. The stalker never came back."

"What did Melvyn do to get rid of him so easily?"

Ella's face clouded. "I don't know, he wouldn't say. But even after that, I kept seeing this guy all over the place. I even think he might have burgled my room and stolen a necklace from me, but I've no proof. Tracey thought I imagined seeing him and I might have done. I'm not sure, now. You know what it's like? You look up and see a shadow and straightaway your mind is full of him. It's really scary. But the season's finished anyway and there's no way they could afford to employ me for the winter, so I left."

Mavis said, "I'm sorry about your necklace. But if it was the only thing missing, how do you know you didn't simply lose it?"

"Melvyn and Tracey's room was trashed but nothing was taken, so we think he was targeting something specific. And as only the necklace went, we reckoned it must have been Mark Winters, the stalker."

"What did the police say?"

"We didn't go to the police. It was the only thing missing and, as I say, no proof. The police would probably have laughed, it was such a petty crime. We didn't think it would come high on their list of priorities, so it didn't seem worth reporting."

"I suppose you're right. A pity, though. Henry and I can remember the time when you could walk out of your house here in Thorpemunden leaving it unlocked. We'd never do it now, though, even in a quiet country village like this.

"Anyway Ella, now that you've left, what are you planning to do in London?"

Ella shrugged. "Don't know. Look for work somewhere, I suppose. I should think I'll pick up some work easily enough. After all, I'm an experienced barmaid now, so maybe I can start a proper CV."

Henry interjected, "Is that how you want to spend your life? As a barmaid?"

Ella hesitated. She didn't detect any undertones of censure in Henry's question, but she was unable to dissemble. "No, not really. I had a year at university studying English, but I had to drop out. What I'd really like to do is go back, but I lost the place and now I can't afford it. I suppose I vaguely thought I might be able to save a bit if I work for a couple of years. Then maybe I can reconsider."

Henry looked at Mavis and began, "Perhaps we could ask—"

But Mavis wasn't ready for that yet. She broke in, "And your family? Where are they?"

"I don't have any family. I never had any brothers or sisters, and my mother died earlier this year."

"So that's why you dropped out? Because of your mother's death?"

Ella nodded. "She was so ill and she didn't want to go into a hospice or anything like that. So I looked after her."

"That must have been very distressing for you."

"Yeah, it was. Seeing her so thin. She was always slight—she was Korean, so I'm half Korean, I suppose, although I've only ever lived in England—but she kinda shrunk before my eyes. I hardly recognised her when she died."

The professional in Henry had taken over. He said gently, "And did she recognise you at the end, Ella?"

Ella's eyes filled and she turned her head away sharply, staring at the carpet. "Yes. She always knew who I was. She didn't go into a coma or anything like that. She just—died. Pneumonia or something at the end, so the doctor said."

Mavis said, "Couldn't they have done something about that? Antibiotics or something?"

Ella shook her head. "Her immune system was shot to pieces by then. Nothing worked."

There was a silence as Henry and Mavis digested this information and the pain behind it. Mavis fleetingly wondered whether it was the truth, but there was such an ingenuousness about Ella that she didn't doubt for long.

She said, “And your father?”

“I never knew him. I don’t know anything about him. To be honest, I don’t even know his name!”

“It must be on your birth certificate, surely?”

“I don’t know. Maybe. My mother didn’t leave much. After she died I went through the handful of papers I found, but there was nothing about me, anywhere. So I’ve never seen my birth certificate.”

Mavis wanted to say, “Should be easy enough to get a copy,” but she felt that was a bit too intrusive at such an early stage in their relationship, so stayed silent, contenting herself with nodding understandingly.

***

The rectory doorbell jangled through the house at around four o’clock. Mavis went to answer the door, returning with Polly in tow.

Polly’s eyes widened in surprise as she glimpsed Ella. “Hello!”

Mavis hurriedly introduced them, before anyone else could say anything untoward. “Polly, meet Ella Wim. Ella, this is Polly Hewitt, Henry’s curate.”

“And doing all the work at the moment as I’m off sick,” Henry added in a good-humoured voice.

Polly’s eyebrows rose in astonishment. She had been procrastinating over this pastoral visit for several days, always discovering something new to do which would prevent her calling at the rectory. But today she had felt she couldn’t put it off any longer. She had dreaded the visit because she had expected to find a morose and silent Henry together with a miserable and tight-lipped Mavis, who would probably criticize her either for calling at all or for not calling sooner, and she had expected the conversation to be like ploughing through treacle. But here was a brighter, more animated Henry than she had yet experienced, someone who seemed to Polly to have suddenly discarded his priestly façade and was apparently normal both in attitude and in health. Mavis, too, seemed warmer than usual. And who was this fantastically pretty visitor?

"Are you staying long?" she asked Ella.

Mavis said, "We just picked Ella up from the station. She's only just got here."

"Oh? Where are you from, Ella?"

"I've come from Yarmouth. I was working there over the summer."

"Oh," said Polly, assuming, as Mavis had intended, that Ella was a niece or relative of some sort. She turned to Henry. "How are you, Henry?"

At the same time, Ella said, "Are you sick? I didn't realise."

Henry replied to both of them. "I have been off work for a week or two, hence it has all fallen on Polly's shoulders. But as you see, I'm much better now and expect to be returning to work before too long."

"What?" Mavis was both pleased and alarmed by Henry's casual statement. She, too, had detected something strange about Henry. The stolid, dependable pillar of the church seemed to have been replaced at the moment by someone altogether more frivolous, someone unpredictable whom Mavis didn't know. "You may be feeling better, Henry, but you have at least another week. The doctor laid you off for a month, remember?"

"And I have no intention of returning before then, my dear. Polly, perhaps we could catch up some time next week with all that's been going on in my absence?"

Polly nodded. "It's great to see you looking so well, Henry. You sound quite different." She forbore to add "lighter" or "happier," although that was what she thought. "The weekly bulletins just say you're 'resting,' which doesn't really tell us anything but doesn't sound that encouraging."

Henry laughed. "Well, now you can see for yourself and tell the world. Can't get rid of me that easily!"

Polly said, "Oh! No, um, I didn't mean—" Then she, too, laughed. She would have to get used to this new, relaxed Henry.

She said tentatively to Ella, "If you're staying for a while, perhaps we could meet up? Go to the cinema or grab a meal or something?"

Before Ella could reply, Mavis said, "We haven't discussed Ella's length of stay yet. But we are hoping she'll be with us for some time, aren't we, Henry? So that's a splendid idea, Polly. It would be lovely for Ella to go out from time to time with someone of her own age. Should Ella ring you?"

"Er, yes, okay," Polly said, somewhat bemused by this show of co-operation from Mavis. But she had immediately liked the look of Ella and welcomed the idea of a companion for a while, if only for one outing. She stood up to go. "Ring me then, when you're ready? See you soon, Mavis. Take care, Henry, and we'll meet next week, yeah?"

***

Ella followed Mavis to the kitchen, helping to carry the used crockery. "What did you mean about staying here?" she asked. "I thought I was only here for tonight."

"I know it must seem strange as we've only just met, but for me that meeting was most fortuitous. In fact, I'd go so far as to say that I think I see the hand of God in it."

Ella drew back. "Oh dear! I—"

Mavis patted her arm. "Perhaps I shouldn't have put it quite like that. I don't mean to alarm you. Let me explain. You see, Henry hasn't been at all well lately. He was under a lot of stress from the job; a vicar's work is never done, and priests have to cope with so much raw emotion with funerals and hospital visits and so on. And if there are difficulties within the parishes as well, it can be too much. Henry has always been so conscientious, which means he works far too hard, always giving out to other people but never taking enough time for himself.

I'm afraid his system just seized up. I thought he was having a heart attack. He had pains in his chest and he couldn't breathe properly. The doctor put him off work for a month, but without his work he's been a bit down. He lives for his work, does Henry. When he picked you up after you more or less fell onto the platform, I saw the old Henry back again. You've really cheered him up. He seems to have regained his spark, just from being with you. Perhaps it's having some youthful company. So you see, if you felt you could stay for a while, just until he gets back on his feet again properly, you'd be doing us both a great kindness."

"Well, I'm not sure…what if it all goes wrong and he relapses or something? I'd hate to be responsible for that."

"No, no, you wouldn't be responsible for anything, Ella. Apart from perhaps spending a little time with Henry. He does seem to have taken to you and I think he would enjoy just getting to know you a bit. As would I, of course. No. What I'm proposing is that you stay here for a time as our guest and we just take each day as it comes. Obviously you'd be free to come and go as you please, although I'd have to ask you to be a little careful about coming in late at night. We do retire to bed quite early and I wouldn't want Henry to be disturbed. But other than that, there would be no restrictions on your movements. You could do whatever you pleased."

"Well, I don't know. I don't like to take advantage of your hospitality. You've been very kind taking me in for the night, but I—"

"If it makes you more comfortable, think of it as unpaid work. I need someone to spend a few hours a day entertaining Henry. I can't afford to pay you, but I can house you and feed you as part of the family. And by 'entertain' I mean talking to him or maybe going out for a walk, going out for lunch, that sort of thing. If you like, why not think of yourself as our niece? Just act as you would with a favourite uncle. Please, Ella. Please say you will, if only for a few days."

"If you're sure… But you must promise to tell me if at any time you want me to go. If things change, like."

"Bless you, dear. You see, I was right. I knew it was God answering our prayer. He never answers as we expect. Come on now, let's go together and tell Henry that you'll stay for a while. He'll be so thrilled."

***

For the first time in her life, Ella attended church. She sat at the back with Mavis and Henry, and after the service found herself surrounded by people all eager to greet Henry and to meet with her.

She had already met Polly, who was leading the service and preaching, but Henry introduced her to the elderly clergyman who had performed that strange ritual far away at the table at the end of the church, where Mavis had led her and where she had had to kneel down with her arms at her side. The old vicar had put his hands on Ella's head and mumbled a few words which she couldn't make out, but she had felt a terrific heat through her head from his touch. It had thrown Ella, who had never experienced anything like it before. She wondered why Mavis and Henry and everyone else there had been given funny little wafers, which they had put in their mouths, and what exactly they had been drinking from that silver cup which was passed around. The old priest had muttered something about blood which Ella had found somewhat disconcerting. She was rather glad she was apparently not expected to drink from the cup.

Father Brian held Ella's gaze as he shook hands with her. "Delighted to meet you, my dear. I hope you have a very happy stay with Mavis and Henry. You certainly seem to be doing him good."

Ella smiled.

The old man said shrewdly, "Have you known Henry and Mavis long? Of course, my old memory's not so good, but I can't recall either of them mentioning you before."

Ella said, “When you put your hands on my head, it felt hot. Why was that?”

Father Brian smiled. “Perhaps it was the warmth of God’s Holy Spirit filling you. You don’t know God, do you? But God knows you and is using you for his own purposes.”

And he moved away, leaving Ella gazing after him with a very perplexed and anxious expression on her face.

Chapter Seventeen

Ella took her "work" seriously. She liked Henry, so it was easy to spend plenty of time in his company. He offered her the loan of any books in his study or anywhere else in the house, so as well as indulging in her taste for detective novels and thrillers, a taste she found she shared with Henry, she also began to delve into some of his easier theological books. She discovered Hans Küng's *On Being A Christian* and, wanting to know more about this religion which determined Henry's life, devoured the book, which she found fascinating. It was an old book—all Henry's theological books were old—but to Ella it was like a door into a new life. She had heard about Jesus in primary school and vaguely remembered something about a baby and an ox and a donkey and some lambs at Christmas, but other than that it was hazy. And long ago she had consigned Christianity to the waste bin along with Santa Claus and other discarded fantasies of childhood.

She began to question Henry about his beliefs, conversations which Henry found immensely stimulating for he seldom had the opportunity to discuss his faith with someone who knew nothing about it. Ella's questions, based on what she read from Hans Küng, ranged over politics and philosophy, science and technology, humanism and ethics, and how Christianity related to any of these. Some of her questions were incisive and observant, causing Henry to think deeply about his own response and occasionally to question things he had always taken for granted.

Ella was particularly concerned about the ethical relationship between Christianity and wealth. "You have this lovely house, Henry, paid for by the Church. But half your parishioners live in much smaller, rented property. I mean, it's lovely living here and I'm really enjoying it, but I don't understand why the Church spends all this money on it. There are people living rough in Norwich and Yarmouth. Why doesn't the Church care about them? And after all, there's only you and Mavis living in this rectory. You rattle round in here. Why doesn't the Church buy you somewhere smaller, rent out this place, and give the money to the homeless?"

"Maybe the diocese doesn't want to become a landlord."

"But it could have two or three homeless families living in here. It wouldn't exactly be a landlord. More of a philanthropist."

Henry laughed at the absurd picture this created in his mind. He was aware of the ambivalence of the Church of England, which jealously guarded its assets whilst decrying poverty, but he was also aware that the Church relied on income from its assets to survive so that if all the assets were sold, the Church would probably fold very quickly, causing untold misery to its employees and to its parishioners. And he knew that whatever outsiders like Ella thought, because it was reliant solely on voluntary contributions from the faithful, money was actually very tight within the whole Church, with several dioceses already on the verge of bankruptcy. That recalled him to uncomfortable thoughts about the Parish Share, so he quoted some words of Jesus about the poor being always with us and changed the subject.

"Come on, Ella. Let's play chess."

Having been taught to play as a child by her mother, Ella was good. She was quicker than Henry to see the moves and able to look ahead rather better than him, so she usually won. And Henry encouraged her, finding himself as pleased by her success as if it had been his own.

***

Despite her growing fondness for Henry and her enjoyment of his company, Ella felt restless. She helped Mavis whenever she could, taking on most of the heavy cleaning so that Mavis only had to dust. Mavis insisted on cooking for them all, but she did permit Ella to help by preparing vegetables and washing up afterwards. Ella would have loved to help in the large rectory garden, too, but even with nearly two acres of land to cover, Mavis jealously guarded her gardening, her only solace in difficult times, and was reluctant to allow anyone else to participate. Henry kept the lawns short with the ride-on mower and Ella had one or two goes on that, but she was aware that the ride-on was one of Henry's pleasures and was loath to snatch it from him. Anyway, now it was well into October, and few more cuts would be required.

So try as she might to fulfil her remarkably easy role, Ella was bored. She broached the subject with Mavis one day when they were washing up.

"Mavis, I've been here nearly three weeks now and Henry seems well. I'm wondering about looking for a job. I mean, I can't stay here forever without paying you rent. But maybe I could get a job in the evenings or something."

Mavis' face fell. "You're not thinking of going, are you, dear? Please don't do that. Henry's been a different man since you came. And you know the doctor gave him another three weeks, so obviously the doctor still thinks he needs more time. I'm so afraid he'll have a relapse if you go."

"No, I won't go yet, I promise. You've both been brilliant to me. But what if I got a job in a pub like before? I might be able to help out in The Crown or The King's Head in Mundenford, just working evenings."

Mavis was reluctant to allow her niece (she had so nearly convinced herself that Ella was a relative that she now thought of her only as a niece) to work in a pub. She didn't think bar work was quite the thing for any member of the rector's family. But neither did she want to lose Ella either completely or to a full-time day job, and there was no other form of evening work in the vicinity. So she agreed as graciously as she could, and Ella started to look for work in the Thorpemunden area.

***

Although Henry gave the impression of being completely well now, Dr. Lambert was not entirely happy about his patient's progress. He felt that from near enough the depths of depression, Henry had swung too far the other way. Henry himself seemed unaware of any incongruities in his behaviour, yet on one occasion he had taken Ella into Norwich with him, emerging with three floral shirts in different primary colours, a pair of jeans, and two pairs of trainers. Hence he turned up for his appointment with Peter Lambert dressed bizarrely in clothes suitable for someone half his age and which the old Henry would never have contemplated.

"You look different from the last time I saw you, Henry," Peter wryly observed.

"I'm proud to acknowledge that I am different, Peter. I think I've been finding myself over the last few weeks and our Ella has helped me. She's a wonderful girl, you know. Have you met her? Just the sort of tonic a chap needs, eh?" He laughed.

"Hmm. I don't think you're quite ready for work yet, are you?"

Peter expected a protest from Henry, but there was none. "If that's what you advise, Peter, of course I shall go along with it. I'll stay off as long as you suggest."

Peter stared. This was utterly unlike Henry, who was so renowned for his conscientiousness that his parishioners worried about him overworking. And since he had been Peter's patient, Henry had never before taken time off work.

"What's going on, Henry?" Peter asked quietly.

Henry frowned. "What do you mean? It was you who said I was ill and needed to rest."

"This girl, Ella. You're not falling for her, are you, Henry? Because it seems to me that your judgement is seriously impaired. I can't recommend any return to work for you until you settle down. You're far too euphoric for a man in your position and as you're not on any tablets, I presume there's some other cause."

"She is a lovely girl, Peter, and I do feel quite different when she's around. She brings me alive, you know? But you're wrong about me being euphoric. This is the real me, Peter, the one that's been crushed under years of the Church. Look at me now and see the real Henry Winstone."

But Peter merely harrumphed and said, "Are you sure you won't have any tablets? Because in my professional opinion you need to get back on an even keel pretty quickly."

***

When Ella went out with Polly on the promised cinema visit, she confided her difficulties to Polly. "They're lovely, Polly. I really like them. But I want something to do. I feel as if I'm just lounging around doing nothing."

"Are you staying then? Can't you go back home?"

Ella shook her head. "Don't have a home. Since I'm alone, I just go where I want and make that into home."

"Oh! No family, then?"

"My mother died and I never knew my father."

"Like me," exclaimed Polly. "Well, not exactly, but close enough. My mother is still alive but she's an alcoholic—don't tell Henry or Mavis, they'd have a fit—and my dad cleared off when I was three. S'pose he couldn't stand it any longer. I've got a little brother, Toby, but we don't have the same father. My mother had loads of blokes."

Ella was surprised. "Me too. About the blokes, I mean. Some of them were okay, but they changed so often I stopped taking any notice of them. Except the ones that hit me, and my mother soon got rid of them."

"Lucky you! It was my mother that did the hitting. Not that she knew what she was doing, since she was always drunk. Didn't hurt any the less, though."

"Do you still see her?"

Polly grimaced. "Not if I can help it. We don't get on. To be honest, it wouldn't worry me if I never saw her again."

"What about Toby?"

"I hardly know him. He's only ten, so I'd left home before he was born." She turned to Ella. "You know, you're the best thing that's happened since I've been here. Henry's quite different since you've been here. He was so old-fashioned and straight-laced, but look at him now. He fairly rocks!" They both laughed and Polly added, "Let's be friends, Ella. It's such a relief to have someone of my own era to talk to."

Ella smiled. "Know what you mean. I'm sure we will be friends. I liked you the first time I saw you. How about making this a regular date for as long as I'm here, shall we?" When Polly nodded enthusiastically she added, "I'm going to look for work. I want to work in a bar. It's good work and only evenings and you meet people. So if you hear of anything, could you let me know?"

"I'll do better than that," Polly replied. "I'll come with you and give you a hand. I know some of the landlords, so I can introduce you. Let's meet again in a day or two for a pub crawl."

***

The appointment with Dr. Lambert made Henry think. He became aware that his feelings for Ella were stronger than he had realised. She had roused in him dormant emotions which he only faintly remembered from long ago. Henry felt like a young man again and his new dress choice reflected that feeling. From there it was but a short step to imagining himself in love with Ella. He feasted his eyes upon her, longed to have her with him, and pined whenever she was away from him. His waking moments were filled with thoughts of Ella, his sleep was filled with dreams of her, and he had little time for anyone or anything else.

Although Henry said nothing about all this to anyone, Mavis was disturbed by her husband's erratic behaviour. She constantly watched Henry, alert for physical signs of his illness. Mavis knew how to deal with those. She was much less confident about dealing with her husband's emotional attachments and quite incapable of recognising her own emotional issues. She was aware of feeling old and frumpy beside Ella, but she had grown fond of the girl and, thinking of her only as a niece, it didn't occur to Mavis that Henry could have anything other than avuncular feelings for her. Mavis sometimes felt left out, but justified this because of her busyness in the house and garden. She had specifically invited Ella to spend time with Henry, so could hardly complain when she did exactly that.

But Mavis was worried by Henry's lack of reality. Since he had never been ill before, she had no idea how long the Church would continue to pay him his full salary. She presumed it would go on forever, with perhaps the State taking over if he was away from work too long, but she didn't know. What she did know was that parishioners were already looking askance at Henry. He had been very open about Ella's presence, and the joy it afforded him was plain to see. After initially welcoming this clear improvement in his condition, people were now beginning to grumble under their breath, asking why he couldn't come back to work if he was well enough to go gallivanting around the countryside with his niece. Mavis wasn't privy to the worst comments, but had noticed that even the Mothers' Union now fell silent when she entered the room, so their topic of conversation was self-evident.

And Henry showed no understanding of the need to return to work. He seemed utterly content to continue in this holiday style forever, even to his new clothes, which Mavis abhorred so strongly that she could hardly bear to look at them. But she didn't say anything for fear of causing a relapse. Even more abhorrent to her than the new gear was the thought of him growing morose and silent once again.

Rather against her better judgement but not knowing where else to turn, Mavis resolved to call on Polly. Mavis felt unable to speak to any of the Church hierarchy about her concerns since they were all Henry's bosses, his line managers. She couldn't go to any parishioners, not even her friends in the MU, for it would soon be broadcast far and wide. Neither did she think Father Brian would be much help, since his memory loss was getting worse. So there was only Polly.

***

Polly welcomed Mavis in, trying to suppress her start of surprise at her visitor. She led Mavis into the lounge, which although far from neat according to rectory standards, at least now had armchairs and was reasonably presentable. She swept the *Eastern Daily Press* off one of the armchairs, slinging it haphazardly onto the floor, and invited Mavis to sit down.

"Coffee? Milk and no sugar, isn't it?"

Mavis nodded. It was the first time she had been in the curate's house, but where she might previously have looked around with some disdain, now she was too concerned with her own problems even to notice evidence of Polly's careless housekeeping.

Polly gave her an opening. "How's Henry?"

"As a matter of fact, Polly, that's why I'm here." Mavis was nervously twisting a handkerchief in her hands. "I don't know quite how to put this."

Polly sipped her coffee, waiting with what she hoped was an encouraging smile on her face. But when Mavis seemed unable to continue, she said gently, "We're all missing him, Mavis."

That opened the floodgates. Mavis said, "That's just it. I'm sure he needs to get back to work, but he just doesn't seem to have any get-up-and-go, if you know what I mean. Henry's never been one for holidays—we both enjoy our home and don't see the point of going away from it—but now it's as if he's on holiday all the time. It's as though he doesn't even recognise that he's on sick leave. More like he's forgotten about work altogether."

"Will he talk about it?"

"He doesn't talk much to me at all." She added hastily, "Oh, he's perfectly all right with me, I didn't mean… Anyway, he chats away to Ella—they get on so well together. Polly, what am I going to do?"

To Polly's dismay, Mavis' face crumpled. But she made a valiant effort to stem the tears. Polly said, "You're really worried about Henry."

Mavis wept into her handkerchief. "I am, Polly, I am! I don't know what's going on. I have no experience of—of—mental illness. We've never had anything like this in our family before, so I don't know what to do for the best."

"You're providing him with a secure and stable background. That must be important."

"Yes, but it doesn't seem to be enough. And what if Ella goes? Henry's so wrapped up in her, I'm sure he'd withdraw again if she went."

"But she can't stay forever. Is that what you're afraid of?"

Mavis blew her nose. "I think she's restless, Polly. After all, it's no life for a young girl like that. She's already talking about getting a job in the evenings. What if she goes altogether?"

Polly said, "Suppose you were to gradually wean him off Ella. Do you think that might help?"

"Whatever do you mean? How could I possibly do that?"

"Well, you've already said Ella's looking for an evening job. That would help, because there'd be some times when she wasn't there. Suppose you take that a bit further? Suppose Ella wasn't living with you any longer but was in the vicinity, so she and Henry could meet whenever Henry wanted?"

Mavis looked thoughtful. "Polly, are you suggesting that Ella comes to live here?"

"It's an obvious solution, isn't it? I don't need a whole three-bedroom house to myself, and Ella and I get on well together. If she came to live here, she could still come over to the rectory every day if necessary, but there'd be a bit of distance. Mind you, she'd have to get a job. I don't earn enough to keep the two of us."

"Hmm. Well. That's certainly an idea. Are you sure you wouldn't mind, Polly? After all, she isn't your niece."

Polly shrugged. "Why would that matter? Why don't you sound out both Ella and Henry together? If he doesn't have entertainment on tap all the time, so to speak, it might just encourage Henry back to work."

"It might at that," Mavis said, a spark of hope in her eyes. "Thank you so much, Polly dear."

Well! thought Polly as she closed the door behind Mavis. *So now I'm "dear" to her. There really is a God after all!*

***

Henry was initially resistant to Mavis' suggestion, but Ella's eyes lit up. She turned to Henry. "I'd still see you loads, Henry. I could borrow Polly's bike, or walk, or buy a bike of my own. And you could walk over to Polly's. That would kill at least two birds with one stone. You'd be walking like the doctor said, you could sort out the parishes with Polly like you said a couple of weeks ago, and you and I could play chess or go out for a walk together."

Mavis held her breath as she watched Henry's reaction. He said, "Don't you like it here, then? I thought we got on well."

Ella knelt beside him and took his hand in hers. "Of course I like it here! You've both been brilliant to me. But I do have to find work, and you have to get back some time, Henry. If you were walking about the parish again visiting like you told me, you could pop in any time. We'd probably see just as much of each other as we do now." She added, "And if I'm going to settle in the area, I must find somewhere to live as well as regular work."

Henry said, "You could live here, like you are now."

Mavis interjected, "But you know Polly needs support, preferably someone of her own age. We mustn't be selfish, Henry, keeping Ella all to ourselves. I think this is the perfect solution, don't you?"

And Henry, unable to think of any further arguments against the idea, reluctantly nodded.

Chapter Eighteen

Ella's move was scheduled for the Monday morning, to give Henry the weekend to get used to the idea of the new arrangements and to allow Mavis to inform the parishes in her own way about the impending change, rather than having to counteract innuendo after the event. This she accomplished by informing Daisy Mansfield and Bunny Sterling, both Mothers' Union members who lived in Thorpemunden. Mavis knew that by lunchtime the whole MU would know and, through them, all those parishioners who might be interested. Mavis had no problems with this means of conveying information. It had been used since time immemorial and Mavis merely continued in a long and hallowed tradition when she and Henry first came to Thorpemunden. The downside was that messages were invariably embellished, sometimes causing real difficulties, but Mavis considered that the advantages far outweighed the disadvantages. She knew she could sit at the computer and inform many people at the same time with one touch of a button, but quite apart from the fact that few of the MU members could use a computer, sending an email would deduct the storytelling element and the personal contact. Many of the members were widows living alone, so giving them a bona fide reason for ringing round was like giving them a slice of birthday cake. Mavis was aware that the other side of this coin was village gossip, but as neither she nor Henry had ever been the subjects of such gossip until recently, she had always rather enjoyed it. Now she wasn't quite so sure, hence her decision to send round the message in her own way.

***

Since all her belongings fitted into the backpack and two carrier bags, Ella was all set to walk the three miles or so to Mundenford. But Henry insisted on driving her there. "You can't possibly walk all that way with all those bags. Besides, I want to see you properly settled."

So Ella had agreed. Polly was there to greet them and offer them coffee ("Polly put the kettle on," Henry sang, but both girls ignored him) while Ella took her bags upstairs to her new room.

Ella was rather relieved at the new arrangements. She was beginning to find Henry's constant attentions a little oppressive and longed for more freedom. Now she was no longer living under the rectory roof and therefore no longer obliged to spend all her waking hours with Henry, she felt more in control of her own life. She already had the offer of bar work in The Rose and Crown at Middlestead and was determined to take it up. Polly had offered the use either of the car or the bike until Ella was able to provide her own transport, so the five-mile distance was no real barrier, although Polly was uneasy about her friend cycling home after midnight along unlit country roads. Other than saying, "Don't tell Henry or Mavis. They're bound to object, they've taken me under their wing to such an extent," Ella, having only known well-lit town streets, had laughed at Polly's fears but promised to invest in a reflective jacket.

***

Realising that Ella's departure marked the end of an era, albeit a short one, Henry resolved to return to work. Without Ella, there was no point in idling away his time at the rectory. He'd rather be up and doing. Consequently he took himself off to Peter Lambert's consulting room at the end of the week, a week in which he had seen Ella most days and had thought about her constantly. At the back of Henry's mind was the hope that if he was out and about in the parish, he'd have more opportunities for dropping in on Ella.

Peter took his blood pressure and listened to his chest through the stethoscope, but was more concerned with Henry's emotional state. "How are you feeling now, Henry?"

"Much better. I want to go back to work. You know Ella's moved out? She's living with Polly now."

Peter sighed. Although Henry was more soberly attired than he was at his last visit, Peter was dismayed to hear Ella's name mentioned so soon in the conversation. Peter was no psychiatrist but he did know the rudiments of counselling. "How does that make you feel, Henry?"

"Fine," declared Henry, who knew a little about counselling, himself. "It will enable me to get back to work if I'm no longer responsible for entertaining Ella. She'll still be able to see me when necessary and it'll do young Polly a good turn, having Ella living there."

"Hmm," Peter said, not knowing quite how to cope with Henry's version of the relationship between him and Ella. "Do you think you're ready for a return to work?"

"I think so. I've been off for what? Six or seven weeks now? That's given me a good rest. I feel quite ready to pick up the strands again. No chest pains now and no shortness of breath. And I've been walking so much that I feel quite toned up. I think I'll try and keep going with the walking. I can certainly feel the benefits."

So Peter nodded and signed him off, ignoring the slight unease he felt.

***

Upon his return to work Henry was greeted with evident relief by many of his parishioners, especially by Jonathan Eckerby, the churchwarden of Kirkby Thorpe. "It's this new service, Henry. We took it on, but I'm not entirely happy about it. Although it started well, the numbers have decreased every week, so now we're lucky to get five or six people attending. And it's decimated the morning service. As you know we only ever had around eight in the congregation, but what with being expected to bake for the afternoon and with Rosemary Grant's departure, we're now down to two or three. Nobody likes unaccompanied singing, and the fewer there are, the more of an ordeal it is. There are lots of mutterings, Henry. I don't know what to do. Perhaps you could talk to Polly?"

"Rosemary's gone?" Henry was horrified. "Gone where?"

"Well, nowhere really. She just resigned after that bust-up with Polly and hasn't been seen at church since. Diana Courtney went round, but she didn't get anywhere. Rosemary was so angry and now she's backed herself into a corner. If she comes back she'll lose face and she'll consider that Polly has won, so she can't come back. At least, I think that's how she sees it. None of the rest of us do, but that doesn't help. I wonder, could you go round, Henry? I'm certain she'd come back if you asked her."

Henry nodded. "Of course I'll go. Poor Rosemary. She must be lost without her church." But he was determined to seek out Polly first. What in Heaven's name had she been doing?

***

"Why, hello, Henry, come in." Polly held the door wide for him. "I'm afraid Ella is out at the moment. I'm on the computer, trying to catch up with some of the paperwork. But I can make you a pot of tea if you want to wait."

"It's you I've come to see." Henry pushed past her into the study, then turned to face her, his mouth drawn in a grim line.

"What's up?" Polly was confused. He suddenly looked as though he was the old Henry again, prim and puritanical and, at the moment, angry. Yet the last time she had seen him he had been the new Henry, laid back, somewhat over the top, but otherwise quite good company.

"What's been going on behind my back? What have you been up to? How dare you change everything in this benefice in my absence?"

Alarmed at the rage in his voice and the increasing redness in his face, Polly said hastily, "Sit down, Henry. I'm going to make a pot of tea whether you want any or not. Make yourself at home."

She escaped to the kitchen to gather her wits but found she was shaking, her usual response to displays of anger since her abusive childhood. Polly would then react either by becoming aggressive herself or by running away. "Fight or flight" she had read in an old *Reader's Digest* in the dentist's waiting room years ago, and she had instantly identified her own reactions.

She took her time making the tea but carried it back to the study with that uncomfortable feeling of fear deep in the pit of her stomach and legs which were trembling. But apart from being unable to quite still the shaking in her hands, Polly hid her inner churnings.

She handed Henry a mug of tea and said much more calmly than she was feeling, "Now, Henry. What is all this about?"

Henry was still red in the face. "It's about you changing everything in my absence. You're a curate, Polly. You don't seem to realise that that means you're here to learn, not to initiate. Your job in my absence was to keep the parishes running smoothly, no more, no less. But you've failed to do that. You've been here five minutes but you thought you knew the benefice better than me. You thought you knew what was needed here to bring people back to church. I hope you can now see that you have been utterly and completely wrong. And I might almost add, criminally negligent. People are unhappy, Kirkby Thorpe's usual eight have dwindled to almost nothing, they've lost a loyal and hardworking organist who's been in the parish all her life, and they're full of resentment. How do you equate that with the gospel?"

Polly could feel her heart hammering in her chest. "But there are new people coming to the informal afternoon service. Didn't Christ say something about going out and spreading the gospel, not keeping it wrapped up in a museum?"

"And how many of these new people are there now? Is the service increasing in number or decreasing? Well?"

"It's early days, Henry. Even you must know that it takes a lot of time and effort to get these things established. So while I've been running around keeping the show on the road—thank God for Father Brian, I couldn't have done it without him; he's been a star—I have also spent hours preparing the informal service and the Pram Service and visited the sick, taken three funerals, and baptised two babies. I haven't exactly been idle for nearly two months. A thank-you would be nice."

Henry snapped, "If you'd done what you ought to have done instead of trying to change the entire benefice in a fortnight, you'd have had plenty of time to do the job properly. Then I might have felt moved to offer you a word of thanks. As it is, I find myself having to spend hours clearing up the mess you've made, and I can do without that, having just returned from sick leave. Did you even visit Rosemary Grant?"

"How could I? If she wanted to resign that's her business. I didn't sack her." But Polly's tone was defensive and she couldn't meet Henry's eyes.

His tone softened. "Look, Polly. Ministry isn't easy. It's not all about putting on wonderful services which attract the whole neighbourhood. In these country areas it's just as much, if not more, about talking to people, listening to their concerns, reassuring them. You have to make change slowly here in the country. Many of these people have lived in the same village for generations. They have a folk memory going back to the Civil War and beyond. These are their churches, not yours or mine. We are privileged to be here for a short period, to do what we can to lead them slowly—note that word—slowly forward in their Christian living.

"Kirkby Thorpe church is Rosemary Grant's life. She has nothing outside the church. You should have visited. I know it would be difficult. She was angry and you would have had to face her ire. But you should have gone."

"Even though she resigned?"

"Even then. Not to beg her to come back. Lord knows, she's a terrible organist. But maybe that's all she has to offer to God. She should be allowed to make a reasoned choice, not to throw everything away in anger. You should have given her the opportunity to make that choice. And did you consider the knock-on effect in the village? In the benefice? Rosemary Grant has lived in that same house all her life. She was born there. Everybody knows her. There are people in the village who have known her since she was born. Who do you think they will support? Her or you?"

Polly stared unseeingly at the carpet. "I—I'm sorry. I didn't realise. What shall I do?"

"We'll go together," Henry decided. "You'll need to apologise to her. Although we both know she has no talent whatsoever at the organ, she is a good and reasonable person. I think she will allow you to mend bridges, and I think she'll be pleased you've dared to face her. We'll go today, after lunch."

***

Polly's sick feeling was so acute that she was unable to face any lunch. She kept rehearsing in her mind her apology to Rosemary Grant, an apology which she thought needed to be sincere but not grovelling. After all, she hadn't done anything to force Rosemary out. She had merely failed to discuss the new plans with her. But however much Polly worked at it, the conversation she was having in her head with Rosemary just wouldn't come out right. In the end she gave up, asked God's help, and with Henry waited on the doorstep with dread in her heart for Rosemary to open the door.

Rosemary's sharp face lit up at the sight of Henry and she seemed to include Polly as a kind of extension of Henry. "Come in, come in. How lovely to see you. Come and sit down. Henry, how are you? We've all missed you so much, but it's wonderful to see you looking so well now. The rest has done you good."

She continued to chatter as she showed them both into the lounge. Polly wedged herself into a small wooden chair with a cane seat, which was set back from the two armchairs and the sofa. Henry, who had been many times before, went straight for the chintz armchair by the fireplace, which looked, Polly reflected, as though it was "his" chair. Rosemary herself sat on the matching sofa, hunched up to the arm and perched on the edge of her seat so that Polly wondered with some amazement whether she was nervous too.

It was a fussy room, crammed with the paraphernalia of ages. A china cabinet looked to Polly's unpractised eye to be full of antiques, and there was barely room in the lounge for the dark wood table and dining chairs upholstered in what appeared to be a fine needlepoint design. A needlework sampler hanging on the wall and, according to its legend, sewn by Isabella Brownstone, aged ten in 1851, summed up the room.

Rosemary spotted Polly glancing at the sampler. "My great grandmother," she said with pride. "My family have lived in this house since it was built in 1737. I was born here."

Polly said, "What about when you were married?"

"Dear Walter. He was our lodger, after the war, you know. Father died in the early days of the war, in 1939. He was a pilot and his plane was shot down over Germany. I was only two at the time. Mother had a struggle, I can tell you. She had to earn her own living so she took in lodgers. Walter came in '52, I was fifteen. We fell for each other immediately, but Mother made us wait until I was twenty-three before she would consent to our marriage. But it was so perfect, don't you see. We all carried on living together until Mother died in '89. But sadly, dear Walter died as well, just two years later."

"That must have been awful for you."

"It was, of course." She added pointedly, "But I had my faith and my church. I don't know where I would have been without them."

Henry cleared his throat. "We were both so sorry to hear about your retirement as organist, Rosemary, but quite understand. One does reach the point where one feels a change is needed. We've come together to express our gratitude for all the years you've given to us through the organ and to wish you well for the future."

Polly said quickly, "And I would like to say that I'm really sorry if you felt I'd gone over your head with the band from Diss. It was just that I didn't want to impose on your good nature any further—you do so much for the church."

Rosemary pursed her lips. "We'll say no more about that, then. What's done is done." She turned to Henry. "I understand there hasn't been any organist at Kirkby Thorpe since I left? The last thing I wanted to do was to cause you any difficulty, Henry. I'd be happy to step in until you can find someone else."

"That's more than generous of you, Rosemary." Henry smiled warmly at her. "You must know how we've missed you. Can I take it we'll see you back at your usual seat on Sunday morning, then?"

And Rosemary, who clearly idolised Henry, smiled and simpered and flushed with delight.

***

Mavis was concerned. She was pleased that Henry was returning to work, but his very first encounter with Polly had seemed to upset him. Although he hadn't revealed any details to her, Mavis had noticed his heightened colour and his irascibility with alarm. Never having been entirely convinced by Peter Lambert's explanation of "stress," she wondered whether Henry had perhaps had a mild heart attack which had left no obvious traces. If so, would his blood pressure rise every time he had a disagreement? Or was it just that wretched Polly who got him so wound up? And he seemed so volatile, one minute up in the air, the next down in the depths. The old Henry, who had been on an even keel ever since Mavis had known him, was no longer anywhere to be seen.

And he hardly spoke to Mavis. The rectory, from having been alive and happy with Ella's presence, was again a place of gloom. Henry came and went without informing Mavis where he was going or what time he would be in. This thoughtlessness was unlike him and Mavis both resented it and feared it.

She tried to engage him in conversation. "Have you had a good day? What have you been doing all day, dear?"

He said shortly, "Sorting out Polly's mess." Then he turned on Mavis. "Why didn't you tell me that Rosemary Grant had resigned? If I'd known sooner, I could have done something to prevent this awful build-up of resentment in that parish."

Mavis stared at him. "I did tell you. Don't you remember? You didn't seem to care at the time."

"Don't accuse me of not caring. I'm the only one who does care around here. If you'd cared, you wouldn't have sent Ella packing."

"But you agreed! You thought it would be the best solution all round. Anyway, I didn't send her packing, as you put it. She was delighted to go. Didn't you realise that? And it has got you back to work."

But this riled Henry further and he stalked out, slamming the door behind him.

At this, something broke in Mavis. She had always supported her husband in every endeavour. Indeed, she firmly believed that it was the job of a wife, especially a clergy wife, to be there for her husband, to comfort and succour him when needed, to make sure his home was warm and clean and that he was well fed and to provide for his physical needs when necessary. This latter had not been necessary too often in Mavis' experience, for which she was profoundly thankful. She grew up in the days when having a baby out of wedlock was considered to be deeply shocking and scandalous, and her mother had impressed upon the young Mavis that such an act was the worst sin a woman could commit and could never be forgiven by God. Mavis had entirely agreed with her parents' views and was both pleased and relieved to have met Henry, her father's curate, at the right time, for she knew a curate would never foist unwelcome attentions on her or try to persuade her to a course of action which she would later regret. The only problem had been that Mavis had then found it difficult to make the adjustment to married life. Although she never voiced it, she was unable to understand how sex could be so vile and wrong one moment, but the next, after a half-hour wedding service in church, was not only all right but was suddenly desirable and a duty.

Mavis had done her duty when required, but she had never enjoyed it, and although the lack of children was a constant sadness to her, she was hugely relieved when Henry seemed to lose interest in the physical aspect of marriage.

Now, she found the resentment, which she had suppressed since Henry's illness began, rising to the surface. She saw both Polly's and Ella's freedom, a freedom she had never experienced as a young woman. She had given her life to Henry in the best way she knew and he was throwing it back in her face. Mavis felt used and abused, jealous and resentful.

Chapter Nineteen

"I'll get it." Ella was sitting in the lounge watching daytime television with her feet tucked under her on the sofa when the doorbell rang. Polly was at the computer in the study, working on the next informal service.

Ella opened the door, expecting to see Henry on the doorstep, but instead found herself face to face with a middle-aged woman, a peroxide blonde with grey roots showing through. Her hair was short, straggly, and looked unkempt, in need of a wash. She was wearing tight jeans, quite unsuited to her spreading figure, and a tired green fleece. Heavily made up with layers of caked face powder, thick black eyeliner, and bright blue eye shadow, her mouth was a scarlet slash in her face. She reeked of stale cigarette smoke, and Ella involuntarily looked down, expecting to see a ground-out butt on the doorstep. She didn't spot a cigarette stub, but she did notice a suitcase on wheels, just behind the woman.

"Hello," Ella said. "Can I help you?"

"You're not the vicar," the woman said.

"No. The vicar doesn't live in this village. But I can give you directions to his rectory, if you like."

"I don't want no man. I want the lady vicar, the young one, about your age. But you're not her."

"Oh! You mean Polly?"

"Polly Hewitt. Yes, that's the one. I was told she lived here."

"Yes, she does. You'd better come in."

Ella opened the door wider and showed the woman into the lounge.

The woman looked round at the aging brown leather suite, which Polly had liberated from a charity shop and brightened up with large scatter cushions in bright greens and yellows. It went well with the beige patterned carpet, left by the previous occupant, and the flamboyant curtains again in greens and yellows, bought by Polly from her diocesan moving grant. "This is nice." She sat down in Polly's armchair.

"Mm. We like it."

"Who are you, then?"

"I'm Ella. I live here. We share, Polly and me."

"Oh! It's nice," the woman repeated. "Better than where she grew up."

"You know Polly from before?"

"'Course I do," the woman said. "I'm her mother. I've come to stay. Amanda Hewitt. Pleased to meet you." She held out her hand.

Ella limply touched it, then sat down heavily on the sofa. She searched the woman's face for any traces of resemblance to Polly but could find none.

The woman said, "Are you gonna sit there or you gonna call her?"

"Oh, sorry." Ella went through to the study at the back of the house. "Polly, you've got a visitor."

Polly sighed. "Just when I was getting into this. Doesn't it always happen? Why can't they come when I'm doing nothing, or better still, why can't they email or something? Who is it this time? Some old dear from Kirkby Thorpe to complain she can't afford a bag of flour to bake a cake?" Then she noticed her friend's face. "What? Who is it?"

"Polly, she says she's your mother."

Polly's face drained and her mouth fell open. She whispered, "It can't be! Are you sure? What does she look like?"

"Blonde, about your height, a bit fat, lots of makeup, smells of cigarettes?" As Polly gloomily nodded, she added, "Polly, she's got a case with her. She says she's come to stay."

Polly swivelled off her computer chair, shunting it back against the desk. She pushed past Ella, into the lounge.

"What are you doing here?"

"That's a nice greeting for your mother, I must say. No kiss for your poor old mum? Where are your manners? Too hoity-toity now for the likes of me, are you? Bit too posh for your own mother who brought you up? If it wasn't for me, you wouldn't be here."

"I'm here in spite of you," Polly shot back. "What do you want? 'Cos you're not staying here."

The woman smiled. "Oh, but I am! See, I've brought my case and the taxi's gone, so I'll have to stay, won't I?"

Polly's lips set. "What have you done with Toby? Is he here with you?"

"Oh, him!" Her mother's tone was dismissive. "Sent him back to his father. Getting to be a right little tear-away, he is. Needed a man's hand. No, I'm free now, Polly, and I want to live with my only daughter."

"Live?" Polly was aghast. "You can't live here. This is a clergy house provided by the Church. I'm not allowed to have other people living here."

"What's she doing, then?" Amanda Hewitt nodded towards Ella.

"That's different. And none of your business."

"S'pose it might be someone's business, though? If they knew?"

Polly glanced helplessly at Ella, the despair she felt showing on her face.

Ella looked at her watch. "It's already after four. Why don't you stay to supper, Mrs. Hewitt—"

"Call me Mandy," interrupted Polly's mother.

"Mandy. And stay the night. Then we'll talk tomorrow. How about that?"

Polly said, “But we’re both out tonight. You’re working and I’ve got a PCC at Hamblestead.”

“That’s all right, love.” Amanda Hewitt was already peeling off her fleece to reveal a skin-tight, bright blue shirt with ruffles at the neck and cuffs. The collar had an obvious powder stain around the inside, and there were dark circles under the arms, just above the tightly encased rolls of fat. “I’ll be fine. You two go off. I’ll watch some television. Don’t you worry about me.”

Polly said, “There’s no drink in here and you’re not to smoke in here. We don’t want our home stinking of stale smoke and booze. If we come back and find you’ve been smoking or drinking, you’ll be straight out whatever time of night it is. Is that clear?”

“Yes, ma’am!” Mandy raised her pencilled eyebrows and smirked at Ella, who turned away into the kitchen.

“I’ll do supper tonight,” Ella called over her shoulder. “You two must have plenty to talk about.”

“Don’t you believe it,” muttered Polly. But she picked up her mother’s case and carried it to the foot of the stairs. “You coming? You can make up the bed yourself. I’ve got work to do.”

In the spare room she faced her mother. “I’m opening this case. I know you. It’s probably stashed with bottles of vodka which I shall throw down the sink. Give me the key.”

She held out her hand. Her mother started to protest but thought better of it. She fished out a key from her capacious handbag and sullenly handed it to Polly. “You won’t find nothing.”

Polly carefully searched the case but found it clean, packed only with a jumbled mass of clothes and shoes and a couple of copies of *Hello* magazine. “Now your handbag.”

“Hey! You can’t go routing through my handbag. A girl’s handbag is private. No one touches that.”

Polly picked up the case. “Good-bye. Have a great life. I’ll take this down for you.”

"Oh, all right then! But you should be ashamed of yourself, treating your own mother this way. I dunno what your vicar will say when I tell him."

"You won't tell him because you won't meet him. You're going tomorrow, remember?"

There was the glimmer of tears in her mother's eyes. Despite herself, Polly could feel the old manipulation working again. Her mother knew exactly which buttons to press.

Polly said stiffly, "The bathroom's along there. You'd better come down when you're ready."

***

"You live in Streatham, Mandy?" Ella handed her a plate of beef stew with mashed potato and initiated the conversation while Polly picked at her food and stared at her plate.

"Did, love." Mandy began to eat with relish, as though she hadn't been fed properly for several days. "Don't anymore. I'm homeless, see. That's why I come here."

"Homeless?"

"My partner, Graham. Well, I should say, my ex. Terrible temper that man has. After all I done for him." *Here we go*, thought Polly. "Been together twelve years, we have, but it don't mean nothing to him. Twelve years of my life. Took my youth, he did, and look at me now."

Tears of self-pity began to gather in Mandy's eyes. Polly said hastily, "Is Toby with him?"

"'Course he is. He's his father, isn't he? Let him look after the little toe-rag. I've had enough. Don't do nothing I tell him and when them police come round—well! You'd think it was me doing the shoplifting."

Polly looked at her mother in dismay. "Toby's in trouble with the police? He's been shoplifting?"

"Him and that gang he runs around with. I told the police. I said, 'There's nothing for them to do round here. What do you expect?' I said. 'Course, they don't care. Just want to get these kids banged up, that's all they want."

Polly was confused. "So Toby's in a gang, he's been caught shoplifting by the police—why are you up here? Why aren't you at home with him, looking after him?"

"Don't you start. That social worker was bad enough, sticking her nose in where it don't belong. Just 'cos she discovered the odd bottle. What was she doing, poking around in the waste bin, I'd like to know?"

"What about Graham? What did he say?"

Mandy sighed. "Just 'cos they fetched him home from work. He threw a wobbly. You don't know him. I thought he was gonna kill me." She looked beseechingly at the two girls from under her mascara lashes. The effect was slightly revolting.

"He threw you out, didn't he?" Polly said in a resigned voice. "You didn't send Toby off to his father at all. His father threw you out and now you think I'm going to look after you."

"Well, look at you! My girl a vicar! Who'd have thought? You have come up in the world. Surely you can spare a bit for your old mum? Isn't that what your lot are supposed to do? Care for the oppressed?"

Polly said, ticking off on her fingers, "First, I'm not a vicar, I'm only a curate. And if anyone meets you, I'm likely to remain a curate forever. That's if I don't get slung out the moment they set eyes on you. Second, curates aren't paid squat. Third, who are 'my lot'? If you mean Christians, yes, we do care for the oppressed, but you hardly fit into that category."

As the tension sharpened between mother and daughter Ella said pacifically, "I've just got time to wash up before I need to leave for work. Mandy, why don't you give me a hand? Then Polly can get ready for her meeting."

Polly shot her a grateful glance and excused herself from the table. Surprised by Ella's invitation, Mandy began to stack dishes and followed her out into the kitchen.

***

"You understand don't you, love?" Mandy began, as soon as she and Ella were alone. "I can see Polly's ashamed of me. She's got a bit lardy-dah with this posh job. But you. I could tell you were different, straightaway. You ever been homeless, love?"

As Ella nodded, Mandy homed in. "You know what it's like, then. No money and nowhere to go. You just need someone to give you a hand up, then you'd be all right. I think this could be the turning point for me. Polly tell you I haven't brought any booze with me? I'm gonna stop the drinking right now. And I'll never smoke in the house here. I'd never do that."

She waited for a response from Ella, but Ella merely looked sombrely at her with liquid, dark brown eyes.

Mandy Hewitt seemed confused. "I will! I promise. I really will. No need for you to look at me like that. So if you could just have a word with Polly… Tell her I've changed, like. Tell her what it's like to be homeless—and with the winter coming on too—maybe she'll let me stay. Just for a short time? Week or two at the most?"

Ella said, "I'll talk to Polly." And they finished the washing up in silence.

***

Inevitably, Mandy Hewitt stayed, as Polly at some deep level had known she would. Polly avoided her as much as possible, using Ella as a kind of shield.

"We're off to Tesco's," Polly announced on the Saturday morning. As she had no priestly duties that day, she and Ella had fallen into the habit of doing the weekly shop.

Mandy said, "Shall I come?"

"No," Polly said shortly.

Left to her own devices, Mandy was about to turn on the television when there was a long and imperious ring at the doorbell.

She opened the door and her eyes gleamed at the sight of the visitor, tall and good-looking with floppy silver hair and dark-rimmed glasses. She smiled. "Hello."

Henry stared. He had no idea who this woman was. He had come because he was desperate for a top-up of Ella, whom he hadn't seen for three days. The lack of Ella was like coming off drugs. Henry described it to himself as "cold turkey," but he'd reached a stage where he couldn't stand it any longer.

As a way of legitimating his presence he said, "Where's Polly?"

"Out. She and Ella went shopping. They shouldn't be too long. Won't you come in and wait?" She held out her hand. "I'm Amanda Hewitt, Polly's mother. Everyone calls me Mandy."

"Her mother?" Henry was astonished.

Mandy giggled girlishly. "I know. Difficult to believe, isn't it? Lots of people think we're sisters. I was very young at the time. But do come in. You are?"

"Oh!" Henry shook hands. "I'm Henry Winstone. Canon Henry Winstone, actually. I'm the rector here. You could say Polly works for me."

Mandy waved him to a chair. "You're Polly's boss? I'm so pleased to meet you. Polly loves it here. I'm just thrilled to see my baby so happy."

"It's, er, good to hear that. Welcome to Norfolk, Mandy. How long are you staying?"

"We haven't decided yet." She sighed, theatrically. "You know what it is with mothers and daughters. We don't like to be apart for too long."

Henry said stiffly, "I don't have any children, myself."

"You're not married, then?" There was a little too much eagerness in Mandy's voice.

Henry retreated. "Mavis and I have been married for nearly forty years. We were not blessed with children."

"I'm so sorry! They are such a blessing, aren't they? I don't know what I'd do without Polly. But where are my manners?

May I offer you a cup of coffee? It is rather special coffee, I'm sure you'll like it."

"Thank you," Henry said gravely, wondering how long he would have to endure this silly, superficial woman. No wonder Polly was such a trial.

But it was a tiny cup of surprisingly good coffee with an underlying flavour which Henry was unable to identify.

"This is delicious. Is it a new brand?"

Mandy giggled coquettishly and shook her head. "My own recipe. I add a little something. Would you like some more? The cups are awfully small because it is rather rich."

Henry nodded. Both he and Mandy had several refills, which seemed to loosen Henry's tongue. By the time Polly and Ella returned, Henry and Mandy were chatting and laughing like old friends, although Henry was hard put to remember anything they had talked about.

"Henry? Mandy?" Polly said, refusing to use any terms of endearment for her mother. "What are you doing?"

At that Henry and Mandy glanced at each other and rocked with laughter, leaving Polly and Ella mystified.

"What's funny? If I didn't know better, I'd think you were both drunk. Oh no! Come on, Ella."

Polly took her friend out into the kitchen, where the evidence was easy to find. A nearly empty bottle of vodka lay half hidden under a tea towel beside the coffeepot.

"I knew it!" Polly's face was grim. "I knew she couldn't keep off it for long. But Henry! I wouldn't have thought it of him, no matter how laid back he's been over recent weeks."

"Do you think he knew?"

"Probably not. May have just thought he was drinking cup after cup of black coffee. Come to think of it, why didn't the coffee counteract the alcohol?"

Ella said, "That's a myth, isn't it? That black coffee makes you sober? At least, that's we're told in the pub trade. We're supposed to make every effort to ensure that people who have been drinking don't drive home, and we're very firmly told that filling them with black coffee won't work."

"That's a point. How are we going to get Henry home?"

"Maybe if you drive his car and I follow behind with yours? You've got fully comp owner-driver insurance, haven't you?"

"Mm, yes. Let's do that. Then she's going, and nothing'll change my mind. I was a fool to let her stay in the first place. Come on, let's dump him on the rectory doorstep and let Mavis deal with him."

***

But when they returned from delivering Henry, which they managed to do without encountering Mavis, by opening the rectory door and gently pushing Henry inside before scuttling back to the car like two guilty schoolgirls, Amanda Hewitt was nowhere to be seen. Polly went through the house and out into the large garden, but she wasn't there.

"She's gone to buy booze," Polly said through clenched teeth. "I'm not opening the door when she comes back. She can crawl back under whatever stone she emerged from."

Ella said nothing, merely looking anxiously at her friend.

Polly stomped upstairs to pack her mother's case and clear out her room. But when Amanda failed to show by evening, even she began to worry.

"She was so drunk. I know it didn't show much with her, but that's because she's always three sheets to the wind. It's not so obvious with her as it was with Henry. Suppose she staggered out of the house and fell in front of a car or something?"

Ella reached for her reflective jacket. "I'll take the bike tonight. Sorry I have to go now, Polly. But why don't you cruise round all the pubs? She might have gone on a bender. And I know it's tempting to leave her smashed out of her skull, but what will she say when she's utterly stewed? Could be really embarrassing for you."

Polly sighed. “I know. I bet that’s what’s happened. She’ll have been drinking all day. She’s probably gone from one to the other. All the pubs in the benefice. Whatever will I do? Henry will definitely want to get rid of me after this.”

Chapter Twenty

Mavis found her husband snoring in his favourite armchair with his feet on the footstool when she returned from shopping. She tiptoed into the kitchen, pleased to see him sleeping so peacefully and loath to wake him. Anyway, it was immeasurably easier to prepare the meal without him getting under her feet.

Mavis had invited James and Daisy Mansfield to dinner as a way of mending bridges. She wasn't sure quite what James Mansfield had made of Henry's illness or of his subsequent behaviour, but she was very aware of James' influence both in the benefice and in the diocese. So it seemed like a good idea to ply James and Daisy with good food and wine in a sociable context, proving how fit and normal Henry was.

Since cooking was one of her few pleasures, seldom indulged as Henry preferred to eat midday, Mavis set to work with a will. She was determined to offer a gourmet meal certain to impress James and put him in an expansive mood. Laying the table carefully with the best silver (polished that morning while Henry was out), Mavis added little touches like the matching serviette rings and table runner she had won in the diocesan MU raffle three years ago. A scented, floral candle in an elegant wrought silver candlestick (one of the few items of any value in the rectory) completed the table to her satisfaction.

Having Googled the menu, she made canapés of prawn and guacamole blinis courtesy of the BBC Good Food guide, to have with pre-dinner drinks. For starters, she thought something light since she didn't want her guests overloaded with food before they sampled the pièce de resistance, so decided upon goats' cheese, sun-dried tomato, and rocket risotto, which she thought would be different and quite colourful. The main course was to be fish, something easy on the digestion as they were all advancing a little in years, so she chose baked salmon with a parsley caper dressing. The desserts, she felt, were less important as by then her guests would hopefully be surfeited. So she went for a choice, offering individual crème brûleés served with mixed berries, which would slip down easily, or a good old English apple crumble and custard. To finish there would be finest cheeses from around the world, coffee, and mints.

As Henry was still asleep in the lounge and therefore continued to be out of the way, things ran smoothly. Even the crème brûlée managed to set without curdling, something of a minor miracle in Mavis' estimation.

She roused Henry an hour before the visitors were due. He took some tablets as he had a thundering headache ("I expect you've been asleep too long in an awkward position, dear," Mavis said) and they both went to change. Mavis was exhausted from all her efforts but was running on adrenaline, as she was anticipating the evening.

She dressed carefully in her best peach jersey wool with the narrow belt. It was a simple style, but she felt it accentuated her best points of slender hips and bust and a tiny waist. Despite his grumbles, she made Henry wear a collar and tie.

"Not a dog collar, dear," she explained, "that might look as though it was a pastoral occasion. This is a lovely evening with dear friends, but you do need to be smart."

It was something of a disappointment that James wore slacks and a sweater and Daisy a skirt and jumper, but Mavis made nothing of it. Perhaps the invitation had sounded casual. And it was nice that James and Daisy regarded them as such good friends that they felt they could pop over without dressing up too much. That, surely, was a sign of intimacy.

The evening went well, with the Mansfields complimenting Mavis on her culinary skills. As they moved in exalted circles and must therefore have enjoyed the very best of cuisines, Mavis glowed under their approbation.

Even Henry made a concerted effort, although Mavis glanced at him anxiously once or twice after his wineglass was refilled for the fourth time. He began to get unusually jovial, in her opinion. But as James matched him glass for glass, Mavis wasn't too concerned. Obviously Daisy would be driving, since her husband allowed her only one small glass of wine.

It was a very pleasant evening, which Mavis considered successful when eleven-thirty arrived before James got up to depart. He kissed Mavis on both cheeks, causing her to blush with pleasure, and shook hands with Henry.

"Splendid evening, Henry. Good man. Thank you too, Mavis. Come along, Daisy."

Daisy fluttered and kissed both Mavis and Henry before hurrying out to chauffeur her husband back to the manor.

And Mavis roused herself to begin the clearing up, feeling more contented than she had for some months.

***

When ten o'clock arrived without any communication from her mother, Polly began to grow seriously worried. She was partly apprehensive that Amanda might indeed have suffered some injury and be lying helpless in a ditch somewhere, but even worse (and more likely) she might be paralytic in some bar saying God knows what about her daughter.

At least, Polly assumed God knew. She wasn't very happy with God at the moment. The least he could have done was to keep her mother out of harm's way, by which Polly meant that he could have kept Amanda's alcoholism hidden from Polly's community. Why couldn't God have stopped her going out? After all, God knew what she was like. Now everyone else would know as well, to Polly's shame.

Polly slipped into her anorak and picked up the car keys. She had no options left. She would have to go out looking for her mother, calling into every bar in the area until she found her. And then inevitably there'd be some rowdy scene as undoubtedly Polly would be forced to drag her mother out.

It took longer than Polly had anticipated. She started with the furthest villages, omitting Middlestead since Ella would be keeping her eyes open there. But Polly drew a blank at all the pubs she visited. She was just turning into Thorpemunden along the Diss road when she thought she spotted a figure lurch across the Mansfields' drive at Thorpemunden Manor.

Cautiously, Polly drove all the way up the winding drive, peering as best she could into the darkness beyond the reach of the headlights. But she saw no one and the house itself was in darkness apart from one light burning in the hall. She turned in the area in front of the house, peering again on the way back, but still to no avail. Perhaps it had been a trick of the light.

Polly was further unnerved by James and Daisy's headlights as they turned into the drive after their evening at the rectory. Narrowly missing a collision but unwilling to stop and explain herself to them, she swerved violently, averted her face, and sped on her way.

Polly hadn't been home long when Ella returned accompanied, partly to Polly's relief and partly to her fury, by Amanda.

Polly rounded on her mother, who was supported by Ella and looked glazed.

"Where have you been? How could you do this to me! You're a complete embarrassment. I took you into my home and gave you every chance and look how you've repaid me. First you get my boss—the rector of these parishes—drunk without his knowledge, which is deception, then you just disappear without a word and come back pie-eyed!

"I'll tell you this. You're off in the morning. I've already packed your bags and I'll be driving you to the station myself and making sure you get on the train. And don't bother coming back."

As Polly turned on her heel, Amanda began to giggle. "She—she'sh angry, ishn't she? Wonder why she'sh angry?" She began to sing to the tune of Frère Jacques, "Polly's angry, Polly's angry. Wonder why? Wonder why? Doesn't get her clothes off. Doesn't get her clothes off. There's no guy. There's no guy," then collapsed into helpless giggles again.

Hot tears of hurt, fury, and humiliation burned Polly's eyes. She strode into the kitchen without a backward glance, slamming the door behind her.

Her arm still around Amanda, Ella said, "Ssh, now! That wasn't very kind. Come on, Mandy, I'll help you upstairs. Let's get you to bed."

When Ella came down some half hour later, Polly was sitting in the lounge, staring stonily in front of her.

She looked up at her friend. "Thanks, Ella. I'm so-o-o sorry! I told you what she was like, but I didn't think she'd go on a blinder down here. Where did you find her? I've been out looking all evening but didn't find a trace."

Ella sat on the sofa and tucked her long legs under her. "Don't worry. She wasn't too bad. She was in The Rose and Crown when I got there. I would have rung, but we were so busy, it being a Saturday. And the landlord's a bit funny about personal calls."

"Was she terribly embarrassing?"

"Not at all. She sat by herself in quite a dark corner and I made sure I served her, so I know exactly how many she had. Don't know how many she'd had before I got there, but she seemed okay. She wasn't talking to anyone. I'm not sure she's quite as drunk as you think."

"You heard her! And you had to practically carry her in!"

Ella smiled gently at her friend. "I think she may be putting it on a bit for your benefit. It's strange. She's really proud of you, but it's as though now you're a vicar (as she thinks) you've changed positions so that you're the adult and she's the child. She may be testing you to see how far she can go. Like kids do."

"If that's the case she just found out," Polly snapped. "Thanks for keeping an eye on her, Ella. And for bringing her home. Did you leave the bike? Can I pay you for the taxi? No? Well, thanks anyway.

"The damage mightn't be as bad as I feared. But I can't risk it. She has to go. I can't cope with this happening every five minutes, I'd have no career left. As soon as I've finished church tomorrow, I'm taking her to the station whether she likes it or not."

***

Polly was as good as her word. After enduring the morning services (for she was unable to concentrate and quite unable to worship), she bundled her mother into the car and drove her to Diss Station. She purchased a ticket to London for Amanda and sat with her in silence until the two seventeen from Norwich arrived. Once her mother was safely ensconced in a seat facing the engine, Polly waited until the train departed non-stop for Liverpool Street. It was only then that she allowed herself to breathe a sigh of relief.

"How was she?" Ella asked when Polly arrived home.

Polly shrugged. "Dunno. Didn't ask. She seemed all right. We didn't speak."

"Not at all? Not to say good-bye?"

Polly shook her head. "Nothing to say. Except that I never want to see her again and I'm glad she's gone."

But she didn't seem glad. On the contrary, Polly was irritable and scratchy for the rest of the day, as Ella noted. Ella said nothing more, doing her best to be there unobtrusively for her friend without getting in the way.

***

It wasn't until the Monday morning that James Mansfield went into his study to empty his safe prior to visiting the bank. He put his hand under the illicit whisky bottle in the second drawer of the desk and drew out the key to his petty cash tin. But when he opened the petty cash tin in the top drawer of his filing cabinet, to his horror he found that it was empty. James simply stared for a moment, unable to believe his eyes but aware of a feeling of violation. Someone had been into his house, touching his things and rifling through his desk. And since the thief had obviously known the whereabouts of the key and had taken the trouble to relock the box and return it to the filing cabinet before departing, James felt sick in the pit of his stomach.

He swung the portrait of his Great Uncle Samuel away from the wall. The safe, too, was closed and locked, but James keyed in his birth date with dread in his heart. When he opened the safe and found that the dread was justified, he collapsed, shouting at Daisy to come quickly.

Daisy ran into the room, but seeing her husband on the floor started shaking and sobbing.

"Oh for God's sake!" he said. "Ring 999. Call for an ambulance. Then you'd better call the police."

"Police? Why? Oh James, what shall I do?"

"I've just told you what to do. Stop wringing your hands and get on with it."

"Oh! Yes, of course." As she turned to pick up the phone from the desk, Daisy noticed the open safe. "James! There's nothing in the safe!"

James ground out from between his teeth, "Yes, you idiot. Get the ambulance and the police. We've been robbed."

The paramedics arrived first, tested James in a variety of interesting ways, and pronounced the possibility of a heart attack. They had just loaded him into a stretcher chair when the police rolled up, sirens blaring.

"Wait!" James beckoned the police officer over. "We've been burgled. My safe and my petty cash tin. Both empty."

"Anything else touched, sir?"

"Don't think so. Very neat." James paused to inhale. "Several hundred thousand in the safe, though."

The sergeant whistled. "That's a lot of money, sir. May I ask why you keep so much cash in the house?"

James said shortly, "Do you trust the banks?"

The paramedic interrupted, "We must get you to hospital, sir." He said to the police officers, "Norfolk and Norwich. You can see him there."

The police sergeant turned to Daisy, who was still shaking and sobbing. "What about you, love? You going with him?"

"I don't know," wailed Daisy. "James, what shall I do?"

The sergeant said, "What if I take you up to the hospital in the police car? I need to ask your husband some more questions when he's ready. My constable, PC Dachery here, can call out the scene of crimes people. She'll need to be here some hours, so I can bring you back whenever you want."

Relieved of the burden to make any decisions, Daisy climbed into the back of the police car where she continued to utter little sobbing gasps from time to time.

The ambulance roared off with lights flashing and sirens screaming, with the police car in hot pursuit.

***

James was allowed home after a week in hospital trying to get his tablets into balance. His mild heart attack had upset his diabetes, and the addition of Warfarin, while preventing a further heart attack, had apparently increased the potency of his anti-diabetic tablets, lowering his blood sugar a little too far. But this was soon sorted out, so James was sent home with instructions to take rest and exercise in sensible proportions.

When he discovered that after a week the police were no further forward in tracking the perpetrator of the burglary, James was incensed, his blood pressure rising alarmingly. He rang his friend the chief constable, demanding an explanation. Shortly after that Sergeant Hooper turned up with PC Dachery in tow.

Sergeant Hooper could be obsequious when he chose. "We do have this incident as a priority, sir. May I offer you my best wishes for a very speedy recovery and bring you up-to-date on our investigation?

"Our forensic people have dusted for fingerprints and we have taken your wife's prints for elimination purposes. We may need to take yours too, sir, but we are fairly certain the suspect was wearing gloves, as the same three sets of prints are throughout the house. That's you, your wife, and your son. There are no signs of forced entry and as you were in all Sunday evening, we suspect that the burglary occurred on the Saturday evening when we understand you were out with your wife? Is that correct, sir?"

As James nodded, he continued, "I also understand that as your son was in the house at the time, you did not set the alarm. So anyone could have come in through one of the back entrances?"

"Only if they knew the house and knew we were going to be out," James protested. "We always set the alarm when it gets dark unless one of us is going to be out. So it's unusual for it to be off."

"Quite so, sir." Sergeant Hooper flicked open his notebook. "We are conducting house-to-house enquiries and have covered the Thorpemunden area. We'll extend enquiries now to the surrounding villages."

"Has anything come up?"

PC Dachery, eager to prove herself but earning an irritated look from her superior, broke in. "Three people reported seeing a suspicious car in the vicinity."

"Suspicious? How?"

Ignoring the sergeant, PC Dachery consulted her notebook. "It was driving very slowly circling round and appeared to be on the lookout."

"An accomplice? A driver, do you think? Or someone who was waiting for us to go out?"

With a quelling look at his constable, Sergeant Hooper said, "It's too early to make any judgments, sir. Could have been someone looking for an address in the dark. But we are following up the lead.

"Now, sir. Your son, Frank."

But James interrupted, his eyes bright. "We saw the car! I'd forgotten. Just as we were driving in through the gates on Saturday night, this car came roaring out, headlights blazing. It nearly hit us. I think the driver turned his face away. Must have been him, Sergeant. There's your culprit. Find the car and you'll find your thief!"

Sergeant Hooper frowned. "Your wife didn't mention any car, sir. And your son didn't mention seeing or hearing any vehicles."

James dismissed his objections with a wave of the hand. "Daisy's stupid, Sergeant." Then, with a slightly apologetic glance at Grace Dachery, "Well, you know what women of a particular age are like. They can be silly creatures sometimes. Heads full of fashion and bodies full of hormones. Dear Daisy wouldn't notice a charging rhino until it was a foot away from her. And I don't want you disturbing Frank. Is that clear? My son can't tell you anything. He watches television in his room while we're out, so naturally he wouldn't see or hear anything. He was in bed asleep when we returned. My wife checked on him as soon as we came in."

Sergeant Hooper stood up. "We'll need to speak to your wife again, sir. Just to see whether she remembers the car."

James stood up with him. "Of course." He went to the door. "Daisy! Daisy, come in here a moment, would you?"

Daisy appeared, wiping her hands on a tea towel depicting Beautiful Villages of Norfolk.

Before the sergeant could speak, James said, "Daisy, when we came back from the rectory on Saturday night, do you remember nearly driving into a car which shot out of the gates?"

"Polly's car? Yes, I remember."

James' mouth fell open. Sergeant Hooper said, "Excuse me, madam? Are you telling us that you recognized the driver?"

"Not exactly. I couldn't see who was driving because the headlights blinded me for a moment." She turned to James. "That's why we nearly crashed, dear. Because I couldn't see just for a moment."

He said testily, "Yes, yes. Get on with it."

"Oh! Yes, of course. I'm so sorry. Now where was I?"

"You didn't recognize the driver," prompted the sergeant.

"No, I didn't. I think it was Polly, but I couldn't be sure. It was her car, you see."

"How do you know that, madam?"

"Oh! Oh dear! Well, now I'm not so sure. But it had that fluorescent fish stuck to the front bumper like Polly's does. Mostly you see them stuck on back bumpers or in the rear window or something. But Polly's is on the front. So I thought it was her. That's why I didn't mention it earlier. Because it was only Polly."

"Fish, madam?" The sergeant was confused.

"Yes, you must have seen them. It's a Christian symbol. Just the outline of a fish. Lots of cars have them. I asked Polly about it once. She said it comes from the first century, when it was a secret symbol. It denotes—"

"Yes, yes, Daisy. I'm sure the sergeant has no desire to know the meaning of the symbol. The point is, did you actually see Polly?"

"Well, no, but I think it was her. She turned her face away, you see. But I noticed her hair. That lovely blonde frizz. It's unmistakable, isn't it?"

"This Polly," Sergeant Hooper said slowly, "it wouldn't be that same Polly who had a run-in with your son a few months ago, would it? Only it's an unusual name, if you see what I mean."

"Of course it's the same person," James snapped. "Polly Hewitt. I might have known!"

"Oh? Why's that, sir? Only it would be unusual for a—" he hesitated slightly, "—a lady of the cloth to go round burgling houses at night. Especially houses in her manor, so to speak."

"If you're looking for a motive, I can tell you that. She was furious over that previous episode, angry and resentful. She's had it in for me ever since. She'd do anything to get back at me."

Daisy said reproachfully, "Oh James!" but he ignored her.

"Go round to Polly Hewitt's," he advised. "She'll be behind this, you mark my words. Her and that other girl who's living there now. I don't think you need look any further, Sergeant. It's as clear as day. There's your villain. Polly Hewitt."

Chapter Twenty-One

Like the rest of the benefice, Polly had heard about James' heart attack and the burglary at the manor. Tales had varied from "five million in used bank notes" along with speculation as to how James had acquired such huge sums in the first place, to "stocks and bonds" relating to unknown companies but again affording vast wealth, to "all Daisy's jewellery," which it was observed she was never permitted to wear. All seemed to think that a hitherto unsuspected fortune was involved.

Along with this was delicious speculation as to the culprits. These ideas, too, varied widely, from "an inside job" to "gypsies from across the border" (the border being the Norfolk/Suffolk county line) to "ram raiders from Norwich." Polly enjoyed the gossip as much as anyone but kept any ideas of her own to herself. She was more concerned with James' health and relieved to hear that his heart attack had been only mild and that he was now home again.

She had visited Daisy while James was in hospital and found her strangely calm and sensible without James, refuelling Polly's conjecture that here was a woman who was emotionally abused on a regular basis. She discussed the situation with Ella.

"She's so normal when he's not around. But the minute he walks through the door she becomes silly and nervous. As though she's terrified of him."

Ella said, "But there are lots of women like that. Didn't it used to be like that in the old days? The man's word was law and the woman had to obey? Didn't women have to promise to 'love, honour, and obey' in the Marriage Service? And in return they got protected and cared for. Isn't that how it was supposed to work? You should know!"

"Mm. I guess so. Still, wouldn't it be great if James himself had set it all up to get the insurance or something? Then she could be rid of him for a few years!"

"Oh, Polly! Good job I know you! And good job I don't repeat any of this outside. You'd be had up for libel or something. And he'd never forgive you."

Polly grinned and went to answer the insistent ringing of the doorbell.

She was surprised to see Sergeant Hooper and PC Dachery, both of whom she remembered, standing on the doorstep with straight faces.

"Hello! Long time no see. You both look serious. Think I've robbed a bank or something? Or did I park on a double yellow line? Oh no. I forgot. There aren't any in Mundenford, are there?"

Sergeant Hooper's lips pinched and PC Dachery looked at the ground. Neither of them smiled.

Sergeant Hooper said, "May we come in, Reverend? There's something we need to discuss with you."

Polly shrugged and stepped aside to allow them to pass. She showed them into the lounge and introduced Ella.

"We're house-mates," she explained. "We share the house. It's too big for just one."

Ella said, "Do you need me? Or shall I make coffee?"

"A cup of coffee would be very nice, miss," the sergeant said. "White, please, for both of us."

When Ella had gone he said, "Reverend, can you tell us where you were last Saturday evening?"

"The night of the robbery at Thorpemunden Manor, you mean? Yes, I was here."

"Alone?"

"Yes. Ella works at the Rose and Crown in Middlestead in the evenings. She went out at about six-thirty."

"So there are plenty of witnesses to vouch for her. And you were here all evening? You didn't go out?"

Polly hesitated slightly, then said, "No. I was in all evening."

Both police officers noticed the hesitation.

PC Dachery said, "You're sure you didn't drive round Thorpemunden, Polly, at around…" she consulted her notebook, "eleven or eleven-thirty that night? Only a car resembling yours was spotted by a number of people in the vicinity."

Polly laughed. "Have you seen my car? It's a Ka. The design hasn't changed since they first started making them in the nineties or whenever."

"That may be so," acknowledged Sergeant Hooper, "but how many have a fluorescent fish stuck to their front bumper?"

Polly cleared her throat. "Several, I should think. It's a very common symbol."

"Less common round here, Reverend. And I understand most fish appear at the rear of cars, not the front. In the light of which, would you like to think again about your response? Now. I'll ask you again. Where were you last Saturday evening, Reverend Hewitt?"

Polly said firmly, forcing herself to maintain eye contact with him, "I was here. All evening. Alone."

"Thank you, Reverend," Sergeant Hooper said politely, closing his notebook. "I think that's all for now. If you should wish to revise your statement or you think of anything you haven't mentioned, please give me a ring at the station." And they departed before Ella had time to bring in their coffee.

Ella slowly set down mugs of coffee for herself and Polly. She looked at Polly, a disturbed frown on her brow.

"Why did you say that?"

Polly looked sheepish. She was already ashamed of herself. "Wish I hadn't. But it kinda slipped out before I thought and then I was stuck with it."

"Yes, but why? What was the point?"

Polly sighed. "I just didn't want anything to get out about my mother. I'm so terrified of it getting back to the bishop."

"But why would he care about your mother? It's you he's interested in, surely?"

"Yes, I know. But you know what the Church is like. It's all old-school-tie and moving in the right circles. If your face doesn't fit, you never get anywhere. I've already seen it. And look what happens. You get disappointed priests like Henry who think they should have made archdeacon or bishop but who end their days puddling about in places like Thorpemunden, feeling frustrated and resentful."

"I thought you liked Thorpemunden?"

"I do! Of course I do! But I'm only twenty-eight. I don't want to spend my whole life here. I'd like to maybe get a big city-centre church one day. And I'd like at least the possibility of making archdeacon or bishop, if that ever comes to pass for women. I don't want to be a curate my whole life. And I don't want to be thrown out of the race at this early stage just because of my background."

Ella switched track. "So what was he talking about? I know you went out to look for Mandy, but you weren't anywhere near the manor, were you?"

As Polly merely looked at her, she groaned, "Oh no! Polly, tell me you didn't drive into the manor? Why would you do that?"

"I didn't think they'd seen me. I hid my face and it was Daisy driving. You know what she's like. I didn't think she'd notice anything and James was half asleep. I thought I saw someone flit across the drive and for a moment I thought it might be Amanda. So I went to look. But there was no one there."

"It might have been the real thief. You should tell the police. What are you going to do now?"

"What can I do? I can hardly go running after the Old Bill to say, 'I was lying.' I'll just have to sit tight and hope nothing further comes of it. After all, it was only a white lie and I wasn't doing any harm. And it's none of their business. Nothing to do with what happened that night. I only caught a glimpse and it might have been nothing. A trick of the light, it was that quick. I can't say anything that will help their investigation. You will back me up, won't you?"

Ella said, "Polly, please don't ask me to lie for you. But you were in when I left that evening and home when I got back, so what else can I say to the police? If I said anything else it would be hearsay, not evidence. I'll just give them the facts if they ask me. But all the same, I wish you'd been honest with them. I do hope this doesn't come back to bite you."

***

Daisy Mansfield found herself the centre of attention at the monthly MU meeting. Her friends crowded round firing questions at her, for Thorpemunden had seen nothing more exciting for many years than random vandalism in the form graffiti daubed on the sports pavilion wall. And everyone had known who had been responsible for that.

The subject was not approached directly.

Bunny Sterling, as a Thorpemunden member, felt it incumbent upon her to open the discussion. "Daisy, darling! We're all so sorry to hear about poor James. How is he now?"

"Much better, thank you. He came home at the end of last week. But he has to take it easy." She added with a wry smile, "He keeps me on my toes. Doesn't like being an invalid, so I have plenty to do."

There were murmurs of sympathy all round. Rosemary Grant said, "Did you get the flowers?"

"Oh! Yes, thank you all so much. They were beautiful, such wonderful colours. I put them in the lounge where James can see them. They've lasted well. Some of them were just beginning to go, but I resurrected them and added fresh water and a soluble aspirin and now they're good as new again. Such a kind thought from you all."

It was a long speech from Daisy, but still hadn't elicited the desired information. As the rector's wife, Mavis took over.

"Daisy, it was too awful. Especially as you'd been dining with us that evening. Henry and I felt almost responsible. If only we hadn't asked you out that evening."

Daisy turned an anxious face upon her. "But you shouldn't feel like that! It wasn't Polly, I'm sure it wasn't. I mean, I thought it was her car, but it can't have been, can it?"

There was a stunned silence. Then Mavis said cautiously, "Polly?"

"Well, you know. That car we nearly bumped into as we turned into our drive. But it can't have been Polly. I told that policeman that I must have been blinded by the headlights."

"What made you think it was Polly?"

"I saw her. Well, I thought I did at the time. You know, the hair. Even though she turned her face away. And the fish on the bumper. But I'm sure I must have been mistaken. It was so dark and she says there are lots of cars with those fishes."

Bette Jarrold said, "I hope nothing much was taken. I mean, none of your personal jewellery? Your house wasn't damaged?"

"Oh no, thank you. Nothing like that. It was just the petty cash tin—James keeps that in his study and it's always locked—and the safe. We didn't think anyone knew where that was."

"What was taken from the safe, then?"

"Oh dear! Well, you know James. He doesn't trust the banks, especially after all that trouble with the credit crunch or whatever they call it. So there was rather a lot of money in there even though it was all in fifty-pound notes."

Diana Courtney probed gently, "So you must have lost a few hundred pounds. How awful for you."

Daisy said, "I'm afraid it was much more than that. James had over three hundred thousand in there. He's awfully worried about it."

There was a sort of collective gasp from the gathered MU members. Then the speculation began.

"But Polly! Who'd have thought it?"

"A curate, too!"

"No, it can't have been her. Daisy must have been mistaken."

"Do the police have any other leads?"

"What about that girl who's been staying—oh! Sorry, Mavis. I forgot she was your niece." Dorothy Mudd reddened.

Mavis said coolly, "If you've all finished tea, ladies, we should start our meeting."

But it was looked upon for years afterwards as one of the best meetings the MU could remember.

***

Henry was in despair. "Not again," he groaned to Mavis. "Just when I seemed to be getting back on an even keel. What am I going to do now?"

"You'll have to inform the bishop. James will certainly have contacted Percy already. You know what he's like."

Henry did know, although he wasn't entirely clear whether Mavis was referring to the bishop or to James.

"Shall I ring him? After all, we don't know whether the police will take this any further. And I really can't believe Polly would be involved in anything like this. She's a very honest girl. So they can't possibly have any evidence. If they did, she'd have been arrested."

Mavis said carefully, "One of my concerns is that Ella could get dragged into this, simply by virtue of living with Polly."

"Ella! You don't think—no, that's quite impossible. I know Ella even better than I know Polly. She'd never be party to anything dishonest. I'll go round and talk to Ella. She'll tell me what's been going on. Do you know whether that woman's still there?"

Mavis frowned. "What woman?"

"Amanda. Polly's mother. You know, she came to stay with Polly. But I must say I'm not over eager to spend the morning in her company."

"I don't know anything about her. When did you meet her? What's she like?"

"A bit blowsy, if you know what I mean. What my mother used to call 'common.' As a matter of fact, I believe I met her the day James and Daisy came to supper, so the day of the robbery."

Mavis said, "Well, it's either risking seeing her or ringing the bishop. But if she was there, surely Polly has an alibi. It would be worth finding out about that. If I were you, I'd try Ella and Polly first. Get the story straight before you approach Percy."

***

But Henry's plans were put on hold by the ringing of the telephone. An agitated Maud Tinton from Middlestead said, "Oh, Rector! Thank goodness I've caught you. Oh, it's too awful. I found him, you see. I don't know what to do. I think you may be too late already. Oh dear, oh dear."

Henry said, "Maud? What is it? What's happened?"

"I just called in on him this morning like I always do on Tuesdays. To get his shopping, you know. He always has a little list ready, then I go to Diss—he likes me to shop at the co-op because of their ethical policy—and I buy his stuff and mine, then I take it back and we always have a bit of a sit down and a coffee and he opens the packet of bisc—"

Henry interrupted. "Yes, Maud. How lovely. Now who is this you're talking about?"

"Father Brian, of course. I thought you knew!"

"Father Brian. Of course. You help him with his weekly shopping. Has something happened to Father Brian?"

There was a gulp on the other end of the phone. Maud's words came out in a rush. "He's dead. When I went this morning he didn't answer the door, and that's so unlike him that I peeped in through the back window, although I wouldn't usually do such a thing. He's on the kitchen floor. I'm sure he's dead. Please come quickly, Rector."

Henry said, "Maud, listen to me. I'm going to get into my car and come straight over. But you need to ring 999 and ask for an ambulance and the police. Have you got that?"

A tearful Maud said in a small voice, "Yes. Yes, thank you, Rector. Yes, I'll do that. But please hurry."

Stopping only to appraise Mavis of the situation, Henry ran to his car, musing how often the emergency number had been called in the last few months. He couldn't recall ever having used it before. *Ever since Polly came,* he thought. *Although if Father Brian has died, I don't suppose that can be laid at her door.* And he sped off towards Middlestead.

***

Father Brian's sudden demise superseded the gossip about the Mansfields' burglary, which even with the possibility of Polly's involvement faded into oblivion. Everyone began to feel a little bit mortal, and uncomfortable questions arose like, is there any life after death or is it total annihilation?

Polly visited Arthur Roamer, thinking that the sudden death might have hit him more than most, recalling for him painful memories about his wife's sudden death so many years earlier. Ivy Cranthorn was sitting in Arthur's kitchen when Polly arrived, and the three of them shared their sadness over Father Brian.

Polly said, "When I came, I was terrified of meeting him because I thought he was going to be anti-women. But he was so sweet. He always encouraged me and he stood up for me, too, on occasion. Not that he could ever remember doing so, afterwards. His memory did leave a bit to be desired."

They laughed and reminisced about Father Brian's services. Arthur said, "Knew his gardening, did Father Brian. We used to chat about the garden from time to time. I picked up a few tips from him."

"Arthur Roamer! I don't believe it! There's no one on this planet could touch you for gardening, no matter how holy they were!"

"That's because you've tasted my tomatoes, Ivy Cranthorn." He turned to Polly. "Ivy here loves her tomatoes. I think that's why she comes, for the tomatoes, not me."

Ivy smiled and said, "Tomato season's over now, Arthur, so you'd better find something else quick to entice me. Polly, when's the funeral? Do you know yet?"

"Next Friday, at Middlestead, naturally. In the afternoon to give the family time to get here."

"Did he have family? I never heard him say much about any family."

"He had a niece he was very fond of. I think she kept in touch. But his sister died years ago, so it's only the niece and her husband and children. They've got three, I think. All grown up now. Two of them have partners and children of their own. But I don't think any of them are churchgoers."

"Who's taking the funeral? Is it different when a priest dies? Do you have to have a bishop or something?"

Polly laughed. "No, Ivy. Although I think Percy's going to take part in the service. Pronounce the blessing or something. Henry's taking the service and I'm actually allowed to read the lesson and lead the prayers. So there'll be three of us robed. And I expect there'll be other priests from the Chapter, but probably they won't robe. Will just sit in the choir stalls or something. The coffin's turned the other way when a priest dies. Did you know that?"

"How do you mean?" Arthur scratched his head as he contemplated the picture in his mind of a coffin turned sideways on to the altar.

"You know how usually the feet are towards the altar for the service, then the bearers turn the coffin at the end of the service and carry it out feet first? But when a priest dies, the head is towards the altar."

"Whatever for?" Ivy was as perplexed as Arthur.

"Apparently it's because a priest is deemed to be ready to meet with God. Doesn't need turning, if you see what I mean."

They caught one another's eyes and began to grin. Soon the three of them were laughing so hard Ivy had to wipe the tears from her eyes.

"Oh!" she gasped at last. "I didn't mean to be disrespectful. But I think poor old Father Brian would be quite amused himself. He was such a gentle soul. He'd never have thought himself nearer to God than anyone else."

"It's a lot of nonsense, isn't it?" agreed Polly. "As if being a priest confers an absolute right to enter Heaven, or something."

"Not sure I believe in Heaven or Hell," Arthur said. "What about you, Ivy? What do you think?"

"I'm up and down. Sometimes I believe, sometimes I don't. I mean, if anything goes on I think it must be our soul or spirit. Never did know the difference between those two. But I can see how spirit could go on to some other existence in a different dimension."

Polly said, "Like the real 'me,' do you mean? That part of us deep inside that no one else knows?"

Ivy turned to her eagerly. "That's it! That's exactly what I mean. I think that bit returns to God. But if we don't know anything about God in this life, perhaps we don't recognize God in the next life. Perhaps that's what Hell is."

Arthur got up and filled the kettle. "It's all a bit deep for me. But I do know this. If there is a Heaven, then Father Brian will be there already. He was a good man, one of the best."

And they all agreed with that.

Chapter Twenty-Two

Because Father Brian had died so suddenly, there had to be an inquest. It was some time before the body was released, so the funeral service was held on Friday the eighth of November, just before Remembrance Sunday.

The niece, who lived in Scotland, was coming down for the funeral with her husband and one of the adult children, but was not able to arrive prior to the Friday, so all arrangements had to be made via email. Fortunately, Father Brian had planned his own funeral years earlier and had specified the type of service he wanted.

Polly had already taken a number of funerals, some directly at the crematorium, some in church, and some split between the two. She liked these latter the least, because the journey to the crematorium from the Thorpemunden area took between a half and three-quarters of an hour, and once there, the final committal part of the service was over in just a few minutes. Then there was the long return journey, and if family and friends had been invited to the local hostelry for refreshments as usually happened, they had all long since gone home by the time the family arrived back. It was most unsatisfactory. More recently the funeral directors had been suggesting to bereaved families that the whole service should be held in church, even if the deceased was to be cremated. The funeral directors would then take the coffin to the crematorium while the family enjoyed refreshments and a chat with their guests.

But none of this applied to Father Brian, who had specified a Requiem Mass and burial in Middlestead churchyard, followed by a party at the Rose and Crown at his posthumous expense. Polly had never attended a Requiem Mass before, but discovered that it was the normal funeral service with which she was familiar, within a service of Holy Communion. Bishop Percy would preside at the Communion part of the service and distribute the communion wafers, while she and Henry were to act as chalice assistants, distributing the wine.

Middlestead Church, which seated around one hundred and twenty, was soon packed. The churchwardens and spare able-bodied parishioners carried chairs over from the Rose and Crown and were able to seat a further thirty. The remaining dozen had to stand throughout the service, but Polly noticed that even they managed to perch on the steps of the font. It was just as well, since the service lasted for an hour, twice as long as the usual funeral.

The mood was sombre and although Henry included one or two amusing anecdotes (culled from the niece) which prompted muted laughter, there were a number of tears. Father Brian had fumbled and bumbled his way through services, which had irritated many, but he had also been deeply loved as the numbers present showed. He had an innate understanding of the human psyche, and the unique ability to make everyone feel as though they were the only person of any importance and that their views really mattered. And he had represented stability. He had been there for as long as anyone could remember, so his sudden demise was an uncomfortable reminder of the fragility of life, especially for the many churchgoers who were approaching their eighties and nineties.

Ella sat with Mavis at the service, but was required to help out behind the bar in the Rose and Crown afterwards. Father Brian had directed that all drinks should be free along with a substantial buffet, and the guests made the most of his generosity. Ella was kept busy all afternoon pulling pints and serving spirits.

Percy had offered his apologies and hurried off after the service to officiate elsewhere in the diocese, but both Polly and

Henry tracked over to the Rose and Crown in their cassocks. Only a small pub, it was packed, making movement difficult, but Polly and Henry managed to circulate, passing the time of day with all the guests. Although Polly found it easy to talk to people she knew, she found it more difficult to approach strangers, so had developed a few opening gambits. She discovered that any one of these, accompanied by a warm smile, soon broke down barriers and enabled her to chat with perfect strangers as though they had been friends forever.

She sidled up to a group of businessmen sat on stools at the bar. "He was a good old boy, wasn't he? Are you friends of his?"

They responded immediately. "Lovely service, Vicar. Yes, poor old Brian, wonderful man! We've all known him for years. Used to drink in here whenever he could and played bowls down at the green. But what a send-off. This is like a real, old-fashioned wake. Terrific. He'd have loved this."

Polly smiled and nodded. "All his idea. He wrote down instructions years ago and this is the result. So make the most of it. No expense spared. That was his wish."

She was interrupted by an angry voice. Until then, she hadn't noticed James Mansfield among the bevy of business suits.

He snarled, "Yes, you like money all right, don't you! I should warn you, gentlemen, that our curate here, the Reverend Polly Hewitt, has an interesting attitude to money. Especially other people's."

Polly was stunned. For a moment she couldn't think. Then she noticed the way James was freely tossing back whisky.

She said, "James, shall I fetch you a plate of food? It'll make you feel better to have some food inside you."

He turned on her. "You keep away from me, you Jezebel! How dare you approach me after what you've done? You should be unfrocked. Driven from the Church."

By now all other chatter had ceased. Everyone was staring at Polly and James. Polly felt her cheeks burning. She had no idea how to handle the situation and was not entirely sure what James was talking about, although she assumed it must be something to do with the robbery. Surely he didn't think she was responsible? Even if her car had been at the manor that night, he couldn't think she would be involved in anything illegal, could he? But what awful trouble he was causing for her. This was so embarrassing. Polly wished Father Brian was here in person. He would have rescued her. He always knew exactly what to say at times like this. She searched round for Henry, imploring him with her eyes to come to her aid. But Henry turned his back, moving over towards Mavis as though he needed protection himself.

There was nothing else for it. Polly said clearly, "I think you should be very careful what you say, James. There are many witnesses here and I won't be afraid to take you to court if you slander me."

There was a gasp from the gathered crowd, but Polly didn't care. Not waiting to discover any further reaction, she pushed her way out of the pub and stumbled back to her car, collapsing into the driving seat and only then allowing the tears to fall. She felt very frightened, for she had sensed evil surrounding the influential James Mansfield and she knew she was the focus for it.

Like everyone else, Ella had heard the exchange with dismay but was trapped behind the bar, unable to get to Polly to offer support or comfort. So she listened as best she could to the reactions, thinking that at least she would be able to appraise Polly of how the majority were thinking.

But James' outburst had spoilt the moment. The atmosphere had soured, with the result that people were hurriedly finishing their drinks and beginning to disperse, embarrassed to have witnessed such a vicious exchange between members of the church. Henry and Mavis disappeared quickly, avoiding James as well as Polly. The suits left soon after and some of James' Masonic friends took him by the arm and ushered him out.

When the pub had largely emptied, those few who were left began to talk.

"What was all that about?"

"He called her 'Jezebel.' Wasn't she that queen in the Bible who committed adultery all over the place? What did he mean by that? Has our Polly been playing away from home?"

An elderly man nursing his beer said, "My wife's in the MU. She said James Mansfield suspects Polly of carrying out that robbery last month because the Mansfields saw Polly's car at the manor when they came home that night."

Another said stoutly, "What rubbish! How could Polly possibly be responsible for that?"

But one or two began to exchange glances, as though the idea was not entirely unfeasible.

"Someone said it was an inside job. Polly's hardly an insider up there. James Mansfield can't stand her, never could."

"But they haven't got anyone else for it, have they? There aren't any other suspects, as far as I know. Perhaps she had an accomplice."

"Yes! That girl who's—"

The speaker was hushed up by the others, and all eyes turned to Ella behind the bar. She returned their gaze coolly.

"Any more orders, gentlemen? Father Brian's instructions were to serve you drinks for as long as necessary."

Most of them had the grace to look sheepish. They finished their drinks and scurried away.

Ella rang Polly to ask for a lift and to reassure her that the pub was now empty.

"I'll fill you in on what happened after you left," promised Ella. "See you soon."

***

The numbers in the pews were noticeably down on the Sunday following Father Brian's funeral, even though it was Remembrance Sunday, normally an occasion which saw the British Legion parading and villagers flocking into church.

Arthur Roamer confided to Ivy Cranthorn next day, "It's all down to that appalling exhibition in the pub on Friday. James Mansfield should be thoroughly ashamed of himself. So should all those supporters of his. That toffee-nosed lot from the Lodge."

Ivy agreed. "I felt so sorry for Polly. That attack was completely unjustified. If there was any evidence against Polly—and there can't possibly be—she'd have been arrested long ago. I heard the chief constable was really putting pressure on the force to get a result, but nothing's happened yet. They don't seem to have any clues."

"But to go after Polly like that, in public! It made me ashamed to be a churchgoer. And I'm certain that's why there weren't many in church yesterday. They're all so disgusted by what they witnessed. I actually heard people say in the car park afterwards, 'If that's how they behave in church circles, I don't want to know.'"

Ivy gave a last flick of her duster to the pews in Mundenford Church. She cleaned the church voluntarily every Monday morning, and lately Arthur had joined her, to help with the heavy work of vacuuming. In return, Ivy joined him at Middlestead Church when he was due to clean there.

She said, "Mind you, it is cold now. I always think winter begins at Remembrance Sunday. It's always freezing. The wind whistles round the marketplace where the parade starts, and it's not much warmer when they get into church."

"True. But it's always like that and it hasn't affected the numbers before. No, I think it's a lot more than that. I shouldn't be surprised if we don't soon see the whole benefice dividing into camps either for or against Polly."

Ivy sucked in her breath. "Do you really think so? That would be terrible. Especially after Henry has worked so hard over the years to unite all our parishes. Poor Polly. She doesn't stand a chance against James Mansfield and his lot. They're powerful men. They run just about every business in the whole benefice. But surely even they can't do anything without proof?"

Arthur laughed without humour. "Did you spot anyone looking for proof on Friday? No. They're avid for gossip and they don't care tuppence whether or not it's valid. Don't much care who it hurts, either, just so long as they get their entertainment."

Ivy said, "Arthur, you're so cynical. Not everyone's like that, you know. Some of us care. And some of us support our Polly, too. At least you and I will do our best to make sure she's not driven away by malicious tittle-tattle, won't we?

"So come on. I've had enough of church cleaning for one day. Let's go to mine for a cuppa."

***

Polly was more disturbed by the events at the wake than she cared to admit, but Ella was well aware of her friend's distress.

"Why don't you give Sue a ring? It helps, sometimes, to get a different perspective from someone who's well away from it all. Can give you a bit of space."

Polly nodded. "You may be right. Anyway, I haven't spoken to her for a while. I'll give her a bell."

She hit speed dial and in a moment was chatting to Sue. "Hey, Sue! How's it going? Haven't heard from you in ages."

"Polly! Great to hear from you. What's up? You okay?"

With an attempt at flippancy Polly said, "Why would you think something's up just 'cos I ring my old friend?" Then, as Sue murmured, "Uh-oh!" she added, "Okay, there is something, but I didn't ring only 'cos of that. Honestly."

Sue said, "C'mon then. What is it?"

And Polly began to pour out the whole story. She left out nothing, even admitting to her friend that she had lied to the police and finishing with the events after the funeral.

She concluded with, "Sue, I don't know what to do. If I go to the police now they'll be even more suspicious and think I really have been hiding something. Besides, they haven't been near me again, so maybe I should just let things rest. You know, give it all time to simmer down.

"But it's James Mansfield. He's started all this dreadful gossip about me and he hates me. I think he's determined to get rid of me. And he's so powerful. He has the bishop's ear and he influences everyone around here. Henry's scared to death of him, not that he'd ever admit it. But he does everything James says, so I can't see him backing me."

"Have you spoken to Henry to check that out?"

"What, you expect me to go up to Henry and say, 'Henry, are you under James Mansfield's thumb?' I don't think so."

"You don't have to put it quite like that. Even you could be a little more subtle, Polly. You could, for instance, express your concern for James. I take it you are concerned for him? He is a parishioner, after all, and one who has been ill. It sounds to me as though James has been acting somewhat irrationally. Perhaps you could tease that out with Henry?"

Polly was dubious. "I'm not sure. Henry himself is still pretty irrational. One minute he's as nice as pie, the next he's tearing strips off me, quite unpredictably. I wouldn't mind if I'd done something wrong, but I haven't. Not this time. At least, I don't think I have."

Sue thought, *Actually, you have. One little white lie has dug you into a pit so deep that you can't yet see the bottom,* but she didn't think this was quite the time to voice her thoughts. She concentrated on supporting Polly.

"You've talked to Ella?"

"Yes, she's being great. I'm so glad she's here. I don't know what I'd do without her."

Sue said, "I'll pray for you, Polly. And you might try that route yourself. But I think in the end you're going to have to brave it. You must talk to Henry. Tell him how you feel. Tell him everything, Polly—and I mean everything—like you've just told me. You may find he's not as unsympathetic as you fear."

Polly sighed. "Okay. Thanks, Sue. Can't make any promises, but at least I'll think about it."

But she was frowning as she replaced the receiver. She felt uneasy about approaching Henry, mostly because he was so friendly with James, and although she hesitated to admit it even to herself, Polly didn't quite trust Henry.

***

With Ella's encouragement, Polly did go to the rectory. The two girls went together, for Polly was well aware that Ella's presence would be invaluable when dealing with both Henry and Mavis. But it didn't work out quite as Polly had envisaged. She had imagined a polite cup of coffee with Mavis and Henry, then leaving Ella with Mavis while she herself went off with Henry to his study. But it seemed that things had changed since Henry's illness. Now, Mavis was constantly on the alert for anything which might upset Henry, and Polly Hewitt definitely counted on that list. So all discussion had to take place within the presence of both Mavis and Henry.

At least Ella was there too. But even her presence didn't help quite as Polly had foreseen, for Henry was unable to take his eyes from Ella, drinking her in to such an extent that Polly felt quite discomfited by him and unsure that he would hear anything she had to say. She felt awkward for Mavis, too, and wondered what Mavis felt about her husband ogling Ella so overtly.

Still, she should at least do her best. She cleared her throat. "Um, I um, just wanted to apologise for that awful scene in the Rose and Crown on Friday. I don't know what got into James. It was so embarrassing."

Henry ignored her, which Polly put down to not having heard a word, but Mavis said in a tart voice, "It was wholly unedifying. I can't imagine what the non-churchgoers thought of you."

Polly stared. "Of me? I didn't start anything. James verbally attacked me, in front of everyone."

"Polly, surely you've learned by now that you don't go around blaming other people for your own misdemeanours. Whatever was or was not said—and I can't imagine that James Mansfield would have said anything untoward; he's a very well-respected man in this area and a close friend of the bishop—you must learn not to retaliate. Turn the other cheek. Have you never read your Bible?"

Polly exchanged a glance with Ella, who jumped to her rescue. "I think James had perhaps had one too many. What he said to Polly was really rude."

Mavis tossed her head. "The poor man has had a lot to cope with. We must make allowances for him. He's been very ill and he's lost a great deal of money. I expect he's worried sick."

Polly said, "He practically accused me of stealing his money. I couldn't believe it."

"Clear it up then," Mavis said, briskly. "Tell him where you were that evening. After all, Henry says you had your mother staying—although why you didn't bring her round to meet us is beyond me—so she can vouch for you, surely? Just tell them and sort the whole thing out once and for all."

Polly said, "Mm," because she couldn't think of anything else to say. But Mavis was immediately suspicious.

"You did have your mother staying, didn't you?"

"Oh yes. She went next day."

"So tell them, then. What's the problem? That's what I mean, Polly. You don't help yourself. It's no good blaming James when all you had to do was tell the truth. You really are a strange girl.

"Now, I'm sorry, but I have to ask you not to come here again bothering Henry with frivolous things like this. He has enough on his plate sorting out the parishes without anything extra. He's still not strong, you know. I don't want a relapse."

Privately, Polly thought Henry looked as though extremely healthy red blood was coursing through his veins the way he was fixated on Ella, but she thought it politic not to say so.

She contented herself with saying in a conciliatory tone, "I'm sorry, Mavis. I didn't mean to upset Henry—or you. It's just that I was a bit concerned as to how the parishes might react. I thought the numbers were quite low in church for Remembrance Sunday and wondered whether it had anything to do with the incident in the pub."

Mavis dismissed this suggestion. "When you've been here a year or two, Polly, you'll realize that numbers do fluctuate from week to week. There are all sorts of reasons. The weather, for one. It was bitterly cold and the British Legion are no longer as young as they were. And people now have different priorities for their Sundays. Lots of them visit families on Sundays. So I shouldn't think your little contretemps had anything to do with it at all, no thanks to you."

And with that, Polly had to be content.

Chapter Twenty-Three

Towards the end of the week, Polly received a phone call from Bishop Percy's secretary.

"Reverend Hewitt? Bishop Percy would like to see you in his office on Monday afternoon at two-thirty. Will that be convenient for you?"

Polly was taken aback by the summons. "Um, well, yes, I suppose so. Why? What does he want to see me about?"

"I couldn't say. The bishop just asked me to ring you and Canon Winstone to fix a date. That's all I know."

"Canon Winstone? Is Henry going too?"

"Yes, he can manage Monday afternoon. Didn't I mention that? The bishop would like to see you together."

"Oh. All right, thank you. I'll be there."

The phone rang again as soon as Polly had replaced the receiver.

"Hello, Henry. Are you ringing me about this summons to the bishop's?"

"You know already, do you? Obviously we'll go together. I'll pick you up at five to two on Monday."

"Okay. Thanks. Listen, Henry, do you know what it's about? The secretary wouldn't tell me."

There was a pause. Then Henry said, "She didn't tell me, either, but I can only think of one issue which might interest the bishop, can't you?"

"You mean that trouble after the funeral?"

"And all its ramifications. Everything leading up to it."

"What do you mean by that?"

"Well, did you tell him you'd been interviewed by the police, for instance?"

"No, of course not! Why should I? They only asked me a few questions. They asked everybody. They were doing house-to-house enquiries. I'm surprised they didn't interview you."

"You should have told the bishop. Or at least told me. How do you think I've felt learning all these things second hand?"

"What things? Really, Henry, there's nothing to learn. Do I have to spell it out in words of one syllable? I haven't done anything! There, does that suit you? Or do you prefer to rely on gossip?"

"Polly, I strongly advise you not to park your cannons on the front lawn when we see the bishop. This belligerence will not help anyone, least of all you. I don't wish to discuss this any further now. But for goodness sake, get your act together before Monday, or we'll both be in trouble."

***

Neither of them felt very talkative on the journey to Stoke Holy Cross. Polly was trying to work out in her own mind what to reveal to the bishop, which was difficult since she had no idea what he already knew. She was desperate to dig herself out of the hole she had created but needed to do so without making matters worse. And if Henry revealed Amanda's presence to the bishop, Polly wondered how on earth she was going to foil him without the whole sordid story of her mother's alcoholism becoming public knowledge.

Henry felt depressed. It was bad enough trying to cope with a wilful curate and a churchwarden full of righteous indignation, without the bishop on his back as well. He wondered whether he should seek early retirement, for in the space of a few months he had gone from a vocation he loved to a job he wasn't far short of hating. He had put in sufficient years for a full pension, but wouldn't be able to draw it before the age of sixty-five. So it was difficult to see how he and Mavis could survive without money coming in, unless he was invalided out, which began to seem like an attractive and viable option the more Henry thought about it.

Not for the first time recently, Henry tried to analyse what he really thought about God. He found himself wondering more and more whether God really existed, and if he didn't, how that affected Henry himself.

Not just me, either, thought Henry. *My work, my house, probably my pension, my life, and my wife, but also around two and a half thousand parishioners and especially the hundred and twenty or so churchgoers. What would it do to all of them if I dared to express what I think I might feel about God?*

The thought didn't bear exploring, so Henry pushed it to the back of his mind as best he could. But he couldn't help wondering whether it was this erosion of his faith which had caused his earlier depressive illness or vice versa. Whichever it was, Polly Hewitt was certainly the catalyst, and Henry was aware of a growing resentment towards Polly because of the way she had contrived to ruin his life.

***

Bishop Percy's round face was grave. "Shall we start in my chapel? We should pray together and ask God to be with us during our discussions."

Henry chalked it up as a bad sign that the bishop led the way into his small private chapel, built in the traditional style, with gothic arches and an altar at the east end. Usually it was a quick prayer in the study before a meeting started, not serious worship in the chapel. It reminded Henry of a visit long ago when he was twelve years old to the headmaster's study, a visit he did not care to dwell upon.

The bishop invited Henry and Polly to kneel at the altar rail while he stood behind the rail in the sanctuary, making Henry even more uncomfortable and certain in his own mind that sin and forgiveness somehow would creep into the prayer.

Using his resonant preaching voice Percy intoned, "Lord Jesus Christ, be with us in our prayers and our deliberations. Enable us to recognise our own faults and to take responsibility for them, and dear Lord, forgive us for our sins as we forgive all who sin against us. May we walk always in your ways, never straying from the path of truth and righteousness. For your name's sake. Amen."

"Amen," echoed Henry and Polly.

They were about to move when the bishop said, "I'll give you each a blessing."

He stood over first Henry then Polly, placing his hands on their heads and muttering some words of sanction almost, Henry thought, like a magic formula. Henry felt sickened by what he saw as a charade, designed to put Percy in a position of power and to point out the faults of his subjects by invoking God's forgiveness. He glanced at Polly, but her eyes were shining.

As they returned to the bishop's study Polly whispered to Henry, "Wasn't that amazing? I felt a terrific heat when he put his hands on my head. Honestly, I thought I was going to go up in flames."

Feeling suddenly old, Henry thought, *You probably will, if that charlatan has anything to do with it. I never realised before how manipulative prayer can be. The old so-and-so's using it entirely for his own ends, and it sounds to me as though we're in for a storm.*

As they sat down in the study, Bishop Percy wore what all his clergy described as his "saddened" face. He launched into the business at hand without offering them any refreshments, another bad sign in Henry's estimation. Although Henry had not been the recipient of the bishop's sadness before, he had heard enough from his colleagues in the Chapter to know exactly what was coming.

"Since the advent of the Clergy Discipline Measure in 2006," the bishop began, "any complaints against clergy have had to be taken much more seriously. Gone are the days when a bishop could dismiss a complaint by ignoring it. Now there is a procedure which has to be followed whenever a bishop or archdeacon receives a written complaint against any of his clergy, however trivial that complaint might seem to be and however much he himself might wish to dismiss it. He is obliged to investigate."

Henry said, "Written complaint? By whom? And about what?"

The bishop continued as though he hadn't spoken.

"The complaint is first scrutinised by the diocesan registrar, who will advise the bishop. That in itself is likely to take a month, so the whole procedure is long and drawn out and extremely unpleasant for all parties, including, I might add, the bishop.

"Now, I want to say first that it grieves me deeply to have to invite you both over here. I want you to know that I very much regret that under the circumstances, I feel there is no other course of action open to me."

Here we go. He's about to pretend it's hurting him more than it's hurting us! thought Henry. He determined not to help the bishop out. Let him squirm as he imparted whatever the bad news was to be.

Percy continued, "You will know that James Mansfield is a very dear friend of mine, as also is the chief constable of Norfolk. Therefore I am privy to recent events in Thorpemunden. I confess to some measure of personal pain that neither of you have seen fit to confide in me, your father in God.

"Polly, of course, would go first to you, Henry, but I would have expected some communication from you. How can I defend my clergy if they fail to approach me? That's why we bishops and archdeacons are in post—to support you. But we cannot do that if you feel unable to share with us."

Henry said, "Share what, exactly, Bishop?"

The bishop's voice took on a sarcastic note and Polly noticed that he was unable to keep his hands still. He kept interlocking and unlocking his fingers in a manner she found quite distracting.

"You may remember that I was at Father Brian's funeral. Did you think I would not be appraised of events afterwards?"

Polly's heart sank and she stared at the bishop's carpet. But Henry was not about to let the bishop off the hook.

"And what events were those, may I ask?"

The bishop flushed. He was unused to this sort of challenge from Henry, who had always been one of the most biddable of his priests. It just showed, reflected the bishop, that you never really knew people.

He said stiffly, "I refer to the altercation in the Rose and Crown, brought about, I might add, because neither of you saw fit to address what is clearly a serious underlying problem. This is what happens when problems are ignored. Other people get hurt and the reputation of the Church is eroded by yet another notch."

Polly burst out, "But that had nothing to do with Henry. He was on the other side of the room. It was just me. And I didn't start it."

"Now you sound like one of my grandchildren, Polly. That's what I hear from them, 'It wasn't my fault, it was him,' or 'I didn't start it, he did.' But they are aged six and eight. I do not expect such a childish reaction from one of my clergy. And I think it only fair to mention at this point that your elevation to the priesthood is in serious doubt at this moment in time."

Polly blanched. Henry wanted to say, "Elevation? I thought we were always told that the diaconate was an important ministry in its own right!" but he tucked that thought away for future reference.

Instead he said, surprising himself in his support of Polly, "What Polly says is true. I was over the other side of the room. But it so happens that I had a good vantage point there and was able to observe everything that went on. I can vouch for Polly unreservedly. She was doing what any good priest" (he lingered on the word "priest") "would do. Circulating throughout the room, speaking to both friends and strangers. I saw her approach a group of men at the bar and begin chatting to them when James Mansfield suddenly erupted. He was well to the rear of the group and I'm quite sure Polly had no idea he was there.

"I know he's your friend, Bishop, but I have to say how it was. He had had several whiskeys—the barmaid at the Rose and Crown can tell you the exact number—and I'm afraid he was drunk. Polly, quite rightly in my opinion, stopped him before he actually slandered her."

Percy said, "Your desire to defend your curate is commendable, Henry, but as I have just said, I do not want to pursue any idea of blame over this issue. I'm sure I don't have to spell out for either of you how damaging an episode like this can be in the life of a parish. Unfortunately it is not the first time I have had to speak to you like this. I had hoped the two of you were pulling together now, but when a curate can respond in such an aggressive manner to possibly the most important lay person in the community, it does raise questions about both of you.

"Polly, are you suitable material for leadership in the Church? I have to tell you that I had my doubts right from the beginning. You came with a less than satisfactory reputation, but I made sure you were given a chance. I put my trust in you, Polly, and so far I'm disappointed in the result. Unless you can show me for the remaining seven months or so of your diaconate that you have developed priestly formation, I'm not sure that I shall be able to recommend you for priesthood. I know you have been questioned by the police—for the second time in your short stay in the Thorpemunden area—and I sincerely hope it will be the last. You must know that I will have no option but to suspend you if this matter should go any further."

Polly swallowed. She felt physically sick and fought to quell her rising nausea. She was also aware of a huge anger building somewhere inside her. But with Henry's words of caution ringing in her ears, she fought to quell that too. Not trusting herself to speak, she moistened her lips but continued to stare at the carpet.

With no response forthcoming, the bishop turned to Henry. "Henry, as I have told you repeatedly, you are responsible for your curate. Whatever she does or fails to do reflects upon you. I have serious doubts as to whether we should have given you a curate in the first place. You are supposed to be training Polly, guiding her to become a good priest. I'm not impressed by your efforts. Unless things improve dramatically, I shall be forced to remove Polly from your influence. And I hardly need tell you what that will mean in terms of your status in the Church.

"Do I make myself clear to both of you?"

Henry said coldly, "Very clear."

Polly nodded. Her fists were clenched so tightly that her fingernails were digging into her palms. But better that than either exploding in anger or bursting into tears.

"There's just one more thing then," said the bishop. "You will both consider this an official verbal warning. I have not yet had a written complaint from your churchwarden, but I have so far had two verbal complaints. If this thing escalates into a written complaint I shall have no option but to invoke the Clergy Discipline Measure. And that, I'm afraid, may well result in suspension, at least during the time of the hearing."

Hardly able to believe what she was hearing, Polly was unable to speak.

But Henry said, "On what grounds, Bishop? As I recall there are only four grounds on which a complaint may be considered." He ticked them off on his fingers. "Acting in breach of ecclesiastical law, failing to do something which should have been done under ecclesiastical law, neglecting to perform or being inefficient in performing the duties of office, or engaging in conduct that is unbecoming or inappropriate to the office and work of the clergy."

The bishop's eyebrows rose at this accurate verbatim recital. Henry continued, "Which of these could possibly apply to our present situation in Thorpemunden?"

Bishop Percy's mouth pinched as his colour heightened. "I think 'conduct unbecoming,' don't you? Or do you consider that your curate has acted in any way commensurate with her office?"

Henry leaned back in his chair, steepled his fingers, and smiled lazily at the bishop. "My dear Percy. I think you'll need something a little more concrete than that to go to a tribunal! I therefore assume that all this—" he spread his hands, "—is nothing more than a threat. It really is too bad of James to involve you in his petty machinations, especially as they are totally without foundation. No doubt he has tried to bring equal pressure to bear upon your mutual friend, the chief constable, but perhaps the chief constable is less—what shall we say—malleable?"

Polly was staring at Henry with open-mouthed admiration. She hadn't expected any support from him, nor such a knowledgeable response. He had swept the rug from beneath Percy's feet (as Percy, by the anger now etched on his face, clearly knew) and had lifted Polly's spirits from the depths of despair to something approaching triumph. She couldn't help grinning at the bishop.

It was a mistake. As Percy got to his feet in dismissal he snarled at Polly, "You'd better watch your step, young lady. I don't think you're aware of a bishop's power. If I think you're unsuitable for ministry, you will never work as a priest."

As Polly gulped, Henry said smoothly, "Was that a threat, Bishop? I think you should be aware that I shall be recording this conversation as soon as I reach home. And no, I'm not threatening you. Merely pointing out the facts. Good-bye, Bishop. Thank you for your time."

Polly waited until they were in the car before turning breathlessly to Henry, her eyes shining. "You were brilliant, Henry! Thank you so much. I don't know what I would have done if you hadn't been there."

But Henry seemed plunged into gloom. "You'd better save your thanks. This isn't over yet, not by a long chalk. I've only managed to stave it off for a short while. And he's now alert to the fact that I'm a danger to him. He made a mistake, asking us both here together, but I don't think he'll make the same error twice. He's not stupid. Would never have made bishop if he was. No, he's clever and manipulative and ambitious. And that's a dangerous combination. I may not be in a position to support you again, so you should pay heed to what he said and keep out of trouble."

"Henry, I'm really sorry. I didn't mean to get you into this mess."

"Don't worry about me. I've got the freehold. There's not much the Church can do to me."

"The freehold?"

Henry sighed. "I've told you before—it more or less means I can do exactly as I please. Surely they taught you about the freehold in theological college? It means I can stay in the rectory until I'm seventy and not even the bishops can get me out. Retirement at seventy is mandatory, but until then, the rectory is effectively mine although it belongs to the diocese. It's a safeguard for clergy if events such as this should ever arise. We don't have a trades union of our own. Mind you, even this protection is being eroded. When you're given a parish of your own, expect to be made a priest-in-charge, not a vicar or rector."

"What does that mean?"

"It means you do exactly the same job as a vicar or rector and are paid the same, but you're not, strictly speaking, the incumbent. You're just there at the bishop's pleasure. You don't have the freehold, so you can be moved on at any time through any whim."

"How would I get the freehold?"

Henry shrugged. "You might be offered it after a few years doing the job. Some people never get it. Not that it makes much difference in practice since bishops don't normally go around slinging people out. But our circumstances at the moment show just how vulnerable clergy can be if vicious parishioners decide to get rid of them."

Polly said, "I'm really confused. I came into this job to serve God, but I'm coming up against prejudice and spite such as I never experienced in the world outside. Is it me?"

Henry smiled. "You certainly seem to be a catalyst for change, if nothing else. But people dislike change, especially if they're in positions of power. For some it's so threatening that they'll do anything to avoid it. Put it like this, Polly. You seem to be bringing out the best in some people but the worst in others. But no. If I'm honest, I don't think it is you. I think that perhaps God is using you to shake up our area. So don't expect it to be comfortable. Mark my words, there is evil afoot. And remember what happened to Jesus when he stood against evil."

Polly shivered and thought of the times when she had blithely quoted the need of all Christians to face crucifixion. But she hadn't expected it come to her through the medium of the Church. And neither had she expected it to be so agonisingly painful.

Chapter Twenty-Four

Since neither the bishop nor Henry had mentioned anything about confidentiality, Polly poured out to Ella her experiences at the bishop's.

"The strangest thing was, El, when he put his hands on my head I felt as though I really was being filled with God's grace. It was so hot. You've no idea. Honestly, I felt like I could walk on water after that. It was amazing."

Ella was sitting in front of the dressing table in her room applying mascara, while Polly lounged on the bed.

"Doesn't sound as though the rest of it was much fun."

Polly grimaced. "It was awful. I don't know what I would have done without Henry. He was brilliant. He was so calm. I felt like throwing up and bursting into tears all at the same time. Ella, I was terrified. Humpty Dumpty said he'll sack me and I'll never work as a priest."

With that Polly's tears began to fall. Ella sat beside her on the bed and put her arms around her. "So what happened to the magic bit? You know, the hands on head stuff?"

Polly sobbed harder and blew her nose. "That's one of the really worst things. It just kind of disappeared as though it had never been, and I felt bereft, as though God was giving up on me too."

"Can that happen? I mean, can God give up on you?"

"Don't suppose so. At least, that's what I'd tell the congregation. But it felt like it, so I guess I'm not sure when it comes to me. I mean, perhaps I've let God down so badly that he just wants rid of me now."

Ella said, "Now you're fishing! Which means you know that's not true but you want me to reassure you. But doesn't God work in mysterious ways? Haven't I heard you—or was it Henry—saying something like that?"

"Yes, of course. But what's that got to do with me right now, right here?"

Ella returned to the dressing table and ran a comb through her hair. "Look, I've got to go or I'll be late for work. But from what you said, it sounds to me as though God was working pretty hard through Henry. Who'd have expected Henry to react like that? He hasn't exactly been your greatest fan in the past, and he left you to get on with it by yourself in the pub. But there's a lot of hidden depth in Henry. I think he's terrific, I always have."

Polly stood up. "You're right. I never thought of it like that. Listen Ella, just before you go. I've been thinking of going to see the Mansfields myself. You know, bearding the lion in his den, all that sort of thing. Facing my fears. Isn't that what people are supposed to do? If I go and see James, maybe I can at least plead Henry's case. Poor old Henry had an unblemished career until I showed up. I'd like to put it right for him if I can."

Ella paused on the threshold. "Polly, please. Don't do anything yet. You need more advice on this before you go visiting. Can't you ring Sue or your rural dean or someone? You don't want to go barging in if there's any possibility it might make matters worse."

***

Snuggling into her favourite armchair in the lounge and tucking her feet under her, Polly picked up the phone. She dialled Sue's number but reached the answer phone. Unwilling to leave a message, she dialled Charles Burgess, but again encountered the answer phone. She listened to the rural dean's message because she always liked its warm, friendly tone, but again, left no message of her own. This, she felt, was rather too delicate a matter to trust to an answering machine.

With nothing on the television and feeling too restless to read, Polly wondered whether perhaps she should spend the evening in prayer. Somehow she always procrastinated when she had opportunities like this for some quiet by herself. But perhaps, she thought, that was because they always came when she wasn't ready for them. When she was feeling calm and relaxed and in the right frame of mind for prayer, there was never any opportunity. And at times like this, when she was so uptight that she was utterly unable to still her mind or think of anything except her troubles, there was loads of time for silence. It didn't make any kind of sense.

Polly wandered over to the CD player and ran her finger down the rack. She wanted mood music, so selected "Song for You" by Alexi Murdoch. Listening to the song gave her a few minutes of complete silence, as Alexi's words and soothing voice let her mind shut down. For a short time Polly felt she could relax and be at peace. She played it over and over again, allowing the music to seep into her soul, massaging her brain. At the same time, she tried to focus on God and open herself to God's nudge, whatever it might be.

As she absorbed the music, Polly wondered why God was so elusive. Why couldn't you just pray and God was right there? Why did it so often feel as though you were talking to yourself with no one on the other end of the line? Why didn't God answer? And why wasn't God there when you needed him? Then she began to reflect on Ella's words. Perhaps Ella was right and God had been present not so much through the bishop's hands on Polly's head (as she had thought) but more in Henry's solid presence. But if that was so, what was it that she had felt? Did that wonderful feeling of heat coursing through her body count for nothing? Or were both experiences God acting in different ways? Polly felt confused. It had all been so simple and so clear when she had felt the call to ministry and later, in theological college. But now it was somehow muddy and she was unable to see any way at all through the mud.

She found herself praying without really thinking about it, somewhere from within the depths of her being. "Please, God, show me the right path. Show me what I need to do and make me do it. 'Cos I'm really scared about what might happen, and unless you hold my hand, I won't be able to do anything."

By the time Ella returned, Polly was asleep in the chair with the music still going. Ella smiled, pleased to see her friend relaxed for once. She turned off the CD, made cocoa, and gently woke Polly.

***

Polly tried both Sue and the rural dean next morning, but when she failed to contact either of them decided that might be a sign from God. Accordingly she dressed carefully, being aware of the importance of power dressing for an occasion such as this.

Although she rarely wore one, Polly did possess a skirt. She selected her dark green clergy shirt, which she felt sent the message that she was serious yet her own person. It teamed well with the dark brown skirt and matching jacket with the pinched waist. And dark colours drew attention to the white dog collar, showing it off sufficiently to spell out "authority." She worked hard to tame her hair, finally tying it back with a dark green bandana, which again she felt added to the sober effect but contrasted nicely with her blond curls. Then she dug out the shoes with the four-inch Cuban heels, in which she could manage to walk without tottering and which gave her sufficient height to counteract the plumpness of her figure. Finally she applied light makeup. Just enough to enhance her natural colouring but not so pronounced as to shout "outrageous" to anyone over thirty.

Polly surveyed herself in the long mirror in the hall and, satisfied with the effect, set off for Thorpemunden Manor.

***

Daisy Mansfield was alone when Polly called. She was as anxious and fluttery as Polly had seen her and hesitated to invite Polly in.

"James is out. He's on the estate. I don't really know when he'll be back. And I'm—I'm—" she looked behind her, alternately wringing her hands and wiping them on her apron and appearing to search for a valid reason to keep Polly on the doorstep, "—I'm, er, baking in the kitchen."

"I'll come and keep you company then," Polly said easily, stepping through the doorway before Daisy had a chance to edge her out.

"Oh! Yes, of course. Do come in, Polly." But she still glanced nervously about her.

"Is anything the matter, Daisy?" Polly asked as she followed her hostess.

Daisy led her away from the kitchen into the lounge, and Polly noticed that there was no aroma of any baking.

"Would you like a coffee?" Daisy asked politely.

Thinking that busying herself in hostess-like duties might relax Daisy, Polly said, "Thank you. That would be lovely."

Daisy seemed more composed when she reappeared with a tray bearing not only coffee, but two small plates and a selection of homemade biscuits. Since Polly had been half-heartedly trying to restrict her intake of calories she was loath to take a biscuit, but she feared it might send a subtle message of rejection if she refused. And they did look tempting.

She took a bite. "Why, Daisy! These are absolutely delicious. I'd love the recipe. Unless it's a family secret?"

Daisy blushed. "No, no, of course not! I mean, it's not a family secret. Yes, I'll write the recipe out for you, Polly. They're really easy. Oh! I didn't mean—it's not that I think—I'm sure you're a very good cook. I didn't mean to imply that you need easy recipes, I—"

"It's all right, Daisy," Polly said gently. "I understand what you mean." She took a sip of coffee. "You must tell me what blend of coffee you use, too. I find coffee varies so much, don't you?"

"Yes, it does, doesn't it? I usually keep to the same blend. It's Arabica. James likes it. So does Frank."

"How is Frank? I haven't seen him for ages. I don't think he was in church with you the last couple of times. Has he gone away?"

Daisy's hands flew to her mouth. Polly noticed that they were trembling.

She said gently, "What is it, Daisy? What's the matter? You seem so upset."

In a moment of complete stillness which felt, Polly thought afterwards, as though the world had stopped, Daisy held her glance. Then a fat tear rolled down her cheek, followed by another and another. Daisy never moved or blinked. She sat there as though she were made from stone, as the tears tumbled down her face and into her lap.

Polly was taken aback. Although she was used to Daisy's fluttering, she had never seen her cry before. And she had never seen anyone cry like this, silently and without moving a muscle. She wasn't sure whether or not to rush over and fling her arms around Daisy, but something about the older woman's stillness prevented her.

For a while Polly just sat there, allowing Daisy to cry. Then she said quietly, "Is there anything I can do?"

When this elicited no response, Polly thought back to what had triggered the weeping. She said, "Daisy, listen to me. Where is Frank?"

This caused such a renewed onslaught, now escalating into what Polly later described as an "animal howling," that Polly was alarmed. But at least Daisy was moving.

Polly refreshed Daisy's coffee, added a liberal dose of sugar, and held the cup to her lips. "Drink this, Daisy."

Responding to the commanding tone, Daisy swallowed a few sips of hot coffee. The frenzied cries began to lessen. Quietly, Polly sat next to the distressed woman until the sobs ameliorated into the occasional hiccup. But Polly was wary of broaching the subject of Frank again. Having narrowly avoided full-scale hysterics, she had no wish for the situation to deteriorate out of control. She was deeply concerned for Daisy and anxious, too, for Frank. She couldn't begin to imagine what might have happened in that household and was not entirely sure that she wished to know. However, it was clear that something had to be done for Daisy, who seemed to Polly to be on the edge of a breakdown.

But what should she do? With no experience of hysterical behaviour, Polly had no idea. And where was Frank? The house felt empty, apart from herself and Daisy. There were no sounds of anyone else present anywhere in the house, and Frank was not usually the quietest of beings. He could be with his father out on the estate, but from Daisy's reaction, Polly considered that to be unlikely.

All sorts of wild thoughts chased themselves through Polly's mind, each more bizarre than the one before. She tried to empty her mind and shrug aside her fears, but it was impossible. She wanted to ask whether Frank was with his father, but she daren't mention Frank again for fear of precipitating another alarming episode. She sent up an arrow prayer, asking God for help and hoping for the right words to magically appear in her mind, but nothing happened.

Not knowing what else to do, Polly finished her coffee and picked up the tray. "I'll just drop these off in the kitchen for you, Daisy, then I must be on my way. Just called round to say 'hello' and see how you both are. Will you tell James I called?"

Eyes still wide and mournful, Daisy nodded but made no attempt to move. Polly carried out the tray and set it on the kitchen counter, but just as she was turning to go, the back door burst open and James Mansfield stood there with a face like thunder. He was carrying a shotgun, and Polly involuntarily backed away.

He snarled, "What are you doing here? You're not welcome. I thought I told you never to set foot in this house again. How dare you show up here when you knew I was out!"

He pushed roughly past her and shouted, "Daisy!"

Immediately there was a scurrying and a scrabbling which reminded Polly of mice, and Daisy appeared on the threshold, eyes full of fear and hands trembling.

"H—Hello, James. I'm so sorry. I just—I—"

James glared at her, his face an inch from hers. Daisy backed away.

"You stupid woman!" he ground out. "How dare you let her in? What did I tell you?"

"I—I'm so sorry, James," Daisy repeated faintly, her eyes dropping and her shoulders hunching submissively.

This exchange gave Polly time to recover herself. She stepped forward, towards James. "This is nothing to do with Daisy, so please don't bully her. She didn't invite me in. I invited myself because I wanted to talk to you both."

James raised the shotgun and pointed it at her. "Neither of us wants to talk to you, so you'd better go now."

Polly opened her mouth and words came out unbidden. Words she hadn't had time to think about. She said, "Do put that thing down, James, before you do someone a mischief. If you think you can threaten me with that, you'd best think again. I won't be intimidated by you."

There was a gasp from Daisy, who cowered against the wall. Polly added, "I'm going now. But you should know two things. One, I came here with the best of intentions to try and patch things up with you both. And two, if I hear that any harm has come to Daisy as a result of my visit, I shall have no alternative but to report what I have seen and heard to the police."

James raised the shotgun higher, aiming it very deliberately at her. "Get out of my house," he spat at her, "and take your evil somewhere else. You know nothing."

Polly moved towards the back door. With one foot outside she paused and turned back. “Where’s Frank?” she asked quietly. Then she went.

***

The reaction had set in by the time Polly reached home. Her face was white and she was shaking so much she could hardly get her key in the door. Ella came out to see what was going on.

“Where have you been? You look awful. What’s up?”

Polly sank into an armchair and covered her face with her hands. She kicked off her shoes, threw off her jacket, and tore the bandana from her hair, flinging it on the floor.

“I’ve been so stupid, Ella. Oh God, what have I done?”

Ella looked concerned. “What have you done?”

“I know you told me not to, but I really thought I could talk them round. I’m so worried, Ella. I’m absolutely certain Daisy is being abused. You should see her. She’s much worse than she was. And honestly, when James came in I thought he was going to shoot me. And Frank’s disappeared. Daisy wouldn’t tell me where he is and there’s no sign of him anywhere in the house. There’s real evil in that place, Ella, and I’m very much afraid I made it worse.”

“Did you talk to them?”

“I couldn’t. Daisy was in a heap, floods of tears and all that kind of stuff. James ordered me out at gunpoint, so I could hardly stay. There’s something going on, I know it. What I don’t know is how it involves me or where Frank is. I mean, if he’d just gone away, Daisy would’ve said, wouldn’t she? Ella, you don’t think James has shot him, do you?”

“Shot him? Now I know you’re crazy! Of course not. Frank’s his son. Anyway, why would he?”

Polly shrugged. “I dunno. Maybe you’re right. But suppose that robbery was an inside job like people say. Suppose James planned it all as an insurance scam and Frank happened upon him. Frank's incapable of untruth and can't stand up to questioning. If James was scared he'd come out with something incriminating, maybe he'd have to do something about Frank. And I know they're worried about Frank now they're getting older. They won't be able to cope much longer. What'll happen to Frank then? Maybe it was a sort of mercy killing."

Ella said, "Stop right there! Don't even contemplate anything like that. If any of what you've just said were to reach the wrong ears, your recent problems would be as nothing! Please, Polly. Forget the Mansfields. Just avoid James whenever you can and don't do anything to upset him."

But Polly couldn't leave it. "I have to do something, Ella. I'm so worried about Daisy. Do you think I could go to the police about that?"

"And say what? That Daisy, who hasn't a mark on her, has been abused by her well-respected, law-abiding, and upstanding husband, who's a churchwarden to boot? Who do you think the police will listen to, you or James?"

Polly sagged. "I know. Stupid of me. But there must be something I can do. How can I support Daisy without upsetting James?"

Ella said, "Why don't you speak to Henry? Tell him the whole truth about your mother. You could even tell him how she filled him with vodka without his knowledge. That would support your story. Then tell him all about this morning. After all, it might be wise to tell him before James gets to him. I can imagine what sort of a spin James would put on your visit. And you never know. Henry may have noticed something himself, over the years. I keep telling you, he's no fool. It may be that Mavis will be able to help through the Mothers' Union, if she's alerted to the problem."

Polly nodded. "Trouble is, Mavis can't stand me. I can't think she'd take anything I say seriously."

"Well," said Ella slowly, "what if I speak to her? That might work. Especially if you talk to Henry at the same time. Let's sleep on it. We'll go tomorrow."

Chapter Twenty-Five

Before Ella and Polly could approach Henry and Mavis, Polly had to make a visit in the village. She had had a telephone call to say that old Walter Mathers was in hospital and his wife was feeling fragile. Polly had no idea who Walter Mathers was, but had soon discovered when she came to rural Norfolk that Church of England clergy were responsible for everyone in the area except those who had actively opted out by joining another church or religion. But since the ethnic mix of this area of Norfolk was almost entirely white Christian and there were no other branches of the Christian church, in effect this meant that the clergy were responsible for what was quaintly called "the cure of souls" of the whole population. In practice, this boiled down to being expected to visit anyone who had any sort of need, whether or not they ever attended church and whether or not anyone had bothered to inform the clergy of the supposed need. Polly had already been taken to task more than once for failing to visit someone who was ill, even though she had no idea that they were ill nor even of who they were. It seemed as though clergy were expected to possess some sort of second sight.

Still, when Ivy Cranthorn had rung to explain about her neighbour, inviting Polly in for coffee after she had visited, Polly felt she had no option but to oblige. Anyway, she enjoyed meeting non-churchgoers. Some of the older ones, like Mrs. Mathers, were apologetic about their non-attendance, assuring Polly that they watched *Songs of Praise* every week and that they used to be in the choir as children. Polly had heard this so often that she reflected that Mundenford Church must have been packed fifty years ago, with a choir stretching out of the door.

Younger non-churchgoers tended to be much more stimulating, with definite ideas about Church and God which were often theologically illiterate but which at least opened up interesting discussions. Polly was astonished by the number of intelligent adults who still thought of God as some kind of fearsome, elderly Superman with a long white beard sitting on a throne in heaven, writing down all the bad deeds of human beings in a little black book and waiting to pounce as soon as said human beings died. Rather like a vicious Victorian schoolteacher with a swishing cane. There seemed to be little recognition of a God of love, a power for good, filling human beings with love and courage.

She thought there was excellent potential for an Alpha group with some of these younger people, but tucked the proposal away onto the back burner until Henry was more receptive of some of her ideas. She was encouraged by the fact that he had come round to the Pram Service, although even she had to admit that the new service in Kirkby Thorpe had not been entirely successful and was already proving something of a drag. She had discovered early on in Henry's illness that she was exhausted after three morning services, barely had time to draw breath before the new service, and then had to go on to Evensong afterwards. Only stubbornness had kept her going, and she was pleased the new services had dropped to alternate weeks.

Mrs. Mathers turned out to be another elderly lady needing reassurance, terrified that this might be her husband's final illness and that he might never return from hospital. As Walter had apparently done everything from odd jobs around the house to driving the car (his wife had never learned to drive) to managing the finances, Mollie Mathers was fearful of a future without him. She confided to Polly that although they had a joint account, she didn't even know how to sign a cheque. Walter did all that. Happily, by the time Polly visited, Walter was already showing signs of improvement and was expected home within the next few days.

Certain she would have been spotted visiting Mrs. Mathers, Polly called at Ivy's afterwards. As usual, Ivy was delighted to see her and ushered her into the kitchen. Polly was aware that this was a sort of inverted promotion. As an unknown quantity visiting from the church she had originally been shown into the lounge. Now that she was regarded as a trusted friend, it was the warmth and cosiness of the kitchen.

Ivy bustled about fetching mugs and the biscuit tin.

Polly sighed. "Come on, Ivy. You know I'm trying to lose a bit of weight. Don't tempt me with these delicious homemade ginger biccys. I can't resist them."

"Lord love you! You don't need to be worrying about that. I like a bit of meat on a girl. Besides," Ivy peered at her, "you look to me as though you've lost some already. Your face is quite drawn and you've large circles under your eyes. What's going on? Aren't you sleeping?"

Polly smiled wanly at her. "I'm all right, Ivy. Don't you worry about me."

But the old lady was tenacious. "Don't give me that. I know when something's amiss. Is it Henry? What's the old so-and-so been doing now? Giving you a hard time, is he?"

"No, no! It isn't Henry. In fact, he's been quite superb. No, it's not him."

"Well? Who is it then?"

Polly leaned her elbows on the table and warmed her hands around the mug of coffee. "If I tell you, will you promise hand on heart not to breathe a word to a soul?"

"Of course I will. You know me. You can tell me anything. You know that."

Polly took a sip of coffee and absently bit into a ginger biscuit. "It's James Mansfield. I have a real problem with him. I went to see Daisy and he threw me out at gunpoint."

"He what?"

"I'd carried the coffee tray back into the kitchen when he came in through the back door. He had his shotgun with him. He went ballistic—as he always does whenever he sets eyes on me—pointed the gun at me, and screamed at me to get out. So I went."

"I never liked the man, but I can hardly believe that! What did Daisy say?"

"She wasn't there to start with. She was still in the lounge where we'd been chatting. But he yelled at her for letting me in, and honestly, Ivy, I'm sure he abuses her. She was terrified. She cringes like a whipped dog. Do you think he beats her?"

Ivy said grimly, "There are more ways of abusing someone than beating them. A few experiences of James Mansfield in your face and you'd soon turn to jelly. He's a powerful man."

"Tell me about it! I was shaking like a leaf when I got home. Ella was quite worried about me."

Ivy drank some more coffee while she thought about Polly's unsettling revelation. "Why did you go there in the first place, Polly?"

"Ah! That's another story. Do you want to hear it? I suppose I might as well tell you everything now I've come this far."

Ivy remained thoughtful when Polly finished her story. Then she said, "Look, love, I've promised not to break your confidence and I won't. But I'm sure we villagers could do something to support you. Remember what I said all those months ago about the Cauliflower Club? It still holds good. We'll do something. We won't have you victimised like this. It isn't fair."

Polly got up and hugged Ivy. "You're a dear and so are all your Cauliflower Club members. But I don't want you getting into trouble on my account and I don't want anything which might make matters worse."

Ivy bristled. "Don't you trust me?"

"Of course I do! I didn't mean that. But I have to think about the benefice and Henry as well as myself. I wouldn't want anything which might split the benefice."

"And you think a few old ladies might be capable of that? You imbue us with more power than we're ever likely to possess. Leave it to me, Polly. All you need to know is that we're on your side, and that old devil won't get away with it."

***

Although Henry had been so supportive on their visit to the bishop, Polly still wasn't entirely convinced of his intentions towards her. He had been so volatile lately that she feared he might turn completely the other way if she confessed to him exactly what had happened on the night of the robbery. And she was afraid that he would regard her as a hopeless and possibly dangerous fool to have visited the Mansfields, especially as she hadn't discussed her plans with him.

Polly was still a little afraid of Henry and aware that, like the bishop, he, too, had power in his own empire. As far as church hierarchy went, she herself was at the bottom of the pile, at the mercy of those above her. She was honest enough to admit that even as a curate she held some power over her parishioners, but she had resolved long ago never to abuse that power. Having now experienced Bishop Percy in disciplinary mood and Henry's unpredictability, she was less sure that her immediate superiors would hold the same resolution.

But she had talked the whole scenario through with Ella, who was proving to be a wonderful sounding board, and had come to the reluctant conclusion that the truth, the whole truth, and nothing but the truth was her only option.

***

Polly and Ella sat side by side on the sofa in the lounge while Mavis and Henry occupied their usual armchairs. Polly was shivering with cold, as Henry refused to allow any heating during the day even in November.

"It's very nice to see you both like this," Mavis began, "but you said on the phone that you had something important you wanted to discuss with us."

"That's right," Polly said. "It's to do with the Mansfields and the robbery and the bishop and all that. I, um, I want to share with you both what happened on the night of the robbery."

Mavis said, "Yes. You had your mother with you, didn't you? We couldn't understand why you didn't just produce her as your alibi. She didn't leave until next day, did she?"

"No, but there's more to it than that. I didn't want to have to tell you this, but my mother is an alcoholic. She always has been, ever since I can remember. That's why my father took off when I was only three."

Mavis and Henry exchanged glances. "I thought you told us your father died?" Henry said.

"No, I never actually said that. But maybe I did allow you to believe it. I'm sorry—I was so ashamed of my family background, and when I first came I wanted you to think well of me."

Henry raised an eyebrow. Mavis said, "You'd better go on."

"You remember you came to see us on the day of the Mansfields' robbery, Henry? Ella and I were out shopping, and my mother made you coffee?"

"Very delicious coffee, if I remember rightly. Had a particularly distinctive flavour. Most unusual. I meant to ask you about it, but forgot."

Ella said, "It was special because Amanda had laced it with vodka. Do you remember Polly and me taking you home?"

Mavis snorted. "So that's why you slept for hours in the armchair while I did all the work." She glared at Polly. "That's disgraceful."

"I know," Polly said miserably, "and I'm really sorry. I apologise for my mother. I feel responsible for what she did. I should never have left her alone for a second. But I was so angry when I realised what had happened that I packed her off home next day. I'd warned her, you see. I told her she'd have to go if she started drinking up here. She swore to me that she was reformed, but she'll never reform, not without rehab or something like that. And she'd never go there because I don't believe she's ever really wanted to get off the drink. I couldn't take the risk any longer. I didn't want to drag the Church into disrepute so I had to get rid of her."

Henry said, "Is that why you didn't mention her to James? Because she'd make an unreliable witness?"

"Not exactly. When we got back from bringing you home, she'd disappeared. I thought she'd gone on a bender. She could be away for days at a time on one of those. I was desperate to find her before she did too much damage. So later that evening, I went out looking for her."

"You took the car into the manor drive?"

"I thought I saw her. I thought I caught a glimpse of this figure in the grounds there, so I drove up to look. But there was nobody. Then when I was coming out, I almost crashed headlong into James and Daisy returning home from here."

Henry sighed. "Why on earth didn't you tell me this sooner? I've told you before. I can't help you if I don't know what's going on."

Polly hung her head. "I didn't want you to know about my background. I thought this would be a new start for me where people would get to know me for myself, not because of my mother. It was a constant nightmare at home. I just thought maybe I could be free of all that. But it wasn't to be."

Mavis said, "This is all very interesting, Polly, but why are you telling us this now?"

Ella took over. "We need your help. Polly has been to see the Mansfields. Yes, I know," she held up her hands as Mavis opened her mouth to voice her indignation and Henry rolled his eyes, "it may not have been the most sensible course of action, but Polly went with the best of intentions. She was concerned that she'd landed you in such trouble with the bishop, Henry, and she wanted to try to put that right if she possibly could. But she's picked up on a really dodgy situation, which is why we've come to you."

Henry said to Polly, "You actually went to Thorpemunden Manor after all that's been said this past week?"

Polly kept her gaze on the carpet and bit her lip while Ella replied. "It's just as well she did. We need to tell you what's happened. First, Polly was thrown out by James Mansfield at gunpoint. He actually threatened her with his shotgun. But that's not the problem. Polly is certain that Daisy is being abused by James, and Frank has disappeared. Daisy seemed so hysterical when Polly asked after Frank that we think those two things are tied up together. We don't know what to do now. So we've come to you for advice."

Mavis wanted to dismiss the whole absurd story. "Really! I'm not sure you two together is a good thing. You seem to wind each other up. This is ridiculous. We've known the Mansfields for years. They're a very charming couple and the centre of this community. And they do a great deal for charity. This is nonsense. There's nothing the matter with Daisy Mansfield. In fact, without James she probably wouldn't survive at all. He's wonderful to her."

Ella said quietly, "I'm sure he is, in public. But Daisy does show some of the classic symptoms of abuse. And abusers are so clever, aren't they? They usually are charming people in public because the abuse is always in private."

Henry was looking thoughtful. "What are typical signs of emotional abuse, Ella? Do you know?"

"Abusers are always brilliant manipulators. In private with the abused person, who is often a wife, they constantly criticise, are continuously demanding, control every moment, are aggressive, and are often in conflict with the abused person or with others because they start arguments. Then they deny what has or hasn't been said and claim to know what's best for the abused person. They love to dominate, they're unpredictable, they belittle and trivialise the one they are abusing, causing her to lose confidence, and then call her stupid. How's that for starters? Does any of that sound like James and Daisy? You know them better than us."

Henry and Mavis exchanged glances. Still unwilling to believe that something so unpleasant was going on in their neighbourhood, Mavis asked, "How do you know so much about it, Ella?"

Ella said simply, "I've had experience. My mother had a number of partners and I watched her disintegrate under one in particular. I couldn't understand what was going on, so I made it my business to find out. Now I'm quite tuned in to emotional abuse. I haven't seen much of Daisy and almost nothing of James, but what I have seen has certainly pricked my antennae, and Polly's recent experiences have confirmed it for me."

"You think James is trying to abuse Polly as well as Daisy?"

"Yes, Henry, I do. It seems that all Polly's difficulties here in Thorpemunden have James at the root. And as I've said, abusers are masters of fabrication and denial while being eminently plausible. It sounds as though he has a real problem with women and can't cope with any woman in a position of authority. Especially one at his back door, so to speak."

Polly snorted, "Authority! That's a good one. Curates have next to nothing in the way of authority."

The others ignored her. Mavis said, "It's true that James always drives Daisy to MU and picks her up afterwards. But I don't think Daisy drives. And she is very timid and a little bit stupid at MU. Gets very upset if anyone disagrees with her. Always back pedals and apologises and yes, is easy to manipulate. Nobody takes any notice of her opinions because she's like a chameleon. Changes opinion to agree with whoever's talking."

Polly brought the conversation back to a practical level. "What can we do? I can't go round again, he'd probably shoot me for real. But if you ask him about that incident, Henry, I bet he'd deny it."

A thought occurred to Henry. He got up and began to pace restlessly. "What about Frank? Didn't you say something about Frank as well?"

"There was no sign of him, and Daisy got hysterical when I mentioned him. Then James came in with his shotgun and, well, I don't want to put two and two together and make five."

"You certainly don't. Let's agree for the moment that we don't know where Frank is. Polly, this is just between the four of us. You haven't told anyone else, have you?" Then as he saw Polly's face, he groaned, "Oh no! Come on, out with it. How many other people know about this?"

Polly said hurriedly, "Not many. And I only said what had happened. Well, actually I might have suggested that James was abusing Daisy… But Ivy won't tell anyone. She's very tight-lipped. We can rely on her."

"Not Ivy Cranthorn? Polly, are you sure you know her as well as you think?"

Polly paled. "What do you mean? She's lovely. She's always supported me and she gets other people on side, too."

Henry sighed. "You mean that ridiculous so-called Cauliflower Club, of course. What exactly did you tell her?"

"I had to tell someone," Polly said defensively. "I'd just been threatened with a shotgun, after all. Ivy rang me and asked to visit her neighbour, then invited me in for coffee afterwards."

"And you didn't spot that as manipulative?"

Polly's eyes widened. "Of course not! It wasn't like that. I often have coffee with Ivy. She's always been great."

"But not averse to a little gossip," Mavis added.

"It never seemed to matter. I mean, it was harmless, wasn't it? There's never anything malicious about Ivy, so I thought—"

"Here we go again," Henry sighed. "Polly, she may be a lovely old lady, but even lovely old ladies can be dangerous. One of the biggest problems in rural places like this, where there's not a lot to do and everyone knows everyone else's business, is gossip. You really are going to have to learn to keep anything you hear to yourself. Now, what did you tell her?"

Polly said miserably, “Everything. I poured it all out, she was so kind and understanding. And she said, ‘Leave it with me. We’ll support you. That old devil will never get away with it.’”

Chapter Twenty-Six

Henry was vexed. It was difficult to get his mind around the situation Polly had described, especially with Ella sitting there looking, Henry thought, absolutely gorgeous.

Today she was wearing the usual dark blue jeans with an embroidered pattern up the outside of the leg and a creamy polo neck sweater covered by the maroon vest which fastened under the bust with a couple of small buttons. The outfit showed her figure off to perfection while highlighting her shining hair and her olive complexion. With a discreet touch of makeup enhancing her dark brown, almond-shaped eyes and her full lips, Ella was a picture to behold. Henry was unable to help feasting his eyes upon her.

But it was more than simply looks. While she had been living at the rectory, Henry had come to appreciate her keen mind, which had been most obvious during their chess games and their walks, when she would ask searching questions about Christianity. Now, with her calm analysis of the symptoms of abuse coupled with her explanation for exploring the issue, Henry was impressed by a maturity beyond her years and her ability to accurately assess an awkward situation.

He turned to her. "What do you think, Ella? What should we do?"

There was a faintly derisive "Harrumph!" from Mavis, which Henry ignored, keeping his back to her.

Ella said, "Perhaps Mavis could discover what Ivy is about at the next MU meeting. I'm sure Mavis will be able to pick up any undercurrents as to what's going on, won't you, Mavis?"

Mavis was gratified. "I probably do know the ladies better than most since we've met every month for years now. I certainly don't think Henry should get too involved at this stage. After all, he hasn't long been back at work. We don't want a relapse. And I do wish you'd sit down, Henry. All this pacing isn't getting us anywhere."

Henry made an irritated "Tch!" and glared at his wife, but sat down anyway. He said, "Well, that's it, then. We'll rely on Mavis to find out as much information as she can before we do anything further. But this must be on one condition."

The three women looked at him enquiringly.

"None of us is to mention anything else about our suspicions or the episodes that have prompted them. Polly, are you listening? You must not go near Thorpemunden Manor again, and I strongly advise you to make absolutely sure you do not under any circumstances meet with James or Daisy Mansfield on your own. Do I make myself clear?"

Polly nodded. "Yes, Henry."

"We'll leave it there, then, for now. None of us will speak of this again until we have more information. But I do beg all of you to hold all three of the Mansfields in your prayers. If Ella and Polly are right, they need a great deal of help."

The meeting broke up with everyone feeling a little better about the situation and Mavis determined to show them what she could do.

***

Now that Mavis had resumed her duties as Henry's secretary, her life was busy, leaving her little time to spare to mull over how she might obtain undercurrents of information from her MU members. So she put all those considerations to one side while she concentrated on clearing the backlog of communications. Having flipped through the day's mail, she logged on to sort out the daily dose of spam from genuine emails but was interrupted by a call from the local funeral directors, asking for Henry to bury some ashes in Beesthorpe Churchyard the following Thursday. After checking through Henry's diary, she called down to him.

"Henry! Can you bury some ashes at Beesthorpe on Thursday week at three-thirty?"

"Mm," responded Henry, who was reading the paper.

"Sure? Shall I say yes, then?"

"Mm," Henry repeated, engrossed in an article about how to manage your finances without resorting to credit. Henry did possess a credit card but rarely used it, preferring the feel of cash in his wallet. Having grown up just after the war in an age when the "never-never" was considered, at least by Henry's parents, to be a dirty word, he was constantly amazed at the debts people incurred.

He found his mind straying towards Ella. If only he and Mavis could put her through university. What an asset she would be in any walk of life, and what a waste it was to have her merely marking time, working in a bar. Henry wondered how he could manage to assist Ella with the necessary fees, rolling round in his mind ideas as bizarre as a gift (Mavis would never countenance that), offering a loan, or somehow employing Ella in a more worthwhile job. He was tempted to suggest that Ella become his new secretary, paid for by the parishes, but feared not only downright mutiny from Mavis but also a backlash from the benefice, who had never yet paid a penny towards Mavis' expenses.

Henry donned his anorak. "Just going out, dear," he called up the stairs, not waiting for a reply.

He drove to Mundenford with his mind still full of plans for Ella, plans he was determined to talk through with her.

He rang Polly's doorbell, but was a trifle disappointed when Polly herself opened the door. Still, perhaps it was for the best. Henry wasn't sure that he could entirely trust himself alone with

Ella and had retained sufficient vestiges of common sense to realise that any sudden move on his part might frighten and horrify the girl.

At least Ella was home. Polly disappeared to put on the ubiquitous kettle, and Henry settled himself in the armchair.

He started without any preamble. "Ella, I've been thinking. It seems so wrong that you're stuck here with a part-time job that can only bring in pocket money for you. I—that is, Mavis and I—would dearly love to assist you in some way in getting back into university. Perhaps I could start a trust fund for you? Or give you an interest-free loan to be paid back over fifty years?"

Ella's eyes widened and Polly's ears (she was listening from the kitchen) nearly popped. Polly hurried back in as quickly as she could with the tray of tea.

"Henry! That's fantastic! Isn't it, Ella? What a fabulous offer!"

But Ella seemed more anxious. She said carefully, "Why would you do that, Henry? You've been wonderful to me, offering me a home and then seeing me settled here with Polly. You've already gone the second mile. Why would you feel you need to do any more?"

Henry clasped his hands together. He was on a mission. "Ella, you're wasted in the Rose and Crown. You have such talent. I—we—merely wish to see such gifts put to good use, honed and strengthened and made ready for service."

Ella shook her head. She said gently, "It's a wonderful offer, Henry, but I can't accept. Besides, I'm not sure that I'm quite ready to leave here, yet. I have been thinking about another course of study, but I may study online from home with the Open University or do a part-time course at the University of East Anglia or something. I'm still thinking."

"But I could help you! I could fund you, at least for the first year. Do let me help you. Please."

Polly looked from one to the other, aware that something was going on below the surface but unsure what.

"Take him up on it, Ella," she urged. "You know you want to get back to some form of study. Don't look a gift horse in the mouth. You'll never get another offer like this!"

But Ella said quite sharply, "Stop it, Polly. I won't be pushed."

Polly blinked, hurt by her friend's retort. She couldn't understand Ella's reaction, either to herself or to Henry. After all, Henry only had himself and Mavis to support and no Council tax or water rates to pay. Why, if even Polly could afford to live on a curate's salary under those terms, he couldn't be short of a few quid. Why couldn't Ella accept this generous offer in the spirit in which it was meant?

Ella said more gently, "I do appreciate your offer, Henry. But just at the moment I'm enjoying the Rose and Crown. Pubs are good places to be, you know. They're full of people and you get to see human life in there."

Henry frowned. "But you could do so much better."

"You surprise me, Henry," Ella said. "Wasn't your Jesus a carpenter? That's not much of a job either, but he seemed to do okay. He met lots of people, too, and learned a lot about what it is to be human. Maybe I'm learning the same."

***

Henry paid a visit to Pauline Carter on the way home. Not because he particularly wanted to, but as a way of justifying his journey to see Ella. Partly, too, because Pauline lived in Mundenford, so it wasn't out of his way and partly because she was in the MU and he didn't want any gossip to surface about his frequent visits to his curate's house, which he was certain would have been noted.

He was confused by Ella, who seemed to have a knack of putting him at a disadvantage and making him think much more deeply about his own motives than he cared to do. He wondered whether he was a snob. He was pretty sure Mavis was, but had never before included himself in the same category. He had not previously questioned the value of a university background against any other form of life, but Ella's words made him think. Obviously she was right in that Jesus had never gone to university or its equivalent in the first century, but how could part-time work behind a bar possibly be considered in the same league as a university education? Could she be right, in that as a training ground for dealing with people the pub was infinitely preferable to the hallowed halls of a university?

Pauline Carter was delighted to see him. Henry was known for calling in on all his church members from time to time for no particular reason, so she was not unduly fazed by his visit. They chatted about life in general terms, bemoaning global warming and the credit crunch and shaking their heads over those who might soon find themselves without work. Then Pauline suddenly said, "How's Polly these days?"

"All right, I think," Henry said, surprised. "As a matter of fact, I've just come from there. She seemed fine to me. Why do you ask?"

"She did so well in your absence, you know. I didn't know whether you knew that. People take so much for granted, don't they? I just wanted you to know how hard she worked. Everyone was delighted with her. Well, almost everyone."

"Oh?"

Pauline leaned towards him and lowered her voice to a conspiratorial whisper. "There's always one or two. But if anything should be said to the contrary, I just want to put the record straight. We all like Polly. She's such an asset to our parishes, and we love having her live in our village. It makes us feel quite important."

"I'll bear that in mind," Henry said gravely. "If anything should be said, I mean. Thank you for your words, Pauline. I'll tell Polly. I know she'll be pleased."

And he went home wondering whether he had inadvertently stumbled upon Ivy Cranthorn's master plan.

***

Henry mentioned Pauline Carter's remarks to Mavis when he got home. She was not best pleased, immediately feeling usurped in her assignment.

"Why did you go there, anyway?" she grumbled.

Not the most subtle under any conditions, Henry was unable to contain his feelings. "I went to see dear Ella."

"What for? She was here only yesterday. Can't you live without her? Is that it?"

Henry failed to pick up on the sarcasm in his wife's tone. He said, "I don't know that I can, now you come to mention it. She is a most gorgeous creature, isn't she? But she's so intelligent, too, and sensitive with it. I went to see if we could help her in any way. Get her back to university where she belongs."

"You did what?"

"Went to see if we could pay her university fees. Help her on her way."

Mavis exploded. "Without asking me? Without discussing it at all? I'm your wife, Henry. How dare you give away my money!"

Henry was surprised. "What's the matter? I thought you'd be pleased. I said it was from you as well, not just me. I didn't leave you out."

"That's hardly the point! Surely I get some say before you give away our money! Suppose I want to give it elsewhere? Ella's not exactly our charity, is she? I don't know what's the matter with you, Henry. You seem to have lost all reason."

Henry retorted, "I don't know what you're getting so upset about. Anyway, she refused. Why can't we help her? We've got plenty of money and no one to leave it to. Why can't we give Ella a helping hand when she needs it?"

Mavis clenched her fists. Although she had a sharp tongue at times, she rarely lost her temper. But now she turned bright red and shouted at Henry, "Because, you fool, it gives a certain message. No wonder she refused! She probably thought you wanted payment in kind, or something equally revolting."

Henry glared. "Mavis, that's disgusting. You're overwrought. I never thought I'd hear my wife talking like that. If that's all you have to say, I think you'd do better to keep your words to yourself."

And Henry stalked into his study, slamming the door.

***

Mavis simmered. Her anxiety levels over Henry were increasing again. Just as he had begun to seem almost as though he had returned completely to normal, he had to go and do this. Perhaps Polly's most recent revelations had been more stressful on Henry than they had appeared. But Mavis was also furious at being sidelined in such a cavalier fashion and hurt that Henry took her so much for granted. She counted up the ways in which she looked after him; cooking, cleaning, washing and ironing, shopping, coping with all the birthday and Christmas cards and presents, acting as his unpaid secretary, being his friend, supporter, and protector, and when unavoidable, his lover. Mavis felt undervalued and unlovely.

As she always did when feeling under the weather, which usually meant not any physical illness but being generally fed up, Mavis decided to tackle some housework. When it was impossible to get out in the garden, she always found housework provided a necessary solace. Mavis had no patience with those females who mooned about the house feeling sorry for themselves, when a good dose of housework would probably solve all their blues.

But today she was feeling more than fed up. She was angry, too. Accordingly she fetched out the Hoover, making as much noise as she could and deliberately vacuuming near Henry's closed study door, knowing how he hated the noise. She also began to sing at the top of her voice and was gifted enough to be able to sing slightly off-key.

Her antics produced an effect, although not necessarily the desired one. Henry slammed out of his study and out of the front door, going she knew not where.

Mavis was instantly deflated and sat on the bottom step of the stairs with her head in her hands. But she didn't stay there long. She had a strongly logical streak and soon began to work out a fight-back strategy. If Henry thought he could simply pick up on someone younger after thirty-five years of marriage, he would soon learn his mistake.

Unable to leave any job in the middle, Mavis finished the Hoovering and the dusting, then put through a call to her hairdresser. To the hairdresser's astonishment, since Mavis only ever had a trim, she made an appointment for a whole head colour with highlights, a trim, and set. Then Mavis, too, gathered her bags and left the house, determined to try this thing everyone these days seemed to call "retail therapy."

***

The Winstones settled back into their usual routine within a couple of days. They never spoke about the row again, just carried on as though it hadn't happened. Henry continued to visit Ella at every opportunity while Mavis continued to look after him in every possible way.

Henry was out on the day that Mavis visited the hairdresser. She had made an early appointment, which was just as well since she was there all morning. She had expected to be restless and bored during this waste of time, but found herself actually enjoying the relaxation and pampering she received. She even read a trashy magazine while she was waiting for the colour to take, and found herself quite caught up in the goings-on of various celebrities.

With her fading brown hair cut in a simple style which she could wash and run through with a comb, Mavis had never before bothered with her coiffure. As the hairdresser applied the finishing touches, Mavis regarded her reflection in the mirror with some dread. What would she look like? Would she look completely ridiculous? And more to the point, what would Henry say?

In fact, Mavis marvelled at the change wrought in her by a few hours in a hairdressing salon. The hairdresser had chosen a rich brown background colour, close to Mavis' natural colour many years before, and had picked out highlights in three shades of blond and auburn. She had styled the hair so that basically it retained its straight style, thus showing off the highlights, but somehow softly framed her face. The effect was stunning. Mavis looked ten years younger.

She walked out of the hairdressers with a new spring in her step and caught the bus into Norwich, where she spent the afternoon in one of the big stores, enjoying a makeover. Finally, she caught the bus home tired but exhilarated by her day.

As Henry was still out on her return, Mavis dressed carefully in the new clothes she had bought on the day of the row. She had selected a mid-calf-length, lined skirt in a rich brown colour, which matched her new hair, and a pair of three-inch heels in shiny brown leather. This she had teamed with a pink cardigan top gathered under the bust in Ella's favourite style, but with a pink and white striped inset. The white was picked out in a thin strip along the lower end of the cardigan and the cuffs. When she surveyed herself in the long mirror, Mavis was thrilled with the result. And for once, she was not going to cook. Having ascertained that Henry's appointment diary was empty, she had booked a table in a small but expensive restaurant in Diss.

***

Henry sauntered in at around five-thirty as he usually did, in time for his high tea. As they usually ate at lunchtimes, Mavis had deliberately provided a cheese salad with a jacket potato at midday today so that they would both have room for a substantial meal this evening.

Mavis had applied a little perfume and came forward to kiss Henry on the cheek. "Hello, darling. How was your day?"

Henry returned the kiss with a peck of his own and shrugged out of his anorak. “Fine, thank you.” He stretched. “I’m whacked. Thank goodness I don’t have to go out tonight. We can have an early night.”

Mavis said, “Well, I have a surprise for you, Henry.”

He looked at her for the first time. She smiled, waiting for his comments, which she was sure would be appreciative, before telling him about the dinner reservation.

Henry waited too. Then he said, “What surprise? Aren’t you going to tell me?”

Mavis spread out her arms and did a twirl. “Well? What do you think?”

Henry frowned. “What about? I don’t know what you’re talking about.”

Mavis said, “Henry, surely even you can’t fail to notice that I look a little different.”

“Do you?” Henry looked at her properly, struggling to see what had changed. “Oh! Have you bought a new jumper? Very nice, dear.”

Mavis’ shoulders sagged. “Look at me, Henry. Really look at me. I’ve had my hair done; it’s totally different. My face is made up and I have a complete new outfit. And we’re going out for dinner tonight like normal people do. I’ve booked a table at that little place in Diss, the one with the good reputation that everyone raves about.”

“Oh!” Henry said. “Yes, very nice, dear. Well, if you’ve booked it I suppose we’ll have to go. But I was looking forward to a night in for once. I wish you’d discussed it with me first.”

“Like you discussed your plans for Ella with me?” Mavis shot back, deeply disappointed in her husband’s lack of any sort of reaction. “You’d better go and change,” she added. “We’re going out whether you like it or not.”

“And a fine evening we’ll have, too, by the sounds of it,” Henry retorted, bitterly.

Chapter Twenty-Seven

The dinner was not a success. Henry was there under duress and (he felt) a certain degree of deception since it had been arranged without his knowledge. He was therefore uncommunicative and surly. Mavis was in despair at his dismissal of her efforts both in her personal appearance and in regard to the dinner she had so carefully and thoughtfully arranged. Feeling belittled by Henry's evident lack of interest in anything she did or thought, she lost confidence in her new look and determined to revert to the old Mavis at the earliest opportunity.

At least the food was good and the service excellent. And by the time Mavis had plied Henry with several glasses of good quality red wine, he had mellowed a little. But the bill at the end of the evening was a shock, and when Henry fell asleep in the car on the way home, Mavis considered the whole venture a waste of time and money.

Henry woke with a headache next day, which didn't improve his temper. He was aware that he had been both unkind and unfair to Mavis, but strangely, found this made him even more angry with her. All he could think about was Ella. It did occur to him that perhaps his mind was focussing on Ella so that he wouldn't have to think too deeply about the Mansfield problem, but he tossed the thought aside, preferring to live in a kind of daydream world in which he and Ella were alone together.

Henry knew he was in love, perhaps for the first time ever. He had suspected it when Ella was living at the rectory, but when Ella moved out to share with Polly, Henry had hoped such an inappropriate feeling would pass. For a time he had been content to call on Ella from time to time and to chat with her in company with Polly. But ever susceptible to an enquiring mind, Ella's wisdom over the Mansfield episode had reawakened Henry's desires and left him breathless with longing.

Henry regarded Mavis' attempts to woo him with contempt. He wondered whether she was trying to compete with Ella, but if so, he couldn't understand why. After all, Mavis and he belonged together. They looked after each other and had been content to rub along together for thirty-five years. Nothing would change that. But that didn't mean that he had any romantic feelings towards Mavis. He wasn't sure whether he had ever had any, even when he married her. She had been there and eligible for an up and coming young curate and they had got along well together. And after they were married she had become an excellent vicar's wife. He had no complaints on that score. But that was her job, surely. This attempt to make herself look different—well, in Henry's view it was pathetic. He could hardly see the difference except that her hair had miraculously darkened apart from those ridiculous streaks in it. And this was a woman in late middle age. Why try to make herself trendy? It would never suit her and it quite upset Henry. He felt the balance of their lives subtly altering and he didn't like it. He wanted Mavis exactly the way she had always been, like an old but comfortable glove, perfectly fitting his needs. And he wanted Ella for those new romantic feelings which were threatening to swamp him but which were filling his mundane life with excitement. Mavis would never be able to do that for him.

Henry wondered where his Christianity lay in all of this. He didn't consider himself a sinner—at least, no more than he had always been, which was just the usual run of being human—since he had done nothing wrong. He didn't consider anyone could be held responsible for their own feelings, since feelings simply occurred. In Henry's view it was what you did with those feelings that might constitute sin. And he had done nothing wrong, so carried no guilt.

But he was continuing to question his faith. For the first time he wondered how Christianity could possibly pronounce upon affairs of the heart since a celibate leader presumably had not been subject to sexual temptation. Unless the stories about Mary Magdalene and Jesus being lovers were true, which Henry doubted. That led him to thinking more about Jesus. He found himself wondering what use it was to follow a celibate man-God, because such a concept was so far removed from virtually all human experience that it almost negated the humanness of Jesus.

None of these were familiar thoughts for Henry, who was more at home reading learned theological treatises than applying popular theology to his own life. He was uncomfortable with his new thoughts and again began to wonder who he really was. Had he ever really known himself? Or had he accepted a second-hand religion which suited him perfectly but which never really touched the centre of his being?

Without bothering to inform Mavis, Henry donned his anorak and set out for a brisk walk, hoping that the cold air might clear his head. Inevitably the walk took him in the direction of Mundenford and just as inevitably he called in at Polly's for a rest and a drink.

As soon as he stepped through the door, Henry felt more relaxed. It was as though he could be himself here. Unlike Mavis, neither Polly nor Ella seemed to expect anything of him. They merely accepted him and even seemed pleased to see him.

***

Mavis had been in the garden clearing leaves when Henry left. She had heard the slam of the front door, which told her Henry had gone out, but had settled back to enjoy her autumn clean-up in the garden. There wasn't a lot she could do at this time of year, but it was eminently satisfying to collect large heaps of leaves into a huge mound on the rough patch down at the end of the garden, ready for a fire. Mavis enjoyed the occasional bonfire, especially as there were no neighbours near enough to worry about washing on the line.

It was three o'clock before Mavis moved back indoors and took herself off to the shower. Normally preferring to relax in a proper bath, when it was the middle of the day Mavis was quite strict with herself and took a shower to minimise the time she was out of action. She washed her hair, hoping she might have washed out some of the dye, and dressed in clean clothes. However much she enjoyed a bonfire, she was not keen on the smell of wood smoke pervading all her garments.

She was just settling down to a cup of tea and Classic FM on the radio when the phone rang.

"Good afternoon. Thorpemunden rectory. Can I help you?"

A man's voice said, "May I speak to Canon Winstone, please?"

"I'm sorry, he's out at the moment. Can I take a message?"

There was a pause on the other end of the line. Then the voice said, "This is Albert Drysdale of Drysdale and Sons, Funeral Directors. We had arranged for Canon Winstone to bury some ashes this afternoon at three-thirty at Beesthorpe Churchyard. Perhaps he's on his way here?"

Mavis didn't know, but very much doubted it. She had no idea where Henry was, although she could hazard an educated guess. She glanced out of the window and saw that the car was still in the drive, so Henry was evidently on foot. That meant he couldn't possibly have gone to Beesthorpe, and it would take him ages to return home, change, and drive there. Mavis didn't know what to do.

"I'm awfully sorry. I think this may have slipped his memory. I do remember your call, but Henry hasn't been too well lately. I'm so sorry. I'm afraid this may be an example of a senior moment."

"What are we to do, then? The family are all here waiting and the hole is dug. We're all ready."

Mavis said, "I'll try and reach him and get him to ring you. Can you give me your mobile number?"

She wrote the number down and immediately rang Polly.

"Polly, it's Mavis. Is Henry with you?"

"He was," Polly said, "but he's just gone. Can I help at all?"

"I rather think you're going to have to. Henry is supposed to be burying ashes at Beesthorpe right now. He's clearly forgotten. I don't know what's the matter with him these days. Could you go, Polly? You have buried ashes before? It's only a two-minute job, as you know. Could you make it? I'll ring Albert Drysdale and tell him to expect you in fifteen minutes, shall I?"

Mavis was perturbed by this latest example of Henry's state of mind. He was now in his sixties, where occasional lapses of memory were perhaps to be expected, but nothing like this had ever happened before. She thought of that grieving family, standing shivering by the grave in the cold November air, waiting for a priest to appear, and she felt ashamed.

Not one given to impulse, Mavis nonetheless picked up the phone and rang Peter Lambert. She got through to the receptionist. "I wish to make an appointment to see Dr. Lambert."

"Yes, madam. May I ask what the problem is?"

"No, you may not. It's private and confidential," Mavis retorted.

A sliver of ice crept into the receptionist's voice. "In that case, madam, may I ask whether the problem is urgent?"

"I wouldn't be ringing the doctor for anything I didn't consider urgent. So yes. I need an appointment as soon as possible."

"Your name, madam?"

There was an audible grunt as Mavis gave her name. She wondered whether she should complain about the receptionist's unhelpful attitude when she saw Peter. But the receptionist said, "I could try him on the phone, if you like. His last patient has just gone."

"Do that," Mavis replied.

***

"Now, Mavis, what seems to be the trouble?" Peter Lambert leaned back in his chair and scratched his goatee with the tip of his pen, wishing he wasn't having this conversation.

Mavis liked the doctor. She confided, "It isn't me, Peter, it's Henry. I'm so worried about him."

Peter's face lengthened and a frown appeared. He sighed. "Mavis, you know I can't discuss my patients with anyone. I can't discuss Henry with you. I'm sorry."

"Hear me out, Peter, please. You don't have to tell me anything. But I can talk to you, surely? What if I describe Henry as he is at the moment and leave you with that extra knowledge? That's not breaching confidentiality, is it?"

Peter shifted the receiver to the other ear and began to doodle on his notepad. "I suppose not. But I can't comment. You do realise that?"

"But if I then persuade Henry to visit you, you'd have a much better picture of him, wouldn't you? You know what he's like. He'll tell you what he thinks you want to hear. But I really am concerned."

Peter sighed, seeing his early night fleeing into the distance. "You'd better fire away, then."

***

By the time Polly had robed and driven to Beesthorpe at breakneck speed along winding country lanes, the family group had been waiting for half an hour. They were huddled in their two cars looking decidedly grim.

Albert Drysdale was in his car, too, but keeping an eye on the wing mirror. He got out as Polly screeched to a halt behind him.

"Reverend Hewitt. Good of you to come. You didn't find Canon Winstone?"

"I'm afraid not, Albert. But he took the funeral, so I know nothing about this family, not even the name of the deceased. Can you fill me in?"

Albert handed her a form with the details of the dead man and which had to be kept with the ashes.

Polly scanned it quickly. "Okay, thanks. Now, who am I meeting?"

"Come on. I'll introduce you."

Polly clasped the hand of the deceased man's widow and gazed soulfully into her eyes. "I'm so sorry! I don't know if Albert said, but Canon Winstone has been ill. He's only just back to work. He'll be so upset that he's missed being here."

The woman's son was in his mid-thirties, with a black-clad, short-skirted, high-heeled wife clinging to his arm. He had wrenched off his black tie and was stuffing it in his pocket.

Before his mother had a chance to respond, he butted in with, "He'll be upset before we've finished with him! It's disgusting. My poor mother here has been frantic, dreading this day. Do you realise that she's about to bury the remains of her husband of sixty-five years?"

At this, his mother burst into loud sobs. A daughter pushed through to put her arm around her mother, glaring at Polly.

Polly glanced round at the group of eight family members, all of whom were glowering at her with varying degrees of hostility. She moistened her lips and spoke to all of them.

"As I say, I do apologise most sincerely. None of us would have wanted this to happen. I'm sure there will be a rational explanation."

"Yes," interrupted the belligerent son, who appeared to be spokesman for the family, "he forgot. We aren't important enough for the likes of him. He don't care about our dad. Well, we'll see about that. I'm not letting it rest here, so you needn't think you can smooth things over with a few poncy words."

Polly could feel her stomach churning. "I can only repeat my apologies. I am extremely sorry. Would you like to start the service now?"

As they began to move into the graveyard the belligerent son shot over his shoulder, "Don't think you're gonna get away with this. We'll take you to court."

His mother held his arm. "Oh John! It's not this lady's fault. Come on. We need to get your dad properly buried."

Polly took the short service around the small grave in a daze. Without any time to prepare, she had no option but to read through the service exactly as it was set out in the book. It was all over in five minutes.

The family piled back into their cars still shooting angry and hostile glances in Polly's direction. She loitered with Albert Drysdale, hoping for a word of comfort as he filled in the hole, replaced the square of turf, and stamped it down.

Albert obliged. "Don't you worry, Reverend. They'll calm down. You know what it's like when people are bereaved. They find any excuse for their anger. Wasn't your fault. You did your best."

And Polly left, musing to herself that they'd probably inscribe, "She did her best" on her tombstone. She couldn't imagine a greater indictment.

As Polly arrived home and clambered out of her car, a lone figure suddenly appeared from behind next door's hedge. Before Polly knew what was happening a bulb had flashed in her face and a reporter was barring her way, notebook at the ready.

"Reverend Hewitt, we understand you've just buried the ashes of," the reporter consulted her notebook, "James Ernest Bradshaw, whose funeral was a week ago in Beesthorpe Church?"

Polly was too bemused to do other than nod.

"Reverend Hewitt, how do you feel about having to bail out Canon Winstone? Does this happen often? Do you think Canon Winstone is losing his touch? What did you say to the family when Canon Winstone forgot to attend?"

Polly was caught off balance. She pushed past the reporter with a curt, "No comment," entered her house at speed, and slammed the door.

***

At least Henry had the grace to ring Polly later that night and apologise for his oversight.

She said, "Have you contacted the family? Only they were a bit annoyed, I'm afraid. I did my best. I grovelled as much as I could, but it didn't seem to placate them."

Henry dithered. "I don't know whether to ring or not, then. It's late now. Might only make matters worse."

Polly was about to warn him that the family had gone to the press, when he put the phone down. She shrugged. Wasn't her row for once, although needless to say, she was caught up in it.

"Trouble follows me around whatever I do," she moaned to Ella. "Even when I rush over like a mad thing to help someone out, I still land myself in it."

But she was much more concerned on the Saturday, when the free, weekly paper was delivered. Since it was full of adverts, Polly rarely bothered to read the paper even when it was thrust through her letter box. But today, the headlines on the front page screamed at her. And worse, her photo, looking (she thought) quite shifty, peered back at her.

Polly began to read:

> GRIEVING FAMILY DESERTED IN GRAVEYARD
> The family of James Ernest Bradshaw, who died very suddenly at home in Beesthorpe a month ago, have had their grief compounded by the failure of Canon Henry Winstone to bury the ashes. "Waiting in the graveyard for forty-five minutes for someone from the church to show up makes everything ten times worse," said John Bradshaw, the deceased's eldest son. "My mum was shivering with the cold,

> and the stress has made her ill. It was bad enough having to wait weeks for the coroner's report before we could have Dad's funeral. We were looking for a bit of closure. We didn't expect to be treated like this by people whose job it is to care. Canon Winstone should be sacked. This is unacceptable behaviour."
>
> The burial of ashes was eventually performed by the curate, the Reverend Polly Hewitt, pictured. John Bradshaw said, "The service was a mockery. We waited all that time and she was through the service in three minutes. It was as though she didn't care, she just wanted to get it over and done with."
>
> Reverend Hewitt refused to comment. Mr. Bradshaw added that he was going to take the matter further, complaining to the highest authority. "It's only fair," Mr. Bradshaw explained. "We have to prevent this terrible occurrence happening to anyone else. Funerals are stressful enough, without all this. We don't want anyone else to suffer like we have."
>
> The *Diss Tribune* wonders how often something like this happens? If you have any experiences where the Church has let you down, we want to know. Ring 01349 953010 ext.10, or email newsdesk@disstribune.co.uk.

Polly threw down the paper in disgust, wondering why misfortunes in the Church made such headline news. It was strange, she thought, that so few attended church, yet a mistake like this was considered by the press to make such avid reading that it sold papers.

Before she had time to show Ella the paper, there was a tap at the back door. A voice called, "It's only me. Can I come in?"

"Yes, come on in, Ivy," Polly called back, wearily. She didn't want to discuss the damaging article with anyone, but Ivy Cranthorn had a copy of the *Diss Tribune* tucked beneath her arm.

"Oh!" she said in some disappointment as she saw the open copy on Polly's floor. "You've seen it."

"Yes, unfortunately. They've made a meal out of it. It wasn't nearly as bad as the article makes out. That obnoxious son was out to make trouble any way he could. And I don't suppose he'll leave it there."

"Probably looking for compensation," Ivy contributed.

"Well, he won't get much from the Church! Don't people realise the Church has no money at all?"

"Doesn't matter. People's conception of the Church of England is that it's rolling in money. All its investments and its land. And most people think the government pays for the Church anyway, since it's a state church."

Polly groaned. "More trouble. Just when I was hoping we might have seen the back of it. Do you know this guy? Will he take it further, do you think?"

Ivy shook her head. "I don't know him personally, but Beesthorpe's a tiny village. There's only around four hundred. I'll ask Jane Mattock or Joan Rudd. They both live in Beesthorpe and they're in the Mothers' Union. They'll know."

Polly said, "Thanks, Ivy. Look, I've got to go now, but you'll let me know?" Not, she added to herself, that there was a thing she could do about it, but perhaps it was better to be forewarned.

Chapter Twenty-Eight

When the *Diss Tribune* landed on Henry's mat, he read it with increasing fury.

"Look at this rubbish," he snarled to Mavis in tones of disgust, flinging the paper onto the kitchen table. She picked it up and scanned the headline.

"Now you can see what happens when you don't concentrate on the job at hand."

Henry grumbled, "You might have told me. I thought that was your job, to tell me of appointments. You are my secretary, after all. If you're not up to it, perhaps I should find myself another secretary."

Mavis glared at him. "My fault? You're making this my fault? I did tell you. I distinctly remember asking you when the call came through. You said it was fine to book it."

"You certainly did not! I had never heard of this burial of ashes before Thursday evening when I got home. I didn't forget to turn up. You forgot to tell me."

"That's not true, Henry. I did tell you but obviously you've forgotten. That's the trouble with you these days. You don't have your mind on the job. Anyway, where were you on Thursday afternoon? I couldn't get in touch with you. Perhaps now you can see the importance of taking your mobile phone with you or letting me know where you'll be."

Henry snapped, "That's none of your business. You're not

my keeper. Anyway, even if you did mention it, you didn't remind me. How am I supposed to do my job if my secretary fails to remind me of important appointments?"

Mavis stood arms akimbo, eyes blazing. All the hurt and anger of the past few months came boiling to the surface. "That's just typical of you! Blame someone else! It's never you, is it? Always someone else's fault. Who's looked after you all these years, I'd like to know? Who's washed and cleaned for you, shopped and cooked for you and made your life comfortable? And what have I ever got out of it? Blame whenever anything goes wrong. Call yourself a man? You never even managed to give me a baby! Well, I've had enough, Henry. You can just apologise right now and, for once, admit you were in the wrong."

Henry's face twisted into something approaching ugliness. "Don't blame me because you're childless. I would have adopted long ago, but you wouldn't have it. 'I'm not looking after other people's children. Trouble always comes of it,' I seem to remember you saying on more than one occasion. As if trouble is genetic! Just the sort of old-fashioned and misinformed attitude I've come to expect from you.

"And if we're swapping tit for tat, who's provided a home for you all these years? Who's made you the centre of village life? Because without me, you'd be nothing. Look at you. Face it, Mavis, you're old and frumpy and bitter. You live your life through me, you've never had any life of your own. And without me, as Rector of Thorpemunden, you'd be a friendless nobody."

Mavis blanched. She clutched a kitchen chair and sat down heavily as her legs gave way. She involuntarily smoothed her hair with a trembling hand. She couldn't believe what she'd just heard.

With eyes full of fury and hurt, she fired back. "Why don't you clear off, then? Afraid your precious Church might throw you out? Divorce among the clergy isn't exactly popular, is it?"

She could hardly believe she'd uttered the dreaded "D" word. Until then, she hadn't even considered the possibility of separation, let alone divorce. But now the word was out. It hung in the air between them while each of them pondered it with fear and dread, but also with that faint spark of possibility. Perhaps life would be better if they were apart. Henry's mind immediately flew to Ella. Perhaps, if he wasn't married… He hardly dared let himself complete the thought.

As if she could read his mind, Mavis flung at him, "And don't kid yourself Ella will want you. You're no spring chicken and you look ridiculous in all those new clothes you've bought. Talk about mutton dressed up as lamb! I never thought I'd see the day when the Rector of Thorpemunden looked like a common spiv."

"Snob to the last?" taunted Henry. "Nothing better to say? And may I remind you how the word 'spiv' dates you? Nobody uses that expression anymore. Let me tell you, many people have told me how smartly dressed I am these days and how I look ten years younger."

In fact, Alice Thompson from Middlestead was the only person who had commented at all on Henry's new appearance, and he had been uncomfortably aware of one or two snide glances. He even thought he had detected a slight smirk from Peter Lambert, but had decided it was just an itch in the doctor's sandy goatee. So Mavis' words stung.

They also caused him to tune out from her voice. But now he noticed that Mavis was still shouting angrily and gesticulating wildly. He had no idea what she'd just said, so turned his back on her and slammed into his study for a bit of peace.

Other than a few bangs and crashes overhead, which he thought were to be expected under the circumstances, Henry heard nothing more for half an hour, when he reckoned it might be safe to emerge and slip quietly out of the house. There was no sign of Mavis as he tossed on his anorak. He pulled up the collar and opened the front door.

There on the rectory drive in front of him were two suitcases. With an icy hand clutching at his heart and a sudden return to sobriety, Henry stared at the suitcases. But before he had a chance to get to them and confirm his fears, Mavis opened the upstairs window and yelled out, "And don't bother to come back!"

Henry was caught between reasoning with her, thus losing face, or taking the suitcases with apparent aplomb and driving off in the car. He was still sufficiently angry to choose the latter. He opened the boot, slung the two cases inside, and drove off without a word.

***

Although Henry roaring out of Thorpemunden Rectory without a backward glance had been a shock to the system causing her to pause, with panic winding its cutting tendrils around her heart, Mavis remained deeply angry for the best part of the day. She kept glancing at the door, reassuring herself that Henry would return presently, when he was hungry and tired. Mind you, she had expected him to come crawling back indoors as soon as he had spotted the cases. She hadn't thought that he'd really take off.

A couple of hours later she had a phone call from Ella.

"Mavis? It's Ella. Henry's here. I just thought you should know. I don't want you worrying about him."

Mavis snorted, "Worry? Why would I worry? He can do whatever he pleases. He always has, so nothing's different there." She paused, then added in what she hoped was nonchalant tones, "Is he staying with you, then?"

"There doesn't seem to be anywhere else he can go. He can hardly stay in B&B accommodation; it would be all over the parish in minutes. Besides, he couldn't work from there."

Mavis sniffed, "It'll be all over the parish in minutes that he's staying with you and Polly. What do you think the parish will make of that? The rector staying with two young, unmarried girls?"

Ella said quietly, "There'll be a scandal. No doubt about that, Mavis. But we may be able to contain the situation for a few days." She hesitated. "Mavis, it may be too soon to ask you this, but are you committed to this course of action? Are you certain this is what you want?"

Mavis said, "You'd better ask him!" and slammed down the phone.

Her heart was crashing against her ribs and her hands were clammy. She sat at the kitchen table with her head buried in her arms after she came off the phone. In the best part of her mind beyond the pain and anger, she appreciated the call. It was typically thoughtful of Ella to ring, and Mavis reminded herself that she had no quarrel with Ella. It wasn't the girl's fault that Henry was acting like a fool. Mavis wondered whether Henry knew that Ella had rung her. Probably not.

Ever practical, Mavis began to think about the future. Where should she go from here? She wasn't moving out of the rectory without a very big fight, that was for sure. Of course, if Henry left the priesthood, she'd be forced to go. He was right, there. She was only in the rectory because of Henry's job. She had no money of her own, never having worked. Although she and Henry had a joint bank account, which she administered, Mavis knew there was barely enough money for one house, let alone two. And if Henry left the ministry, there'd be no money at all coming in for either of them. They would both be forced into the loving arms of State benefits. It was not an encouraging picture.

Mavis decided that her first course of action must be to open her own bank account and transfer into it a good percentage of the funds from their joint account. Probably, Henry would never notice. For the first time, Mavis began to realise how vulnerable she was. Henry, too, was vulnerable, but from what she had seen in the past, clergy were quickly forgiven by the diocese and merely moved a few miles away to a new post. But what would happen to her?

Mavis hovered her hand over the phone, debating with herself whether or not to ring Bishop Percy. Was it too early to make this official? Or would she be better protected if she got her story in first?

In the event, the decision was taken out of her hands, for the phone rang.

"Thorpemunden Rectory? Can I help you?"

"Mavis, is that you? You sound different, I hardly recognised you. It's Bishop Percy. How are you?"

"Oh, you know. So-so."

"Good, good. Look, I'd love to chat, but I need to get on. Is Henry there?"

"I'm afraid not. Can I take a message?"

Percy sounded testy. "I've just had a copy of the *Diss Tribune* thrust through my door. I don't know who left it, they didn't stay. What's going on now, Mavis?"

"Well, I—" Mavis stopped. Her instinct was to prevaricate, to protect Henry. But she suddenly saw her opportunity.

"Mavis?"

"Oh, Bishop Percy! I'm so glad you've called." Mavis sniffled and allowed her voice to wobble precariously. "I don't know what to do. It's Henry. I think this has tipped him over the top. He's gone."

"Gone? What do you mean, he's gone? Gone where?"

"I'm afraid he took two suitcases of his clothes with him and drove off."

There was a pause. Then the bishop said, "My dear, are you telling me that Henry's left you?"

Mavis began to weep in earnest. Between muffled sobs she managed to say in a small voice, "That's what it looks like."

"But where has he gone? When did this happen? Has he contacted you? Does anyone else know? The rural dean? Any of your churchwardens?"

They will soon, thought Mavis, with some satisfaction. Aloud she said, "It just happened this morning, Bishop. And although

Henry himself hasn't contacted me, I do know where he is. He's staying with Polly Hewitt, our curate."

There was a sharp intake of breath, bordering on a gasp, quickly stifled. "You don't mean—? Surely he isn't—?"

"No, definitely not. There's nothing between Henry and Polly."

"Well, he can't stay there. A single, young girl like that! Tongues will wag."

"She's not alone," Mavis offered. "She has a friend living there. A very nice girl, Ella. So there are two of them."

She could almost see the bishop's mind whirring. "They're not—?"

"Lesbians? No, Bishop. Just friends."

Percy retorted, "I hope she knows it's against her contract to sublet. You cannot sublet any clergy properties. So if she's receiving rent from this friend, there'll be trouble."

"I wouldn't know what the arrangements are. But at least it constitutes safety in numbers as far as Henry is concerned, doesn't it?"

"Hmm, not sure about that. Two young girls. I don't like this, Mavis, I don't like it at all. Henry has been very strange lately. I certainly don't think he can go on living there."

"But can you stop him? After all, he has the freehold. What can you do?"

"He may have the freehold, but Polly Hewitt doesn't. We can move her on any time we like. And with no curate in the house, the friend would have to go too. So would Henry, because we'd let the property. I'll have to get down there, but I can't imagine when. I'm up to the ears, Mavis. Up to the ears."

Mavis murmured sympathetically, although she felt anything but sympathetic. She didn't care about the bishop's workload. She didn't care about anything. Her mind was filled with her own situation, which kept rolling over and over in an endless and debilitating loop.

Bishop Percy suddenly remembered her. “Mavis, my dear, if there’s anything I can do…”

Yes! Mavis wanted to shout. *Get him back! Get my situation back to the way it was this time last year*. She contented herself with saying, “Thank you, Bishop. Very kind of you.”

***

Shortly after the bishop’s telephone conversation with Mavis, the rural dean fetched up on Polly’s doorstep.

“Charles! Lovely to see you. Do come in.” Then, as she noticed his face, “What is it? Oh! You’ve heard already, have you? The bush telegraph is even faster than I thought! I take it you want to see Henry? He’s here. Better take the study. You can have a bit of privacy in there.”

She led him through, introduced him to Ella, offered him tea, which he refused, and left him in the study with Henry.

“Well, Henry,” Charles began when they were both seated. “How are you, mate?”

Henry was immediately irritated. “I’m not your mate, nor ever will be. How do you think I am? My wife throws me out of my own house for no reason at all and within hours she’s obviously informed the whole diocese because my rural dean is on the doorstep.”

“Now just a minute, Henry—”

“No! I suppose you want to convict me of my evil ways. But I won’t listen to your evangelical rubbish. Did Humpty Dumpty send you? Ah! Thought as much. Well, you can just go back to your puppet master and tell him from me that if he can’t be bothered to come himself, I don’t want to know.”

Charles changed tack. “You’re really upset, Henry. You must have had a terrible time.”

“I certainly have. It’s not very pleasant being thrown out of your own home. She’s probably changed the locks by now, the bitch.”

Charles was shocked. Henry had never used that sort of language before and it made Charles very uncomfortable. "Mavis has treated you badly."

"She jolly well has! And after all I've done for her. Anyway, what did she tell you?"

"I haven't spoken to Mavis. Humpty Dumpty rang me. I think she told him that you'd left. She must have implied that you chose to leave, because he never told me any of this."

"I chose—? While I was sitting quietly in my study, praying, if you must know, she filled two suitcases with my clothes and dumped them on the drive. Then when I went out to retrieve them she yelled at me not to come back."

"This puts a very different complexion on things. I'll tell Percy. Did anything precipitate her actions? Doesn't sound like Mavis."

"We'd had a row, if that's what you mean. But all couples have rows from time to time, don't they? At least, that's what I tell my wedding couples. You don't expect this sort of treatment. You expect a bit of maturity from your partner of thirty-five years."

"You certainly do." Charles stood up. "This does change things, Henry. I need to get back to Percy on this. He should know the true picture. Do I have your permission to repeat to him what you've just told me?"

Henry said, "Of course," and shook hands with Charles. *That'll show her*, he thought with satisfaction. *Now we'll see what the diocese does.*

***

The next call to Thorpemunden Rectory was from the Mansfields. Daisy said, "Mavis? We've just heard! We're so sorry. James says, would you like to come for supper tonight?"

"That's very kind of you, Daisy," Mavis said, her heart sinking. She wasn't at all sure she felt up to coping with the Mansfields. "But I don't have a car. I know you're not far, but it's so dark now the nights have drawn in so much. So thank you, but I think I'll have to say no."

"Just a minute." Daisy had put her hand over the receiver, for Mavis could hear a muffled conversation in the background. "Mavis? James says he'll fetch you and take you back. He'll pick you up at seven-fifteen."

"Oh, but—" Mavis was unable to think of a suitable excuse. She ended lamely with, "I don't want to take James out of his way."

"No, no! James insists. We'll see you later."

Mavis sighed. This was getting out of hand and had already, she felt, moved up several gears. She was not naive enough to believe that James Mansfield wanted her company. Clearly he had latched onto an opportunity to sow yet more poison. In view of Bishop Percy's words, Mavis wondered whether James saw it as a chance to get rid of Polly once and for all. Mavis had a brief attack of conscience, but she successfully smothered it. After all, it was only after Polly Hewitt came into the benefice that all these awful things had started to happen. She had to take some responsibility for Henry's altered state of mind. So perhaps it would be best all round if she went. Maybe it was only then that things would return to normal.

***

James Mansfield could be charming when he chose. Despite her forebodings, Mavis thoroughly enjoyed herself. James was attentive and pleasant in a courtly sort of way, leaning close to Mavis when he poured her wine so that she could smell his delightful aftershave as his silver bristle moustache softly touched her cheek.

"May I say, Mavis, how very much I do like your new hairstyle. It suits you perfectly. You look wonderful. Henry is a very stupid man."

Mavis smiled and simpered at him, loving the attention. She had always been attracted to James, and as she relaxed with the wine and the excellent food, she allowed herself to respond to his charisma.

She gave an exaggerated sigh. "You know Henry! His head is so far in the clouds he has no earthly idea of when he's well off."

"How will you manage, my dear?"

"Oh, I'll be fine! I can look after myself."

"Of course you can! I always knew that. It's one of the things I admire about you, Mavis. You're self-sufficient and you're strong. I do so love to see that in a woman." He shot a glance at Daisy as he spoke, but she kept her eyes on her plate.

Mavis, with several glasses of wine plus a strong sherry inside her, giggled. "I do believe you're flirting with me, James Mansfield!"

"If only I dared! But I know you'd see through me in an instant. No, I only tell you the truth, Mavis my dear. You are a very beautiful woman. Did you know that?"

Mavis laughed. "I don't think so! I don't think Henry would agree with you."

"More fool him, then. Mavis, I have to say this. You're not only a very attractive woman, but you are intelligent and poised as well. Henry really isn't aware of his assets, is he?"

"I don't think I'm his asset anymore, James. I'm afraid our marriage is well and truly over, after thirty-five years."

"Oh, my dear! I'm so sorry. But I'm sure you'll be much better off without Henry. Gives you a chance to spread your own wings, and a very pretty spread they'll be, I wager. But tell me, Mavis. What do you think Henry will do?"

Mavis shrugged. "I have no idea. I know what he'd like to do, but I don't think it'll happen."

"And what's that, my dear?"

"Spend the rest of his life with Ella. They're very close. Not that I think—he isn't—you know!"

"I understand." James smiled at her. "And Polly?"

"Well, he's staying there at the moment. But Bishop Percy says he'll have to go soon or he'll turn Polly out."

"Really?" There was a gleam in James' eye. "Well, we must see about that, mustn't we?"

Chapter Twenty-Nine

Following the dinner which provided a very welcome interlude for Mavis, she began to wonder whether perhaps James was right. It had been wonderful to have James to herself; Daisy was so silly and pathetic that she hardly counted. Mavis dismissed any lingering thoughts of possible abuse of Daisy by James as she found herself wondering what might happen if Daisy were not around. Maybe she and James… She didn't complete the thought, but it made her realise that life after Henry might not be all bad. She was strong, she would survive. And she was happy enough in her own company. With the occasional desirable escort like James Mansfield or the occasional invitation out, Mavis reckoned life could be quite good. Maybe even better than with Henry, which had always had its shortcomings even though she had closed her eyes to them.

Of course, it might be different if she was out of the rectory and living in some miniscule cottage miles from anywhere, but Mavis refused to dwell on that thought. All her energies were focussed on not only surviving, but surviving in the best way possible. And that meant getting the better of Henry.

Her first opportunity came on the Sunday. Mavis didn't see why her religious observance should be curtailed in any way just because her husband had walked out, even if he was the rector. If her presence at church embarrassed him, so be it. That was part of the price he had to pay for his actions.

Mavis sat in her usual pew and was rewarded by a warm smile from James Mansfield as he bustled about his churchwarden's duties, and by the presence of Ella, who slipped in beside her. So far, no one other than those in the know would be aware that anything was different. But when the time came for the congregation to receive Communion, as Ella went forward Mavis remained firmly glued to her seat. Since she and Ella always sat near the front, this caused some consternation behind her. Nobody knew quite what to do.

Bunny Sterling leaned over and prodded Mavis, asking in a stage whisper, "Are you going up, dear?"

Mavis responded clearly enough for several rows to hear her. "I cannot receive Communion from hands that are tainted."

There was a sudden hush as this information was digested. Bunny Sterling tried again. "You don't have to receive from Polly, dear."

"I'm not referring to Polly but to the rector," Mavis said, as loudly as she dared.

There was an audible gasp from several people and some feverish whispering which continued throughout the distribution of Communion until drowned out by the organ.

After the service, a crowd quickly clustered around Mavis. Someone thrust a cup of coffee into her hand. Then the interrogations started.

"Is something the matter, dear?"

"Can we help?"

"Are you poorly?"

"Anything we can do?"

"Henry hasn't been himself, has he?"

"If you want to come and talk—"

"—we're always here to listen."

Ivy Cranthorn was put out. She had planned to use this time to spread her own mild rumours about the Mansfield situation and was unaware that the situation had changed. Unusually, she hadn't spotted Henry's car arriving at Polly's house and, since it had been swiftly hidden in the garage, had no idea that Henry was staying there.

She elbowed her way to the front of the small crowd and took Mavis' arm.

"Come and sit down, dear."

Clearing a way through, she led Mavis to an empty pew. "Now then, Mavis. What's all this? What's happened? I thought we agreed I would do something about James Mansfield. You've upstaged me. What's going on?"

Reckoning that attack was very definitely the best form of defence Mavis said, "Henry has gone. He's walked out on me."

The crowd had edged near enough for everyone to listen without appearing to do so, but no one except Ivy was willing to take up the gauntlet.

Ivy said, "What do you mean, he's left you?"

"Precisely that. He took two suitcases full of clothes and walked out. Well, drove, actually. He's taken the car."

Apart from the smothered gasps, the silence from the assembled company was palpable. Ivy said, "Where's he gone?"

"I thought you'd know that, Ivy. He's in your village."

"At Polly's?"

As Mavis nodded, Ivy murmured, "Oh dear! This does complicate matters, doesn't it? James will have a field day."

Mavis responded, "I think Polly was quite wrong about James. There's nothing at all the matter with Daisy. Why, I had a wonderful meal over there and he was quite charming. They both were. Kindness itself. I couldn't wish for a better friend. It's at times like this that you know who your true friends are."

By now, the muttering and whispering had begun and were already swelling in volume. Some people had caught the name "James" and had drawn their own erroneous conclusions, shifting their opinions heavily in favour of Henry. Others had been so incensed by the thought that their rector could walk out on his wife, leaving his proper place in the rectory, that they had hurriedly left church, sliding quickly past Henry at the door, giving him a dark look and refusing to shake his hand.

Henry's spirit was already so crushed that it was unable to drop any lower. When the first wave of parishioners had left the church he wandered back, his usual habit, to greet those who were still drinking coffee. As soon as he approached, a hush fell on the eagerly gossiping villagers and they turned away. Henry was stricken. Just for a moment he caught his wife's eye across the church, surprising the fleeting look of triumph which crossed her features.

When Mavis had so pointedly refused to come to him for Communion, Henry had been devastated. He hadn't expected her to take their fight into the public domain in quite such an overt way, nor so quickly. And how could she possibly include God in their row like that? It had always been an unspoken rule between them that they kept their private business away from church. To find Mavis violating that rule in a way that was certain to cause him maximum embarrassment had shaken Henry.

He had come to church that morning determined to try to patch things up with Mavis. Church, he had reckoned, was the right place for reconciliations and offered the perfect opportunity. With plenty of people around, he could probably treat Mavis as he always treated her; nobody would be any the wiser as to what had happened between them and they could go back to the way they were before this ugly situation arose.

But now his resolve hardened. Mavis might have stolen the initiative, but Henry was rector. He had power and he was determined to use it. He had been charming elderly ladies for years and knew exactly how to manipulate them in his favour. No matter what wicked and malicious rumours Mavis had spread, Henry knew he could counteract them. He had noted those who had walked out without shaking his hand and he would visit them all in the morning. Visiting was his trump card. He was known and admired for it; it would be expected of him and he was confident that he could win back all those who had been taken in by Mavis' lies.

A smile began to play on Henry's lips. He approached the group gathered around Mavis.

"Good morning, ladies, Mavis." He nodded and smiled at them all, making sure to include Mavis in his benign charm. "Cold, now, isn't it? Make sure you all wrap up warm before you go out."

He was rewarded by a few uncertain titters.

He spoke directly to his wife, across the group. "Mavis, I'm a little concerned about the heating in the rectory. I don't want you to be cold. Would you like me to come over and check the oil? Or turn up the radiators for you?"

Mavis was nonplussed. She was so angry with her husband that she had forgotten how charming he could be when he chose. She knew it was a ruse to retain the loyalty of the people of Thorpemunden, but she wasn't entirely sure how to respond. What she desperately wanted was an amusing and light-hearted put-down which would make people laugh, but Mavis had never been quick-witted in that way and she couldn't think of anything to say. If she was nasty to Henry, he'd have won and she'd lose all support. If she was pleasant to him, people would wonder why they were apart. In fact, with that one charm-laden remark they probably already wondered what was wrong with Mavis, that this wonderful man had left her.

Mavis settled for saying lamely, "Thank you, Henry. That would be a welcome change from all previous winters when you've been happy for us both to freeze to death."

But the remark emerged not humorously as she had intended, but as waspish and spiteful.

Mavis caught Ella's eye as she replied. The girl was standing apart, at the back of the group of people but alone and away from Henry. She looked confused and unhappy. Mavis had an unexpected twinge of conscience, almost as though she had let down her own daughter. She reminded herself that Ella was no relation, whatever she had pretended to herself.

Henry, too, had noticed Ella. He glanced at her out of the corner of his eye when he made his charm offensive, hoping to see her face light up with admiration, especially in view of Mavis' predictable response. But like Mavis, he, too, saw the unhappiness etched on Ella's face and he, too, experienced a stab of guilt, which he quickly suppressed. He had done everything in his power for Ella. He owed her nothing. Yet something about the droop of Ella's shoulders told him that somehow or other she, too, was hurting in this ridiculous row between him and Mavis. Which, he reminded himself, was all Mavis' fault. Henry determined to have a talk with Ella as soon as he got home. He had to make her see things his way.

***

Henry had resigned himself to a visit from Bishop Percy with the strong possibility of a summons to the Diocesan, Bishop Gerald Kramer. Not, Henry thought, that he had much to lose. He had no chance of preferment now. That had long gone, if it had ever existed. Personally he thought it had probably only existed in Mavis' mind. Henry was realistic enough to realise that better men than him had never made archdeacon, whatever Mavis' ambitions for him.

Henry still had the freehold so could stay in Thorpemunden as long as he wished. Whether or not he was living in the rectory was largely irrelevant, as far as Church law was concerned. And as long as he continued to take services on most Sundays, there were no grounds for dismissal or a Consistory Court. He was not in any other relationship and he would do his duty by Mavis, making sure that she was cared for properly.

To his surprise, he had a further visit not from Percy but from Charles Burgess, his rural dean. Henry had warmed marginally towards Charles at their previous meeting, having felt that Charles might conceivably have understood enough to be on Henry's side.

He welcomed Charles into the lounge.

"Do you want to speak privately or shall we talk in here with Polly and Ella present?"

Charles sat down in one of the armchairs and smiled easily at them all. "It would be good to talk between all of us, I think. After all, we're all concerned in this to some degree."

Polly offered, "Do you want coffee first? We were about to have one."

"All right, thank you. That would be nice."

They chatted in a desultory fashion over coffee, avoiding the topic which was uppermost in all their minds. Then Charles put down his mug in a determined way.

"I need to tell all of you that the bishops' staff met this week and discussed your situation here. Henry, they are deeply concerned about your health and asked to me impress upon you that you are very much in their prayers. They hold you daily in God's presence."

Henry grinned. "That's all right then," he said flippantly, hoping to raise a conspiratorial smile from the girls. When both concerned faces ignored him, he continued, "No need to worry about my health, Charles. I'm as fit as a fiddle. Better than I've ever been. It's doing me good to have a break from the routine of the rectory, especially with such delightful company."

Polly and Ella looked embarrassed, as though they wished the ground would open up beneath them. Henry knew he was coming across as a little too hearty and feared his remark, meant as a compliment, had been patronising. But in view of his recent past history he was terrified that the bishops might turn this into a mental condition on his part, ordering him to take a long Sabbatical and seek treatment. He looked to Polly and Ella for support, but they were silent, sat on the sofa together, Henry thought, like two Dutch dolls.

"I know, I know." Charles was pacific. "I'll tell them that, don't worry." He leaned towards them, his voice dropping to a whisper. "I think there's something more at stake here. That's why I wanted you all to be present, because I think it concerns you all."

He glanced at each of them in turn. "I think dark forces are at work. This whole unfortunate business is Satan's doing. Satan is very clever. He creeps in where we're most vulnerable and creates havoc. I've noticed a coldness in the rectory before now. I'm convinced evil spirits are afoot. And I think they might be gaining a foothold here, as well."

He leaned back, his eyes shining with fervour.

Henry didn't know whether to laugh or cry. He wanted to laugh because it was such utter piffle, but the better part of him was deeply concerned that a man who was rural dean could peddle such dangerous nonsense. He was about to point out that the rectory was cold because he made a point of conserving his heating oil, but he looked at the two girls to see how they were reacting and lost his opportunity.

Ella was regarding the floor as though her eyes were glued to it. Polly, worryingly, was gazing at Charles with parted lips and glowing eyes.

"Oh Charles! Do you really think so? Things haven't been right in this benefice for a long time, have they, Henry? Ever since I came, there have been problems. And they've just been stupid little things which have somehow got blown out of all proportion. Isn't that how the Devil works, Charles?"

He nodded vigorously. "It certainly is! I'm sure you're right, Polly. There's evil abroad here and if only we can stamp it out and let Jesus in, I'm certain we'll reap untold rewards. This may even be a blessing in disguise. You know, it's all come to the surface like a carbuncle exploding. We need to get rid of all that septic pus."

Henry said, "Satan might make a convenient scapegoat taking responsibility away from me—from any of us—but how do you propose we should do that, Charles?"

"By surrounding this whole situation with prayer and by exorcism. I am experienced, you know. I'm on the diocesan exorcism team."

"Never knew there was one," Henry muttered.

"That's because you've never needed us before. I've brought my equipment, so I'm all ready. I think there may be a focus of evil here that we need to eradicate before we tackle the rectory, which undoubtedly holds the key. We could do it now."

Ella was looking troubled. "Where is the focus likely to be? In a place or a person?"

For the first time, Charles shifted uncomfortably in his seat. "I can't say at this stage. That often becomes apparent after we've started."

"But usually?" she prompted.

He mumbled, "Well, it can be in a person." Then he hastened to add, "Almost always unbeknown to them. It's almost never conscious. The spirits take over a person without their knowledge or their will."

Ella dropped her eyes again. They were full of pain. "It's me, isn't it? You think it's me. This has all happened since I came. I'm the focus of evil."

Polly cried out, grasping her arm. "Don't say that, Ella! That's ridiculous! That's not what Charles meant at all, is it, Charles?"

But Charles' mumbled, "Of course not," sounded unconvincing, even to Polly.

Henry stood up. "This nonsense has gone quite far enough. I hope you can see, Charles, how dangerous this rubbish can be. Just look what you've done to Ella. I won't have it. I think you'd better go."

"But don't you see," cried Charles. "This is exactly how Satan works! He sets us against each other so that we take no action. That's how evil flourishes."

Henry took Charles' arm and propelled him towards the door. "There are other ways of working this out," he said, not unkindly. "You and I will never see eye to eye theologically. I can't allow you to frighten these girls and I won't have Polly's head filled with such claptrap. I'm sorry, Charles. I believe you mean well, but I will never agree with your methods."

When Henry returned to the lounge, fat tears were trickling down Ella's cheeks. Polly was doing her best to comfort her friend.

"He didn't mean that, honestly, Ella. If it's anybody, it's me. These troubles all date from me first arriving in Thorpemunden, not you. When you came, you helped enormously. You made Henry better, didn't she, Henry."

"You certainly did, Ella," Henry agreed. "But listen, you two. This is all complete twaddle. Evil is a human construct, not some supernatural spirit which inhabits people's bodies. We have free will. We choose whether to go along the path of evil or the path of righteousness."

Polly argued, "But if there's a God and he can inhabit people's bodies or souls or minds or whatever, why can't there be a Devil who acts in the same way? After all, isn't the Devil supposed to be Lucifer, the bringer of light? A fallen angel?"

Henry sighed. "You need to stop being so literal, Polly. God isn't a person and neither is the Devil."

"No, God is a spirit, the spirit of love and truth and goodness and all that. I know that. But I don't see why there can't be the opposite spirit. A spirit of darkness and evil and hatred and so on. Plenty of people think there is and lots of them have experience of Satan just as we have experience of God."

Henry frowned. There was a logic to Polly's argument that he was having difficulty in refuting. Yet he knew he didn't believe in the Devil or Satan or Lucifer or whatever name people used, any more than he believed in Hell. Now he wondered why. What was the logical conclusion? That there was, or could be, a spirit of evil? Or was it that God himself was a human construct, designed to make people feel secure and warm and cosy? At the moment to his chagrin, Henry didn't know.

Ella, meanwhile, was gazing from one to the other in utter confusion. "How can you both be Christian ministers and Charles, too, yet all believe something different? I don't understand. But I still think I should go. Whatever it is, I think it's me. I think I attract evil, although I don't know why. I think, if you're all to have a chance to settle down, I have to go."

Chapter Thirty

Bishop Percy was smarting. He had not enjoyed the bishops' staff meeting, at which he had been publicly held to account by his superior, Bishop Gerald.

Gerald, who at fifty-one was one of the youngest diocesan bishops in the country, had risen to high office via a chaplaincy route. Groomed since his early twenties for high office, he had been chaplain to two diocesan bishops prior to a brief sojourn as chaplain in the higher echelons of the army and had finally landed the job of chaplain to the Archbishop of Canterbury. After that he was promoted to suffragan bishop for a few years, being appointed Bishop of Norwich six years previously at the tender age of forty-five.

As a youngster in the grey-haired House of Bishops he had had to fight his way. It was either that, or be overlooked. He chose the former. Here his stint in the army proved to be of sterling worth, for he found that army disciplinary techniques (such as an exceptionally loud and commanding voice together with an authoritarian manner which brooked no opposition) served him well in the House of Bishops.

Bishop Gerald was at home in a hierarchical system, especially when he himself was at the peak of the pyramid. Aware that his two suffragans, Bishop Percy and Bishop John, were his seniors by several years, Gerald drew upon his experience of the army hierarchical system to establish his position despite his youth. He developed hard eyes which could quell with a glance and a reputation for stinging harshness. Since he managed successfully to wrap this up in ecclesiastical language, he was usually credited with being firm but fair as long as you didn't cross him. If that happened, rumour had it that you were in deep trouble.

Fortunately, Bishop Gerald was not at home too much. As he sat in the House of Lords, he was considered to be a very important person and was therefore in great demand as a speaker at various different events. He was a master of publicity who delighted in posing for the press, making sure that he was reported across the spectrum of human activities with plenty of photographs involving classes of schoolchildren or beautiful celebrities.

As one of the country's senior bishops, Gerald had only one mountain left to climb. His final remaining ambition was to be appointed Archbishop of Canterbury when the present incumbent, who was sixty-four, retired. The whisper in the House of Bishops was that Archbishop Leslie intended to go the moment he was sixty-five, so Gerald's present strategy worked on that assumption.

The strategy depended on presenting to the world a harmonious and fully functioning diocese, one which was financially viable and which was seen to be growing steadily despite the downturn in worship habits by the majority of the population of England. Bishop Gerald wanted to be able to point to his diocese with pride, knowing that it was considered to be one of the best dioceses in the country, despite its rural nature. Hence he was less than pleased to see in the local press an account of a country parson who had neglected to turn up for the burial of ashes.

He ran this past Percy at the staff meeting in a deceptively mild manner. Percy, who should have known better, was lulled into presuming that his relationship with Gerald actually constituted some form of friendship which counted for something. Percy discovered his mistake when he admitted to the gathered personnel that the problem at Thorpemunden ran rather deeper than merely forgetting to attend a service.

"What do you mean, 'he's left the rectory'?" Gerald's voice was still mild, sounding inquisitive rather than threatening.

Percy sighed. "These incumbents today! They think they can get away with anything. But what can we do?"

As he pictured national headlines and television coverage, Gerald's black brows drew together, belying his ingenuous youthful appearance. He ran a hand through his black college-style hair. "Very simply, I suggest you get down there and sort him out. Make it extremely clear to him that he will not 'get away,' as you call it, with anything. I expect exceptionally high standards of my clergy. If they cannot conform to those standards they must go."

"But he has the freehold! We can't force him to do anything."

"I'm not advocating force, Percy. That shouldn't be necessary. I assume you are able to make it clear to Canon Winstone that should he choose not to return to the rectory and sort out his parishes in a suitable manner, there will be exceedingly serious consequences. This is your patch, Percy. Work it properly, as though you mean business for once. Do I make myself clear?"

Percy had glanced round at Bishop John and the three archdeacons, searching for support. There was none. All were averting their faces and avoiding eye contact, since those who came into Bishop Gerald's line of fire were invariably left to fight their own battles. And Keith, the Archdeacon of Norfolk who was supposed to work in conjunction with Percy, had a self-satisfied look about him. Percy wished he'd designated Keith to sort out the Thorpemunden mess. That would have wiped the smugness from his face, gaining bonus points for Percy at the same time.

But it was too late for recriminations and Gerald was waiting. Percy nodded. "I'll see to it."

"I take it you have been down there?"

Percy ran his tongue over his lips. "Well, I have been inundated with work. Important appointments which I simply could not miss. You know how it is. But I spoke to his wife on the phone and I have spoken with the rural dean. He's been round."

There was a charged silence as he was subjected to one of Gerald's piercing glares. Then came the mini explosion. "You spoke to his wife but not to him? What are you about? I cannot believe that you have been stupid enough to leave something of this magnitude to a rural dean. Do you not know that rural deans support the clergy first, before ever they give a thought to anything their bishops might require? This is dereliction of duty of the first order. Had you been on top of the job, Percy, none of this would have happened. You would have known what was going on in your own patch and you would have taken steps to counteract it. As it is, you've allowed a situation to develop to such an extent that it may now be difficult to contain. Where do you keep your brains, Percy? Or have you been in the job too long? How long is it now until you retire?"

Percy reddened and squirmed uncomfortably. He muttered an apology. "I'll go first thing in the morning."

"See to it that you do."

***

As he stood on the doorstep of the curate's house at Mundenford, Bishop Percy was seething inwardly. He continued to smart over his lecture from Gerald in front of the other members of the staff team and he blamed Henry. He had spent the journey to Thorpemunden running through his opening gambits and deciding in which direction he wished to take the forthcoming interview. He was properly pumped up for the matter in hand, only to be greeted after his peremptory ring on the doorbell by Ella, clad in Polly's scarlet dressing gown, which she clutched around her slender body.

She peered uncertainly around the edge of the door. "Hello?"

Percy deflated like a pink balloon. "Who are you?"

"Ella. Who did you want?" Then, as she noticed Percy's dog collar, "Oh! Are you a vicar? I expect you want Henry or Polly then. They're both out. I don't know when they'll be back. Shall

I tell them you called? I like your shirt, by the way. Polly has some lovely colours, but she doesn't have a purple one like that, I don't think."

Percy was unsure what to make of this. Was this girl deliberately sending him up? Or could it be possible that she was ignorant of the distinctive dress of bishops?

He said stiffly, "That's because Polly isn't a bishop, nor ever will be."

"Oh!" Ella's hand flew to her mouth. "Sorry! I had no idea."

Percy couldn't help his eyes straying as the hand moved from the dressing gown and he wondered fleetingly what was beneath. He resorted to pomposity to distract himself.

"Are you the young lady who's staying here with Polly? I hope you realise that subletting is against Church rules. I would not like to discover that you pay Polly, for that would certainly constitute a breach of the regulations."

Ella's eyes opened wide. "You mean I have to go?"

"You should not be here as a paying guest." He added in a more kindly tone, "But if you're just staying as a friend, there's no problem. Hadn't you better go and get dressed? They're out, you say?"

"Yes. Henry has gone to see some people in Thorpemunden who were at church yesterday and Polly's gone to Beesthorpe to see someone who's ill. That's all I know, I'm afraid."

Percy turned away. "Well, perhaps you'll tell them I called. I may catch up with them later."

***

At a loose end and reluctant either to waste the morning or to have made the journey for nothing, Percy decided to poke around the churches. After all, although there was an unwritten code that bishops waited to be invited into parishes by the incumbent, there was no reason why a bishop shouldn't visit any time he chose.

He pushed at the heavy oak door of Mundenford Church and stepped inside. He paused for a brief prayer. No matter what church he visited, Percy was always surprised by the need he felt to pray. He was immediately enveloped by the prayers of centuries and he wondered rather fancifully whether they were somehow held in the thick, stone walls.

He was on his knees at the altar rail when the door creaked open behind him. Percy took his time standing up. He didn't want it to look as though he was ashamed of being disturbed at prayer.

Ivy Cranthorn crept up behind him. She felt it her duty to keep an eye on the church and generally managed to catch any visitors. "Good morning. Welcome to our lovely church." Then, as Percy turned round and she realised who it was, "Bishop Percy! How wonderful to see you. Lovely of you to visit. Is there anything you want? I mean, did you come to look at the books, or anything?"

Percy smiled, his blue eyes twinkling behind his rimless glasses. He knew Ivy of old. "No, thank you, Ivy. This isn't an official visitation. Just thought I'd pop in for a quiet moment. How is the church? Everything all right?"

Ivy hesitated. "Well, yes, of course! All this business about Henry and Mavis, though. We're all very sad to see it."

"Do you think it's permanent then? More than just a whim?"

Ivy shrugged. "Who knows? They always seemed all right together, but who knows what goes on behind locked doors? Take the Mansfields, for instance. Some people think he abuses her, she's such a little mouse."

Percy drew himself up to his full stature, which although only five foot five, was considerably taller than Ivy.

"I've never heard such nonsense! I know James Mansfield well. Let me tell you, he would never harm a fly. Why, that man doesn't possess an unkind bone in his body!"

Ivy backtracked as fast as she could. "Exactly, Bishop! That's just what I said. I don't know how these vicious rumours start, but I do take pains to scotch them. I won't listen to gossip, myself."

Percy relaxed a little. "I'm pleased to hear it, Ivy. The Church relies on people like you to make sure Christ's work is done. We are his arms and legs, you know, his hands and feet. It's up to us to make sure his message is heard.

"Talking of which, have you any idea how this present difficulty between Mavis and Henry arose? We must do all we can to help them."

It was cold, standing there talking in the church. Ivy shivered and thrust her hands into the pockets of her winter fleece. "We are doing our best, Bishop."

"I'm sure you are. But any little thing you can tell me? It all helps to build a picture."

Ivy frowned. "I'm not sure anyone really knows. We only found out at church on Sunday. But Henry has been having a tricky time, lately. I wonder whether he's not quite over that illness yet? They say depression can make you do funny things and he's at a difficult age for a man, isn't he?"

Percy blinked. Although he thought of himself as considerably younger than Henry, he was uncomfortably aware that he belonged to the same generation. Realising that Ivy was going to be no help at all, he contented himself with smiling warmly at her, thanking her for her help, and making his escape as quickly as he could.

Since it was certainly time for coffee and warmth, Percy drove on to Thorpemunden, to call on the Mansfields. Perhaps James, as churchwarden of Thorpemunden, would know something.

He regarded Daisy covertly as she opened the door and ushered him in, but could detect nothing different in her manner. She was just Daisy, dithering and fussy, but as she always was.

James was reading the paper in the lounge, seated in his armchair in front of a roaring log fire. His face lightened when he saw Percy.

"Percy! Come in, man, warm yourself by the fire."

Percy was happy to oblige. As Daisy disappeared with his coat, he sat down opposite James.

"How are things, James? I hear you've been having a spot of bother down here in the sticks?"

James grimaced. "You could say that! Ever since that wretched woman came. Don't know what she's done to Henry, but he hasn't been the same. Why on earth did you send us a female, Percy? They're nothing but trouble."

Percy laughed. "I know what you mean. To be honest—and don't let this go any further, just between these four walls if you don't mind—Polly was a problem even at college. Got into one or two, well, I suppose we'd have called them 'scrapes' back in our prep school days. We had all hoped she'd settle down with Henry. Dour, dependable, stable Henry! Never thought anything would move him. Thought he'd knock all her silly ideas out of her head and teach her what real, day-to-day priesthood is about. Get rid of all that modern nonsense. But it seems we were wrong."

James wagged his finger playfully. "Bad judgement, there, Percy! But I know what you mean. If I recall, that's why we had Henry in the first place. Because he was so predictable, so traditional. That girl must have some power to have changed him like this. You don't suppose she's a witch, do you?"

They both laughed. Percy said, "Now, now, James! Can't have you referring to my clergy like that!" But his mind flew to the rural dean's report. Charles had seemed convinced that evil was afoot. It couldn't be true, surely? He brought himself back to the present.

James was saying, "The word on the street is that she may not be your clergy for much longer."

"How do you mean?"

Daisy came in with a tray of coffee. Percy helped himself to two of her homemade biscuits and sat back with a contented sigh.

"This is more like it. I've just spent half an hour in Mundenford Church with Ivy Cranthorn. It's enough to freeze the—" he glanced at Daisy, "—nose off your face."

Daisy smiled at him. She glanced at James then said, "Would you like to stay to lunch, Percy? I'm about to start preparing it. We usually eat at one."

Percy consulted his watch. It was already eleven o'clock, with no guarantee that Henry would reappear that morning. Lunch at Thorpemunden Manor was infinitely appealing.

"Thank you, Daisy. That would be grand."

When she had gone, the conversation continued.

"Come on, James, out with it. What rumours are flying round now?"

"It was just something Mavis said. We had her over for a meal when we discovered what had happened. She said you might have to move Polly to get Henry out of the house there. I must say, I think that's a splendid idea."

Percy scratched his ear. "I hope it won't come to that. I'm going to see Henry this afternoon and I hope to persuade him to return to the rectory. But as you so astutely observed, Henry hasn't been himself lately. There's no telling how he will respond. And Polly had previously requested a transfer. She wanted to spend a few months with Charles Burgess over in Diss. It might be that she has to spend more than a few months there. We'll see."

***

After an excellent lunch of poached salmon in a cucumber and dill sauce, served with boiled potatoes, carrots, and broccoli and washed down with a glass of James' best chardonnay, Percy's pumped-up ire had dissipated. He drove to Mundenford in a genial mood.

Henry and Polly were both at home, clearly having been briefed by Ella. They both looked anxious, but invited him in warmly enough.

Ella disappeared, saying she was going to Diss for the shopping and would probably be a couple of hours.

"I'm sorry to hear of all this trouble," Percy began, addressing Henry.

Having expected righteous anger to be poured upon his head, Henry was surprised but not yet willing to lower his guard. "I'm sorry, too. But these things happen in the best regulated households, I'm afraid."

"Quite so. I have spoken to Mavis on the phone and I plan to see her when we've finished here, but may I ask how things are between you at the moment?"

Henry pursed his lips. "Not very good, I'm afraid. I don't think she wants me back."

Percy pounced on this opening. "So you might be prepared to contemplate returning? Under the right circumstances, of course."

"I might. It would depend a lot on Mavis. There would have to be some give and take. She publicly humiliated me on Sunday. I would expect an apology for such unacceptable behaviour."

Percy hastily changed tack. "I believe Charles called on you?"

Polly entered the conversation. "He thinks there are evil spirits at work both here and in the rectory."

Ignoring the snort from Henry, Percy asked, "What do you think?"

Polly glanced at Henry. "None of us can detect anything. But it's a bit unfair on Ella. She now thinks it's all her fault, which is rubbish. I told her, if it's anyone's fault, it's mine. This has all happened since I came."

Percy nodded sagely. "It does look that way, doesn't it?"

"Now just a minute!" Henry was nearly out of his seat. "I won't have Polly or Ella blamed for something which is obviously between myself and my wife. All this talk of darkness is superstitious nonsense. I thought the Church had moved past that in the Middle Ages."

"Don't get upset, Henry." Percy was alarmed by this outburst. "We're just trying to find out the truth, explore all avenues, however unlikely. Look, do either of you have any suggestions as to how we might move this forward? You really can't stay here for much longer, Henry. You either have to move back, or we'll have to move you out of Thorpemunden."

"To some sink parish which will finish me off?"

"Oh, come now! There are some very good parishes in interregnum at the moment. One of them might be a possibility."

Polly burst out, "No! You can't take Henry away from here! Why, he is Thorpemunden. It would make things much worse if Henry went."

Percy said carefully, "There might be a compromise. Suppose we could import a mediator to help you all sort this out? Someone who would listen to both sides impartially and find a way forward."

Polly's eyes suddenly shone. "Sue! Sue Gallagher, my mentor. She's brilliant. And isn't she an old friend of yours, Bishop? You must know her. She's really good. If Sue could come and stay, I really think we might mend some fences. What do you say? Bishop? Henry? Can I ring her?"

Percy and Henry looked at her. "I think that might be an excellent idea, Polly. Don't you, Henry?"

And Henry nodded, thoughtfully.

Chapter Thirty-One

Delighted with the opportunity for a visit from Sue, which was not only officially sanctioned but even sought by those in ecclesiastical power, Polly rang her friend that day.

Reluctant to commit herself, as like all churches her parish was busier than ever on the run-up to Christmas, Sue promised to ring back when she'd had time to think about the proposal. But clearly the network of bishops swung into immediate action, for she soon had a call from her own diocesan bishop strongly recommending that she leave her church in the capable hands of her churchwardens, non-stipendiary minister, and licensed reader.

"It will be good for them, Sue, to take on the responsibility of a busy London parish. And it will be good for you to have a few weeks' reprieve in the country. Work wonders for your health. Think of it as a retreat."

"A few weeks? I don't want to be away that long. And I don't imagine for one moment that it'll be a rest cure. Bishop, I'm not sure that I want to leave my own people at this critical point in the Church's year."

"Obviously you must do as you decide. I can't—and wouldn't—force you in any way. But the Church has trained you with particular skills and those skills are very much in demand at Thorpemunden at the moment. Perhaps I should add that from what Bishop Gerald said to me, Polly Hewitt's priestly career hangs in the balance over this. It sounds to me as though she might well be used as a sacrificial lamb if things don't work out."

"Polly? Oh, this is so unfair! It's blackmail. Surely even the Church couldn't dismiss Polly because her incumbent has fallen out with his wife?"

"But it goes deeper than that, doesn't it? From what I've been told, it sounds as though Polly's presence has had quite a profound effect up there in the backwaters of Norfolk. Obviously they wouldn't dismiss her, but they could move her on, and as you know, an early move like that under, shall we say, questionable circumstances, which would never be explained in order to protect her present incumbent, would dog her for the rest of her priestly life. Still, as I've said, it's up to you. I shan't hold it against you if you refuse."

Sue sighed. "All right, I'll go for a week. But this is positively the last time. If Polly has such problems up there, you should move her down here. No reason why she couldn't be my curate."

"Hmm. Except that she'd never learn to stand on her own two feet then, would she? With your support in the background I'm sure she'll make a very fine priest one day, a priest that can face difficulties and problems without going under. And with the Clergy Discipline Measure making clergy even more vulnerable to malicious complaints without any foundation, a priest who can keep his or her head above water is becoming as rare as hen's teeth, these days."

***

Sue was unwilling to commit to more than a week in Thorpemunden. She reckoned that if nothing moved within that time, the Winstones would have to seek professional help. She knew there were a couple of diocesan counsellors in Norwich diocese, but perhaps the problem was persuading Henry and Mavis that they needed any help. Probably the bishops had decided that it might be quicker and easier in the long run to import Sue as a friend rather than in a strictly professional capacity. And it was good to be staying with Polly for a while.

***

The house at Mundenford was growing crowded. Unlike the rectory with its four bedrooms, Polly only had three. It required some juggling to fit in four adults, and in the end, Ella elected to sleep on a camp bed in Polly's room for as long as necessary. Polly and Henry were usually up first as they continued to say the Morning Office in the different churches. They had already fallen into a routine which suited them well. Since Ella worked in the evenings, she arose when the house was empty.

Sue decided to avoid Morning Prayer, thinking it best to give Henry and Polly that time to themselves, so she, too, stayed in bed until they had gone.

With just the two of them for a leisurely breakfast, Sue and Ella began to get to know each other. Ella revealed her background to Sue, discovering that now time had moved on, she was much more comfortable talking about her mother, especially her mother's death.

"My mother was Korean," finished Ella, "but I've never been there. I don't know if I have any relatives in Korea. I don't have any over here. There's just me. That's why it's been so terrific to meet Polly."

"You don't have a father?" Sue asked.

Ella helped herself to toast and shook her head. "I don't know who he was. I s'pose I'd like to know, but I can't see how to find out."

"Your birth certificate?"

"Haven't got one. Although a friend did once tell me I could get one. Don't really know how, though."

"I could help you. I'm quite interested in family history. I traced my own family back to 1700, so I'm sure I could get a birth certificate for you."

Ella's dark eyes regarded her quizzically. "But what if his name isn't on the certificate?"

"Then I guess we're stumped. I suppose you could have a DNA test, but since there isn't a national register of DNA, I don't see how that would help you. Unless he had a criminal record, in which case it might be better not to know!"

Ella wiped the crumbs from her mouth and shook her head. "I'm sure he hasn't. Because the only thing my mother did tell me about him was that he was a professional man and very kind. Would do anything for anybody."

"Hmm. Didn't do much for you and your mother though, did he?"

"I don't think he knew I existed. My mother was a prostitute, after all. They don't often get pregnant. You know, I always wondered whether she deliberately chose him as someone she really wanted to father her child. Otherwise, why didn't she have hundreds more children?"

Sue said, "You may be right. Leave it with me. I'll see what I can do."

***

The first opportunity for a conversation with Henry came that evening. Ella was out at work and Polly had some paperwork to finish on the computer in the study. Sue and Henry sat over a leisurely coffee, chatting about the weather, the state of the economy, and life in general.

"Talking of those things that contribute to happiness, Henry, are you happy? Is it better away from Mavis?"

Henry made a wry face. "Is the grass ever greener on the other side? It's given us both a bit of breathing space, I suppose. But thirty-five years! It's a lifetime to give up."

"Do you think it has to be given up? I mean, is it final?"

Henry shrugged and swirled the remaining coffee in his mug. "Who knows? I can't get near Mavis. She doesn't seem to want me.

It was her that threw me out not the other way round, in case you're wondering. I've only seen her once since then, at church, where she made it very clear that she wanted nothing more to do with me."

"Have you checked that out? Have you tried to contact her to see whether your assumptions are correct?"

"Not as such, no. The ball's in her court. She can come to me and ask, if she wants me back."

"Would you go, if she did that?"

Henry considered. "I might. It's somewhat crowded here and to be honest, I'm not that comfortable sharing with two young females. I never know when I'm going to come upon one of them dressed only in a nightgown or underwear or something. It's highly embarrassing."

"You're disturbed by seeing Ella or Polly scantily clad?"

"Of course I am! I haven't forgotten that I'm a priest."

"But you're also a man, Henry. What do you feel if you see too much female flesh?"

Henry banged down his mug. "I've just told you what I feel! What is this, the Spanish Inquisition? Have they sent you in here to question me? I thought you were going to help us sort things out, not make unnecessary innuendo."

Sue said pacifically, "I'm sorry. I had no intention of upsetting you. It's just that I need to see clearly how you are feeling. So forgive me if I just pursue this line one step further. How did you feel when you saw Mavis partially undressed? Did you have the same feelings of embarrassment as you do with the girls?"

"I never really saw Mavis undressed. We have separate bedrooms because she can't sleep with me. I'm a restless sleeper and apparently I sometimes snore."

Sue nodded. "Neither of you get a good night's sleep when you're together?

"Henry, would you mind if I go to see Mavis tomorrow? Obviously what we've said together here is confidential, but I think I need to hear her version of events before we all meet together. How does that sound to you?"

"All right, I suppose."
"Any messages for Mavis?"
Henry frowned. "No, I don't think so."

***

Sue tackled Mavis in the morning. The rectory was probably the cleanest and neatest house Sue had ever entered. She felt as though the cushions on the sofa would be plumped up the minute she had gone. It was almost clinical, Sue reflected. A expression of Mavis' unhappiness? Or the way she always was? Sue seemed to remember Polly commenting on the spartan appearance of the rectory back when she had first arrived.

Sue accepted a cup of tea in a bone china cup with a saucer and refused to be intimidated either by the orderliness of her surroundings or by Mavis' faintly defensive and hostile bearing. Mavis was sitting very upright on the edge of her armchair with her feet and legs held tightly together. Her lips were pinched and her eyes bleakly angry.

"Why have they sent you?" she asked. "Henry couldn't face me himself? Is that it?"

Sue smiled warmly, trying to get her to relax. "This is an informal initiative by the bishops. I think they want to see whether there's any mileage in mediation."

"And you're an expert on marriage, are you? Ever been married yourself?"

"I don't think this can be solved by experts, do you? I think the only people who can resolve it are you and Henry. But sometimes it helps to have a neutral body around."

"Huh! When he comes back here and apologises, that's when it'll be resolved."

"Apologises? Does he have a lot to apologise for?"

"Only thirty-five years of my life! I've given my youth to him and where has it got me? Some reward when he goes whoring after other women."

Sue stifled a shock of surprise. She was endeavouring to remain neutral, but couldn't help her own feelings of shock both at the language and the thought behind it. She decided to openly admit to her feelings.

"Wow! I feel quite shocked at that sentiment, Mavis. Can you enlarge upon it for me?"

Mavis set down her cup with a clatter. Sue was pleased to see that she had settled back more comfortably in her chair. Perhaps she was beginning to release some of the hostility.

"I certainly can! It's Ella. You must know he's in love with her?" As Sue raised her eyebrows, Mavis continued, "I blame myself, really. It was that illness of Henry's—not that I'm sure he's over it yet—but at the time, I was desperate. I didn't know how to make him sit up and take notice. He just turned his face to the wall like King Ahab. So I took him to the railway—he's passionate about trains—and that's where we met Ella. He was transformed immediately, back to the old Henry, so I managed to persuade Ella to stay on. I have to say, she was a tonic for him. They seemed to have an instant bond. I just didn't expect him to fall in love with her."

"In love?" Sue prompted gently.

"So he says. But I don't know. Men can be like that, can't they, when they reach a certain age?"

Sue inclined her head as an invitation to go on.

Mavis continued, "For a while he followed her round like a lost sheep, although he seems to be over that bit by now. Well, I suppose he would be, since he's living there. No telling what he's getting up to, with two young girls in the house."

"What would you expect he'd be getting up to?"

Mavis smiled, a little sheepishly. "Nothing, really. Not sure he's capable of anything anymore. But how would I know?"

"Separate bedrooms?"

"Too true. Stopped all that nonsense as soon as I could."

"You and Henry haven't had sex for a while?"

"I wouldn't put it quite that bluntly myself, but yes. To be honest, I never enjoyed it. I remember my mother telling me when I was sixteen how unpleasant and nasty sex was. Of course, at that age everyone was talking about it at school in hushed tones of wonder, so I didn't believe her. But I found out quick enough when I was married. Apparently my grandmother told my mother on the eve of her wedding to my father that she would have to 'lie back and think of England.' I've never forgotten that. I did my duty by Henry, but when it was apparent that we weren't to be blessed with children, I suppose it became too much of a burden. There didn't seem any point, anymore."

"You'd have liked children?"

Mavis glared at her. The question seemed to make her angry. "Of course I would! Wouldn't any woman? That's what we're for, isn't it? To procreate. Well, I'm afraid I've failed in that department. Henry never gave me a child. And he wouldn't go for tests, either."

"Did you go for tests?"

"Certainly not! That was Henry's responsibility and he failed it. He did mention once about adopting, but it wasn't the right time for me and he never mentioned it again. So we just grew old without really noticing. And here we are, two dried-up people in late middle age, with no family to support our old age."

Sue blew out her cheeks. "Phew! That's quite a loss, then. Did Henry feel the loss, too?"

"I don't know, we never discussed it. You'd have to ask him that. Why? What difference does it make?"

"I just find myself wondering whether Henry's bond with Ella isn't love in the romantic sense but something to do with the daughter you never had."

Mavis stared at her open-mouthed for a long moment. Then her eyes filled and tears began to spill down her cheeks.

Sue said gently, "It's been a terrible loss for you, hasn't it? And Ella has filled the gap."

The sobbing increased in intensity. Mavis was unable to speak for a while. Then she managed to articulate, "And now he's taken her away too," before collapsing into a puddle of tears.

***

Sue left it two days before arranging a meeting between Henry and Mavis, with herself as referee. She would have liked to have given it longer, but time was pressing for her, and the rapidly advancing Christmas season seemed like a good target for reconciliations.

She suggested a neutral venue away from prying eyes, so they settled for a small hotel tucked away in the next benefice, where they could have a table in a private corner. It being out of season, the hotel was virtually empty and the dining room had only two other tables of guests.

Henry drove himself to the venue and arrived first, while Sue drove via Thorpemunden and picked up Mavis.

Henry greeted them in a restrained but courteous manner. "Would you like a drink? Gin and tonic?"

"I'll have a white wine," Mavis said, determined to flaunt her new independence.

Henry blinked at this change from her usual tipple, but conformed to her request. Drinks in hand, they were shown to their table, which was covered in an immaculate white cloth, laid with heavy silverware, and finished with a small, three-branched candle stand. The waiter fussed over them, opening serviettes with a flourish and handing over menus. He lit the three rose-scented candles and withdrew.

"This is nice," murmured Mavis, despite herself.

Henry nodded and smiled at her. Sue watched them covertly while appearing to study her menu and was pleased with this mutual effort to be civil.

When they had chosen their meals—medium-rare steak for Henry, chicken in a white wine sauce for both Mavis and Sue—they sipped their drinks in silence.

Sue started the conversation. "Did you go out much when you were together?"

"No," Mavis said shortly. It sounded like a contentious issue, so Sue skirted delicately round it.

"It does make it special when it's occasional, doesn't it?"

Henry admitted, "I get tired these days. After working all day it's a bit of an effort to get dressed up. Sheer laziness, I suppose."

Mavis snapped, "What about me? I slave away in the house all day long, when I'm not running your errands for you or sorting out the MU or something. You never think about me. I'd like a change, now and then."

"Well, you've got one now," retorted Henry. "You can do whatever you like now you're on your own."

Trying not to sound like a school mistress, Sue said mildly, "Perhaps if we could all try to suspend blame just for this evening. Let's enjoy tonight. We've got all tomorrow to blame each other, if you think that would be productive."

They had the grace to look sheepish, but Mavis was not yet ready to let it go. "I wanted to come out like this the other week, but Henry spoiled it all."

Sue said sharply, "It takes two to tango as we all know, Mavis. Please. Leave it for tonight."

Mavis was saved from replying by the arrival of their meal. They ate in silence, but the food was excellent and the wine relaxed them all. Conversation began again.

Sue said, "I want to get back at the end of the week. You know what it's like, this period just before Advent. I don't want to be away too long."

"Me neither," agreed Henry. "Not that I'm away from the job, but to be honest, it's not very convenient living at Polly's."

"Is that all I am, a convenience?"

Henry sighed. "I'm sorry, Mavis. Is that what you want to hear? Whatever I'm supposed to have done, I'm sorry for it. Okay?"

"If you don't know what you've done, how can you be sorry? Empty apologies are no good to me, Henry." Mavis tossed her head.

Henry said, "Look, I don't want to spoil this evening. I've really enjoyed it. And I do want to sort things out between us. It isn't doing anyone any good, all this. Certainly not helping me and you don't seem too happy. And tongues are wagging in the benefice like there's no tomorrow."

Mavis said bitterly, "That's all you've ever cared about, the job."

To his surprise, Henry found himself reaching for her hand. But she snatched it away. He contented himself with saying, "Yes, I do care about the job and I think you care about it too. But I care about you more, Mavis. I really do. I've been hurting away from you. This separation has made me realise how much I need you. It's been like losing half of myself."

Mavis gazed at him with parted lips. Then she said softly, "But you don't love me, do you? There's someone else."

Henry frowned, trying to be honest. "I do care for Ella and for a time I thought I must be in love with her. But now I'm not sure. And no, I'm not 'in love' with you, Mavis. But we have so much more than that, don't we? We belong together. There may not be too much romance in our relationship, but that's only because we know each other so well. And if romance is what you want, stuff like this every so often," he indicated the table with a sweep of his hands, "I'm sure we can manage that. It might be good. What do you say, my dear?"

Chapter Thirty-Two

Satisfied with the results so far, Sue was able to leave on the Saturday so that she would be back in time for her own Sunday services. She felt it best now to leave Mavis and Henry to their own devices. They were grown-up people. The ice was broken; it was time they worked things out for themselves.

"You have my number," Sue told them as she prepared to depart. "Ring me—any of you—if you need me or if you just want to chat. Even if I'm not immediately available, I can usually get back to you the same day if you leave a message on my answer phone."

They were all sorry to see her go. Polly because she was a good friend, Henry because he was aware of a tiny soupçon of anxiety at having to cope with Mavis without Sue's help, and Ella because Sue had stirred up in her a longing to find her father, to discover someone to whom she belonged.

Henry and Mavis had decided to take it slowly. Mavis had indicated a wish to be courted again and Henry, although privately unable to comprehend any purpose whatsoever in this, was prepared to humour her. It was a bore and an effort, but if that was what it took to clamber back into Mavis' good books, then he was prepared to do it. He suppressed his question mark over the balance of power, because it threatened to scupper his return to the rectory. But it left him just a little uneasy.

In a train of thought far removed from his usual pathways, Henry wondered whether this was what sin was really about. Was sin not so much doing or saying or thinking bad things, but more suppressing uneasiness in order to take the easy route? Going with the flow? Would he be better to have it out properly with Mavis, risking either delaying his return or not returning at all, or was it better to set aside unwelcome questions and just get on with it for the greater good? Henry's theological thought had never moved in such a practical direction before and he found himself floundering in this virgin territory. His mind flew immediately to Ella. He might try it out on her. She had good sense and seemed to come at issues from a different direction. Perhaps she would have something worthwhile to contribute.

***

Ella kept in close touch with Sue, determined to keep Sue to her word to search out Ella's origins. Within the week, an official-looking, buff-coloured envelope arrived for Ella. Inside was a copy of her birth certificate together with a scrawled note from Sue. "Sorry—not what you were hoping. Not sure where to go from here, but keep in touch. Love Sue."

Without looking, Ella knew that her search had ground to a halt almost before it had started. She unfolded the birth certificate and saw the word "Unknown" under "Father's Name." She was overwhelmed with such a feeling of grief that it felt almost as though she had actually been bereaved all over again. It was as if her father had died and left her more alone than she had been before she started to hope.

She shared her feelings with Henry and found him more understanding than she had expected. He said, "You know Mavis and I look upon you as our daughter. We both hope you can think of us as your adopted parents. We suffer the same loss but in the opposite direction. We have no children, you have no parents. It makes sense for us to have each other, doesn't it?"

His words brought tears to Ella's eyes. She was immensely grateful to them both and delighted that it looked as though they were going to get back together. But it wasn't the same as having a father of her own.

To take her mind off her own woes she asked Henry how things were going with Mavis.

He grinned ruefully. "She wants me to court her all over again. I'm going to try, but I don't really see why and it doesn't come naturally. May need some help, there. And I wanted to ask you, Ella. If I can't see the point in all this, do you think I should go along with it just to keep the peace or should I stand my ground and tell Mavis I think it's all rubbish? Why can't I just move back in without any of this unnecessary palaver?"

Ella swallowed. "Please don't let Mavis know you feel any of that, Henry. There's a time to keep silent and this is it. Make a fuss of her. Mavis isn't sure that you really love her. She's much more unsure of herself than she appears. She needs you to tell her that you love her and to make her feel that she's the centre of your universe and you can't do without her."

"But how on earth would I do that? I don't know how to do all this stuff anymore. I left all that behind when I was a teenager."

Ella laughed. "With your looks, Henry, you could court anyone at any time. Half the ladies in the parish swoon at your feet whenever they see you! But anyway, it's not so much what you look like, it's what you do and say. Let Polly and me give you some ideas, like buying Mavis the occasional surprise gift and taking her out to the theatre now and again. You'll soon slip into it."

"And I thought romance was dead among you young people," he mocked.

But he took Ella's advice to heart. He rang Mavis each day for a chat and was surprised by how he began to look forward to these exchanges. He took her out for a meal, this time in Ella's pub at Middlestead where they could be seen by parishioners.

"Just as well to spread the word that we're getting back to normal," he explained.

"Are we?" Mavis was still unable to resist the tart replies, but they were becoming less frequent and less acid.

Henry took her hand and gazed into her eyes. "I hope so. I really do. Don't you?"

And she found herself melting under his touch and his evident sincerity. Instead of snatching her hand away she squeezed his hand gently and smiled shyly at him. She almost thought he was going to lean across the table to kiss her, but perhaps that was a step too far for two married people in late middle age. She grinned to herself at the thought.

He smiled, too. "What's funny?"

Mavis laughed out loud. Henry reflected that it was the first time he had heard her laugh properly for years and he felt ashamed if perhaps he had been the cause of her lack.

With eyes dancing in merriment she said, "I thought for a moment you were going to kiss me. Then I thought of what the locals would make of that! The rector kissing his wife in public! It would really make them sit up and think."

Without a word Henry leaned across the table, cupped her face in both his hands, and gave her a long, lingering kiss on the lips. Mavis' eyes opened wide and for a moment, as the old Mavis reasserted herself, she was tempted to pull away. But then, without her volition, her eyes closed and she gave herself up to a sensation she hadn't experienced since she was in her twenties. Neither of them noticed the hush that had fallen on the pub. And neither of them noticed Ella wipe a small tear away from the corner of her eye.

As Mavis had predicted, the news was around the benefice like wildfire. There was a sense of deep relief among many of the churchgoers, but others were less charitable. Some grumbled that such a display in public was disgusting and a disgraceful example to the young, and what was the Church coming to? But most were delighted that life in the Thorpemunden benefice was apparently returning to normal.

One person was not amused. James Mansfield had been relying on the separation to force the removal of Polly Hewitt from the benefice. He had worked on both Bishop Percy and on Mavis and had thought his plan was succeeding. There had been no previous indication that anything was being patched up between Mavis and Henry and he had been quietly working to deepen the rift. For him, this reconciliation was the worst news possible, for it spelt an end to his plans. And the beauty of these plans had been that they could not be laid at his door. Now it looked as though that dream was over. To achieve his desired ends, he would have to start again in a different direction.

James was a complex man, used to masculine virtues in a man's world. Now in his seventies, he was unable to come to terms with women in positions of power. He felt so uncomfortable with women who regarded themselves as his equal that he could barely remain in the same room as them. In his view, women were for adornment, for procreation, and for making his life comfortable. They had no other purpose. Anything more was against nature. His own wife, Daisy, had failed even in that regard, for she had given him an incomplete son.

James regarded Frank as somehow like a piece of his farm machinery in need of repair. In some respects James loved Frank, but he was a deeply disappointed man. He had been so thrilled and proud when Frank was born, but as it gradually became clear that Frank was intellectually deficient, James had withdrawn and left Frank's upbringing to Daisy apart from occasional rides on the tractor and walks round the estate. But Frank had grown. His physical stature was not in the least impaired and he had become too much for Daisy to handle alone. James blamed Daisy for her weakness. That was another problem with women. They were so stupidly fragile, unable to cope with the simplest of difficulties. Ever since Frank's teenage years, James had used strong-arm tactics on him, learned through military service. Frank usually blubbered like a baby, but did as he was told, never daring to refuse his father.

Most of the time, life had fallen into a satisfactory pattern for the Mansfields with just a sporadic blip now and again when Frank flipped. But that was to be expected from someone with

Frank's limited capacity. James always had a stout stick to hand, which he needed only to raise in order to subdue Frank.

Seated in his armchair in front of the log fire with soft music from Classic FM on the radio, James mused over his son and the problem of Polly Hewitt. Too much had changed since Polly's arrival, none of it for the better and all of it traced eventually back to that point. Women had no place in the Church other than to fill the pews, arrange flowers, and clean. That had been the tradition since Christ chose only male disciples and St Paul reiterated that man must be the head of woman. And for good reason, too.

It was clear to James that Polly must go. He seethed all over again when he recalled the way she had set Frank off the day he had disappeared, causing untold trouble for James himself. That brought his mind back to the robbery, which had never been solved. Of course, the police worked slowly (although hopefully methodically) but nonetheless, James thought it high time he put in another call to his friend the chief constable. Perhaps he should have Reg and Kathleen over for a meal. Then he could suggest further avenues of inquiry.

***

"We can't go round arresting people on hearsay," explained the chief constable. Reg Pearson was a big man who dwarfed James' much slighter stature. As always, he and Kathleen had dined well with the Mansfields, but he was only too aware that you didn't get an invitation to Thorpemunden Manor without some hidden agenda. For Reg, part of the fun was challenging himself to discover the hidden agenda before the meal was over and the ladies were ushered away in order to allow man-talk in private.

This evening had been disappointingly easy, for James had mentioned the monthly crime figures before the first course was through. Now they were alone, James was getting stuck in to the nub of the visit.

"I have received compensation," James was saying. "But I'm concerned for the community. If I'm right—and I may very well be wrong, that's for you to find out—to have a thief at the centre of the community will be disastrous. Can you imagine what it will do to people's morale? What it will do to the reputation of the Church?"

Reg's big brows drew together. "But if she's arrested, both those things will happen, won't they? And if we get it wrong, we in the Force will be crucified. James, my friend, I'm never surprised by who turns out to have criminal intentions, but even I find the thought of a crime spree by your—let's face it, over endowed—female curate, difficult to swallow. You know the territory better than I do, but nothing my officers have uncovered so far has pointed them in that direction."

"You're right on one score, Reg. I do know the territory better than you and if I might say so, I know the curate better than your officers. She's sly, that one. Nice as pie to your face, but when you're alone with her, phew! This needs to be cleared up, Reg, for all our sakes."

Reg swirled his very fine Courvoisier and took a leisurely sip. "Please don't think for one moment that the investigation has ceased. We never close cases until they're solved. We are continuing to pursue various lines of inquiry."

"Such as?"

Reg laughed and touched the side of his nose. "Now you know very well that I can't reveal any of that information to you, James! But I will tell you this. Until we find evidence—and I mean evidence, not innuendo or gossip—we cannot arrest anyone."

"And if I were to find you proof by pursuing my own investigations?"

Reg looked at him narrowly from beneath his brows. He said carefully, "If you were to do anything illegal, James, friend or no friend, I would have to arrest you."

"Me?" James threw back his head and laughed. "You'd better have another brandy, Reg! I hope you know me better than that. But if I were to find proof?"

"Then obviously we would follow it up."

***

Polly was feeling left out. Sue had gone home and made it clear that she would not be returning unless there was a real emergency. Ella had been lost in her own thoughts and quite remote since receiving her birth certificate, which although it didn't contain the information she wanted, she nonetheless kept as close to her as though it were the Crown Jewels. And Henry, although he had initially balked at the idea of courtship with his own wife, was now completely wrapped up in her in a way which brought tears to Polly's eyes.

Polly had seen a new side to both Henry and Mavis. The austere, distant, and very correct priest had all but disappeared, to be replaced by someone warmer and altogether more human. Someone who had human foibles and who now joked and teased. Someone who continued to take his work seriously, but who had clearly begun to believe that there was life after Church. Mavis had mellowed, there was no other word for it. She, too, seemed warmer and with the new, gentler hairstyle had treated herself to some new outfits. The polyester dresses with the narrow belts circa 1975 had gone, to be replaced by blouses and skirts and even a pair of tailored slacks. The creases in her forehead, which had given her a permanently anxious and pursed look, were gradually smoothing out as laughter lines around her eyes and mouth became more noticeable. She was softer and seemed to have a new kind of self-confidence, one that no longer depended on being in a position of power over other people.

Polly was delighted to see these gradual developments, but they left her wondering what her role was. With Henry living at the Mundenford house there had been something like a reversal of roles, with Polly and Ella looking after Henry almost like a couple of mothers. But it was clear he would be returning to the rectory soon and Polly found herself wondering what effect this would have on her. She didn't think he would revert to the old grave Henry, but she wasn't sure that her relationship with him would remain on quite the even keel it was now. Perhaps she would again be thrust into the subordinate role of the curate. If so, Polly wondered how she would react. It would be a bit like offering a lollipop to a child, then snatching it away when it had been half licked.

She had kicked off her slippers and was curled in the armchair with her feet beneath her watching whatever happened to be on television, when the doorbell rang. It was unusual to have visitors after dark and Polly felt a moment of anxiety. She padded to the door, opening it just a crack and peering around the edge. Then she threw it wide open in surprise and some degree of genuine delight.

"James! This is unexpected. To what do I owe the pleasure?"

James Mansfield smiled at her with as much charm as he could muster. "Polly my dear! May I come in?"

Polly stood to one side and indicated the lounge. She took his coat and offered him a drink, which he declined.

"Just finished my supper, thank you. Oh, have you eaten? I'm not disturbing you, am I?"

Polly shook her head as she switched off the television and slid her feet into her slippers. "Not at all. I wasn't really watching. Just passing the time."

"All alone tonight, then?"

"Afraid so. Ella's working and Henry is with Mavis. Isn't it brilliant, the way they've got back together again?"

"It certainly is! One might almost class it as a miracle. But that would be more in your jurisdiction than mine." He wagged a playful finger at her in a way that Polly found quite disconcerting. "Did you have anything to do with that?"

"Me? I wish! No, if it was anybody, it was my friend Sue Gallagher. She's a priest in the London area but she's also a trained counsellor. The bishops asked her to come."

"She's gone now?"

"Yes, she went on Saturday, worse luck. She's a great friend. I miss her."

She looked at James enquiringly. "It's lovely to see you, James, but is there something I can do for you?"

James said, "No, no, my dear. It's just that—well, I think you'll agree that things haven't been so great between us. Between you and me. I don't like to have barriers, especially when other things in the benefice seem to be settling down so well. So I've come to see if I can mend a few bridges."

Polly was startled. "Oh James! That's so nice of you. I can't tell you what this means to me. I've never wanted barriers between us either. I don't really know how they've happened, but if we can put them behind us now, that would be terrific."

"That is certainly my wish. If we're both agreed on a fresh start so easily, perhaps I will have that drink after all. As a matter of fact, I've brought a bottle of sherry with me for just that purpose. Let's drink to you and me and a new start."

He fished the bottle out of his jacket pocket. "Do you have any glasses?"

Polly got up. "Yes, I won't be a minute. They're in the dining room. Back in a bit."

She left the room, returning moments later with the two small glasses. But James was on his feet, looking at his watch. "I'm so sorry, my dear. I'd quite forgotten—I promised Daisy I'd call in at the supermarket and I've cut it a bit fine. Can I take a rain check? We'll have our drink some other time, if we may."

"You're going already? Oh! Some other time, then."

But her brow was furrowed as she closed the door after him and she looked carefully around the room. What had James been up to? Why had he come?

She noticed a buff envelope half hidden down the side of the armchair. Fishing it out she saw it was addressed to James and marked "Confidential." Polly turned it over in her hands. What a nuisance. This was probably what he had wanted to talk to her about, but she'd heard the car roar away. Now she'd have to deliver it to the manor and ask him what it was about.

Chapter Thirty-Three

Henry and Mavis between them set a date for Henry's return. Mavis sang as she scrubbed and polished, cleaned and dusted until every surface shone. She bought four bunches of brightly coloured flowers from Tesco and filled six vases with them, placing them at strategic intervals throughout the ground floor of the rectory. Then she prepared dinner. Although for the past ten years Henry had demanded a main meal at lunchtime, blaming a delicate digestion, he had easily fallen into the habit of an evening meal with Ella and Polly, and Mavis intended to keep it that way. She had discovered that even their contemporaries mostly ate in the evenings and she knew it made for a more leisurely meal, one which held the possibility of civilized conversation. Knowing that his favourite food was steak, Mavis had splashed out on prime fillet steak with a selection of vegetables and followed by his all-time favourite pudding of Spotted Dick (which she had made herself and steamed for hours) and custard. And she'd bought a box of chocolate mints to have with coffee afterwards, in the lounge.

Mavis laid the table with the damask tablecloth which had been a wedding present from her chief bridesmaid and which she saved for special occasions, the best cutlery, and a table centre of a small bouquet of fresh flowers surrounding a red scented candle in the silver candle holder. It took her hours, but she was pleased with the result.

Then Mavis showered and dressed carefully in another new outfit, this time a daring affair in blue chiffon of wide evening trousers and a loose top with a low neckline and five rows of sparkling sequins under the bust, flowing over her hips and drawing attention to her slender figure. She wondered briefly whether it was too young for her, but dismissed the thought. Henry wore what he liked without bothering about his age, so Mavis was sure he'd have no idea what garments for women suited which age group. She applied pale pink lipstick, blue eye shadow, and black mascara, but drew the line at the black eyeliner suggested by the girl in Boots. With newly washed hair, brushed until it shone then liberally sprayed to keep it immaculately in place, Mavis surveyed herself in the mirror. She knew she looked good and her heart was pattering like a teenager's, waiting for Henry to arrive. She added dabs of expensive perfume (a treat to herself for this particular occasion) on the inside of both wrists and on her neck.

Henry was due at seven for seven-thirty, but when seven-forty came and went, Mavis began to grow first worried, then deeply hurt and disappointed, and finally, angry. Had it all been a show, then? Had he forgotten so soon? Now he was coming home, did he regard her as some old rag to be tossed aside, uncaringly? Did he not realize that she would have gone to a whole day's worth of trouble to make this a perfect evening? And was he really not aware that when somebody failed to show for an important appointment, those waiting for him worried themselves sick?

Mavis picked up a book and tried to read. But when she had read the same paragraph six times, she threw it down in disgust. Then she turned on the television, but *I'm a Celebrity, Get Me Out of Here* did nothing for her. She channel-hopped for a while, but there was nothing. She switched off.

At eight-thirty, Mavis picked up the phone. Underneath the anger, she was seriously worried by now with visions of Henry's car lying upside down in one of the many ditches lining South

Norfolk country roads. She rang Henry's mobile without much hope that it was switched on. It wasn't. So she called Polly, but after thirteen rings knew the answer phone was going to cut in.

Not knowing what else to do or who else to contact, Mavis put the food back in the fridge and began to clear the table. Then she remembered Ella and ran back to the phone. Looking up the number of the Rose and Crown, she quickly dialled. After only a handful of rings, the phone was answered by a gruff male voice.

"Rose and Crown?"

"Could I speak to Ella, please?"

"Who is it? Is it personal? She's not allowed personal calls during working hours."

"This is an emergency," Mavis said firmly. "Tell her it's about the rector."

Then, as she heard the voice yell out, "Ella, phone. Some emergency with the rector," she wondered whether that had been a wise move. Now the gossip would fly yet again.

As she heard Ella's voice say, "Hello? Who is it, please?" she was unable to speak. Tears caught at her voice as she managed to croak, "Ella!"

Ella took over. "Mavis? Mavis, what is it? Mavis, something has happened to Henry. Mavis?"

Taking a deep breath Mavis stuttered, "No—well—I don't know. Do you know where he is, Ella? I was expecting him," she consulted her watch, "over two hours ago. But he hasn't come. I'm so worried, Ella."

Mavis heard the consternation in Ella's voice on the other end of the phone. "Oh dear! I thought he was with you, Mavis. He seemed so excited to be coming. He was about to get ready when I left. Have you tried Polly?"

"I rang, but she's out. Tried Henry's mobile, too, but no response."

"Well, they may be together. I didn't think Polly was going out this evening, so perhaps there's been an emergency and they've both been called out."

The relief that flooded Mavis at this sensible suggestion was so great that it made her acid again. "Too much of an emergency for either of them to pick up the phone? That takes about ten seconds. But obviously I'm not important enough for either of them to consider. Thanks very much. Sorry to have troubled you at work. Perhaps you won't mind picking up the phone if you hear anything?"

As Ella's warm voice said, "Of course I'll ring you, Mavis. Would you like me to come over when I've finished?" Mavis felt ashamed of her outburst.

She said, "No, it's all right, Ella dear. If he turns up here, I'll leave a message to let you know. You take care now. Lots of love."

She replaced the phone, made herself a sandwich and a cup of hot chocolate, and went to bed. But sleep was impossible. Mavis tossed and turned and tried to read, but to no avail. She couldn't prevent herself listening for the phone or the crunch of tyres on the gravel or the slamming of a car door. She kept fancying that she heard one of these events and her heart would start to pound, only to be disappointed all over again. The phone did not ring and Henry did not appear.

***

Henry had been eagerly anticipating his first evening at home with Mavis and dithered over what to wear. He rejected all his modern gear since he knew Mavis hated it, but neither did he want to go back to the old sports jacket with the leather elbow patches. He didn't want to appear too formal, but neither did he want to be so casual that Mavis would conclude he had made no effort at all. In the end he settled for a pair of light grey "stay-pressed" trousers with a pale blue shirt, an old college tie, and a maroon V-neck pullover he was fairly sure Mavis had given him one Christmas but which he hardly ever wore.

Ella had gone to work. Henry had showered, dressed, and was shaving when the phone rang. Polly answered it. From his room upstairs Henry couldn't hear what was said, but he did hear a note of alarm in Polly's voice as it rose several decibels. He went downstairs as Polly finished the call. She was white and shaky, and Henry looked at her with concern.

"Whatever's the matter? Who was that? What's happened?"

Polly's lower lip was trembling uncontrollably. Then she threw herself into Henry's arms, sobbing uncontrollably. Henry had no choice but to put his arms around her and hold her tight. He waited for the storm to subside.

Polly gulped and freed herself to move away and blow her nose. "Sorry, Henry. It was such a shock. It's Arthur. He's in hospital. That was the ward sister. He's asked for me. And—and—" her voice cracked and rose again, "the sister says to come at once. There isn't much time."

"Arthur? Arthur Roamer? What's happened? Did she say?"

"She said he had a fall yesterday but they didn't find him until this morning. The milkman saw him on the floor when he delivered his milk. He was due to be paid today, so he knocked. You know Arthur. He's always right on the nail with things like that. So when he didn't come to the door, the milkman peered through the letterbox. That's when he saw him and called an ambulance."

"Pity nobody called us earlier, then."

Polly scrubbed at her eyes. "I suppose the hospital staff were busy trying to save his life. Anyway, they wouldn't know who to call, would they? He's been semi-conscious. I don't suppose anyone knows he's in. I'll have to go."

Henry eyed her as she haphazardly searched for her car keys, then remembered Ella had the car. He sighed. "I'll take you. Come on."

"What about your evening out with Mavis?"

"Mavis will understand. Besides, I'll ring her from the hospital. Then I can give her an update on Arthur's condition. No point in ringing twice."

But when they saw Arthur, all thoughts of the telephone fled from both their minds. Arthur was hooked up to machines with tubes and wires, and his breathing was raspy and shallow. His eyes flickered open when Polly leaned over the bed, and he reached out a feeble hand. She gripped his hand in both of hers and stroked his forehead.

"Don't try to speak, Arthur. You need all your strength. Just concentrate on getting better."

But the old man appeared agitated and was trying to tell her something. Henry stood awkwardly in the background. He hated hospitals and avoided visiting whenever he could. He didn't know what to do with himself.

Fortunately for Henry, a nurse appeared and drew the floral curtains around the bed. She placed an extra chair in the little cubicle and Henry sat down with relief.

The nurse addressed Henry in a sibilant whisper. "I'm glad you've come, Reverend. He hasn't got long. Can you do the Last Rites for him? He was adamant that I call Reverend Hewitt—it's the only words he's spoken since they brought him in this morning—but I'm so glad you've come too. Does he know you're here?"

Without waiting for an answer, the nurse bustled forward and leaned over Arthur. She said in a voice loud enough for the entire ward to hear, "Arthur, your vicar's here, too. He's going to talk to you."

Then she whispered to Henry, "Hearing and touch are the last of the senses to go. He'll probably hear you and feel you even though he appears to be unconscious."

Polly moved aside to allow Henry to approach the bed. He had no service books with him, but knew the rudiments of offering the Last Rites. He made the sign of the cross on Arthur's forehead and said clearly, "Arthur, your sins are forgiven you. All those regrets for things you have thought or done or said in this life are wiped away. You are clean and washed and ready to face your Maker. Go on your way, dear friend, aided by angels and archangels and all the hosts of heaven. May your portion this day be in peace and your home the heavenly Jerusalem."

Then he stepped back, offering a silent apology to God for having the wrong words and hoping what he had done was sufficient. But he noticed that Polly had stepped forward again and was saying something of her own to Arthur. Henry leaned forward to listen.

Polly was saying, "You don't have to worry about anything, Arthur. Your wife is there for you and God himself is waiting to hold you in his arms and cuddle you. God loves you more than you can ever imagine and he's longing to meet you face to face. Good-bye, dear friend. I shall miss you so much, but we'll stay with you, Henry and I, for as long as your journey on this earth takes." Her voice cracked but she struggled to contain her grief, anxious that Arthur shouldn't be distressed by it.

Henry was both moved and embarrassed by her words. He knew he would never be able to bring himself to use words like that, but supposed it was different for women clergy. Polly seemed to be able to say exactly what was in her heart without pausing to wonder whether or not it was appropriately dignified for the Church, and perhaps, on occasion, that was entirely right and proper. The idea of someone being "cuddled by God" after their death was a powerful image and he imagined it would be immensely comforting to the old man.

Arthur never opened his eyes again. He slipped deeper into unconsciousness while Polly sat there, holding his hand. Henry was restless and would have given anything to be anywhere else, but Polly had made a promise.

Henry looked at his watch and cleared his throat. "It's after ten, Polly, and we both have work in the morning."

She looked at him with eyes brimming with unshed tears. "You go, Henry. I'll be all right. I'll get a taxi when—when it's over. But I can't leave him. You do see that, don't you?"

Henry whispered, "But it might be hours or days. You can't stay here forever. This is one of the problems when you allow yourself to get emotionally involved with parishioners."

But Polly just smiled and reiterated, "You go. I'll be fine."

Henry sighed silently and leaned back in his seat. It was then that his mind flew to Mavis. He pushed back his chair. "Listen, Polly. I've just remembered Mavis. I must find a phone. I'll not be long."

He padded out of the six-bedded bay and walked round to the entrance of the ward. But once on the long corridor, he was completely disorientated. The lights had been dimmed and there were few people about. Finding the lift, he studied the plan and took the lift to the ground floor. But the information desk was closed and the ground floor deserted. There were no signs for a telephone, so after wandering the floor helplessly for a while he made his way back upstairs to the ward.

Arthur Roamer died at four minutes past one in the morning. In all his long years of ministry, it was the first time Henry had actually been with someone at the exact moment when the soul left the body. He found it a strange experience, something of an anticlimax. One minute Arthur had been unconscious but breathing shallowly, the next the breathing ceased like a puff of wind and his chest rose and fell no more. Henry shivered. But Polly was much more matter-of-fact. She patted Arthur's hand, kissed him on the forehead, said, "Go well, my friend," called the nurse, then said to Henry, "He's gone. There's nothing more we can do here now. Shall we go home? Thanks for staying with me."

***

Mavis fell into a restless sleep in the small hours of the morning, but tossed and turned so much that she felt like a limp rag when she finally woke at six. Unable to sleep any further she got up and dressed, then sat at the kitchen table eyeing the phone. It was too early to ring Polly's house under any pretext, especially as she was sure by now that she would have heard from Ella if anything had been amiss. She made herself a cup of strong tea and ate a slice of dry toast.

The phone rang at seven o'clock, but Mavis couldn't bring herself to answer it. She watched as the little red light blinked, indicating that a message was being left, and waited until the light subsided. Then she picked up the receiver and dialled one-five-seven-one. Ella's whispered tones delivered the message.

"Sorry to wake you, Mavis," (*As if,* thought Mavis) "but Henry and Polly were so late last night and both of them were absolutely wrung out. It was Arthur Roamer. He'd been rushed into hospital and had asked for Polly, so the hospital rang and Henry took her up there. I don't think either of them expected it to be for more than an hour or so, but he was dying and they stayed with him for his final journey as far as they were able. I'm whispering because they're both still asleep and likely to be so for hours. But I knew you'd want to know. Arthur died early this morning."

Mavis played the message through a couple of times. She was genuinely sorry to hear about Arthur, someone whose straight talking she had always appreciated, but relieved to know that Henry was all right. She was also somewhat mollified that it really had been a legitimate emergency, but still both furious and disappointed that in all that time, Henry hadn't bothered to lift a phone to explain to her.

Still, she thought, *two can play at that game*. Fairly certain that Henry would drive over to explain in person that morning, she donned her anorak and caught the early bus into Norwich. If he thought she was going to wait around for him, he had better think again.

***

Henry slept until nine, then stumbled out of bed and into the shower, worrying about how to approach Mavis. Although he had assured Polly that Mavis would understand, privately he wasn't so sure. Mavis would have understood six months ago, but she had been so odd, lately. He dressed and shaved, thinking of his missed evening with regret and pondering over how to arrange Arthur's funeral service. There were no next of kin, as far as he knew. He hoped Arthur had at least made a will and wondered whether he would be contacted by a solicitor to make the necessary arrangements. But that would probably take a day or two. Meanwhile, there was Mavis.

Henry had a bowl of cereal and a cup of tea, then drove over to Thorpemunden. Recalling Ella's words from a day or two ago, he stopped at the garage and bought a bunch of flowers, even remembering to remove the sticky price tag.

He rang the doorbell at the rectory but, as no one answered, let himself in with his front door key. The rectory smelt fresh and clean, reminding Henry of how good it had been when Mavis had looked after him. He had always taken housework and washing and cooking for granted, but after a couple of weeks sharing the haphazard lifestyle of his curate, Henry had come to appreciate domestic order as never before.

Clearly Mavis was not at home and Henry wondered miserably whether her absence was a deliberate message to him. He laid the flowers on the draining board in the kitchen, then thought that it might be a pertinent gesture to put them in a vase. There was only one vase under the sink, so Henry did his best. But the vase was too big and flower arranging was not strong in his list of skills. He left the sad results on the windowsill in the kitchen.

Not knowing where Mavis was or how long she would be, Henry decided to leave a note. He tore a page from the lined pad Mavis used in her little office and wrote,

Dear Mavis,

I'm so sorry about last night. Poor Arthur Roamer has died and I had to go to the hospital with Polly. It took a long time, but he died peacefully. I think our presence helped.

I did try to ring you from the hospital, but everything shuts down at night and I couldn't find a phone. I realize how worried and anxious you must have been and I apologise unreservedly. But I'm sure you can understand the problem. My dearest wish is to be back with you, as we always were. The house looks lovely. I brought you some flowers. They are on the windowsill.

With love,
Yours, Henry.
Xxx

He folded the note and tucked it under a clean mug on the kitchen table. Then, with a last wistful look around he let himself out and drove back to Mundenford, to appraise Ivy Cranthorn of Arthur's demise.

Chapter Thirty-Four

Henry was busy over the next few days, arranging Arthur's funeral. Arthur's solicitor was the executor for his will, but Arthur had left no instructions about his funeral, not even whether he wished to be buried or cremated. Polly offered to chat with Ivy, who knew Arthur better than most.

Ivy was surprisingly philosophical about Arthur's death.

"I shall miss the old so-and-so, of course I will. I used to enjoy our chats together. But when you reach my age," she confided to Polly, "you expect it. You see all your friends gradually disappearing around you. There are few of my contemporaries left now."

"Must be quite depressing," Polly observed.

"Not at all. Can be a bit lonely at times. But I have my faith. It means a great deal to me. I believe in the afterlife, so that's all that matters, really."

"You think Arthur will be with his beloved wife?"

Ivy smiled. "That's a nice, comfortable thought. But I've never been totally convinced about that aspect. I suspect that once you leave this life, memory gradually fades until you become pure spirit, with no shades of earth clinging to you, if you see what I mean. As spirit, we're absorbed into God, who is spirit. So your question really doesn't apply."

"But what about Heaven and Hell?"

Ivy busied herself fetching a notebook and pencil. "I don't think of a physical place where you either go in or stay out. But I guess if your spirit isn't absorbed into God, then that loss might be an agonising experience."

Polly wrinkled her nose. "So although we'll be purely spirit, we'll still have feelings and emotions? We'll still be capable of experiencing pain even though we lose our memories?"

Ivy laughed. "Now you've got me! I don't know. All I really know for sure is that it'll be good unless we choose not to be part of God. That won't be good. Anyway, got my notebook. What did you want to ask me about Arthur?"

Polly grinned. She didn't know all the answers about life after death either. "For a start, we don't know whether he wanted burial or cremation. Did you ever discuss that sort of thing with him?"

"Not directly. But his wife was buried. She's in the churchyard at Middlestead, as you know. I think he wanted to be buried with her. In fact, I'm almost sure he talked about a double grave."

"Of course! I should have thought of that. Any idea about his favourite hymns or readings?"

Ivy consulted her notebook. Polly learned that Ivy and Arthur had had a number of discussions about hymns and music and readings, as well as putting the world to rights. They had never discussed anything in the context of funerals, but nonetheless Ivy had learned Arthur's preferences. Polly stayed for a further half hour, finding out from Ivy all she could about Arthur's inclinations and his earlier life and beginning to put together the rudiments of Arthur's funeral. Ivy said the Mothers' Union would be delighted to provide some sort of refreshments after the service free of charge, so Polly left her in charge of making the arrangements for that.

***

Henry had tried two or three times to ring Mavis, but had been forced to leave messages on the answer phone. In the end he decided to go home to the rectory anyway, whatever Mavis said or did. His final message stated clearly that he would be returning that afternoon, with all his belongings.

He packed quickly, said a fond farewell to Ella after making sure that she would visit frequently, arranged to meet up with Polly the following morning to discuss the funeral, and left straight after lunch. It was with a sense of relief that he motored back to Thorpemunden. Strange how you changed as you grew older, he reflected. Although he had enjoyed the relaxed lifestyle of the two younger women, he had found the general mess and untidiness frustrating and disconcerting. On several occasions he had had to close his lips to prevent himself criticizing the cobwebs and the dust and the mayhem, all of which had hit him with renewed force after his visit to the ordered and spotless rectory a day or two ago. Partly he was aware of what the response would have been, especially from Polly, if he had said anything, so it seemed more politic all round to keep his negative opinions to himself. But to be going home, to peace and order and a wife who looked after him in the manner to which he was accustomed, seemed to Henry to be something approaching paradise.

He unloaded his bags from the boot and opened the front door with his key. He called out, "Mavis?"

Mavis appeared at the end of the hall. She stood silently, arms folded. Henry hesitated, wondering how he should react. Then he dropped his bags, went up to her, and planted a discreet kiss on her cheek. She turned her head away.

Henry said, "Lovely to be home, dear."

Mavis sniffed. "You've come to stay, then? I suppose you think I'm going to move out?"

"No, of course not! I want us to be together, like it used to be."

"So when you failed to turn up the other night, with no message, no phone call, nothing until I heard from Ella next morning, that was your idea of being together, was it? I think 'being together' for you, Henry, means me washing and ironing and cooking and cleaning and you doing as you jolly well please. My advice to you is, find yourself another slave."

Henry sighed. He turned back for his cases. "Let's talk later. I did try to apologise but perhaps you failed to pick up the messages?"

"Oh, my failure, is it?" She turned to go. "Do you want a cup of tea?" When his eyes lit up she added, "The kitchen's there," and disappeared into the lounge where Henry soon heard music from the shows being played at volume.

Henry took his luggage upstairs. Since it was clear Mavis was not going to unpack for him, he did it himself. When he came down he went into the kitchen and made a pot of tea, which he carried through into the lounge. He poured out a cup for Mavis and handed it to her with the warmest smile he could muster. Then he sat down in his usual armchair with his own cup.

"This is nice," he observed.

Mavis didn't respond. Henry drank his tea in silence. Then he put his cup onto its saucer on the occasional table and said in a determined way, "Mavis, we can't go on like this. I've said I'm sorry. I don't know what else to do. Are you going to punish me forever? Is there no way we can talk about this like sensible adults?"

"So now I'm not sensible!" she snapped.

"You know I didn't mean that. I just want to talk. Mavis, tell me what you want. What are you looking for?"

Mavis turned hurt but steely eyes upon him. "If you don't know, why should I tell you?"

Henry put his head in his hands. He said in despair, "I don't know what to do. Please, Mavis. Help me. I can't do without you. I've come to realise that over the past few weeks. I've hated being apart from you. We belong together, you and I, and I really thought we'd sorted it out. I'm so sorry for the other night. I should have lent Polly the car and come over to you in a taxi. But, well, she's never been in that sort of situation before and I suppose I was a bit concerned for her. And it is my job to care for the people of these parishes."

"But that's just it, isn't it? You care for the people of the parishes at my expense. I'm the one who pays the price, not you. You get all the accolades for being a wonderful priest, but who enables you to do all those things? I do! But I never even get a word of thanks. I share your ministry, Henry. I've always supported you, even to running the Mothers' Union and starting the Sunday School all those years ago when we first came here, but I don't think you've ever thanked me. The parishes certainly haven't. They take it all for granted, as something that a rector's wife should do. Nobody cares about me."

Henry knelt in front of her and took both her hands in his. "Mavis, love. I am so sorry. I never realized. You're quite right. And that's what I've discovered; I can't do this job without you. You're always there for me, I pour out my problems to you, you help out when I need someone to do something suddenly, and you never complain. It's going to be different from now on, I promise."

"Like the other night, you mean? Do you know how long it took me to prepare? I spent the whole day cleaning, I chose your favourite meal, and I dressed up for the occasion. And there I sat, watching the clock and waiting for the phone to ring. How do you think I felt?"

Henry looked ashamed. "I really am sorry. When we went up to the hospital I didn't realise Arthur was actually at the point of death. You know what it's like—they call you in but the dying process goes on for days. Arthur was always such a tough old stick. I thought it would be like that. I thought we'd go in, he'd be practically out of it, so we'd murmur a few prayers and leave. Honestly, Mavis, I thought I'd be here by eight at the latest."

"So what happened?"

"He was dying when we got there. Drifting in and out of consciousness, but he was quite agitated at one point. Wanted to say something to Polly, although I don't think he managed to say anything coherent. But she sat there holding his hand and promised him we'd stay until he died. So I was stuck. I did mention about coming home, but she was determined to stay and I could hardly abandon her to take a taxi at that time of night."

"Why on earth didn't you ring and explain all this? I'd have understood. I'd have been disappointed, of course I would. But I'd have understood."

"You know what I'm like. I need a nursemaid at times. When I realized how late it was I trailed all over the hospital looking for a phone. But everything shuts up at night and there's no one to ask. In the end I gave up. And by the time we got home, it was too late. I didn't want to disturb you at two in the morning."

"Huh!" Mavis muttered. "And what about Ella? You going to be happy leaving her and living here?"

Henry looked ashamed. "I think I had a few moments of madness, after my illness. Ella almost seemed like an angel sent from God. She helped me to get through, and for a while, I fancied myself in love with her. She made me feel young again and—and—she made me feel wanted for myself."

"Which I don't, I suppose? Who do you think looked after you through all those black weeks when you responded to nothing, when you hardly opened your mouth? Who was so desperately worried about you that she practically went down on bended knee to persuade Ella to stay?"

"I know, I know. And I'm sorry. I have taken you for granted, Mavis. But I won't anymore, I promise."

"So you're not in love with Ella?"

"I think I probably love her," Henry said honestly, "but no, I'm not in love with her. I love you, Mavis, more than I can ever say. I don't want it to seem as if I'm hiding behind my illness, but I think it took longer to clear than I had appreciated. I am over it now, though. And I'm asking you to give me another chance. I'll do anything you want. I'll be anyone you want."

Mavis' lips were still tightly pinched, but her eyes had softened. "I only want you. That's all I've ever wanted. But it may take me awhile to fully trust you again. Will we be all right together, Henry?"

In answer, he pulled her to her feet and hugged her closely. Then he tipped up her chin and kissed her on the lips with a long, lingering kiss.

"Yes," he said softly, "we will."

***

After seeing Ivy, Polly called at Thorpemunden Manor with the official-looking envelope James had inadvertently left behind. It was the first chance she'd had. She'd meant to ring and warn him that the envelope must have dropped out of his pocket, but Arthur's death had put everything out of her mind and it was only this morning that she had rediscovered the envelope, hidden under a pile of mail.

But the house was closed and silent and there was no car in the drive. Not knowing what else to do, Polly wrote a short note on the back of one of her business cards and pushed it through the letterbox with the envelope. James could contact her again if he wished to do so. There was no way Polly had time to go round chasing after him.

She glanced up at the windows as she climbed back into the car and thought for a moment that she saw a figure flit across the latticed dormer window of the attic. But the window was high and because it was set back a little in the roof, she wasn't sure. It was too far away to see anything clearly. Grimacing as she recalled the last time she thought she had seen a shadowy figure in the confines of Thorpemunden Manor and all the trouble that had caused her, Polly told herself not to be so stupid. It was clear the Mansfields were not at home.

She drove home. It felt almost empty now there were just the two of them again, but Polly felt more relaxed than she had for some time. It had been fine having Henry there and she had got to know him so much better, but his presence had cramped her style. Being in the same age group, she and Ella had similar lifestyles and expectations, which didn't feature pristine orderliness at all times. They cleaned from time to time when it was glaringly necessary, Ella taking the brunt of the work, but other than that lived altogether more casually than Henry or Mavis. Polly was quite certain Mavis would be horrified if she had any idea of the state of Polly's house, even though it was perfectly presentable.

***

James Mansfield had been waiting for Polly's visit. Indeed, he had almost given up waiting, she had taken so long to return the envelope. Since it was only lightly sealed, he hoped she had taken out the contents and had a good look. It would strengthen his case if her fingerprints were on both envelope and contents.

He picked up the envelope by its corner and sauntered into the study, laying the envelope carefully on his desk. Then he rang the chief constable.

"Reg? James here. Remember what we said about proof the other night? I think I've got some!"

Reg sounded confused. "Proof? What about?"

"Have you forgotten my robbery? I thought you assured me you were pulling out all the stops. Just as well I'm doing your work for you."

"All right, James, cut the accusations. I've had a bad week. Now, what are you talking about?"

"It's just as I thought. Our curate, Polly Hewitt, pushed an envelope through my door this morning. It's one that was stolen from my safe."

Reg sighed. "A little convenient, isn't it? The very person you so dearly wish to accuse of theft suddenly turns up on your doorstep with an envelope which you say was in your safe and returns it to you! Well, James, I have some questions about that. One, can anyone corroborate that the envelope was in your safe in the first place; two, why would she return it if she stole it; and three, what do you expect me to do about it?"

Not having thought his plan through to that extent, James resorted to bluster. “Don’t expect me to know all the answers! I would have thought my word—the word of a long-established and trusted friend and ex-Master of the Lodge—would count for something. Surely you can at least fingerprint the envelope? Verify that she’s held it? How else would Polly Hewitt get to handle an envelope addressed to me and clearly marked ‘Confidential’? Whatever else you decide to do or avoid doing, I think you owe me that much. You’ve done precious little else to solve this crime.”

“You know nothing of what we’ve been doing. I can assure you that my officers are still doing all in their power. But we do have other priorities as well. I’m sure you read in the paper about the stabbing in Diss last week? I’m afraid crimes like that must come very high on our list, possibly even higher than your robbery, for which I understand there has been a substantial insurance pay-out.”

“How in the world—?”

“I told you, James. We have not stopped working on it. We are covering all angles. Now if you’ll excuse me—”

“No, hang on a minute, Reg. All I’m asking is that you fingerprint this envelope and take it from there. It might be clean, in which case you need take it no further.”

“It all costs public money, James. I’m not sure this is a good use of resources, especially as you tell me she delivered the envelope back. Of course it’ll have her prints on it. But that won’t prove anything.”

“No, I suppose not. Oh, by the way, Reg, we’re having a shoot the weekend after next. Do hope you can join us? As my guest, of course.”

There was a sudden silence on the other end of the phone. When Reg spoke again his voice was silky. “Why, James! How very kind of you. I should be delighted to join your party. And it just so happens I do have an officer free at the moment. Obviously a set of prints on an envelope is insufficient to make any arrest, but all evidence helps. I'll send someone over for that envelope forthwith."

***

The first snow of winter fell on the first Saturday of December, the day of Thorpemunden Christmas Fayre. An event which was shared between the village and the church, it usually drew a good crowd who spent freely, thus helping to reduce the church's cash flow problem. Henry had always relied on the Christmas Fayre to enable Thorpemunden Church to pay the final instalment of its Parish Share, but as the Share increased year on year, so it was becoming increasingly difficult to fund the shortfall. He looked out at the heavy sky with foreboding in his heart. While most people would brave rain, few of the older folk would venture out in a blizzard. And part of him was glad about that. The responsibility if anyone slipped and broke a fragile bone lay weightily upon Henry.

Nonetheless, Henry himself had to be there, urbanely smiling at everyone, introducing Lord Temstock, who lived locally and had been prevailed upon to open the Fayre, wandering around outside in the freezing weather looking as though a Christmas Market was his idea of Heaven, and spending money he didn't want to spend on items he didn't want to buy. Although Henry escaped to the warmth of the church and a welcome cup of tea and a mince pie as frequently as he could, he was aware that to spend too long inside the confines of the church would provoke criticism and resentment by those who had to suffer outside.

Henry dressed as warmly as he could with extra layers of clothing and set off. It was difficult to see through the falling snow, but it was evident that not many people had ventured out. He wandered round all the stallholders outside on the village green, trying to find encouraging words for each of them. After learning from the first stallholder that sales were miserable, he forbore to ask that question again. But he found himself dipping into his pocket more frequently than he would have wished, just to cheer up the stallholders.

As Mavis was in the church helping out with teas, Henry escaped there as quickly as he could. There were a few more people in the church, sitting at makeshift tables in the pews with their sausage rolls and teas and mince pies, and Henry was relieved to be able to join them.

He looked round for Polly. She, too, was expected to be there and when Henry couldn't see her, he felt his irritation rising.

"Have you seen Polly or Ella?" he asked Mavis.

She shook her head. "Neither of them have been in here. Aren't they outside?"

"No." He consulted his watch. "This is too bad. Polly should be here by now. Surely she realises that we need to support this event? It's our biggest event of the year and we need to keep the liaison with the village strong. I thought things were so much better with Polly, but then she does this! Where on earth has the girl got to?"

Chapter Thirty-Five

Polly woke late on the Saturday morning and scrambled to get ready in time for Thorpemunden's Christmas Fayre. Unlike Henry, she was thrilled to see the snow. Still young enough to enjoy the excitement, she was also aware that snow would bring out the children and their families, and she had visions of making relationships with young people she had not yet met. She sang as she showered and dressed, but by the time she was eating breakfast, Ella had still not appeared. Although Ella rose after Polly, she was always ready for special events and Polly was fairly sure Ella had planned to help Mavis in the kitchen.

Polly called up the stairs as she whisked her toast out of the toaster, but there was no reply. Buttering the toast and stuffing a quarter into her mouth, Polly bounded up the stairs and hammered on Ella's door. When there was no response she opened the door and peeped inside. To her puzzlement, Ella's bed was already made but Ella herself was nowhere to be seen. Polly shrugged and returned to the kitchen to finish her breakfast. Perhaps Ella was out running—although Polly had never known her to go running before—or more likely, she had slipped out for a paper while Polly was in the shower.

But Polly was uneasy. Neither explanation sounded likely to her and she hadn't heard a sound while she had been dressing. She glanced at the clock on the kitchen wall and checked the time against her watch. She could afford to wait for maybe fifteen minutes. If Ella wasn't home by then, she really ought to go.

Polly busied herself washing her breakfast pots, even going so far as to dry them and put them away just to fill in time. But Ella did not reappear. By now, Polly was seriously worried. She didn't dare ring Henry, for such were his feelings for Ella that he'd probably go haywire if he thought she might be missing. Polly returned upstairs and began to look more carefully in Ella's room. The bed was neatly made, but were her pyjamas in it? No, they'd gone. Polly opened the wardrobe. Few if any clothes appeared to be missing. What about shoes? Ella's boots had gone, but Polly wasn't sure whether or not anything else was absent. She particularly noticed the lack of boots because she had admired them only recently, but she wasn't sure whether or not Ella had more than one pair of trainers. There was a pair in the bottom of the wardrobe, but it could be a spare pair.

Polly ran through to the bathroom. Being half asleep at the time, she hadn't taken much notice of anything while she had her shower, but now she looked more carefully, opening the bathroom cabinet to see whether Ella's toothbrush was still there. With a sinking feeling Polly saw that both the toothbrush and a tube of toothpaste had gone, along with Ella's deodorant.

Then she remembered Ella's backpack, the one she took with her everywhere. Polly ran throughout the house, searching in the most unlikely places, willing it to be found, but there was no sign of the bag. Her multicoloured, knitted cloche hat, the one that so defined Ella, had gone, too. Polly sank down at the kitchen table, unable to believe the conclusion she had reached. Ella was gone and had chosen to go.

Polly began to search for a note. She even powered up her computer to see whether Ella had left a message, but to no avail. Trying to comfort herself with the fact that Ella had left almost an entire wardrobe behind, surely an indication that she planned to return, Polly couldn't help the feelings of desolation, abandonment, and deep hurt which filled her being. And she didn't know what to do next.

She rang Ella's mobile but it went straight to the answer phone, a sure indication that Ella was either out of signal or had switched the phone off. She left a message anyway, pleading for Ella to get in touch. Polly felt she could hardly ring the police. They'd laugh at her for reporting a missing person who had taken a toothbrush and a pair of pyjamas with her. Even Polly in her distress could see that Ella's departure was deliberate.

But why? Polly had thought Ella was happy, even though she'd been a little quiet lately. But Polly had put that down to the problems between Henry and Mavis. Obviously Polly would have to inform Mavis at some point, for Ella was her niece, wasn't she? But how would Henry take the news? That reminded Polly about the Christmas Fayre, but she was reluctant to leave the house, just in case Ella came back. And what would she say to Henry and Mavis?

Then she sat up suddenly as a brilliant idea occurred to her. Of course! Probably Mavis had invited her to stay overnight at the rectory to help ease the situation with Henry, and they had all forgotten to tell Polly. Or even more likely, they had told Polly but her mind had been elsewhere at the time and she hadn't taken it in. That must be it.

With a heart now full of hope, Polly fished out her woolly hat and sheepskin mittens and prepared to set out for Thorpemunden, certain she would find Ella already there. How Ella could have got there without the car was a thought which Polly pushed to the back of her mind, preferring not to deflate her optimism. She was already very late, but hoped Henry would understand when she explained the circumstances to him.

It was a difficult journey with the snow still falling, sometimes with blizzard-like ferocity. None of the roads between Mundenford and Thorpemunden had been gritted and Polly had to drive with extreme caution. It was all right as long as no other cars approached from the opposite direction, but Polly's heart thumped whenever she had to pass a parked car or a car moving towards her. The wheels slewed in all directions on the frozen snow. The road entering Thorpemunden from Mundenford ended on a slight rise in a T junction. Normally there was no problem, but today Polly prayed for a clear road. If she had to stop on the rise she wasn't sure that she'd ever get started again. But it was definitely a day for the operation of Murphy's Law. Polly drove up the sloping road as slowly as she dared, but when she reached the junction two cars were coming along the road at the top. Polly was forced to stop. When she tried to drive out onto the village street, the wheels refused to grip. Since she had nothing in the car, no spade or sacking or anything to help drive forwards, it was a choice between abandoning the car in the middle of the road or reversing until she found a suitable driveway where she could turn. Polly decided to reverse, managed to turn without hitting any gateposts, and drove back the way she had come. There was a small passing place half a mile back which she planned to use as a lay-by until she could attend properly to the car. But it all took ages. By the time she had walked back into the village, Polly was extremely late, exceedingly chilled, and very unhappy.

To her disappointment there were few children on the village green, although the presence of a large snowman with a carrot for a nose indicated that the children had been and gone, as had the stallholders. Most of the stalls covered by their gazebos were still standing, but were deserted. Polly trudged into the church, stamping her feet to remove the worst of the clogged snow from her boots.

By contrast, the church was packed with chattering people who seemed to be enjoying the companionship.

"It's like it was in the war," observed Ivy Cranthorn, "everyone supporting each other and making sure the elderly are all right."

Polly hid a smile, thinking that few as old as Ivy would venture out in weather like this. Obviously she'd had a lift and the conditions first thing weren't quite as bad as they were now, but even so. Still, Ivy would never consider herself to be old if she lived to be a hundred.

Polly scanned the crowd but failed to see Ella. She spotted Henry across the church and made her way towards him. Then she changed her mind and sought out Mavis in the small kitchen area at the west end of the church under the tower.

Mavis dried her hands on the tea towel and came out into the church with mugs of tomato soup for herself and Polly.

"Tell me again. I couldn't hear properly in there. What's this all about? Ella, did you say? What's wrong with Ella?"

Polly slurped some soup and warmed her hands round the polystyrene mug. "I thought she might be here. I'm sure she said she was going to help you in the kitchen. But she seems to have gone and I don't know where. She's just gone. When I got up this morning the bed was made but her pyjamas and toothbrush have gone. I thought she'd perhaps spent the night with you? No? Then I think she's just taken off."

Mavis frowned. "Why would she do that? She must have left a note or something."

"I've been all round the house but I couldn't find a thing. I've looked in all the likely places, on the kitchen cabinet, on the cork board in the study, on the coffee table. I've even looked on the computer. But there's nothing."

"Has she taken her clothes? If not, it must be a flying visit somewhere. Perhaps she got called away and didn't have time to tell you."

"But who would call her away? She hasn't any relatives, has she? You're her aunt, you should know."

Mavis dropped her eyes. "I'm not, actually. We met quite by chance one day. People jumped to the conclusion that she was my niece and it seemed easier to leave it that way. But I never actually said that."

Polly was astonished. "Oh! I had no idea. She never said. Well, then. In that case, I don't think she has any relatives at all, so where would she go?"

"Perhaps back to Yarmouth? She was living there before she came to us."

Polly shook her head. "I doubt it. As far as I know, she had no further contact with those people. But then, it appears that I don't know Ella as well as I thought I did. Otherwise I'd know what was going on."

Mavis was looking worried. "I don't know what I'm going to tell Henry. He'll be distraught."

"That's why I came to you first. I don't really know what to do."

"There's nothing you can do." Mavis' common sense reasserted itself. "We just have to wait until Ella contacts us. The good news is that we can be certain she went of her own accord and that she hasn't gone for long. She's entitled to her own agenda and I'm sure she will get in touch when she's ready. We just have to be patient. Don't worry about Henry. I'll tell him and keep him calm."

***

But Henry was anything but calm when he heard the news. His face twisted and Polly was afraid he was going to break down in the church. One or two people glanced his way, realised that something was amiss, and moved off uncomfortably.

Henry was in anguish. He tried to think back over all he had said and done recently, guiltily wondering whether he was to blame. He wanted to rush out immediately to look for Ella, and his voice rose.

Mavis took his arm and drew him away into a quieter corner of the church where they were less likely to be observed.

"Where would you look?" she asked.

"I don't know, but I must do something. I can't just sit here as though nothing has happened."

Polly said, "We don't know that anything has happened, Henry. As Mavis said, all Ella's clothes are still there. She can't have gone for long. Perhaps there'll be a message on the answer phone when we get back. After all, you know what it's like.

When we were at the hospital with Arthur we couldn't phone Mavis. Perhaps Ella's in some sort of situation like that."

But this only served to make Henry worse. "Hospital? Yes, we must phone the hospital to see if anyone has been brought in. What if she's had an accident and has no identification on her?"

The two women looked at each other helplessly. Mavis said, "I'll ring as soon as we get back. If you like, I'll ring the police too. Just to set your mind at rest. But we can't go yet. You must stay here for a bit longer, you owe it to the Thorpemunden people. Come on, do what Ella would want you to do, make her proud of you. Go round and chat to people like you always do."

Henry turned anxious eyes upon her, but rather to her surprise, he complied. He was better moving about than sitting still, but although he strove to act normally, his agitation was clear for all to see.

"What's wrong with Henry?" demanded Bette Jarrold, for whom tact was never a strong point.

"He's just had some bad news," Mavis replied and pointedly walked away.

The gossip spread round the church like a bush fire and since nobody knew what the "bad news" was, they happily used their imaginations. Before long, Henry's sister had been diagnosed with cancer (he had no sister), his best friend had died suddenly, there was a flood at the rectory, and he'd suddenly been told he was to lose his job. Nobody imagined the truth, that Ella had gone.

Both Mavis and Polly had begun to settle, believing that Ella would soon return, but Henry had had more conversations with Ella than anybody. Only he was aware of her pattern of suddenly moving on when she felt the time was apposite. Henry was very afraid that Ella had gone for good. He remembered their first meeting, when Ella arrived carrying nothing more than a backpack, so the information about her clothes remaining at Polly's house did nothing to encourage him. What he found most painful was that she hadn't said good-bye. He had considered himself and Ella to have a special relationship, and no matter how she had left on previous occasions, he had not expected her to leave him without any form of farewell.

***

As churchwarden of Thorpemunden, James Mansfield had had a busy day. When it became obvious that the snow would prevent the usual fun outside, he had invited the stallholders into the church. There was neither time nor room to erect their stalls in there, but everyone had worked with a will, transferring the goods from the stalls into different areas of the church, which soon resembled a market in its own right. Along with the make-shift tables where food was being consumed, the church was packed with barely room to move in the aisles. James was in his element, making decisions for everybody and strutting about the church as though it was his own manor.

He had been well aware that Polly was absent and had mentally added this misdemeanour to the list he was compiling to present to the bishop. He was a little disappointed to see her come in eventually, but his interest was piqued when he noticed her dishevelled appearance and saw her in earnest conversation with Mavis. James lingered close by.

As Mavis and Polly moved across to talk to Henry, James hovered within listening distance while showing enormous interest in the Christmas wrapping paper being sold from the pew on his right-hand side. While talking to the seller of the Christmas paper, James managed to hear all that was said and his mind began to work overtime.

To James, it was obvious. Polly's words to Mavis were all an act. She knew exactly where Ella had gone, because the girl had absconded with the proceeds from James' safe. They'd been in it together from the beginning. Somehow or other, Polly had got wind that the police were about to concentrate their efforts on her again, so she had thought it expedient to get rid of the evidence. Hence Ella had "disappeared" and Polly would no doubt meet up with her at some future point when the coast was clear.

Who was this Ella anyway? If she wasn't Mavis' niece as everyone had thought and if Mavis and Henry had only just met her, where had she come from? James wondered whether the police had thought through that angle at all. Ella had been working in full view of a saloon bar full of people on the night of the robbery, so he was fairly sure the police had not even considered her as a likely suspect. But what if Ella had a criminal record? And what about Polly Hewitt's mother? Hadn't she disappeared at about the same time?

Suddenly, it was all becoming crystal clear to James. No wonder the police had got nowhere in their investigations. It wasn't just Polly, there were three of them in on the robbery. Polly was the one who had been seen at Thorpemunden Manor, so she had stolen the money, but her mother must have been sent away instantly with part or all of the loot, and now Ella Wim had gone to join her. James had no doubt that within a very short time Polly, too, would disappear.

James could hardly wait to get home. He determined to ring Reg as soon as he could. This time he felt he had enough circumstantial evidence to demand a fresh look at Polly Hewitt and her household.

***

Although the snow eased during the afternoon, it was lying three inches thick. Polly prepared to trudge back to her car, but Henry wouldn't hear of it.

"Come and stay with us for the night," he invited.

"What if Ella returns?"

"She'll ring," Henry said, with more confidence than he felt. "Anyway, you can ring your house from the rectory to see if she's there."

Mavis added her voice to Henry's. "You can't go walking off in this. It's nearly dark. What if you can't start your car? Stay with us for the night. The snow will likely be gone by tomorrow."

So Polly had gone back to the rectory, where all three of them felt more comfortable with each other for support and company. Mavis rang the police for reports of any accidents, but although there were a number of minor traffic pile-ups in the county, none of them had been serious and the police had accounted for all occupants of the cars. She had then rung the hospital at Henry's insistence, but again to no avail, to the relief of all of them.

"How did she get anywhere in weather like this?" wondered Polly.

"It wasn't so bad early on. Do you have any idea what time she left?" Mavis poured tea as she spoke.

"No, I overslept. Didn't hear a thing. I only know that she was gone when I got up. For all I know, she could have taken off late last night, after I went to bed."

Henry said gravely, "All we can do is wait and pray and hope she comes back soon. Isn't it amazing how much we all miss her?"

The other two nodded sombrely. Ella had become very much a part of all their lives and they were now unsure how they had managed without her. She had become very precious to them all in different ways, and her absence, together with their anxiety over it and not knowing what had happened to her, was in danger of leaving a large and open wound in the very centre of all their beings.

Chapter Thirty-Six

When the doorbell rang early on the Tuesday morning, Polly was certain it was Ella. She knew Ella had a key and there was no need for her to ring, but Polly's mind so wanted her friend back that it refused to consider such a trivial detail. It had to be Ella, for who else would call at such an ungodly hour?

Polly flew to the door in her fleecy, polka-dot pyjamas, not even pausing to throw on a dressing gown. She flung the door wide, but the delighted grin on her face quickly died, to be replaced by a scowl.

"What do you want? It's not Ella, is it? Don't tell me something's happened to her?"

Sergeant Hooper said, "No, it's not Ella, whoever she might be. May we come in?"

Polly indicated "yes" with a flick of her head and stood aside to let him and PC Dachery pass. The young policewoman gave Polly an apologetic smile as she entered, but Sergeant Hooper strode into the lounge as though he owned it.

Polly said, "You'd better sit down. I wasn't expecting visitors, as you can see. Give me ten minutes to get dressed. Do you want a drink or anything?" She said it in a way that prompted a "no" response and Sergeant Hooper obediently refused refreshment on behalf of both of them.

Polly ran upstairs with her thoughts in turmoil. It was a relief to know that they hadn't come about Ella, but she was unable to think of any other reason for their visit. The only thing she could come up with was that perhaps her car had been parked illegally in the passing spot on Saturday. Maybe someone had phoned in a complaint.

She had a quick shower and dressed in her tan trousers with the bottle green shirt and her dog collar. She wore a dark brown Thorpemunden Church sweatshirt over the top and slid her feet into flat black pumps. She attended to her hair as best she could—it was still never tame—and applied a touch of makeup. Feeling a little more presentable she walked downstairs in a more sedate manner than her usual bound and sat in the spare armchair in the lounge. She sent up a quick and silent prayer and folded her hands in her lap.

"What can I do for you? Sergeant Hooper isn't it? And PC Dachery?"

PC Dachery smiled and said eagerly, "You remember us from last time, then?"

But the sergeant quelled her with a glance, plucking at the ends of his drooping ginger moustache. He spoke in heavy tones. "Reverent Hewitt, do you remember the night of Saturday October the twenty-eighth? Over a month ago now, but you may recall that we visited you soon after that to ask where you were on that evening."

Polly nodded. "I believe I told you I was here at home. It was the night of the Mansfields' robbery, wasn't it? Is that what all this is about? Have you caught someone? But why would you come to me if you have?"

PC Dachery dropped her eyes. She sat on the edge of her chair, twining and untwining her fingers in her lap. Polly thought how Dachery was constantly reduced to the status of a little girl by her sergeant, who was presumably her police partner, without a word being said. Perhaps the long blond hair tied back in a ponytail added to the illusion, although at around five foot nine she towered over Polly. And she looked to be at least twenty-three. Polly repressed the thought of "victims are responsible for their own victimisation," which sprang unbidden into her mind. She reminded herself that Christianity is about unconditional love and that she had no idea what kind of sexism went on in the backrooms of police stations. Then she glanced at Sergeant Hooper with distaste and knew that she herself was several light years away from that ideal of unconditional love.

Sergeant Hooper was saying, "But that wasn't true, was it, Reverend Hewitt?"

Polly had a moment of blind panic. She couldn't remember exactly what she had said, but she knew she had claimed to be at home alone. And nobody apart from Ella and now Henry and Mavis knew that she had fibbed. She moistened her lips, caught between a longing to tell the truth and brazening it out on the grounds that it would look awful if she suddenly changed her story.

She played for time. "What do you mean?"

"We know you were at the Mansfields' house on that evening. What we don't know is why you, a woman of the cloth, are choosing to lie about it. But a great deal of money was stolen on that occasion and new evidence has come into our possession linking you with that crime."

Polly stared, the colour draining from her face. "What new evidence? What are you talking about? I haven't done anything. How can there be any evidence?"

Sergeant Hooper stood up. "If you'll just come along with us, Miss."

Polly noticed the dropping of her title and felt even more afraid. Her heart was beating so hard she felt as if they must notice it. "What do you mean? Come where? Why? I can't come. I have work to do, people to see."

"Come along now, Miss. Don't make this more difficult than it already is. We need you to come to the station with us."

"Are you arresting me?"

"We will, if you don't come of your own accord. At the moment we merely wish to question you further."

Polly hung back. "Question me here, then. I don't want to come to the police station."

Sergeant Hooper's tone became peremptory. "You come now or I will arrest you and take you out to the car in handcuffs. Which is it to be?"

Polly gasped. She thought he was bluffing and doubted that he could legally handcuff her, but she didn't dare risk it. Her eyes filled but she tossed her head and walked out with it held high, grabbing her anorak from the hall stand on her way past. She said no more as she sat next to PC Dachery in the back of the car, but her lips were moving in silent prayer. She needed God now as she had never needed him before.

At the station she was shown into a drab incident room containing just a table with two chairs on either side of the table. A voice recorder box stood on one end of the table. The room was bare, with grey paint on the walls and dark grey lintels and windowsill. There was just one window to the outside world, a window which was so high Polly was unable to see out of it. It allowed a little light into the room, but the overall impression was dreary. The other long, dark window covering most of one wall, Polly assumed from her television viewing of police dramas, was one-way, for her interview to be watched by unknown persons while she was at the disadvantage of having no idea who was there.

Sergeant Hooper indicated where she should sit, then exited the room. Polly was left alone. She wondered whether it was a ploy to soften her up and she wondered who was observing her. She glanced at her watch. Still only seven-fifteen. Having missed breakfast she was hungry and desperate for a cup of tea, but there were no such welcoming signs. She got up and wandered round the room, not because there was anything to see, but merely for something to do.

Sergeant Hooper and PC Dachery returned at five to eight. Polly was sure they had been in the staff canteen and wondered why they couldn't have called on her half an hour later. They failed to offer her anything. Sergeant Hooper sat down with an self-satisfied smirk on his red face, as though now he had Polly on his turf she would immediately crumple. But he had made the mistake of giving her time and Polly's resolve had strengthened. She now had other ideas.

Sergeant Hooper switched on the recorder and entered the time and date, his own name and PC Dachery's. He asked Polly to state her name, which she did clearly and without fuss.

Then he said, "Where were you on the night of Saturday October twenty-eighth?"

Polly said more calmly than she felt, "I have not eaten or been offered a cup of tea. I cannot answer any questions until I have received refreshments."

She noticed the sergeant grit his teeth, but he looked at Dachery and nodded. He said for the recorder, "PC Dachery has left the room," and sat back with his arms folded. He switched off the machine.

Polly said, "I shouldn't wait, if I was you. After breakfast I shall not answer any questions without a solicitor present."

Hooper grinned at her, an unpleasant grin revealing broken teeth stained by nicotine. "So you have got something to hide? The goody-two-shoes Reverend Hewitt is not quite so good after all."

"Not so," retorted Polly. "But I've seen enough television cop dramas to know some of my rights, so I suggest you find me that solicitor."

The grin faded as Hooper opened his notebook. "What's his name?"

"I don't have one. The duty solicitor will do fine, whoever he or she might be."

But she was uncomfortably aware that Hooper's grin returned with full force. Clearly he was pleased, which must be an indication that he considered the duty solicitor to be hopelessly malleable. Polly's heart sank. She was no good at this game. Sergeant Hooper had been playing it all his life, but Polly didn't know the rules. She was guessing at them while trying to find her way in the dark. It was like walking through squelching mud in the fog and she was aware that any minute she might make a fatal slip.

With no plan in mind, she decided to mirror Sergeant Hooper, so sat back on the uncomfortable plastic chair with her arms folded and what she hoped was a supercilious smile on her face.

Polly was also aware that she was entitled to a phone call, but hadn't been able to make up her mind who to phone. The obvious choice was Henry, who had to know at some point anyway and would be missing her at Morning Prayers, but would she be better phoning Sue?

Unbidden, a surprising thought inserted itself into Polly's mind. With a sudden desperation, she wanted her mother. Polly hadn't been in contact with Amanda at all since the day she had packed her off home on the train and she hadn't missed her in the least. But from somewhere deep down in Polly's being came an unexpected longing for her own flesh and blood, her own mother.

Polly gulped back a sob as tears stung the back of her eyelids and she told herself not to be so stupid. Fat lot of help Amanda would be! It was her fault Polly was in this mess in the first place and she would hardly come running in response to a phone call from her daughter. No, she'd probably never want to see Polly again. Besides, she'd be bound to blurt out some compromising sentiment. Much better to forget her.

In the end, Polly elected to call Henry. He'd ring Sue for her, if the shock of Polly's news didn't put him in such a state that he was incapable of doing anything.

She asked for a phone.

Hooper said, "All in good time."

Polly stared, a small frown appearing on her brow. "What do you mean, 'All in good time'? I believe I'm entitled to a phone call and I would like to make that phone call now."

With his beefy elbows on the table, Hooper leaned forward. The unpleasant smirk was back. "See here, Miss Goody-two-shoes. In here you do what I say. None of your lardy-dah attitudes will work in here. See, I don't care that you're a reverend, because I don't believe in any of that God rubbish. I'd like to see your God get you out of this."

Polly glanced towards the one-way window. "I presume no one's watching, yet? I don't think you'd be addressing me in quite those terms if they were."

He made a noise between a snort and a sneer. "My point is, in here you do what I say. I'm your god as long as you're in here and I'll thank you to remember that."

Polly felt sick. She hated to hear such blasphemy, which she would have liked to shove straight back down Sergeant Hooper's throat. Then she felt guilty for such sentiments, which were no better than his. She took a deep breath.

"I wish to make a phone call, please."

"And I wish you to wait," he said, mimicking her tone.

The door opened and PC Dachery entered, carrying a tray bearing a mug of tea and a plate with toast and marmalade. She set it down in front of Polly with a shy smile. Polly smiled back and murmured her thanks. The tea was steaming and Polly took a scalding sip. She ate her breakfast slowly, determined not to give the odious sergeant any further advantage and hoping that the duty solicitor would appear before too long. But she'd wait all day if she had to. There was no way she was going to say anything without legal representation.

A police officer came into the room at eight-thirty and whispered in Sergeant Hooper's ear. Polly strained to catch the words without leaning forward and looking too obvious, but she was too far away. She remained leaning back in her chair, trying to appear uninterested.

Sergeant Hooper said shortly, "Your brief is here." He looked at his watch. "You get ten minutes with him. Better make the most of it. You're going to need it."

Polly thought of retorting, "Are you bullying me?" but he was already leaving the room and she decided it wasn't worth it. She should save any ammunition she might possess for a more serious moment.

As the solicitor entered the room, all the police officers left. Polly stood up, but her heart sank. She now knew exactly why that self-satisfied smirk had appeared on Hooper's face. This solicitor looked as if he was straight out of college. About five foot ten in height, he had a teenage boy's slight physique. His dark hair was gelled in spikes, which made his cherubic face even more babyish. The effect was enhanced by dimples at either side of his mouth, which had full, rosy lips like a girl's. Polly wondered whether he was gay.

He introduced himself as Tom Curtis and held out his hand. Polly took it and was marginally reassured by his firm handshake.

She said, "Look, I'm in trouble here and I need help, which is why I asked for you. But I may as well be straight with you from the start. You don't look as though you've had much experience with this sort of thing. Can you help me or should I look for someone older right now?"

Tom Curtis laughed. His dark eyes lit up and danced, and the dimples became more pronounced. He indicated that Polly should sit and sat down himself, opposite her.

"I like clients who are straight with me. It makes my job a great deal easier. So I'll be straight with you, that's only fair. This is my first criminal case. I have worked with colleagues on other criminal cases and loads of civil cases, but to be honest, I'm more interested in criminal law."

"So I'm a kind of guinea pig? To see whether criminal law is for you? By the way, I think I should point out that I am certainly not a criminal and I resent that tag. I've done nothing wrong, nothing. This is all ridiculous, but you must know how embarrassing it is for me. I do wonder whether that's the bottom line. To thoroughly embarrass me in the eyes of the community."

She expected Tom Curtis to dismiss her claim, but he seemed interested. "Why would the police want to embarrass you?"

"Not the police, they're just doing their job. Although I have to say, there are different ways of doing a job. And if that Sergeant Hooper tries any more of his bullying tactics, I shall probably thump him right on his bulbous red nose."

A grin twitched the corners of the solicitor's mouth and activated the dimples. Polly liked the effect and grinned with him. He said, "If he's been too heavy-handed, you could put in a complaint. But I might have to advise you against thumping his bulbous red nose."

Polly laughed and he laughed with her. "Okay. I won't hit him. But he is repellent. Perhaps they need a repellent policeman. You know, the good cop-bad cop routine. PC Dachery's sweet. I really like her."

"Mm. I know exactly what you mean." His eyes twinkled again and Polly decided he definitely wasn't gay. He added, "Can you tell me about all this? What happened?"

Polly nodded and leant on the table. Then she glanced at the windowed wall. "Can they hear us? I need to speak confidentially. I don't want them listening in."

He got up. "Just a minute." He banged on the door and spoke a few words to the young policeman who answered his summons. In a couple of minutes PC Dachery appeared and escorted them both out of the interview room and into a much smaller, cosier room with a window, armchairs, and a coffee table. Polly crossed to the window and gazed out onto the forecourt of the police station. It wasn't an inspiring view but she drank it in, suddenly aware of something of what it must be like to be locked up in a windowless room for twenty-three hours a day, every day.

Tom Curtis was watching her. "It's been grim in here?"

She nodded, her throat burning at the unexpected gentleness in his voice. "They got me out of bed. I wasn't even dressed. It was humiliating. Then they left me in that awful room for half an hour. I'm sure they went for breakfast, but they didn't offer me any. I had to ask for it. And by the way, I haven't had my statutory phone call, although I have asked for it."

He wrote something on a pad of A4 lined paper which he fetched out of his black leather briefcase. "I'll see to it. Don't worry too much. I'll get you out of here."

Polly was surprised by the relief which surged through her. "I'll cooperate in any way I can. What do you want to know?"

"Why don't you start at the beginning? I'll just listen."

So she began. He sat quietly, listening to every word and occasionally writing notes on his pad. When she had finished he looked at her very deliberately and asked, "And the bit you've left out?"

Polly gasped. "How on earth—? How did you know?"

He smiled. "Training. I know what to look out for. The 'non-verbal cues,' they call it. You must tell me everything. I'm not your judge, but unless I know the whole story from beginning to end, I can't help you."

Polly nodded. "I'm sorry. It's just—well, I'm ashamed. I did lie to the police and it's got me into such trouble. But I was afraid and it seemed the simplest solution at the time. I had no idea all this would escalate."

He frowned. "From what you've told me already I think you have enemies. But we'll talk about that later. The first thing is to know the truth, the whole truth, and nothing but the truth." He grinned to soften his words.

Polly was amazed by the confidence she already felt in this young man. From thinking he was just out of high school she had moved in five minutes to a deep respect and liking for him. She realised how glad she was that Tom Curtis was her solicitor.

She took a deep breath. "I was at Thorpemunden Manor on the night in question. I had my mother staying with me, but she'd disappeared. She's an alcoholic, so I didn't want the whole neighbourhood knowing. I went out in the car to look for her and while I was passing the gates of the manor I thought I saw someone in the grounds. It was only a passing glimpse, but I drove in to take a look, then drove out again. As luck would have it, the Mansfields were driving back in as I drove out. We nearly collided at the gate. Daisy Mansfield recognised my car."

"So you lied to protect your mother?"

Polly nodded miserably. "It was the stupidest thing I've ever done, and that's saying something. I've been in trouble before, but nothing like this."

Chapter Thirty-Seven

Tom Curtis said, "You've told me about the evening of October the twenty-eighth and James Mansfield's subsequent wild accusations or, at least, insinuations. I gather he hasn't gone so far as to accuse you of anything?"

"No. In fact, the other day he was all sweetness and light. He came round to my house, completely out of the blue. He's never done that before, it's not like him. I thought he'd come to make things right between us. That's how he started, at any rate. But then I went out to get a couple of glasses since he'd brought a bottle with him—to toast our new relationship, I think—and it seemed churlish to refuse. But in the second or two it took me to fetch the glasses, he seemed to have changed his mind. He suddenly upped and said he was going."

A small frown appeared again on the solicitor's face. "Have you mentioned this to the police? Do you remember the date?"

"I don't think I've told anyone. And no, I can't remember. My mind's been all over the place. My flatmate, Ella, has disappeared and I'm really worried about her. But James came round while both Ella and Henry were staying, although they were both out at the time. As a matter of fact, I found an envelope of James' which must have fallen out of his pocket, stuffed down the side of the chair. It was a day or two before I took it back because poor old Arthur Roamer died and Henry and I were at the hospital for hours. And then we had to organise the funeral."

"I know about the envelope and so do the police, although I suspect their take on it is somewhat different from yours. But your flatmate, did you say?"

"Well, housemate, I suppose, if you want to be pedantic. We share. She's not a priest or anything. She's a friend of Henry's. Canon Henry Winstone, that is. He's my incumbent and my boss. Ella was staying with them, but she's been with me for a while now."

"I see." But Tom Curtis looked perplexed, as though he didn't see in the least.

Polly added, "It's complicated. But it has nothing to do with all this."

"Was Ella with you that evening?"

"No, that's the funny thing. Ella works in the Rose and Crown at Middlestead in the evenings. It seems that my mother was in the bar there all evening on the night of the robbery and Ella was keeping an eye on her. How my mother got there I can't imagine. I suppose she must have walked. She was away all day, so it's not beyond the bounds of possibility. Soon after I got in, they arrived home together."

"Where is your mother now?"

Polly shrugged. "At her home in Streatham, I guess. I'm afraid I sent her back next day. In this job and in these villages I can't risk having a drunk relative about. It would do untold damage to the Church." She was aware it sounded pretentious but hoped Tom wouldn't notice. He did.

"And untold damage to you, too?" he observed, dryly.

Polly blushed. She wouldn't get much past this young man, however cherubic his appearance.

Tom was speaking again. "I want you to take your mind back further. Can you think of any reason why James Mansfield might want to implicate you in the robbery? Apart from the fact that he saw your car there, I mean?"

Polly grinned. "There is that! Well, I get the impression that he doesn't approve of women priests. He's rather old-school. Very county and all that."

"Would that be sufficient for him to take such a drastic step?"

"Probably not. Some pretty awful things went on when women were first ordained, but all that bad behaviour seems to have died a death. There's still a school of thought which claims that women can't be priests, but they mostly protest through the proper channels, like General Synod. I don't think James would take any action against me on that score alone. But there was a previous incident ages ago in the summer, soon after I came here. James and Daisy have a mentally handicapped son, Frank. He'd be in his forties, I should say. Frank went missing and Daisy rang me up in a panic. I went over and offered to go looking for Frank. They both seemed really pleased at the time, but it all went horribly wrong. I found him in the amusement place here in Diss and he had a great wad of money with him. I mean serious money. A really thick wad of twenties and fifties. He was peeling them off like there was no tomorrow, and that oily little weasel who runs the place was giving him ten- and twenty-pence pieces in exchange, to play the machines. Frank thought it was brilliant, but goodness knows how much the bloke had had out of Frank before I got there."

"Did you report this to the police or tell James?"

"It got complicated. I went to take the money and Frank pushed me. At least, I think that's what happened. I must have fallen and hit my head. The next thing I knew, I was in hospital and I'd lost a day, I think. A few hours, anyway. The police came to see me and practically accused me of trying to steal Frank's money. I think that's what James must have told them. Anyway, he was furious with me. They'd had unpleasant run-ins with the police before over Frank and it's not the sort of publicity the county set want. James had impressed on me when I went looking for Frank that the police mustn't be involved, but unfortunately they were. I don't know whether the police actually arrested Frank, but they certainly took him to the station. So all hell was let loose as far as James was concerned, especially over me. And needless to say, the thieving little weasel supported Frank."

"I see." Tom tapped his pen against his teeth, looking thoughtful. "And you think James has had it in for you ever since?"

Polly nodded. "I think it dates from there. He complained to the bishop—they're great buddies, so it was inevitable—but I think now he'd like to get rid of me, and I suppose this is a pretty neat way of doing that. And the problem is, the bishop has said he won't ordain me if I get into any more trouble. If he's hears about this, I'm done for."

"I thought you were already ordained. You wear a dog collar."

"Everyone is ordained deacon for the first year. But deacons can only do half the job. They can't preside at Communion, for instance. I'd never get another job if I remained a deacon. I'd have to leave. Priests don't get paid much more than curates, but you couldn't live on a curate's salary for long, even though the house is thrown in. Okay for a single person like me, but must be hell for married curates with families."

Tom stood, gathering his papers together. "Let's not jump to any conclusions just yet. Stay here for a minute. I'm going to get you out of here, but you may need to answer some of their questions first. Don't worry," as he saw her anxious look, "I'll be in there with you. If I nod, tell the truth even if you think it might incriminate you. If I don't nod, refuse to answer. Okay? Trust me. It'll be all right."

Polly did trust him. When she was interviewed with Tom seated beside her, she had much more confidence. She apologised to Sergeant Hooper for misleading him over her actions on the twenty-eighth of October and clearly stated the reasons for her deception, for the record. She answered all the sergeant's questions, but when he began to get aggressive over the envelope with her fingerprints on it and to go back over the events of October the twenty-eighth again and again, Tom intervened.

"Reverend Hewitt has answered all your questions, and she will sign a statement I have prepared for her."

When did he do that? wondered Polly.

"Unless you are going to arrest Reverend Hewitt—and I would strongly advise against that move as you have no evidence whatsoever linking her to any crime—she will now leave. For the record, she came here voluntarily to help you with your enquiries, which she has done in full detail and in a spirit of willing cooperation."

Sergeant Hooper scowled at the table but knew when he was beaten. He dismissed them with a flick of his head, but Tom was having none of that.

"Perhaps you could ensure that Reverend Hewitt has all she needs? A car to take her home, for instance?"

But Polly didn't want to spend another moment in police company, however helpful. She shook her head. "I don't need a car, thanks." She held out her hand, which Sergeant Hooper reluctantly took. He glowered at her as if to say, "We aren't finished yet," but managed to squeeze an approximation of a smile and opened the door for them.

When they were safely outside, Polly breathed in a lungful of fresh air. She felt suddenly shaky. It had been a scary experience, being at another person's mercy with all her freedom curtailed.

Tom noticed her shivering. "Come on," he said. "I'll take you home, if you'll allow me."

Polly turned to him. "Thank you so much for all you've done. I'd have been lost without you. How much do I owe you?"

He took her arm to steer her to the car and she didn't object. "Nothing. I'm the duty solicitor, remember? The State pays me on your behalf. You contribute to me through your taxes."

"Thank goodness for that! Look, you don't have to do this. I can get a taxi."

But he just smiled and walked her to his car, which was parked at the front of the station. It was a silver Volvo and Polly sank gratefully into the plush front seat, inhaling the smell of leather.

"This is more like it," she remarked.

"Press that button if you want proper luxury. It heats the seat."

Polly leaned forward and pressed the button on the dashboard. As the car purred smoothly onto the road, the seat began to warm. She snuggled down, enjoying the rare treat.

Tom switched on the radio. "Radio Two, Classic FM, or Radio Norfolk?"

"Hmm. I think Radio Two today. Don't feel like anything too heavy. Something light and upbeat, please."

With music and warmth to speed them on their way, the journey was over all too soon.

Polly said, "Will you come in for a coffee?" She checked her watch. "Actually, it's near enough lunch time. I can fix you a sandwich or beans on toast. The largesse of clergy living."

He laughed. "I'm okay, thanks. But a coffee would be nice."

As he followed her into the house, Polly glanced round hurriedly, hoping the house was reasonably tidy. She hadn't done any housework since Ella had disappeared but, with only one person now living in the house, trusted it wasn't too disastrous. Somehow, she wanted to impress Tom Curtis.

While she was waiting for the kettle to boil Polly checked the answer phone, but there were no messages.

Noting her slightly crestfallen face Tom said, "Your friend still hasn't been in touch?"

Polly shook her head. "Afraid not. I just hope nothing's happened to her. It seems strange, to go off like that without a word. But I kind of think that's the way Ella is, so I guess I'm less concerned than I might have been. She didn't have much of a childhood, I don't think."

"What do you know about her? I'm only asking because of the juxtaposition of events. She was with your mother on the night of the robbery, your mother disappeared next day, and just as further so-called 'evidence' has come to light in the form of the envelope and James' version of it, Ella has disappeared. You see how it might look once the police winkle that out?"

"Only to the stupid who are out to get me," retorted Polly. Then her hand flew to her mouth. "Whoops! Sorry, didn't mean you. Was thinking about the police and James."

He grinned. "So you tell me. But I know what's really in your mind!"

Polly grinned back. "I think I'd better make the coffee before I dig myself in any deeper. But would you mind if I just ring Henry? I should have been at Morning Prayer with him about four hours ago, so he may be wondering what's happened."

But Henry wasn't wondering. When he heard her voice on the phone he said, "Ah, Polly. They've let you out, then?"

Polly was astounded. "How did you know?"

"You don't think anything as exciting as a police raid at dawn with the curate being taken out to the car in handcuffs would go unnoticed, did you?"

Polly gasped. "That's been well and truly elaborated! No raid, not exactly dawn, and no handcuffs. Otherwise relatively accurate."

Henry laughed. "The main thing is, are you okay? I rang the station, did they tell you? They said your solicitor was with you and you were leaving very soon, so I didn't pursue it."

"What time was that?"

"Oh, around a quarter to nine, I should think. Why?"

"I've only just got home. The so-and-sos! They knew they wouldn't be holding me, but they made me think I was going to spend the rest of my life in jail!"

"It's called 'mind games,' Polly. But you're all right now? Was your solicitor okay?"

"He's here now, as a matter of fact. He brought me home and we're just having coffee." Polly grinned across at Tom. "He's not only excellent, but very nice with it." Suddenly anxious she added, "You do believe me, don't you, Henry? That I had nothing to do with that robbery?"

"Of course I believe you! You're an ordained deacon. Why wouldn't I believe you?"

It wasn't quite the answer Polly had wanted, but it would have to do for now. She said good-bye to Henry and replaced the phone.

Tom was still drinking his coffee. "Tell me more about Frank Mansfield. What is he like?"

Polly shrugged. "There's not much more to tell, really. I haven't seen him for ages. In fact, now I come to think about it, I don't think I've seen him to talk to since the robbery. I'm not sure anyone has seen him." She frowned in an effort of concentration. "I'm sure I remember someone remarking on it. On Frank's absence, that is. But I can't remember who or when."

"You said he's in his forties. What does he look like?"

"Yes, early to mid forties I should say. He's tall and muscular, very strong. Has this dark hair which kind of flops over his forehead. Looks completely normal, but has a mental age of around eight or ten, I should think. I reckon Daisy's quite frightened of him. She's only slight. As a matter of fact, I think she's frightened of James as well, but that's another story."

"Sounds like a spectacularly dysfunctional family."

Polly chuckled. "You'll think I'm daft if you meet them. They don't seem the least dysfunctional. James is very wealthy, churchwarden of Thorpemunden Church, and right in the centre of upmarket civic life. And Daisy kind of adorns him. They've been married forever. You'd think they were the perfect couple."

"And Frank?"

"James is solicitous and caring towards him in public. Takes him out for walks and takes him on the estate, all that sort of thing. And I wouldn't know how he treats him in private, I've never been there socially."

"This guy from the Amusement Arcade. Do you think he's still in the picture?"

Polly shrugged again. "I've no idea. I've never seen him again. I don't even know if he still works there. Jobs like that, they come and go. All I can tell you is that Frank regarded him as a bosom pal and James seemed quite taken with him. But that may only have been in contrast to me, if you see what I mean."

Tom nodded. "Still, it may be another line of enquiry. Certainly worth investigating and I shall suggest as much to the police."

"It won't get you very far. There's no way James will allow Frank to be questioned. And James is best buddies with the chief constable, so I'm afraid it won't happen."

"Is he now?" murmured Tom. "Well, we'll just have to see what pans out." He drained his cup and set it down on the table. Then he stood up and held out his hand. "Nice to have met you, Reverend Hewitt. I don't think you have any cause for worry, but I will pursue this further and help out in any way I can. Thanks for the coffee."

Polly had a wild desire to hang onto him. But she had to make do with the thought that if he pursued her case, she might meet him again. So she merely took his hand and replied formally, "Thank you, Mr. Curtis. I appreciate all your trouble."

But still holding his hand she couldn't help bursting into laughter. "You've been calling me Polly all morning and I've been calling you Tom. What is all this?"

He laughed with her and his eyes danced. He gave her hand a little squeeze. "Okay. See ya, Polly." And with a wave and a grin he was gone.

Polly felt quite deflated by his absence. She wondered whether she really would see him again. Hopefully not in this context, but if not, probably they'd never meet again. She was surprised at the disappointment this notion caused her and mentally told herself not to be so stupid. This caused her to miss Ella all over again, for she and Ella would have discussed Tom Curtis for hours and that was such a good thought. She wondered all over again where Ella was and what had happened to her and sent up yet another prayer for Ella's safe return.

Feeling distinctly sorry for herself and very alone, Polly picked up the phone and dialled. The phone rang for so long that she was about to replace the receiver when the phone was answered.

A child's voice said, "Yes?"

"Toby? Is that you? How are you, mate? Is Mum there?"

The uncertain voice on the other end said, "Hel—hello?"

"Toby, it's me, Polly. You remember me, don't you? Your big sister."

"Er— I'll get Mum."

The phone was dropped and Polly heard, "Mum!" screeched throughout the house. Several moments later Amanda picked up the phone.

"What on earth do you want?"

Polly's heart sank. Some chance of support from this direction! She said, "Mum? Just wondered how you are?"

Amanda snorted. "Still alive, although much you care and I don't suppose that's what you want to hear. What you really ringing for?"

Polly sighed. "Look, Mum. Can't we put all this antagonism behind us? I am your only daughter, after all. Anyway, listen. Are you back with Graham? Or is it just you and Toby?"

"What's it to you? And while we're about it, Miss, I seem to remember the 'antagonism,' as you call it, came from you."

Polly said patiently, "I'm just trying to be friendly. To make conversation, if you like."

But Amanda Hewitt was suspicious. "What's going on up there? You in some kinda trouble?"

Despite herself, Polly gulped. She blurted out, "I've been questioned by the police. They think I stole some money, but I didn't."

Amanda roared with laughter. "Is that all? Don't need to cry about that, girl. I've been questioned by the police more times than I've slept with strange men and that's saying something. You get used to it. Don't mean nothing. When they arrest you, that's when you need to start worrying. But questioning, that's nothing. It means they don't have anything on you and they're wanting you to give them the evidence. And if you haven't done nothing, you can't, can you? So you're home and dry. No contest."

To her surprise, Polly felt comforted and supported by her mother's words. For the first time, she felt the glimmerings of gratitude, rather than disgust at her mother's lifestyle. Her mother had come from a good family which had rejected her when her alcoholism became pronounced, and Polly began to realise how much hurt that must have caused, sending Amanda deeper into her illness. It was a short step from there to Polly beginning to see how much pain she herself must have caused by her rejection of her mother for similar reasons. And yet she had turned to her mother the moment she was in need, and here was her mother, supporting her in a way that she didn't deserve.

Who, Polly wondered to herself for the first time, *is the Christian here?*

Chapter Thirty-Eight

She met with Henry next day at Morning Prayer, but Henry wasn't a bit interested in Polly's experience at the hands of the police.

"You don't think it'll get to the bishop, do you?" Polly asked anxiously.

Henry dismissed the thought with a wave of his hand. "Stop worrying. You haven't done anything so nothing will happen to you."

"Didn't hold true for Jesus," Polly muttered.

"I don't think you're quite in that category," Henry reproved her.

Polly thought his attitude was verging on the euphoric. He didn't seem to take her situation seriously at all and she wondered why that was, since he was certain to be involved in any row surrounding her. But when he asked in a deceptively casual manner, "Have you heard from Ella?" she realised where his mind was stuck. He was so concerned about Ella that he had no space for any other thoughts, let alone problems. Polly wondered how Mavis was taking yet another indication of his fixation, which they had all thought had faded into insignificance.

She shook her head. "Not yet. I expect she'll reappear when she's ready." But Polly was feeling less confident than her words suggested. She missed Ella more than she could say, but there was also a hardening kernel within her which felt angry and resentful at Ella's treatment of them all. Why couldn't Ella have picked up the phone? Surely she must realise how concerned they all were and how helpless they all felt?

Polly wondered whether she could pursue her friend's disappearance with Tom Curtis. There was absolutely no way she could possibly approach the police, but Tom had seemed interested. Then an unworthy thought inserted itself into Polly's mind. What if Ella really had been implicated in the robbery in some way? What if that was why she had disappeared? Had she sensed that the police were closing in?

As soon as it surfaced, Polly dismissed the thought. Ella was working that night. It could not have been possible for her to have been at Thorpemunden Manor at the same time. Besides, Amanda had been with her.

Yes, a little voice insisted inside Polly's head, *but they were each other's alibi. Suppose the person in the grounds of Thorpemunden Manor that night had been Amanda, and Ella had somehow got her out? Or could they have been in it together? They certainly seemed to get on well together . . .*

Polly shook herself. There was no point in stupid, baseless fantasies. She had mentally castigated the police for doing exactly that. Now here she was indulging in the same nightmare world herself.

Henry's long face drew her out of her reverie. The light had gone from his eyes and she instinctively sensed an inkling of the pain he was feeling.

She touched him gently on the arm. "She'll come back, Henry," she reiterated. "Trust me."

Henry turned sad brown eyes on her and ran a hand through his silver hair. Polly was reminded of a spaniel begging mournfully for a treat and wondered irreverently whether Henry would scamper in delight when—or if—Ella returned.

Hoping the question would jerk him back to reality, she asked, "How's Mavis?"

Henry blinked and seemed to make a conscious effort to attend. "All right, I think."

"Is she missing Ella, too?"

Henry frowned a little then nodded slowly, as though he had only just realised that Mavis, too, was fond of Ella. "I think she might be," he responded. He checked his watch and stood up. "I'd better get back to her, if you don't mind. She'll be wondering how you are. I need to let her know everything is all right with you, at least."

He closed the prayer book, muttered a final blessing, and left the church. Polly lingered for a moment or two enjoying her own space, but it was cold in the church and she soon followed suit.

***

It was two days later that Polly received an unexpected phone call. Daisy Mansfield was sobbing in a such a flustered and uncontrolled way that Polly was seriously worried.

"Slow down, can you, Daisy? I can't quite make out what you're saying."

There was a snuffling and gulping on the other end of the phone. Daisy was so upset she could hardly speak. All she could say was, "Please, Polly. I don't know who else to ask. Please come." And with that she hung up.

Polly didn't know what to do or who to consult. Tom Curtis had made it very clear that she must have nothing whatsoever to do with the Mansfields under any pretext, and Henry had told her some time ago not to go near James Mansfield. But Daisy had sounded so needy and clearly had not thought she could approach Henry.

Was she walking into a trap neatly laid by James Mansfield? Polly wondered. On the other hand, could she leave Daisy to suffer alone when she had begged for help? Had James become violent towards her? Or had something happened between James and Frank?

Polly fetched her jacket. She wondered whether to ring Henry or to leave some sort of message in case she never returned, but decided that was far too melodramatic. She was probably making a mountain out of a very tiny molehill and would find that it was just Daisy being Daisy. But she knew she needed to find out, if only to settle her own conscience.

Polly parked boldly on the circular gravel drive in the front of the manor. She had decided that she might as well be thoroughly open about her movements on the grounds and that complete openness would leave less room for manipulation of the facts.

She rang the bell and hammered on the door as well, to advertise her presence. Daisy must have been waiting for her, since the door was opened immediately.

Daisy's wispy grey hair was even less contained than usual. Escaping tendrils framed her face at wild angles and the French pleat at the back was scarcely more than a gathering of hair stuffed with straying pins. Tears had streaked Daisy's face and she wore no makeup. She looked so much older without the help of cosmetics that Polly wondered whether she was perhaps over eighty. Today she seemed particularly frail, old, and bent.

Without thinking, Polly put her arms round Daisy and hugged her. For the first time she realised how slight Daisy was, as she felt Daisy's ribs under her hands. Daisy buried her face in Polly's shoulder and shook with tears.

When the sobs began to subside, Polly said gently, "What is it, Daisy? Can you tell me what's happened?"

Daisy pulled away and blew her nose. "It's J—James—I—"

"James?" prompted Polly. "Is he ill again? Has he been taken into hospital? Where's Frank, Daisy? I haven't seen him for ages."

At this the sobs renewed and Daisy turned away. Polly followed her into the kitchen, where she automatically reached for the kettle, filled it, and stood it on the Aga.

Polly sat down at the kitchen table. "Daisy?"

Daisy nodded and lifted a hand as if to say, "Give me time." She busied herself setting out cups and saucers and a plate of biscuits, until Polly wanted to scream. But she knew it was no good trying to hurry Daisy, for that would only result in more tears and even less ability to articulate.

Eventually, when they were drinking coffee and Polly had reluctantly helped herself to a biscuit just to quieten Daisy, the older woman began to speak, haltingly at first but with increasing strength as she went on. Polly listened carefully, not daring to respond in case she broke the flow.

Daisy said, "I've known for some time that things weren't right. Oh, everyone thinks I'm stupid and maybe I am. I've given that impression over the years. But I do notice things that not everybody sees. I noticed your car that night and I knew it was you driving, but I wished I hadn't said anything. James hadn't noticed, you see, and if only I'd kept quiet, perhaps none of this would have happened. He doesn't like you, I'm afraid."

Daisy gave a tight, apologetic smile but was unable to lift her eyes to Polly. She continued, "James knew straightaway what had happened. We both did. But we were afraid, you see. I was afraid for Frank. He'd never survive prison and I didn't want him taken away to some dreadful place where they don't know him. And James, well, I think James was afraid for his reputation. He has standing in this area. He knows all the top people and he has always feared the loss of their friendship. That's why you never see much of Frank. James is so ashamed of him. He keeps him—he—since the robbery—he—"

Daisy faltered so much that Polly thought she might be unable to go on. She wanted to reach across the table and clutch Daisy's hand, but thought that such a move might open the floodgates again. So she simply remained very still and utterly silent.

Daisy took a couple of deep breaths to steady herself. "He keeps Frank locked up, now. That's why you haven't seen him for such a long time. James keeps him locked up on the top floor. I'm not allowed to go up there. James says I mustn't in case Frank attacks me. He says Frank has become much more violent lately. So

I put his meals on a tray and James takes them up." She glanced at Polly, stronger now that the shameful secret was out.

Polly struggled not to show her dismay in her face. She was appalled at what she had just heard, but not altogether surprised. She said quietly, keeping her tone as even as she could, "Does James control Frank with the stick?"

Daisy nodded miserably and her gaze fell again. "I don't think he uses it on Frank. Not often, anyway. He has no need. He's used it in the past and poor Frank is terrified. One glimpse of the stick and he's a shivering wreck. He'd never dare disobey James. But James had to use it, in the early days when Frank was a boy. It was different then, forty-five years ago. That's how everyone controlled their children. James was no worse than anyone else. He wasn't brutal, nothing like that."

Polly made no comment. She longed to ask whether James had ever used the stick on Daisy, but she didn't dare. She contented herself with nodding and raising her eyebrows with a slight turn of the head, to indicate that Daisy should continue.

Daisy said, "Where was I? Oh yes, the so-called robbery. As you must have guessed, Frank let somebody in. We didn't know who, to start with. James was sure it must have been you. But he found out soon enough. Frank can't keep any secrets. It was that friend he met at the Amusement Arcade in Diss, Sidney something, I think his name is. Yes, Sid Ellis, that's it. Frank has never had a friend before, so we rather encouraged it. I didn't like him much, but James said I was being silly and we should do all we could to help the friendship along. Well, he was right, of course. Frank does need friends.

"But when this happened, James was so angry. I think he may have beaten Frank on that occasion, but he can hardly be blamed for that, can he? I mean, Frank does know it's wrong to steal. Anyway, James confronted this Sid, but he just laughed at James. He told him to claim on the insurance and that if James said anything, he'd tell the police exactly what had happened and Frank would be put away for good.

"I begged James to do something. It didn't seem right to allow that nasty man to get away with it and I thought with us getting older, perhaps a nice home might be found for Frank, and once he was safe, then perhaps we could tell the police everything. I'm not happy about Frank being upstairs all the time. He doesn't get any fresh air and it's not right that he should be alone all day. He needs company. But I'm afraid James had other plans. He told me Frank would be sent to prison for years and I couldn't have that, so I said nothing. James thought he could get rid of you at the same time and it all escalated. I'm so sorry, Polly."

This time Polly did reach for her hand. "Daisy, you mustn't blame yourself. James is a strong personality. Whatever you said, I guarantee he'd do what he liked."

Daisy gave a mirthless laugh. "I'm afraid he does. He doesn't listen to me. But I am rather stupid."

Polly squeezed her hand. "No, Daisy, I don't think you are. But can you tell me why he's so eager to get rid of me? That's the only bit I don't quite understand."

"You stood up to him. Nobody does that to James. Most people kowtow and do exactly as he says. He saw you as a threat because you weren't afraid of him and you asked awkward questions. You had to go, or his plan would be scuppered. And since he's always been opposed to women priests, he focussed his hostility on that. Sounded more likely, I suppose. I'm so sorry."

"So where is James now?"

Daisy's eyes welled, but she held back her tears. "The police came for him this morning. I don't know how they found out, but they took him away so they must have put two and two together and figured it all out somehow. He was shouting and raving about his friend the chief constable, but I'm not sure that Reggie Pearson will save him this time. Reg likes to shoot, you know, and James invites him as a guest. It's a kind of bribe, really. But it has helped in the past, when the police have cottoned on to Frank."

"Where is Frank at the moment?"

"Still up in the attic. And that's the problem, Polly. I don't know what to do. I know he's my son and I love him to bits, but he's so big and strong. He's been locked up there for ages and I haven't seen him. I think he may blame me for that. I'm afraid he may attack me of I go up and if he does that, there'll be no one to feed him and he may do something terrible to someone else. Does that sound awful?"

Polly thought it did sound awful but she wasn't about to say so. "Didn't the police ask about Frank? Surely they'd want to question him as well as James?"

"James refused to tell them where he was. If they question Frank, everything will come out and James has already had the money from the insurance company. That must be wrong. I'm afraid that James might have to stand trial. He'd never cope with that. So obviously I couldn't tell them where Frank is."

Polly frowned. "They're bound to find out sooner or later, aren't they? What do you want me to do, Daisy?"

Daisy clutched her arm and looked beseechingly at her. "Could you take Frank away somewhere? He likes you, he always has. He'd be all right with you, I know he would. He trusts you and so do I."

"But Daisy, last time we met, Frank was quite violent towards me. If you remember, he pushed me and I ended up in hospital. And I'm not sure that he does like me very much. I don't think he liked me very much then."

"Oh, but he was so sorry afterwards! He said so. Please, Polly. I know he'd be all right with you."

Polly sighed. "Daisy, I'd love to help, you know I would. But I just don't think that's the way to go about it. Everything is going to come out in the end. It sounds as though the police are already nearly there. If we take Frank away, we'll be perverting the course of justice or aiding and abetting or something like that. At the moment, you can't be held responsible for anything. But now that James is in police custody, even though it may be only temporary, you need to tell the police everything you've told me. And it may be the best possible thing for Frank. There are some excellent homes for people with learning difficulties, places where they're taught a trade and can earn money for themselves. And they're looked after with expert care and a lot of love. Don't you think the time might have come to get Frank settled somewhere like that, where you can visit him as often as you like and where he'd have his own friends?"

Daisy nodded miserably. "I suppose you're right. But James would never allow it. If James comes home, he'll stop all that. Do you really think he might be released soon?"

Polly thought back to her own brief time in custody. "I'm sure James must have an excellent lawyer who will get him home as quickly as possible, especially if he's only being questioned. He wasn't actually arrested, was he?"

"I don't know. Oh dear, what shall I do? I just know he was taken away. I don't know—"

"It's all right, Daisy. Don't worry. I think James will certainly be released. At the worst, he'll be released on bail and will have to return at some future date. At the best, there'll be no evidence against him and he won't be charged with any offence."

But Daisy was still wringing her hands and looking even more anxious.

"Daisy, do you want James home?"

"Well, of course! But it's Frank. I don't like him to be left up there, it's not good for him. If James comes home—"

"—you won't be able to do anything for Frank, is that it?"

Daisy nodded. "Please help, Polly. But we have to be quick. He could be home at any time. If he finds you here, I don't know what he'll do."

Polly made a quick decision. "Come on. Let's go and collect Frank and we'll take him over to my place. And you'd better come, too, Daisy. Frank will need his mum."

Daisy led the way up three flights of stairs. The final flight was hidden behind a locked door, but Daisy had the key. Polly noticed that Daisy's hand was trembling as she fitted the key into the lock and she realised that Daisy really was afraid of her son. Polly wondered just what had been going on over the months and years behind the imposingly calm façade of Thorpemunden Manor.

As soon as the key turned, noises could be heard at the top of the stairs. Not speech, but more like animal grunts. Daisy called out, "Frank, it's me, Mummy. I've come to take you downstairs. Where are you, Frank?"

They climbed the last flight of stairs to the attic floor of the house where presumably the maids had once resided. There were several small rooms, one of which was clearly Frank's bedroom. They followed the winding corridor to the end room, where the door was ajar. Frank Mansfield was cowering at the far side of the room.

Daisy gasped and ran towards him, her arms outstretched. "Frank! My poor baby, what has he done to you?"

But Frank continued to cower away from her, emitting strange noises, a cross between a yelp and a squeal. Polly was shocked by the sight of him. He was gaunt and pale and unkempt and the room smelt terrible. She suspected he hadn't washed or changed his clothes for days. She wondered for a moment whether, like a cornered animal, he would attack them. But Daisy was gently stroking his hair and he seemed to be slowly responding to her murmurings.

All we have to do now, thought Polly, *is get him downstairs and spirit him away before James gets back. That's all!*

Chapter Thirty-Nine

Polly moved slowly towards Daisy and Frank with a wide smile on her face and an outstretched hand. She had no wish to spook Frank and was entirely unconvinced that he had any happy memories of her, no matter what Daisy fondly thought. She halted a couple of feet from him and spoke gently.

"Hello, Frank. It's good to see you again."

Frank whimpered and continued to cower with his head turned away, but didn't make any attempt to back off from her.

Polly continued, "Would you like to come for a ride in my car, Frank? It's a red car. You could sit in the front, if you like." A voice in her head was telling her not to be so naive. She had no idea how Frank was going to react. He could be very unpredictable at the best of times and this was probably the worst of times. It might be extremely dangerous to have Frank in the front. But they had to get him downstairs somehow and bribery seemed like the best bet. Time was ticking inexorably; James could be home at any moment.

She was rewarded by a brightening in Frank's eyes. He looked nervously at his mother, who nodded encouragingly. "It's all right, Frank. You remember Polly, don't you? Remember how you like Polly?"

Frank gazed from one to the other of them, an uncertain expression on his face. He spoke for the first time. "D—Dad? Where's Dad?"

"Daddy's not here at the moment, Frank. He'd want you to come." Daisy lied smoothly.

Polly edged closer and took his other arm. He didn't pull away. "All right, Frank? Come on now. My car's just outside."

But he hung back, resisting their urging. "Daddy angry with Frank."

"No, Frank. Daddy isn't angry anymore. Daddy wants you to come with us. Daddy has gone away just at the moment. Come on now. You've been up here long enough. Time to go out for a nice ride."

They began to edge him towards the door and the corridor. Polly thought there might be a blip at the top of the stairs when he looked terrified at the thought of venturing down. With a shudder she was unable to suppress, Polly wondered exactly how Frank had been persuaded to stay in the attic for so long.

Progress was agonisingly slow and Polly kept imagining she could hear a car drawing up outside on the gravel, discharging James. But eventually they got Frank outside, where he shielded his eyes from the sudden glare.

It must be like emerging from a coal mine after weeks underground, Polly reflected. *The dormer windows are so small, it makes everything dim and dingy in that loft.*

They helped Frank into the front seat of Polly's Ka and applied the seat belt. As it was only a two-door car, Daisy climbed into the back with some difficulty. She wasn't used to clambering about and at her age was considerably stiffer and slower than she used to be. Polly kept glancing round, anxious to get going before James returned, and she breathed more easily when she herself was strapped in and they were able to roar on their way down the drive. Frank gave a small, delighted chuckle and Polly was surprised at how relieved she felt to hear this early sign of the beginnings of a return to normality. She drove quickly, wanting to put as much distance as possible between themselves and Thorpemunden Manor and rather dreading that history might be repeated and she would nearly collide with James at the entrance. But they managed to get away without any sign of a car approaching the manor.

Polly drove home. She didn't really stop to think about it, for there seemed to be no alternative. She had to get Frank and Daisy out of harm's way and there was nowhere else to take them. Plenty of time to think about what to do next when they were all out of immediate danger.

Although he kept close to his mother, Frank was visibly relaxing. Polly showed them into the lounge, where Frank and Daisy sat huddled together on the sofa. Polly turned on the television for CBBC for Frank, to give herself time to think and to discuss with Daisy what they should do next. She knew she had to persuade Daisy to call the police and hoped that perhaps Daisy might be more open to that suggestion now that she had seen for herself the harm her husband's treatment of Frank had caused. But it was a delicate subject and she approached it with caution.

"Daisy," she began, diffidently.

But Daisy interrupted her. It was the first time Polly could ever remember Daisy having the confidence to interrupt anyone. But she seemed to have suddenly developed a new strength.

"I know what you're going to say and the answer is 'yes.'"

Polly's eyebrows rose in astonishment. "What was I going to say?"

"That I should contact the police."

"Well, yes, as a matter of fact! Are you sure that's okay with you? You do know what it means? That Frank will be questioned by them? And maybe you, too?"

Daisy nodded, a new steely glint in her tired eyes. "Frank is incapable of lying. That's why James hid him up there, he knew Frank would tell it how it is and he couldn't risk that. And I'm so ashamed that I've been complicit in that." She gave a small shudder. "But now I've seen for myself, and I want my son to testify against his father. I want the world to know how James has treated Frank all these years. And I wish to make a personal testimony against my husband. I want to explain about his calumny in regard to you, Polly, and to tell the world about his mistreatment of me over many years."

Polly stifled a gasp, trying to remain calm and professional. "Do you want to tell me about it, Daisy? Would it be easier to talk to me before having to express it all to a stranger?"

But as Daisy opened her mouth to respond, there was an imperious ring at the doorbell. Both women froze, although Frank continued to watch the television without any outward sign of concern.

Unable to still the thudding of her heart, Polly moistened her lips. But before she could reach the door, a key was inserted in the lock and the door was opened.

A voice called out, "Hello? Polly?"

Polly shot out into the hall and flung her arms around Ella in an agony of relief. Ella wasn't alone. Behind her stood Sue and behind Sue were Henry and Mavis.

Polly said wonderingly, "What is all this? What's happened? Where have you come from? Why didn't any of you tell me?"

But her words were muffled in hugs and laughter and joy. They all piled into the lounge, but stopped uncertainly when they saw Daisy and Frank. Henry's brows drew together in a frown.

"It's a long story," Polly said. "Let me get some more chairs, then perhaps we can catch up with one another."

"I'll get one," called Henry, disappearing into the dining room and returning with an upright chair, which he placed close to the armchair where Mavis had sat down. Sue took the other armchair while the two girls adorned cushions on the floor.

"Now, then," Polly said. "You first. Then Daisy and I will fill you in on what's been happening." She turned to Ella. "Why didn't you ring?"

Ella smiled, but there was an apology in her dark eyes. "Can you remember the last time you received a telephone call, Polly?"

Polly frowned in an effort of concentration. "Now you come to mention it, I don't think I've had any for a while. Not until Daisy rang this morning."

"Any answer phone messages?"

"No. Kept listening for one from you, but you didn't ring."

"But that's just it," cried Ella. "I did ring. I left countless messages, sometimes two a day. I thought you didn't want to know. I thought maybe you were glad to get rid of me. It wasn't until those pips sounded, showing that your message tape was full, that I began to wonder. I thought perhaps you'd gone away."

Henry took over. "We were as surprised as you, Polly, when Ella rang us late last night. So I tried ringing you, as it was too late to visit. There's a fault on your line. You can ring out and it sounds at your end as though everything is okay with your phone, but when anyone rings in they get the engaged signal. And clearly the messages left aren't being relayed to you. We contacted the phone company and they must have sent out an engineer and rectified the fault, if you had a call this morning. They do promise twenty-four-hour service. Perhaps they actually do work during the night—unless someone else had tried to ring you, realised there was a problem, and reported it earlier."

Polly looked reproachfully at Ella. "Even if my phone was wrong, you could have rung my mobile."

"Have you tried your mobile lately? I think you're out of battery. Every time I rang your mobile it went straight to voice mail. And since I'd left so many messages and you hadn't responded, I didn't dare leave any more. I thought you were getting the messages I left on your landline. I'm really sorry, Polly. When I didn't hear anything, I just assumed you were glad I'd gone, so I stopped ringing. I didn't want to embarrass you or put you under any pressure to have me back."

Ella sounded so unsure of herself and so forlorn that Polly was tempted to throw her arms around her friend. But she desisted until she knew the whole story. "Where have you been and what have you been doing? And how come Sue's here?"

Sue said, "I realised something was wrong when Ella arrived on my doorstep last night and we tried again to ring you. I knew what you felt about Ella and that you would never ditch her like that. So we thought the best thing was to come straight up and explain in person. We couldn't get in touch with you, so we called Henry first to let him know we were on our way."

Polly turned to Ella. "But what have you been doing? Why did you go in the first place?"

"I was searching for my father," Ella explained. "I thought you knew I needed to do that. I thought you'd realise how important it is for me to find my father. Sue had always said she'd help me.

"I went back to the place where I grew up for the first few years of my life. I figured that if there was still anyone there who remembered my mother, they just might have some recollection of my father. I couldn't think what else to do."

"And was there?"

"The madam of the brothel turned out to have been a friend of my mother's years ago. They started out together, penniless, foreign teenagers who were desperate. Neither of them could get work, so they turned to the only alternative they had, prostitution. Felicia did well for herself and rose through the ranks, so to speak. But apparently my mother always hated the work. She was there for a few years, but met this one special man. Felicia didn't know his name, but said he was tall and handsome with thick, wavy blond hair and he was so kind. He treated my mother like a human being with thoughts and aspirations, who had a right to life. He was very gentle and apologetic that he was using her, but unlike so many of the others, determined not to abuse her. And he was a professional man. That's all Felicia could remember. My mother fell in love with him and was sure he loved her back. Felicia thought my mother chose to get pregnant by this man, but he only came a couple of times. My mother was heartbroken. She was very young at the time. I think she had dreams of this man marrying her, but of course that wasn't to be. So she moved on when I was very small. She told Felicia she wanted a better life for me."

"So you haven't located your father?"

Ella shook her head. "I realised then that it was hopeless, so I called on Sue. I thought she might have been able to dig something up."

"But I haven't," Sue finished. "And I knew how you must all be worrying, so the quickest solution seemed to be to drive up as soon as we could. So here we are."

Polly glanced across at Henry. He looked entirely different, relaxed and happy, although there was an expression of concern on his face as he listened to Ella's story. He sat close to Mavis with his hand resting lightly on her shoulder, but his eyes were fixed on Ella.

Polly jumped up. "I should make a drink. Then we'll fill you in on what's been happening at this end—if that's okay with you, Daisy?"

Daisy gave a quick nod and for the first time the others seemed to become aware of her presence. Frank was still focussed on the television, which Polly had turned down in order to hear the conversation, but was huddled even more closely against his mother. Polly felt concerned that such a crowd of people might be overwhelming for him after so many months in solitary confinement. She walked over to him and knelt at his feet, taking both his hands in hers.

"Frank," she said gently, "would you like us all to go into the study and leave you here in peace with your mum? You can watch television for as long as you like."

Frank met her eyes briefly but reverted immediately to the screen. Then he gave an almost imperceptible shake of his head.

Polly said, "You'd prefer us to stay?"

This time he nodded more strongly. Henry, Mavis, and Sue were watching this exchange with concern, realising that something was wrong. Ella was already in the kitchen and could be heard clattering china and filling the kettle.

Henry followed Polly into the kitchen. "What's up?"

"I'm sorry, Henry. I know you told me not to go near the Mansfields, but I had such an urgent call from Daisy this morning. She was so upset—you know how Daisy can get. I knew it might be a trick, but I went anyway. I figured I don't have much to lose by now. Henry, it was terrible. James has been keeping Frank locked away in the attic and he beats him with a stick to keep him in order. As you can see, Frank is severely traumatised."

"Where is James? Surely he didn't just stand by and watch you and Daisy abduct Frank?"

"It's not exactly an abduction, is it? I haven't kidnapped anybody! Frank came willingly—with Daisy's help. And Daisy certainly came willingly.

"James is in police custody. Daisy didn't know whether he'd been arrested or just taken in for questioning, like me. But whichever it is, I reckoned he'd have the best lawyer in town and be out almost before he'd got there, so speed was essential."

"And the charges?"

"According to Daisy, Frank was involved in the robbery. It was that guy from the amusement place in Diss. Frank let him in. Of course, James soon got it out of Frank, but decided to claim on the insurance anyway. I believe Daisy said James had met up with Sid Ellis, who refused to return the money and blackmailed James into keeping quiet. So he needed a scapegoat, which is where I fitted in. I don't know how the police cottoned on."

But her thoughts flew to Tom Curtis and she wondered whether he had been working solidly on her behalf.

Henry looked bemused and let out his breath in a long sigh. He took the tray from Ella and carried it through to the lounge.

The room fell silent as they sipped their coffee. Ella disappeared again and soon returned with a plate of sandwiches, which she handed round. Frank was starving and ate voraciously, taking one after the other. Daisy made to restrain him, but Polly shook her head.

"Let him have as much as he wants. He's been starved of company for so long. Just let him get used to us again. There's plenty more. We can make more sandwiches."

She glanced round at the others, but they'd all had sufficient. When they had finished and the pots were cleared away, Henry took centre stage.

"We need to decide what to do. Daisy, you and Frank can't return to Thorpemunden Manor, that much is obvious. But what are our options?"

Mavis said, "If James should come home and somehow discover that Frank and Daisy are here with Polly, there's no saying what he'd do. I think the two of you should stay at the rectory for a while. James has nothing against us."

"That's very kind of you, Mavis, but I need to contact the police first." Daisy spoke firmly. "I've had enough of lies. I don't care what happens to me, I need to tell the truth at last. James and I have been married for over fifty years and for all that time, I've kept silent. I was too afraid. I suspected that he was abusing Frank, but I wasn't sure what constituted abuse. Times have changed. Something which was considered a just and reasonable punishment for a child forty years ago is now classed as abuse, but I haven't really been able to understand that. Not until now, that is. When I saw the conditions in which poor Frank has been living, I changed my mind. I never want to see James again, except across a courtroom. I want to find somewhere decent for Frank to live. Somewhere he can be happy and make friends of his own. I want to see him settled before I die."

Henry regarded her with a new respect. "We'll help you, Daisy, you can be sure of that. What do you want to do first? How do you want to play it?"

"Ring the police. They'll want to question Frank, of course they will. And me, too, I shouldn't wonder. I want to be with Frank and make sure they treat him properly. I want social services involved at long last, to get Frank thc hclp hc needs."

Mavis said, "I'll come with you, if you like. To the police station. Two will be stronger than one. We'll go together."

Henry ran a hand through his silver hair. "It sounds as though we're sorted, then. We'll take Daisy and Frank back to the rectory. You can ring the police from there, Daisy. And we'll try to persuade them to question you at the rectory. But if they insist on you going to the station, Mavis will come with you and support you." He smiled fondly at his wife, surprised by her unexpected generosity, and gave her arm a gentle squeeze.

He stood up. "Ella is home, thank goodness. Daisy and Frank are away from James, and it sounds as though for once, Polly is out of trouble! I had thought that maybe God and heaven were both spent, but now I really begin to believe that God is in his heaven and all's well with the world, after all."

They nodded and laughed, buoyed up by his words and the new hope flooding through all of them. And Polly tried to quell the fluttering of unease she felt at his words.

Chapter Forty

Not over keen to have Frank staying for long in view of the possible ramifications once James found out, Henry was relieved when Daisy rang the police station and offered to go in with Frank. Henry decided to drive them into Diss, but Mavis made it clear that they did not need him to stay. He dropped them off, introduced them to the desk sergeant, making sure the officer knew that he was Canon Winstone, and was pleased to note that the sergeant appeared duly impressed. Henry hoped his status would help the cause, if only subliminally.

He had taken his mobile so that Mavis could ring to be picked up when their business was done, but meanwhile Henry decided to meander round the shops in Diss. Christmas was rapidly approaching and his mind turned to gifts. Not that he ever bought any gift save for some little token for his wife, and that was usually something she had suggested in unsubtle hints for several weeks prior to Christmas.

But Henry felt differently now. He was happier than he had been for ages. Ella was home, Polly appeared to be exonerated from all blame, which might have the knock-on effect of restoring Henry's standing with the bishop, and Henry was back with Mavis, albeit with some continued reluctance on her part. Henry remembered something Ella had once said about buying a gift for Mavis just to show that he cared, rather than only buying for Christmas or birthdays.

He thought of starting with the flower shop, but being a gardener Mavis was fussy about flowers, especially flowers that had been forced in a hothouse and were exorbitantly expensive. And flowers wouldn't last. Henry wanted a present that would be significant, something to mark a new turn in their relationship. Something, he supposed, to show his continuing love. So that ruled out chocolates as well, which left Henry rather at a loss.

He wandered round the department store, but had no idea of Mavis' dress size or of the styles she preferred. Finding himself in the lingerie section—how had that happened?—he averted his eyes and moved quickly on. He couldn't quite envisage Mavis in frilly underwear or black lace.

This buying of presents was more difficult than Henry had imagined. He had vaguely expected to walk into a shop, see the right gift, buy it, and come out, all in around five minutes. The reality was proving to be more of a hurdle. He looked at brooches in the jewellery section of the store, but couldn't remember ever seeing Mavis wearing a brooch.

Increasingly despondent, Henry wandered back into the street. As he gazed somewhat hopelessly in shop windows, he was hailed from across the road. Turning, he spotted Charles Burgess, the rural dean.

Charles hurried across the road towards him. "Henry! So good to see you. How are you doing? Quite better now, I hope?"

Henry shook hands. "Fine, thank you, Charles. And yourself?"

"What brings you to Diss? Christmas shopping well in hand for the festive season, eh?" He gave Henry a playful dig in the ribs.

Henry winced. "Not really. Although I am looking for a gift for Mavis. Can't think what to get her."

"You want to visit Sam. He's brilliant. Staunch member of my congregation" (Henry groaned inwardly) "and a wonderful eye for what the ladies like. He has the little antique shop on the corner. You know it?"

Henry did know it. Although he knew nothing about them, he did like antiques. They always felt so comforting and safe, symbols of a bygone age when life moved more serenely. Or so Henry fondly thought.

He perked up. "That's an idea. Thanks, Charles. I think I might go there."

"Just mention my name," called Charles with a cheery wave, as Henry set off. "Sam'll give you a discount on my behalf."

But Henry had no need to name drop, since Sam took one look at Henry's dog collar and became obsequious. Henry took full advantage.

"I'm looking for a special gift for my wife. Something meaningful, something that speaks of lasting love."

"Of course, Reverend." Henry half expected him to rub his hands like Uriah Heep, but Sam merely held them together as though he were about to resort to prayer. "Something for the home, perhaps? That both of you could enjoy together? I have this very nice vase from 1843, best porcelain."

Henry inspected the vase, white with a rose pattern and beautiful but unwieldy, with a narrow base and wide lip. He shook his head. "I don't think so. I was thinking of something more personal, something just for her, you know?"

The hands flew open and fluttered, palms up. "I have just the thing! If you'd kindly follow me, Reverend."

Henry followed him to the back of the shop, where Sam drew out a tray of rings from under the counter.

"An eternity ring, perhaps? To demonstrate your undying love for the dear lady? We have all types, shapes, and sizes. A square set with diamonds, perhaps? Or this magnificent opal?"

Henry was uncertain. He had no idea of Mavis' ring size and wasn't sure that she liked rings. Her hands were gardener's hands, broad and square; strong hands which Henry liked, but probably unsuited to rings. Henry rejected the rings, but out of the corner of his eye he noticed a gold pendant necklace.

Sam fetched it out. It was a beautiful antique gold, a solid oval inscribed with floral swirls, and Henry immediately fell in love with it. This was exactly right. The perfect gift for Mavis to prove his love for her.

"I'll take it," he decided, before even inquiring the price, which turned out to be hefty. But Henry didn't care. He knew he had to have the necklace and accepted immediately when he was offered ten per cent discount.

Sam placed the locket in an attractive box lined with dark blue velvet and slipped the box into a small gold carrier. "Here you are. No need for any further wrapping, unless you wish, of course. I'm sure your dear lady will be delighted with this."

"I rather think she might be," Henry said and left the shop, whistling.

***

Henry drove home. With Christmas coming up, he wanted to put the finishing touches to the carol services and make sure he had everything ready for tomorrow's Advent Communion. With Polly remaining a deacon until the summer, he had to take all the Communion services himself, which with six parishes meant considerably more work during Advent when he offered a mid-week, morning Eucharist in every parish. He wondered whether it was worth the bother since no more than six people ever attended, but felt it was the right thing to do. After all, he told himself, worship was for God just as much as for human beings. And Advent was a good time to be putting himself out for God.

It was late afternoon when Mavis eventually called. Henry drove back to Diss to pick her up and was secretly relieved to see that she was alone, although he enquired solicitously after Frank and Daisy.

Mavis chuckled. "Frank really spilled the beans, so they're keeping James in custody. Presumably he'll be charged when they confirm Frank's account. But they didn't know what to do with Frank and Daisy. That's why I've been so long. They called social services, who took Frank away to some place for vulnerable adults and allowed Daisy to go with him just to see him settled, but they wouldn't let Daisy go back to Thorpemunden Manor in case James is released. They're taking her to a women's refuge, but wouldn't even give me the address. It has to remain highly confidential, in case violent husbands discover its whereabouts. It seems James has been emotionally abusing Daisy all their married life and occasionally has escalated into physical violence."

Henry grimaced. "Poor Daisy. I wish we'd noticed. I feel quite guilty about her. All these years, and we thought she was ecstatically happy. You never know what goes on behind closed doors, do you? Doesn't matter how well you think you know someone. How on earth could I have had James as my churchwarden all these years and not have known he was abusing his family?"

"I don't think we can blame ourselves, although something like this makes us all feel guilty. But Daisy and James were adept at keeping it all hidden. When they held events they were always the perfect hosts. No one could have guessed."

Polly did, Henry thought. But he didn't want to spoil the rare moment of intimacy. He took his hand off the wheel to reach across and squeeze Mavis' hand, lying loosely in her lap. "I'm glad we'll be alone tonight. I want to take you out to dinner. Somewhere special. I've got something for you." But he refused to reveal what it was. "I want it to be a surprise."

Mavis was intrigued and, despite herself, quietly excited. She had asked Henry to woo her again and it seemed he was taking his task seriously. With Ella home, the Mansfields' situation temporarily sorted, and the Christmas rush still a couple of weeks off, she was determined to relax and enjoy whatever Henry had in mind.

Mavis dressed carefully in one of her new outfits, this time a low-cut, midnight-blue dress in a lightweight jersey wool with three-quarter sleeves, which she teamed with a beige wool jacket to keep out the cold. As an afterthought she reached for a light blue silk scarf and tucked it into the neck of the dress. It needed something, she thought, just to finish it off.

Henry had ditched his dog collar in favour of a pale blue shirt and blue and gold striped tie. It wasn't an old school tie but it looked like one, so he wore a navy blazer over dark grey slacks to complete the college image.

They drove to a small country pub in the next diocese of St. Edmundsbury and Ipswich for their meal. Henry had seen The Ratcatcher advertised in the Good Pubs Guide and fancied the name, although he wasn't sure what Mavis would make of it. But it would be well away from prying eyes, and from the prices quoted, the food ought to be first rate.

They were shown to a table near enough to the log fire to appreciate its warmth but not so close as to roast them. Nonetheless, Mavis slipped off her jacket while Henry retained his. The waiter was already hovering with menus in leather covers offering a substantial choice. He handed over the menus before flicking open crisp white damask serviettes for each of them. Then he brought drinks and tapas for them while they chose their meals.

As it was so near Christmas and something of a celebration, they both opted for the seven-course Christmas menu of baked goat's cheese followed by smoked salmon, then lemon sorbet and turkey with all the trimmings. Mavis doubted she would manage a sweet, but Henry had his eye on Christmas pudding with custard and cream.

They ate slowly, relishing the different flavours and enjoying each other's company. After the sorbet they pulled their crackers like a couple of schoolchildren, giggling at the silly jokes and ridiculously pleased with a plastic tape measure (Mavis) and a pencil sharpener (Henry). Mavis laid her tissue paper crown to one side, not wishing to disturb her hair, but Henry put on his purple crown.

"Note the Episcopal colour," he teased. "Perhaps it's a sign from God that I shall soon receive preferment." But they both laughed as he said it and he soon tore off the hat.

Henry made room for dessert while Mavis sat back to digest her meal, before they both prepared to finish with a mince pie, coffee, and a mint chocolate.

"Would you like an armchair by the fire in the lounge for your coffee?" the waiter asked.

They moved through into the lounge and sank into deep armchairs with thick, down cushions, on either side of the fireplace.

Henry smiled contentedly at his wife and reached into the inside pocket of his jacket. He fished out the small gold bag and handed it to Mavis.

"With all my love," he said quietly.

Mavis frowned. "It's a bit early for Christmas, isn't it?"

"Not a Christmas present. You don't get that until Christmas Day. This is just a message to say, 'I love you.' I wanted to give you something that will last. Not for any special occasion, but just because I want to. I didn't want to wait until Christmas because then it would be a Christmas present. I wanted something special for now." He gazed into her eyes and was thrown to notice a tear escape. She wiped it away hurriedly and opened the bag.

Withdrawing the box, Mavis held it for a moment or two, cradling it in her hands. It was the first spontaneous gift Henry had bought her in thirty-five years of marriage and she wanted to savour the moment.

He said, "Aren't you going to open it?" so she lifted the lid and looked inside, greeting the pendant with widening eyes and a sharp intake of breath.

Henry looked anxious until she said, "Oh Henry! It's so beautiful. Thank you. I've never had anything like this before. I shall treasure it forever."

"Shall I put it on for you? You'd like to wear it?"

Mavis nodded and pulled off the silk scarf, stuffing it into her handbag. Henry rose from his armchair and took the necklace from her. He placed it gently round her neck and fastened the catch. Then he kissed her, a slow and lingering kiss.

"There! That looks splendid. I'm so glad you like it."

Mavis said, "I must see it! Excuse me a moment. I'm just off to the ladies'."

To Henry's eyes it looked as if she was glowing when she returned a moment or two later.

She said, "It's perfect, Henry. Just what this dress needed. I absolutely love it."

He took her hand and said, "And I'll always love you. You do know that, don't you?"

And Mavis did.

***

Mavis wore the necklace all the time after that. It was as though she couldn't bear to be parted from it, and as it had a comparatively long chain, it went with every outfit, from the low-cut dress to jumpers and jerseys and blouses with collars.

Not someone who normally wore much jewellery, Mavis' new necklace was quickly noticed. The Mothers' Union members crowded round at their Christmas meeting, which was held in Bette Jarrold's conservatory and consisted of carols round the Christmas tree, enhanced by mulled wine and mince pies.

"What's this?" asked Bette, fingering the pendant. "An early Christmas present?"

"Just a gift from Henry," Mavis replied airily, as though such things happened all the time.

Everyone wanted to see. Little Alice Thompson from Middlestead suddenly said, "What's inside?"

Mavis frowned. "Inside? What do you mean?"

"It's a locket, isn't it? I just wondered whether you had a picture of Henry in there." She laughed girlishly.

Unaware until then that the pendant was a locket, Mavis tried to prise it open with her fingernails, but to no avail.

"Perhaps it doesn't open after all," suggested Ivy Cranthorn. "Maybe it just looks like a locket but is actually a pendant as you thought, Mavis."

In the end, Mavis slipped the locket off and it was passed round the circle of ladies, from hand to hand. They handled it gently and most of them had a go at gingerly inserting a fingernail under what appeared to be the rim, but no one could open the locket until it reached Diana Courtney. She felt carefully all around the edge and discovered a tiny catch, which she sprang with a fingernail.

"Here. My mother used to have a locket similar to this. There's a hidden catch—see, just under here—then it opens quite easily. You don't have to force it."

"Is there anything inside?" Mavis asked.

Diana handed it back to her. "Mm, look. A woman's head and shoulders. It's very tiny, but definitely a photograph. Looks a bit Oriental, if you ask me. Nothing on the other side, though. You could take this out and put a picture of yourself on one side with Henry on the other."

Mavis retrieved the necklace and squinted at the picture. "So I could. You know, she looks vaguely familiar, I don't know why. Perhaps she looks a bit like that picture that was all the rage back in the sixties, where that Chinese woman was painted green. What was it called?"

Ivy said unexpectedly, "I know the one you mean. There's a number of them, all painted by Vladimir Tretchikoff. He lives in South Africa. He was unusual in that he readily allowed his paintings to be made into prints. He wanted his work to be accessible to ordinary folk, not just rich, highbrow types. Hence, as you say, every house had one back in the sixties or seventies."

They all looked at her in surprise. "Where did you learn so much about art, Ivy?" Bette Jarrold asked with an edge to her voice, slightly miffed that she herself hadn't known anything about the artist.

Ivy was unruffled. "I used to have one of those pictures in my lounge. To be honest, I never liked it, so it found its way to the nearest jumble sale in due course. I suspect many of them ended up in similar places."

"They were somewhat kitsch, if I remember rightly," Bette said waspishly and felt better.

Mavis replaced the pendant around her neck, and the talk moved on to discussing the Mansfields. Ivy Cranthorn, Pauline Carter, and Peggy Masters, all of whom lived in Mundenford, had all spotted Polly arriving back home with Daisy and Frank in tow, and Peggy Masters, who had remained glued to the window for several hours, had also seen the arrival of Henry and Mavis, Sue and Ella.

"What's been going on, Mavis?" she asked eagerly. "Do tell. Is everything all right?"

Mavis was unwilling to break any confidences and unsure how much Daisy would want her to say. So she contented herself with smiling enigmatically and replying, "You'll need to ask Daisy about that. I expect she'll be at our next meeting," knowing full well that the story would have broken long before then.

***

When she got home, Mavis spoke to Henry about the necklace. "It's a proper locket and there's a photo inside, Henry. A bit like those pictures from the seventies that you never liked. Ivy Cranthorn did tell us the name of the artist, but I've forgotten. There's a hidden catch, which you have to spring to open the locket. The photo was probably left there by the last owner."

Henry murmured, "Mm." But clearly his mind was elsewhere. He said, "I've been thinking about the Thorpemunden carol service. Do you think we might invite Ella and Polly to come back afterwards? Could you lay on some refreshments? Mince pies or sausage rolls or something?"

Mavis sighed. She hated it when Henry ignored her, even though she was aware that he simply hadn't heard. But she put aside her own thoughts in order to consider Henry's suggestion.

"Good idea. It would be nice to have a bit of a party. I can do mulled wine if you like, and a proper meal if you'd prefer?"

"By that time of the evening I suspect everyone will have eaten, so probably we wouldn't want too much. Better make sure Ella isn't working, though. Wouldn't want to leave her out."

No, thought Mavis, rather more darkly than she had intended. She said, "Ella has already said she'll be coming to the carol service, so I don't think she can be working. But I'll check it out. Leave it to me, Henry. I'll get it sorted."

Chapter Forty-One

The Thorpemunden carol service was packed. The church was decorated by greenery and red berries and lit only by hundreds of candles, imparting an atmosphere of awe and mystery and stretching back across the centuries. The three purple candles on the Advent ring burned brightly, leaving only the pink candle, denoting the dawning of a new age, to be lit on the last Sunday before Christmas and the white candle, depicting the light of Christ coming into the world, to be lit at the Midnight Mass on Christmas Eve.

The six-foot Christmas tree, covered with gold and silver baubles, tinsel, and white fairy lights and topped by a large gold star, was stationed near the pulpit at the chancel step. It took your eye as soon as you entered church and was greeted with gasps and excitement by children young and old.

Flying from the roof of the church were two angels blowing trumpets and covered in gold foil. As they were suspended on thin wire, they moved whenever the heavy oak door opened, disturbing the air in church.

Underneath the altar was the crib scene. The backdrop of a stable was painted on card, but the wooden manger was filled with straw, and the figures of Mary and Joseph and the baby were made out of plaster and were almost lifelike. A donkey and an ox completed the scene, but the magi on their camels and carrying their gifts of gold, frankincense, and myrrh were at the west end of church near the door. They would gradually move up the church to arrive at the manger on Twelfth Night, the feast of the Epiphany. The awe factor was definitely present.

As always, the village had turned out in full force for the carol service, and the choir were on top form. This was their big event of the year and they made sure that they looked the part, with their Virgin-Mary blue robes and their starched white collars.

Everyone in the congregation was given their own individual candle in its cardboard drip collar and the lights were turned off for the service, which was entirely in candlelight.

Millie Sterling, aged eight, with long golden ringlets, cherubic looks, and the pure voice of an angel, was chosen to sing the solo first verse of "Once in Royal David's City" and was greeted with emotional, stunned silence from the congregation and tears of pride and joy from her grandmother, Bunny.

Henry settled back to enjoy the service. Apart from the Bidding Prayer at the beginning and the Blessing at the end, he had no further duties in the service, which flowed automatically. So it was a rare opportunity for Henry to soak up the worship himself.

Polly had robed and was sitting opposite Henry in the curate's stall. She was both pleased and proud to be reading the final lesson from the first chapter of John's gospel, since that was usually the prerogative of the incumbent. She loved being up front and had practised reading "In the beginning was the Word and the Word was with God and the Word was God" before the mirror at least six times in at least six different cadences to try to impart proper significance to the words.

Mavis and Ella sat together towards the front of the congregation, both experiencing a sense of the numinous at this special time of the year but for different reasons. Mavis was still glowing, hugging to herself her dawning realisation of Henry's love for her, in which she was now beginning to trust, and touching her necklace from time to time, just to make sure it was still there. Ella was transported by her first real experience of a carol service. She had attended carol services at school, but they hadn't meant much to her and she could barely remember them. Her mother had never paid much attention to religion and Ella vaguely thought she might have had Buddhist leanings, if anything. But she couldn't remember her mother ever attending any type of religious service and certainly not at Christmas. In fact, the only thing she remembered about Christmas was envying other children at school who seemed to be filled with excitement over it.

It was a magical service, transporting the congregation into the hidden mysteries of God. But for the whole church, a sour note crept in at coffee after the service when there were grumbles and complaints that James Mansfield—as churchwarden—was absent. Some people wondered whether his nose had been put out of joint because the church looked so amazing. When James was in charge, there were no flying angels and no candles, on health and safety grounds. Henry explained to any who would listen that James had not taken umbrage but that the Mansfields were away.

"You'd have thought they might have avoided going away for the carol service! I've never heard of such a thing! The churchwarden going on holiday on the very occasion the church is certain to be packed," grumbled Bunny Sterling, who had wanted the whole world to hear her darling Millie sing. "Anyway, where have they gone? I thought they never went away during the shooting season. Too busy playing hosts and raking in the cash."

Henry was saved from having to reply by Dorothy Mudd, who seized the opportunity to reprove Bunny.

"Now, now, Bunny! It is the season of peace and goodwill. We mustn't begrudge them a little time to themselves. James does work awfully hard for the church. Wonderful man, don't you think?" She turned to Henry. "I'm sure the rector agrees?"

Henry coughed into his fist, muttered, "Excuse me," and turned away. Although he should have been prepared to field questions about the Mansfields, in fact he had failed to anticipate the backlash. But he soon recovered. By the time he reached the next query, Henry had his explanation in place.

"No James, Rector?" asked the organist. "Never known him to miss one of these before."

Henry said smoothly, "We must remember that he's getting on in years now, Barry. The Mansfields are all away." He didn't want to say anything that would be adversely recalled when the news broke, as it surely would within the next week or so, and was glad when folk began to drift away and he could escape to the rectory.

***

The three women had left only minutes before Henry and he caught up with them as they opened the door to the rectory. Mavis hurried off towards the kitchen to cook sausage rolls and to finish the laying of the table with the buffet she had prepared. Polly hung her coat on the stand in the hall and followed her, while Henry made up the fire in the lounge and Ella poured drinks for all of them.

When the food preparation was complete, Mavis and Polly came into the lounge and the four of them stood with raised glasses.

"Happy Christmas to all of us," toasted Henry.

But as they raised their glasses Ella stifled a gasp, her eyes fixed on Mavis' locket.

"Your necklace, Mavis! Where did you get it?"

Mavis looked surprised. "Henry gave it to me. It's lovely, don't you think?"

Ella's hand holding the glass was trembling. "I had one just like it. At least, I think it was like it. Can I have a closer look? It may not be quite the same."

"Of course." Mavis put down her drink, slipped off the pendant, and handed it to Ella, who cradled it in her hands, turning it over almost reverently.

"Mine had a tiny catch under the rim, invisible to those who didn't know about it. I kept my mother's picture in the locket. It was the only thing I had of hers. I really treasured it." Her voice caught and her eyes glistened.

Mavis said, "As it happens, this one has a photo in it and a catch under the rim. They must be from the same era. Possibly the same manufacturer. Why don't you take a look?"

They all crowded round as Ella slipped the catch with her fingernail. The locket sprang open.

Ella gasped. "It's my picture! This is my mother! This is my locket. It was given to my mother by my father, the only man she ever loved and the only gift he ever gave her, as far as I know."

Polly frowned. "That's some coincidence, isn't it? Didn't you tell me your locket was stolen when you were in Great Yarmouth, Ella?"

"That's right. I always suspected that creep Mark Winters, who used to follow me around. But I could never prove anything. And I never went to the police. I didn't think they'd want to know about something so trivial to them. So very important to me, but not to the rest of the world. Oh!" She caught her breath. "You don't suppose he's here, do you? That awful Mark Winters?" She looked round wildly as if expecting to see him emerge from behind the sofa.

Henry put his arm around her shoulders and gave her a gentle squeeze. "Of course not! He'll be long gone, now he's sold it on. And we don't know where he sold it, either. I bought the locket from an antique shop in Diss, so it's not such a stretch, Polly. All these antique dealers know each other. It's quite within the bounds of probability that Sam, the antiques man in Diss, bought this off some antique dealer friend from Yarmouth. I don't suppose Sam knew it was stolen. May I look at the picture? I didn't realise there was a photo inside."

Mavis groaned. "I did tell you, but as usual you were on a different planet. Well, Ella, I suppose if this is really yours, obviously you must have it back." She looked archly at Henry. "But I'll expect Henry to replace it with another one."

As the attention turned to Mavis, only she noticed the colour drain from Henry's face. But when he collapsed into a chair, his breathing shallow, sweat beading his forehead, and the necklace slipping from his fingers, they were all over him.

"Henry! Are you all right? What's the matter?"

"Give him some air, he can't breathe."

"Shall I call an ambulance?"

At this last Henry recovered sufficiently to say, "No! No ambulance. I'm fine. I'll be fine in a minute."

He took some deep breaths while Mavis regarded him with anxious eyes. Ella quickly poured out a small glass of brandy, which Mavis held to his lips. They had taken on a bluish tinge, which Mavis didn't like.

"Drink this, Henry." She used her most peremptory tones and Henry obediently sipped the brandy. Colour began to return to his cheeks and his breathing settled.

After a while Mavis said, "How are you feeling now? Any better?"

Henry nodded. "I don't know what brought that on. Perhaps the stress of the season. You know what Christmas is like for clergy."

Mavis eyed him askance and felt his pulse. "Shall I call the doctor? Are you settling now? Perhaps you need food. We haven't eaten since lunchtime."

"Perhaps that's it," Henry agreed. "Come on. I don't want to spoil the party." He held up the locket. "I don't know what to do with this. It seems it belongs to two of my favourite women now!"

It wasn't the best attempt at humour, but they dutifully smiled.

Mavis said robustly, "You take it, Ella. It was yours before it was mine. And it's so precious to you. You must have it. I'll enjoy seeing you wear it."

As Ella hung back, hesitating to take something which Mavis loved, which had been given to Mavis, and which was therefore still technically hers, Mavis stepped forward and fastened the locket around Ella's slender neck.

"There! Now you're complete again."

Impulsively, Ella hugged her. "Thank you so much, Mavis. It is special. You've been so good to me, I can never repay you. But perhaps I can buy you a new necklace to replace this one?"

Henry intervened. "No, you won't! If it helps, regard this as our Christmas present to you. I shall be pleased to buy another necklace for Mavis." He turned to his wife. "Perhaps this time we could go together and you could choose? Besides, I want a word with Sam in the antiques shop. I want to be certain he was unaware that he was receiving stolen goods and I want to know where he bought this locket."

Ella blanched. "Do you really think Mark Winters might still be around? What will I do?"

Henry shook his head. "No, please don't worry. I'm sure he isn't. Otherwise you would have seen him long before this. He doesn't sound the kind of guy to keep out of the limelight. No. I think he would have found his way to the Rose and Crown if he had tracked you down this far. My guess is that once he realised you were out of his life for good, he sold the necklace for the best price he could get and Sam picked it up cheaply at an antiques fair or an auction or something like that. It was sheer luck it ended up in Diss."

Ella added quietly, "Or the hand of God. Ever since I came here I've had this feeling that God has his hand on my life." She gazed at them all. "You're the first real family I've ever had. And I don't think that's luck or coincidence. I think it's because God works through you all in ways you scarcely realise."

Polly said, "If that's true of us, Ella, it's certainly true of you. You've made a huge difference to us and I think we've all changed because of you.

"But come on, everyone. The sausage rolls will be cold if we don't eat soon, and I for one have had my fill of theology for today. Let's eat."

***

Henry was off colour for the next few days and Mavis was anxious about him. There seemed to be a return to the old listlessness and lethargy and she feared that he was again descending into depression.

Henry himself was tortured. He had instantly recognised the photo inside the locket, the shock of which had led to his near collapse.

Memories of the long Windsor Course came flooding back, the time when he was away from Mavis for six weeks.

He had met Ayoung Wim quite by chance in an art gallery, although he had never known her surname. They were both enjoying the paintings when Ayoung had fainted. As the only other person in that particular room, naturally Henry had attended to her. She had soon come round, but it was apparent that she needed food and a hot drink. Henry had taken her to the café and fed her, which is how it had all started. By the time the meal was over, he was in love. Ayoung was so beautiful and so vulnerable, in need of manly protection, or so Henry thought. Small and slight, with flowing black hair, almond eyes, and high cheekbones, she had a flawless complexion and the most amazing smile Henry had ever seen. A tiny rosebud mouth revealed neat, even white teeth, and her soulful eyes lit up when she smiled.

With old-fashioned courtesy, Henry had insisted on escorting Ayoung home and there he had been powerless against her practised charms, which were her only way of repaying his kindness. He had returned a week later when he was able to escape the Windsor Course for a couple of hours and had declared his undying love for her. He had again made love to her, but when she had shyly asked him for money afterwards, had realised exactly what sort of a house he had entered. Not that this realisation had stopped him, although it had made him pause. He was already an incumbent and knew all about conduct unbecoming to a man of the cloth. But he was so besotted with her that he had returned once more, this time with a gift for Ayoung and had insisted that she put her own photograph in the locket.

Henry had never learned Ayoung's surname, and after his second visit the torture inflicted upon him by his own conscience had got the better of him. He had confessed to one of the more approachable tutors on his course, who had taken a very dim and horrified view of Henry's dalliance and had extracted a promise under threat of exposure that the liaison would cease immediately.

Although he had thought about her daily for more than two years, Henry had reluctantly kept his promise. He had wrestled with himself over giving up his ministry in order to seek out Ayoung, but the thought of the scandal involved both in relinquishing his vocation, in consorting with a prostitute, and in divorcing Mavis was too much for him. On his knees before God, Henry had vowed to put the past behind him and devote all his energies to the service of God.

When he had been the given the post of Rector of the Thorpemunden Benefice, he had finally been able to say good-bye in his own mind to the girl he had met and loved and put her memory to one side. He had had no idea that she was pregnant and had rarely thought about her since.

But although he hadn't realised it at the time, Henry was now aware that by turning his back on love, something had died within him. And through that little death, he had killed something in Mavis too. He had originally blamed his fall from grace on Mavis' frigidity, telling himself that he would never have slept with Ayoung if his sex life with Mavis had been satisfactory. But with more mature vision and the undoubted benefit of hindsight, he slowly began to realise that he had been unfair to Mavis. She had been even younger than him at the time of their marriage, and coming from a strict Victorian background as the daughter of a vicar with very strong ideas about morals, Henry had vaguely been aware that she had been terrified of sex, but had thought no further than his own needs. In retrospect, he should have helped her. He should have been gentle and patient and kind, instead of taking it for granted that Mavis should do her duty whenever he required her to do so. The result had been that their marriage had become cold and loveless, with Mavis hiding behind a spotless home without any hint of intimacy about it and Henry devoting all his energies to the parish. Since this was exactly how it had been for Mavis during her childhood, she had accepted the situation without complaint, assuming that this was the norm for clergy.

But first Polly's appearance as curate, challenging and questioning Henry's usual way of doing things, and then Ella arriving on the scene, had thrown both the Winstones into turmoil.

Reflecting on how near he had come to falling in love with his own daughter made Henry feel slightly sick. But that feeling was swallowed up in the immense pride and deep love he felt for Ella. He knew something had passed between them the first time they had met, a kind of recognition, but he had misinterpreted that unacknowledged recognition and feelings of fatherly love for feelings of amour. Having no idea that he was a father, how could he have done otherwise?

Now, for the first time in twenty-three years, Henry questioned whether he should have confessed his failings to Mavis at the time. Perhaps if he had had the courage to be honest then, their marriage would have been the better for it. But he had preferred to remain on a pedestal of perfection, which had resulted in some remoteness between them but which had been easier and more pleasant to handle than the truth. If he had told Mavis the truth, would she have stayed with him all these years? Or more to the point, if he revealed the truth now, how would Mavis react? On the other hand, was it fair to Ella to continue to keep the truth hidden?

Chapter Forty-Two

Polly was always a last-minute person. Ella was usually more organised but, having been down in London with Sue until so recently, hadn't got round to thinking about Christmas presents. The two girls decided to go shopping together in Norwich on the Monday of Christmas week.

Strangely enough, the parish tended to quieten down during Christmas week until Christmas Eve, when Polly was responsible for the Crib Service at six o'clock, which was likely to be so packed with children high on Christmas excitement together with adults desperate for an hour's peace, that Polly would be exhausted after it. But exhausted or not, she had to be on duty again at Midnight Mass, although Henry would be leading the service. Then Polly and Henry had two services each on Christmas morning before they could take time off and, Polly hoped, sink into oblivion for at least two days until the next Sunday service.

So the Monday morning was a good time to tackle Christmas shopping. Polly drove, but they decided to use the Park and Ride facility on the Ipswich road rather than fighting through the traffic and queuing for hours for a parking slot in the city.

Ella and Polly had decided to club together for gifts for Mavis and Henry, but had no idea what to buy. Ella was all for separate gifts. Perhaps a pendant necklace for Mavis as she clearly liked pendants, even though it would hardly replace Ella's necklace, and a book token for Henry. Polly thought a book token was the most boring present she could imagine and was eager to prevent Henry's relapse into boredom.

"Why don't we look for an ornament of some kind?" she suggested. "A turned wooden bowl, or one of those china birds or something? We could give it to both of them from both of us. Then we could afford to spend more for it and get something really cool."

Ella was already peering in the window of a jewellers-cum-china shop in the mall. "Look." She pointed at entwined figures. About twelve inches high and fashioned from white porcelain, they were long and slender with beautifully flowing lines, their arms around each other making an unbroken circle. "How about that? Doesn't that say something about Mavis and Henry's new relationship? It's a real token, don't you think?"

Polly did think and they entered the shop. The figurine was not only good to look at, but smooth and tactile as well. The two girls made up their minds immediately and the ornament was duly purchased and carefully wrapped.

Polly had spotted a photograph album which she thought would be perfect for Ella, but she needed to evade Ella for ten minutes in order to buy it. It was time Ella had some proper family memories, Polly thought, and since she and Mavis and Henry were now the nearest thing Ella had to a family, Polly intended to fill a few pages of the album with some shots of them all and the churches and anything else she could find. She hoped such a treasure trove of memories might minimise the risk of Ella disappearing again.

She suggested they should migrate to the bookshop for coffee, then was able to slip away while Ella was still finishing her latte, promising to keep in touch by mobile phone. Ella was more than happy with the arrangement as she wanted to purchase gifts for Melvyn and Tracey back in Yarmouth, and Siobhan in the flat in Essex. Feeling more settled in her own life, Ella now felt more secure about keeping in touch with her former friends.

She also wanted to buy a surprise gift for Polly. She had her eye on a quirky ceramic set of a teapot in the shape of an elephant, a cup and saucer, and a packet of Sri Lankan tea. It was fun as well as useful and she thought Polly would laugh when she opened it. And she wanted to buy some flashing Christmas earrings, which she was determined to challenge Polly to wear to both services on Christmas Eve. Surely even the Church of England would smile at Christmas tree earrings with flashing lights on Christmas Eve.

Polly had one final gift to buy, something for Sue. In an unexpected, spur of the moment online decision, she had already ordered a hamper to be delivered to her mother back in Streatham (for the first time ever) and had sent a Game Boy for Toby. Somehow, she had warmer feelings towards her family than she'd ever had before. Perhaps it was something to do with the Christmas spirit, which in her mother's case, Polly reflected wryly, would probably be vodka.

Anyway, she knew she wouldn't deliver Sue's gift until after Christmas. She didn't think Sue would object, since they had already arranged that Polly should visit for a few days in the new year. Like all clergy, Henry would have the week after Christmas off, leaving Polly to take the following week. So if she wished, she could use the post-Christmas sales for Sue's gift. But when she discovered a purple scarf with a velvety touch, Polly bought it immediately for Sue. There was something Episcopal about it, so Polly reckoned it would appeal to Sue's imagination and sense of humour.

With a few rolls of wrapping paper and a couple of extra packs of Christmas cards just in case, Ella and Polly's shopping was complete. They drove home discussing exactly when they should deliver their gift to the rectory.

"Why don't we go during the evening of Christmas Eve?" Polly suggested. "You've managed to get the time off—although I can't imagine how at this time of year. Must be that winning smile—and we'll all have a few hours to fill in before the midnight. Why don't we go then?"

Ella agreed and promised to help Polly with the Crib Service. Children were invited to come dressed as shepherds or angels, so that all of them took part in the service. It was mainly a question of marshalling them to the crib at the right time while proud parents and grandparents got busy with their camcorders. Inevitably, Millie Sterling was going to play Mary and bring her favourite doll with her for baby Jesus, while Dorothy Mudd's grandson Kevin Smith, who happened to be staying for Christmas, had been roped in amid protestations, reluctance, and bribery to play Joseph.

It wasn't so much a service, Polly reflected afterwards, as unadulterated Christmas mayhem. With over fifty children of all ages and around two adults per child, Mundenford Church was straining at the seams. There were shepherds and angels everywhere, running up and down the aisles, standing on pews, climbing over the altar rail, and playing precariously with the ancient plaster figures of the Holy family. And all of this at maximum decibels. Even with a microphone it was as much as Polly could do to make herself heard. In the end, after managing to stagger through "Away in a Manger" and "While Shepherds Watched," she gave up on any further carols or Bible readings, contenting herself with telling the Christmas story by smiling and nodding and moving children from place to place in the church. She couldn't believe that there had been any Christmas message whatsoever in the service, but everyone seemed to enjoy it and eventually dispersed to hang up Christmas stockings and await the arrival of Santa Claus.

Ella insisted that Polly rest for an hour after the service and prepared supper for them both. They made their way to Thorpemunden to the rectory at around eight-thirty and Polly took her robes with her to save having to return home before Midnight Mass.

Mavis seemed both pleased and strangely relieved to see them. Polly couldn't figure out the relief until they entered the lounge and saw Henry. He was slumped in his armchair, failing to get up to greet them and just acknowledging their presence with a grunt. His complexion was grey and he looked unshaven. Although he was wearing his dog collar so evidently expected to be taking the Midnight service, he looked incapable.

Polly's heart sank and she and Ella looked at Mavis with concern.

"What's happened? Is he ill?"

Mavis lifted her shoulders helplessly. "He's been like this since the carol service on Sunday. You remember how he nearly collapsed? I think it's a relapse. I don't know what to do."

Ella crossed to Henry and knelt at his feet. She took both his hands in hers, massaging them gently, and spoke quietly but firmly to him. "Henry, it's Christmas Eve. Polly and I have brought you and Mavis a gift. We hope you like it. Would you like to open it?"

Henry stirred himself enough to return her look. Then he dropped his eyes, but not before she had witnessed the pain in them.

"Henry, what is it? What's the matter? Are you in pain? You must tell us. Perhaps we can help. We could call the doctor for you."

He shook his head. "No one can help."

Mavis whispered, "He's been like this all day. He won't respond to me. I don't know what's worrying him."

Ella cupped Henry's face in her hands. "Please, Henry," she begged. "Please. We can't enjoy Christmas with you like this."

He stroked the side of her face and to her dismay, a tear gathered in the corner of his eye. He blinked it away impatiently.

Polly said brightly, "Why don't you open our present, Mavis? Perhaps that will cheer Henry up."

Mavis looked as though the last thing she wanted to do was open a gift, but she took the wrapped box from Polly with dutiful exclamations of delight.

"Look, Henry! How lovely. Shall I open it?"

Since Henry seemed incapable of responding, she opened the present anyway and lifted out the porcelain figurine, greeting it with a gasp of pleasure.

"Look, Henry!" And this time her tone was quite genuine. "Look! Isn't this lovely? Thank you so much, both of you. It—it says something really profound, don't you think, Henry? Something about us?"

At this, Henry roused himself to respond to the gift. When he saw it his eyes widened, but almost immediately tears began to fall. And somehow, as though it were a sign he had been expecting, the gift also opened the floodgate of Henry's words. He began to speak, his words falling over themselves in his eagerness to share his burden and relieve his own aching.

"I've something to tell you all, something of which I'm ashamed. It concerns both Ella and Mavis and it all happened a long time ago. Around twenty-three years ago to be precise." He looked meaningfully at Ella, but she was as perplexed as Mavis and Polly. They waited for him to go on, but the atmosphere had taken on a strange quality of dread.

Henry continued his tale, explaining about the Windsor Course and his excursion to the art gallery. When he spoke about Ayoung and mentioned her name, his eyes were on Ella, whose mouth opened in a big round "O" of comprehension. But there was a look of horror and disbelief in her eyes. She wrenched her hands free from his and flew out of the room.

Henry's head slumped. He looked piteously at Mavis, who exchanged a glance of consternation with Polly.

"I'll go," decided Polly. "You look after Henry."

She ran after Ella, catching up with her in the kitchen. She had never seen Ella, usually so calm and controlled, in such a state.

Polly waited while Ella paced the kitchen, agitatedly wringing her hands. Then she said, "What is it, Ella? Can you tell me?"

Ella burst into a storm of tears. "He—he's my father," she managed to croak.

"Henry? What do you mean? He can't be! Are you sure? Didn't you tell me your mother was—"

Polly's voice trailed as she realised the enormity of what she had been about to say, but Ella completed the sentence for her.

"—a prostitute, yes. Don't you see, it all fits. My father was a professional man, tall and straight with blond, wavy hair and the kindest man she'd ever met. That's all I know about him and that's Henry to a T. It's just that I never noticed before. That's why he collapsed when he saw my mother's photo in the locket. He recognised her. He must have vaguely recognised the locket from all those years ago. That's why it attracted him so much and he bought it for Mavis. Obviously he has a habit of buying it for women he loves. I wonder how many more there've been? No wonder he's been ill, it's a guilty conscience. This is my worst nightmare, Polly. I didn't expect it to be like this when I found my father. Now I never want to see him again."

"But, Ella, you've been searching for your father all your life. And you don't know for certain that you're right. You need to check it out with him and—and Mavis, I guess. If you are right and Henry is your father, he's here for you now. But surely it has to be too much of a coincidence? Things like that don't happen in real life."

"Where has he been all my life? Why didn't he care about me or Mum? Why didn't he ever come back? He's been living a lie all these years. And he left us destitute. My mother died of AIDS. You should have seen her at the end—Henry should have seen her! He should know what he did to her, the sort of life he forced her to lead. If he'd had any compassion at all or been true to his own integrity, she'd still be alive today and we'd have been a proper family. I hate him, I really do. I hate him."

Not knowing how to answer, Polly put an arm around her friend's shoulders and hugged her. "At least he's telling the truth now. I expect he's trying to break it to Mavis at this very moment. That won't be easy, especially considering the way their relationship has been lately. Oh Lordy! It looks as if this could turn out to be an interesting Christmas."

For want of any better ideas, Polly brewed a pot of tea. When she reckoned they'd left Henry long enough for him to reveal the story to Mavis, and Ella had subsided into a well of misery without the tears, Polly stacked the tray with mugs and took the tea through, dragging a reluctant Ella along with her.

One look at Mavis' horrified face was enough to confirm that the story was out. Strangely enough, Henry seemed better; brighter and perkier. But Mavis took one look at Ella and turned away.

"I hate you," she muttered in a strangled voice, although whether she meant Ella or Henry or both was hard to tell. She turned back to Henry.

"How could you do such a dreadful thing? You, who preach from the pulpit Sunday after Sunday! You disgust me. You're filthy, unclean." In her vituperation she failed to notice Ella's stricken face. She went on, "All I ever wanted was a child and you—you oh! How could you do this to me? A prostitute! Henry, how could you?" And she ran from the room, slamming the door behind her. A moment later they heard the bedroom door slamming too.

Henry held out his arms to Ella, but she shrank from him.

"All these years!" she cried accusingly, letting the sentence hang in the air between them.

Henry shook his head as though to clear it. "I'm so sorry," he said softly. "But I loved you the moment I set eyes on you. I didn't know why at the time. I thought it was just an old man feeling rejuvenated by youth and life and beauty. But there was something between us, you can't deny it, Ella. It's just that neither of us knew what it was. Now I've found you and—oh, my dear! I love you so very much. I want to be a proper father to you, to make up for all the years. You do realise I had no idea your mother was pregnant? You do know that, don't you? I'd never have deserted her if I'd known. But at that time, status and society and conscience and the Church—they all got in the way. I loved your mother so much. She was the most beautiful, gentle, serene creature I had ever met. She opened up a new world for me. But I'm ashamed to say I turned my back on it and on her.

"At the time, I thought I was doing the right thing. I was told I had acted against God's laws, and maybe I had. It didn't feel like it, though. It felt so right, so perfect. I was in love, you see, and love wipes out all manner of sins. At least, that's what I think now. But I was young then and told I must repent and I had no other career. If I'd left the Church I would have been penniless. That wouldn't have worried me too much, but I couldn't drag Mavis down there with me or cause such scandal to the Church I still loved. Remember we're talking nearly a quarter of a century ago. Things were different then. None of this is any excuse, I know that. I'm just trying to explain as best I can and to ask for your forgiveness.

"Ella, darling Ella, can you do that? Can you ever forgive me?"

But Ella couldn't bear to look at him. She said shortly, "You'd better go to your wife."

Polly was growing increasingly anxious. She glanced at her watch. "Henry, It's already ten forty-five. The service starts at eleven-thirty so we need to be there by eleven, don't we? After all, James won't be there so we need to make sure everything is in place. Henry, please. We have to go in fifteen minutes."

Ella said to her, "I don't think I can go. Not now."

"But what will you do? If you take the car and go home I'll be stranded. Couldn't you just come and slip in at the back? We could leave as soon as the service is over. Please, Ella, please. Do it for me."

Ella hesitated, feeling trapped and longing to run far away. She wanted nothing more than to be left alone, to try to sort out her feelings. She wasn't sure she could face any of the jolly Christmas banter which she was certain would come their way after the service, and she was well aware that it would take Polly at least half an hour at the door wishing everyone a merry Christmas, before they'd be able to escape. And the thought of being anywhere near Henry, especially being forced to sit and listen to him delivering a Christmas sermon, filled her with revulsion. How could he have been so hypocritical all these years?

But it was clear that Polly needed her support. She said abruptly without looking at Henry, "I'll go now, then, if you don't mind. I'll sit at the back." And with that she left the rectory to slip through the gate into the churchyard. The church was likely to be empty for another ten minutes or so before the midnight worshippers began to drift in, and Ella wanted the time and the space.

Polly was seriously anxious. Her first priority, she felt, was to get Henry functioning sufficiently to go through to the church and preside at the service. Otherwise she would be trying to cope with a packed church and no one who could give Communion. She didn't care about a sermon and didn't think the worshippers would care much either. They just wanted to make their Christmas Communion and go home to their families and their parties. But there had to be someone there who could preside and there was only Henry.

"Come on, Henry. We must go. The church will be full and everyone wants to hear you. Have you got your robes together? Any books you need to take? Shall I lead intercessions? Come on, do come. Please."

She made no further mention of Mavis, reckoning that if Henry chased after Mavis now he'd never make the service. Feeling like a shepherd or perhaps someone with a recalcitrant donkey, she pushed and pulled and prodded and cajoled until Henry eventually got to his feet. Then Polly collected his robes, pushed his books into his hands, and opened the front door. Henry meekly followed her out of the rectory.

Chapter Forty-Three

It was like dressing a child, Polly thought later. Having hustled Henry into the vestry, she took off his jacket, helped him into his cassock alb, placed his gold stole around his neck, and draped the gold chasuble over his shoulders. Henry looked magnificent, but stood there as she administered to him just as though he were a puppet, waiting for his strings to be pulled. He had such a spaced-out look in his eyes that Polly wondered exactly which planet he was inhabiting.

Fortunately, from his scribbled notes, Mavis had typed his sermon in full on the computer and printed it out, so all he had to do was read through the entire service. Polly hoped he was capable of that, with a bit of help from her prodding him in the right direction at the right time.

Thorpemunden Church soon filled with merry revellers, especially those who came straight from The Crown in the village. Polly was relieved to notice Ella hidden in the shadows at the west end of the church. The knowledge that Ella was in church and therefore secure until after the service, freed Polly to concentrate on the matter in hand. She hoped and prayed that Henry would be working on autopilot. He had led this service every year of his ministry, so should know it backwards. Nonetheless, Polly knew she would remain anxious until the service was over and she could return Henry intact to the rectory.

The congregation was much noisier than the usual Sunday gathering and Polly knew only a handful of the people there. She wondered where they all fitted into the grand scheme of things. Some were obviously student children and grandchildren returned to the family nest for Christmas, but others were complete strangers to her even though she thought she knew most of the people living in Thorpemunden and surrounding villages. Clearly there was something romantic about Midnight Mass which appealed to the popular imagination.

Henry seemed to be energised by the full church and to Polly's relief, launched into the service with aplomb. He greeted everyone by wishing them a very happy Christmas to which they responded in ecclesiastical terms from long ago, "And with thy spirit," making Polly grin despite herself.

She had a moment's qualm when Henry stood up in the pulpit to preach and started with, "Something strange has happened to me this Christmas." Polly held her breath. Surely he wasn't going to use this occasion for a public confession? It was bad enough revealing the awful truth to his wife on Christmas Eve, but in Polly's opinion, to involve the whole community would be the most appalling form of self-indulgence. Besides which, it would be certain to end his career. She wished he'd kept his former misdemeanours to himself, especially in view of Ella's unexpected reaction.

But in fact Henry's words were simply an opening gambit, prelude to a mild joke which was less than funny but which had the congregation rolling in the aisles. Amazing, Polly thought, what a visit to The Crown prior to the service could achieve. Henry read straight from the script in front of him, speaking about the reality of God within every human person, revealed by the babe in the manger. It was a standard Christmas sermon, unlikely to fire anyone up but also unlikely to antagonise.

Polly began to relax. Perhaps they'd get through it all right after all. It was even better when the people came up to the altar rail row by row to receive communion. Polly was concentrating so hard on offering the chalice to slightly inebriated parishioners without spilling a drop and somehow tilting the chalice underneath the rims of large hats (you could tell instantly who the occasional churchgoers were, she thought) that she had no idea who was in the congregation. Then, as she came to a bowed head of gelled, spiky black hair, her heart did a curious flip, compounded when the head lifted to reveal dancing brown eyes and two dimples on either side of full lips in a cheeky grin.

"Tom Curtis," she breathed and was unable to prevent herself returning his grin with a delighted smile of her own. As her eyes met his, something electric passed between them and her heart soared. She felt like dancing to the next worshipper at the rail and offering the chalice while singing at the top of her voice, but recovered her composure sufficiently to continue with the dignity demanded by her task, contenting herself with watching out of the corner of her eye so as not to miss a moment of Tom returning to his pew.

It's going to be all right, she thought, with a new confidence. *It's Christmas, God's in his heaven, and all's right with the world.*

But she was wrong.

All was far from right in the insular world of Thorpemunden and it was doubtful whether God was in his heaven after all, for even as the thought entered Polly's head there was a huge commotion as the great oaken west door of the church swung open and crashed back against the stone wall. Everyone turned at the ear-shattering clatter. For a moment Polly thought the wind had caught the door and somehow prised it open, but then she saw the silhouette of Mavis outlined against the light pouring from the church.

With a cry which held every worshipper spellbound, Mavis dramatically stretched out her arm and pointed straight at Henry.

"That man is an impostor," Mavis cried at the top of her voice. "How dare he offer you food from the Lord's Table? He's filth, nothing but filth, I tell you. I denounce him before God."

There was a stunned silence, punctuated only by a few nervous giggles. Some people evidently thought it was a set-up. Every breath was held, every eye was on Mavis. Henry had paused with a wafer from the paten halfway to the next worshipper's mouth, which remained open in a round "O" of astonishment. Polly nearly dropped the chalice. All attention was focussed upon Mavis, the moment breathlessly suspended in mixed excitement, anticipation, and trepidation.

Her heart filled with dread, Polly was also aware of a sneaking moment of admiration. Who'd have thought Mavis Winstone had it in her to disrupt the biggest service of the year with such a brilliant move? It was like something straight out of *Pride and Prejudice*.

Polly was the first to recover but was too far away from Mavis to be able to do anything. Henry was in a state of shock. For once, Polly longed for James Mansfield. As churchwarden he would have reacted swiftly to the situation and hustled Mavis out before she could do any more harm. But James, as far as she knew, was in police custody. And Ella, who would normally have sprung to Mavis' side, had just been rejected by Mavis. Polly prayed that someone would have the gumption to do something before Mavis started again.

Someone did. As Mavis began to march purposefully up the aisle towards the altar rail, Tom Curtis slipped out of his seat. He neatly grabbed the startled Mavis' outstretched arm, turned her around in one fluid movement, and marched her back out of the church before she knew what was happening.

Polly expelled her breath in a long sigh of relief. But Henry was still transfixed, staring after his wife, his face like chalk. And the congregation was beginning to buzz, alive with delectable gossip too good to miss. There were already sidelong glances at Henry as brain cells began to whirr.

Polly sidled up to Henry as surreptitiously as she could and nudged him gently. He appeared not to notice. As Henry's pause lengthened into embarrassment, the buzz of whispered conversation grew louder until it threatened to become a roar. The situation was rapidly getting out of hand at what should have been the most solemn moment of the entire year.

"Henry!" Polly hissed urgently. "Come on. Say something or carry on with Communion or something!"

But Henry was incapable of movement. Polly glanced round wildly, wondering whether she should wrench the microphone from Henry's lapel or lean over in a somewhat undignified manner and speak into it. Somehow she needed to recover the situation. She caught the organist's eye as Trevor Smith, Dorothy Mudd's son-in-law and Kevin's father, who was a churchwarden at his own church and was staying for Christmas, hurried up the aisle towards the sanctuary.

Without more ado the organist launched smoothly into "God Rest Ye Merry Gentlemen," which made Polly want to giggle but had the desired effect on the congregation. Everybody rustled through their carol sheets until they found the correct carol, then obediently stood up and began to sing. Trevor Smith slipped into the sanctuary and took the paten from Henry. He beckoned to Bunny Sterling, who had received Communion and had been in the act of returning to her seat when the drama began, and whispered to her to take Henry into the vestry. Trevor swapped the paten with Polly, taking the chalice himself, and the Communion continued. Polly gave the wafers, Trevor gave the wine, and Polly took Henry's place for the remainder of the service, which more or less ran itself, leaving her a little space to think of what she was going to say at the end. It was clear she would have to make some sort of announcement to go at least some way towards satisfying prurient curiosity, but what?

As the final strains of "O Come All Ye Faithful" died away, Polly pronounced a Christmas blessing from the altar. Then instead of recessing, she asked the congregation to sit. They sat expectantly, eager faces turned towards her.

Polly took a deep breath. "I'm sorry to have to tell you that there have been problems in Thorpemunden over recent weeks, which some of you may already know about. I'm sure many of you have noticed the absence of the Mansfield family, both from the Carol Service and now again from Midnight Mass. I'm not at liberty to reveal to you the full extent of the difficulties, but suffice it to say that if you haven't yet heard, I think you will all become aware very soon of the events which have led up to this. Until then, I'm afraid I cannot break any confidences.

"Obviously, all of this has been highly traumatic for Henry our rector, who was so ill only recently and has not long been back at work. Mrs. Winstone—Mavis—is the person who has had to cope with all of this, and I think with the added pressures of Christmas—it is the busiest time of the year for clergy with many extra services—it has clearly been too much for her. Sadly, she has become rather confused, but I'm absolutely certain this is only a temporary affliction. I'm sure you will all join me in wishing both her and Henry a speedy recovery and a happy and healthy New Year. I know you all wish them well, but perhaps you could limit your good wishes to cards rather than telephone calls at this time. And most of all, Mavis and Henry and indeed the Mansfields need your prayers if they are to recover their health as soon as possible.

"I will keep you informed of their progress via the weekly pew slip. And now, it merely remains for me to wish you all a very Happy Christmas."

She spread her hands. "Let us go in peace to love and serve the Lord."

"In the name of Christ. Amen," they dutifully chorused.

Polly was aware of every eye on her as she walked the length of the aisle to the back of the church. She stationed herself at the west door to say farewell and shake hands with every worshipper as they left, hoping no one would notice the trembling of her hands or press her further. She hadn't exactly lied, well, not in so many words, but she was well aware that the implication had been untrue. In view of all James had done to harm her in the past, she persuaded herself that her action was probably justified, especially as she was trying her best to protect Henry and Mavis. And James was finished anyway. Polly convinced herself that protecting the Winstones' reputation was the least he could do in reparation.

On the way out, one or two expressed sympathy for the Winstones, clearly hoping to draw more information from Polly, but she simply smiled and said she would pass on their good wishes. Most were eager to get away in order to indulge in gossip with their own friends and discover whether anyone knew what had happened to the Mansfields. The mysterious disappearance of the squire and his family had now become almost as exciting as Mavis Winstone's dramatic entry, which was certain to go down in the annals of Thorpemunden Church history.

Ella didn't pass Polly at the door, so by the time everyone had gone and the church was empty save for Trevor in the vestry with Henry, Polly realised that Ella must have slipped out earlier. She wondered where Ella might have gone. Probably not far, since they were sharing the car and it was now well after one in the morning. But Ella was the least of her concerns at the moment. First she had to get Henry back to the rectory and find out how things were with Mavis. She assumed Tom had taken her back to the rectory since there was nowhere else to go at that time of night, but rather dreaded what she might find. And if Ella was there, too, it might be a hundred times worse.

By the time Polly got back to the vestry, Trevor had sent Bunny Sterling home with her family, had already disrobed Henry, and was waiting. He insisted on accompanying Polly and Henry back to the rectory, taking the great iron key from Polly to lock the west door and carrying it back to the rectory for her.

"I can manage," Polly protested, somewhat half-heartedly. Henry was completely docile and she was sure Trevor must want to get back to his family at his mother-in-law's.

But he shook his head. "I'm not allowing you to walk through the churchyard by yourself at this time of night. Besides, you don't know what you're going to find. I'll stay until we're sure everything has settled." And Polly was secretly glad of his support.

By the time they reached the rectory, Henry had recovered sufficiently to be able to fish in his pocket for the front door key. But as he inserted the key in the lock the door was opened from within by Tom Curtis. He smiled easily at Trevor, thanked him for escorting Polly and Henry, and looked thoroughly at home.

The house was quiet. Polly tried to sense whether it was an ominous, brooding silence or just peaceful. That, she thought, was probably wishful thinking. And she couldn't pick up any vibes anyway, which may have been something to do with the presence of Tom Curtis, standing so disturbingly close to her.

"How's things?" she asked in an urgent undertone.

He grinned. "Fine. No problems. See for yourself." And he opened the door of the lounge with a sweep of his hand.

Polly ushered Henry through first, afraid that if she preceded him he wouldn't enter at all. Mavis was sitting in one of the armchairs, her shoulders hunched, staring at the floor, somehow folded in on herself, but quiet. Ella was stood leaning against the wall, just out of Mavis' line of sight. Each of them held a glass generously filled with what looked like brandy, but neither of them seemed to have imbibed very much.

Polly was relieved when Tom took the floor. Obviously he was used to this sort of situation in court, if not in a private home, so at least he knew how to handle antagonists. He suggested they all sat down, then poured out drinks for Polly and Henry. Polly swirled her brandy in the glass but declined to sip any. She hated brandy. She eyed Ella and decided Ella had done the same. Henry took a hefty mouthful before raising his eyes to Mavis.

Before Tom could begin, Henry said, "I'm truly sorry, Mavis. I should never have opened my mouth, on this night of all nights. I have compounded my sin by relieving my conscience, because my relief has been at your expense."

Mavis stared at him stonily. At least she was looking at him, Polly thought.

Henry continued, "Of course I've done wrong, I acknowledge that. But did you really have to humiliate me so publicly?

You certainly got your own back, didn't you? You do realise this will all come out now and I may lose my job? At the very least we'll have to move from Thorpemunden. They'll put us on the other side of the diocese for sure, in some run-down, sink parish which has no hope. Is that what you want?"

Mavis erupted. Her eyes flashed. She took a swig of brandy and spluttered, "How dare you make out everything is my fault, you filthy whore-monger! You have no right to stand in any pulpit pretending you're God's gift to the earth. Why, you're worse than any man in the congregation. No decent man would do what you've done. And why are you talking about the future for us? There is no 'us'! You destroyed 'us' by your revelations tonight."

Sitting on the sofa next to Ella, Polly could sense Ella shivering. She put a hand on her arm. "But there has been a 'you' despite Henry's—er—youthful indiscretion, hasn't there? I mean, before you knew about all this? So you're not different people or anything, are you? The only difference is that something which was between you and must have been some sort of deep down barrier is now out in the open. Can't that be a good thing? A fresh start?"

Henry and Mavis both glared at her and she wished she'd kept her mouth shut. Mavis said icily, "You're far too young to know anything, and you've never been married. So I'll thank you to keep out of it, Polly Hewitt. It has nothing to do with you. Mind your own business for once."

Polly's face fell, but not before Tom had winked at her. He said easily, "Would you like us all to go? So that you can sort things out between yourselves?"

He made to stand up, but Henry forestalled him. "No, you stay. We may need a solicitor." He turned to Ella. "How are you, love? This affects you just as much as it affects Mavis and me—"

He got no further. There was a loud snort from Mavis, who said bitterly, "That's right. You look after the tramp's daughter, not your wife. Anything rather than me, is it Henry? How many more did you have? Is it still going on? Slip away to the red light district in Ipswich, do you? It's a wonder you weren't questioned when all those prostitutes were murdered in Ipswich."

Henry shot to his feet. "How dare you speak about Ella like that! She's been nothing but good to you. None of this is Ella's fault, so don't take your bad temper out on her. And for your information, it was a one-off. I wasn't using a prostitute. I fell in love with a beautiful woman, Ella's mother. Inappropriate for a married man and a priest at that, but it happens. It was a long time ago and she's dead now, anyway. Get used to it."

"Bad temper?" Mavis was on her feet, too, her body rigid with fury. "Is that what you think all this is? Post menopausal, perhaps? You disgust me, Henry Winstone. And let me tell you this. If you'd ever been a half decent lover, you wouldn't have needed to go a-whoring at any time. I loved you, Henry. I really did. But you've destroyed everything. Now I hate you, Henry. My love has turned to hate."

Just as Polly was thinking, *She really is a drama queen underneath that austere exterior. I never suspected*, Ella stood up. She hadn't said a word all evening. But now all eyes were upon her as she marched purposefully to the mantelpiece. She picked up the figurine which she and Polly had given to Mavis and Henry only hours earlier. She held it high above her head. And then she sent it crashing into the hearth, where it smashed into a thousand tiny fragments.

Chapter Forty-Four

They were all on their feet now, staring at Ella and shocked into horrified silence. Polly was mortified. They had chosen the ornament so carefully and it had cost more than she had anticipated from her hard-earned salary, leaving her credit card distinctly red.

Ella looked very deliberately at Mavis and Henry. She said so quietly that they had to strain to hear, "Is that what you want? Both your lives smashed into a thousand tiny pieces which can never be reassembled? This is what you're both doing and it doesn't just affect you. It affects the whole benefice. You have no idea of the repercussions which will arise. You have each other and over thirty-five years of love. Do you really want to shatter that? I have nobody. No family of my own. Take it from me, it's a lonely place to be. I would give anything to have just a taste of what you two have."

Mavis gave a strangled sob. Tears began to trickle as conflicting emotions of hurt and sorrow, grief and shame chased themselves across her face. Henry looked stricken, his eyes shifting from Mavis to Ella and back again. He held out his arms to Mavis and she fell into them. They hugged as though they would never let go and Henry kept murmuring against her hair, "I'm so sorry. I'm so very sorry."

Mavis patted his face and shook her head. "No, it's me. I'm the one who should be sorry. I've been terrible to you and to

Ella. I'm so ashamed. Can you ever forgive me?"

Neither of them noticed a downcast Ella edging towards the door. But Polly sprang ahead of her, leaning against the door so that she couldn't escape.

"Not again, Ella Wim," she declared. "You're not going anywhere."

With that, Mavis moved out of Henry's arms and ran to Ella, enveloping her in a bear hug. "Welcome to your home, Ella. I've always wanted a daughter; God has heard me and sent you. You're Henry's flesh and blood and now, if you'll let me, I want to be a proper step-mum to you. Can you forgive me? I spoke in the heat of the moment and I'm so very sorry. But Ella, I loved you the moment I first saw you and I'll love you forever. I knew you'd been sent for a special reason. I just didn't know what it was until now. Please forgive me and make a family with Henry and me."

In answer, Ella returned the hug with shining eyes and a stifled sob of her own. Henry went to them, holding them both in his arms. "Our family," he breathed. "At last. We're a family together now and nothing will ever change that. I promise."

Polly and Tom exchanged a glance.

"Might as well join in," murmured Tom. "I've been wanting to do this ever since I met you, and I've a sprig of mistletoe in my pocket just in case. Come here, Polly Hewitt."

And as Polly melted into his arms, giving herself up to his long and lingering kiss, she thought, *Hmm. Perhaps God is in his heaven after all. Perhaps he's been there all along but I never noticed.*

And she sent up a little prayer of thanks.

Lightning Source UK Ltd.
Milton Keynes UK
11 July 2010

156809UK00001BA/46/P